Withdrawn from Stock

KU-616-420

Also by David Gemmell:

nai Saga:
ghts of Dark Renown
ningstar
ander
ander 2: In the Realm of
Wolf
ander 3: Hero in the
adows
irst Chronicles of Druss
Legend
egend of Deathwalker
Wolf
d
eyond the Gate
or Lost Heroes
Warriors
ords of Night and Day

si Tales:
Macedon
ince
ing
ord of Power
hadow
Guardian
ne

Hawk Queen Duology:
Ironhand's Daughter
The Hawk Eternal

Rigante Quartet:
Sword in the Storm
Midnight Falcon
Ravenheart
Stormrider

Troy Trilogy:
Troy: Lord of the Silver Bow
Troy: Shield of Thunder
Troy: Fall of Kings

Dark Moon
Echoes of the Great Song

Rhyming Rings

WHITE K
BLACK

Withdrawn from Stock

WHITE KNIGHT/ BLACK SWAN

DAVID GEMMELL

GOLLANCZ
LONDON

First published in Great Britain in 1993 under the name Ross Harding.
This edition first published in Great Britain in 2017 by Gollancz
an imprint of the Orion Publishing Group Ltd
Carmelite House, 50 Victoria Embankment
London EC4Y 0DZ

An Hachette UK Company

1 3 5 7 9 10 8 6 4 2

Copyright © David Gemmell 1993

The moral right of David Gemmell to be identified as
the author of this work has been asserted in accordance
with the Copyright, Designs and Patents Act of 1988.

All rights reserved. No part of this publication may be
reproduced, stored in a retrieval system, or transmitted
in any form or by any means, electronic, mechanical,
photocopying, recording, or otherwise, without the
prior permission of both the copyright owner and the
above publisher of this book.

All the characters in this book are fictitious, and any resemblance
to actual persons, living or dead, is purely coincidental.

A CIP catalogue record for this book
is available from the British Library.

ISBN (Cased) 978 1 473 21996 0
ISBN (Export Trade Paperback) 978 1473 21997 7

Typeset by Deltatype Ltd, Birkenhead, Merseyside

Printed in Great Britain by CPI Group (UK) Ltd,
Croydon, CR0 4YY

MIX
Paper from
responsible sources
FSC   FSC® C104740
www.fsc.org

www.orionbooks.co.uk
www.gollancz.co.uk

White Knight/Black Swan is dedicated with great affection to Tony Fenelon, Acton's 'Mr Chips', who never gave up on a kid because he had rough edges, or a bad family background.

And to Roland Woodward, Peter Chilton, Tom Hodd, Brian Flower, Ray Scott, Peter Phillips, Tony Brown, Richard Allen, Robbie Fairman, Jim Lally, Michael Ort, and Valerie Ballard, some for the trials of friendship, some for the gift of enmity.

And to Guiseppe and Laurette Bertolli for the sheer perfection of the *Sundial*.

The big man in the torn track suit top watched the black swan building her nest on the island at the centre of the pond. Two years ago vandals with air rifles had killed the swan's mate and all four of her cygnets. She had also been shot in the head, and her right eye was now blind. To the man called Bimbo the eye was deeply beautiful, for it was grey and shimmered like a pearl set in the bird's ebony face.

Now, as the mating season neared, the swan once more built her nest. A pointless exercise, made more sad by the fact that she would also sit on her sterile eggs, keeping them warm, and waiting for them to hatch.

High above, the clouds drifted in a light breeze and the sun broke clear. Bimbo opened a brown paper bag, taking out a small granary loaf.

'Hey, princess!' he called. The swan ceased her work and waddled gracelessly to the waterside, becoming majestic as she breasted the water. The big man rose from the park bench and walked to the two-foot-tall iron fence, watching her glide through the reeds and turn, in order to see him with her good eye.

'There's my girl,' he said, softly, tossing chunks of bread to the water. Several ducks torpedoed in but the swan scattered them with arrogant ease.

'Hello Bimbo,' said a little girl in a Spiderman track suit.

'Hello darlin', where's yer mum?'

'Wiv Simon at the swings. Can I frow some bread?'

'Yeah.' He handed her the remains of the loaf, but the swan moved away and Sarah fed the ducks that swarmed in. With the feeding over, Bimbo returned to the bench and glanced back along the north path to the outer gates. It was empty. Still, it was early yet, he thought.

Sarah joined him and he ruffled her short, mousy hair.

'Aint your 'ands big, Bimbo?'

'Yeah. Bunches of bananas,' he said, grinning.

'I was seven, Sunday.'

'Happy birthday. Did you get some presents?'

'I got a doll from me mum, and a packet of Maltesers from Simon. But he et them.'

'It's the thought that counts, sweetheart.'

'Your princess is building a nest again.'

'I know.'

'Is she going to have babies?'

'No, darlin'.'

'How can you tell?'

'There's gotta be two of them. Husband and wife. Mummy and Daddy.'

'I aint got a daddy.'

'It's different with swans,' he said, lamely.

'Why do you call her Princess?'

'Dunno. Seems to fit though, eh?'

'Is she a real princess? Like magic?'

'No. She's just a bird.'

'She's got a magic eye. All grey and foggy.'

'Yeah,' said Bimbo, glancing up to see Sarah's mother walking along the broad path, a sturdy five year old beside her. Bimbo stood and opened his arms. Simon squealed, tugged clear of his mother's hand and raced towards him, shrieking with delight as Bimbo tossed him into the air, catching him expertly.

'I wish you wouldn't do that,' said Sherry Parker, sternly.

'How ya doin, Sher?' said Bimbo, gently releasing the boy.

2

'No point complainin' is there?'

Bimbo shrugged. Sherry was short and dark haired, her face still pretty despite the harshness the last few years had brought. Her eyes were tired, her complexion pale, her body becoming overweight, her shoulders round.

'You're doin a great job with the kids,' he said. 'Pair of diamonds.'

'Yeah. Real diamonds,' she said. 'Come on you two, time to go.'

'Can't we stay for a while, mum?' pleaded Sarah.

'No. Mrs Simmonds is coming round.'

'Nice to see you, Sher.'

'Was it? You still with that pig Reardon?'

'Yeah,' he answered. 'It's a livin'.' She nodded, and he looked away, embarrassed .

He watched them until they reached a bend in the path, then called out to Sarah, waving her back. She sprinted to him, her thin arms pumping. Obligingly he tossed her into the air. Then he knelt beside her and produced a £10 note from the back pocket of his faded jeans.

'When you get home you give this to your mum. All right?'

'Can I buy sweets with it?'

'No. That's grown-up money, that is.' He delved in the pocket of his track suit top and gave her a fifty pence piece. 'That's sweets money for you and Simon.'

'Thanks Bimbo. Why don't my mum like you?'

'Cos she's got good sense. Go on. She's waitin'.' Sarah swung away, and then looked back.

'Simon says that Bimbo's a funny name for a man. Is it your real, true to God, name?'

'Nah. It's John. But when I was about your age I used to go and watch this cartoon. Fell in love with it, like. *Dumbo*, it was; all about an elephant. So the other kids started callin' me Dumbo. But I didn't like it. Then they changed it to Bimbo.'

'And you liked *that*?' asked Sarah, giggling.

The big man smiled. 'It means somethin' else now, sweetheart. But back then it made me ... different, you know what I mean?'

'No,' she admitted. 'And Simon says it means a woman with big tits!'

'Sarah!' shouted her mother. 'Will you get a bloody move on?' The child pulled a face, then grinned at the man before sprinting away.

Bimbo's smile faded as he returned to the bench. He and Sherry had been in the same class at school, two desks apart. All the lads fancied her. But it was well known that, as a good Catholic girl, she didn't screw. It made them fancy her all the more. Bimbo was no different. But girls always seemed to go for the slim, athletic type. Not bloody giants with big, ugly faces. And, like all the kids from the Home, he had nowhere to take girlfriends, except the hut at the back of the Rec. Two years after he'd left school he heard that Sherry had married that scumbag Wilks. He was now living with a barmaid on the estate and Sherry was struggling to bring up the kids on her own. It was Bimbo's dearest wish that Wilks would get on the wrong side of Mr Reardon. Just once.

Another hour passed and the distant factory hooter sounded. Bimbo rose and walked to a covered, white-painted seating area. He leaned against the wall and watched the gate. A tall, broad-shouldered man in blue overalls entered the park. Bimbo moved back out of sight. The man was whistling as he walked. Bimbo judged the moment of his arrival and stepped out, grabbing the man by the shoulder and spinning him into the building.

'You bin a naughty boy, Tony,' said Bimbo. The man hit the far wall, steadied himself then drew a flick-knife from his pocket. The blade clicked into place.

'Don't be a prick, son,' said Bimbo, moving forward.

4

'I'll cut you, you bastard.'

'You said you'd have the money by Thursday. That was yesterday,' said Bimbo, still closing.

Suddenly the man lunged. Bimbo grabbed his arm and twisted it. There was a sickening crack and the knife fell from his fingers. He slid to his knees.

'You've broken me bleedin' arm!'

Bimbo shook his head. 'You aint never gonna learn, are you, son?' He held out his hand. The man scrabbled at his pocket and produced a tightly rolled bundle of notes. Bimbo took them, removed the elastic band and slowly counted them. 'You're twenty light.'

'I'll have it Monday. But leave us with something, Bimbo. There's a game tonight.'

'There always is. Monday. And don't make me find you this time. Be at the Stag around seven.'

'Seven. Right.'

'I should get to the hospital, son, and have that plastered up.'

Tony's face was grey, but he nodded and Bimbo helped him to his feet, watching as he stumbled away, clutching his arm to his chest.

Bimbo wandered back to the pond. The black swan was sitting on her new nest, partly hidden by the bushes.

'See ya, princess,' said Bimbo.

Bimbo didn't much like the High Street any more, not since all those Asians had opened their shops and deli's and Tandoori take-aways. He had tried to explain it once to Esther, back in the early days. 'You're a racist!' she had said, spitting out the word like it tasted lousy on her tongue. Bimbo thought about it a lot after that. Maybe he was. But he didn't like people chipping away at his memories. Old Mr Booker's sweet shop was long gone, and, instead of Mars bars, the shop now had mangoes outside and a sweet, spicy smell wafted from the interior.

Bimbo had liked old Mr Booker. Not that he didn't like the Singhs. Always smiling them people, and you could shop there at night. But Booker's was history. All the kids went there for paper rounds and their first, real, honest to God pocket money.

And Mr Reardon liked the Asians. They knew how the world worked, he said. They never quibbled about paying their way.

Bimbo made his weekly collections from the Six Bells and the Barley Mow and stopped at the Eel and Pie for a mug of tea before heading for the Anchor. The pub was crowded and a juke-box was playing Sinatra's *Strangers in the Night*. Bimbo eased his way to the bar and beyond to the narrow corridor which led to MacLeeland's office. Mac was sitting at the small desk, holding a phone to his ear. He waved Bimbo to a seat.

'No, I'll be home around eleven. No, eleven. Then leave it in the microwave. Jesus! What do you expect me to do? We'll talk later. Yes, I've got the pills. See you. No, I'm not being snappy, but there's someone waiting for me. See you later.' He replaced the phone and leaned back. Bimbo stared at the fat man, wondering how he could still be alive. Two heart attacks and a mild stroke, and yet MacLeeland still drank like a fish, and smoked sixty cigarettes a day. Grossly overweight, and permanently bathed in sweat, even in winter, Mac was a living monument to man's progress in the late twentieth century.

'You're looking fit, Bim.'

'Can't complain. How you doin', Mac?'

'Bloody rat poison they're giving me now. Warfarin. Can you believe it? "Take it easy, Mac. Rest, Mac." What the fuck do they expect me to do? You know anybody who works for Mr Reardon who takes it easy? Now we've got the spades kicking up rough on the estate. That Silver has started his own racket! Pimpin'. Bleedin' American idea. Six girls he's got. Calls them his "String". And there's a tough crowd moved in down the Bush. Gonna have trouble with them. On top of that the old Bill are always sniffin' around. Take it easy?'

6

'I saw Tony.'

'I heard. You broke his arm. That's good. Flash git.'

'I didn't mean to break it.'

'We won't say nothing about that. Mr Reardon is very pleased with you.'

'He had a knife, see. And I grabbed his arm. It just bent.'

'Spare me the details. Get the cash?'

'All but twenty. He'll have the rest Monday.'

'You believe that?'

Bimbo shrugged.

'We'll see,' said Mac. 'Any other problems?'

'Nah.' Bimbo took the day's collections from his track suit top and handed them to the fat man, who counted the notes swiftly, then returned ten £5 notes to Bimbo.

'You staying for a drink, Bim?'

'Nah. I'm off down Stepney's. He's teaching me chess.'

'Chess? Why?'

'Why not?'

'What's it good for?'

'It don't have to be good for nothing, Mac. I just like the old man's company.'

'You watch it. He'll have you down for a bar mitzvah or something.'

'What's that then?'

'Some Yid festival. Aint given him no money have you?'

'Why should I give him money?'

'He's a Jewboy. He must want something from you. And it can't be a chess partner.'

'See you, Mac. Take care.'

'Take rat poison, more like. Enjoy your game.'

Bimbo stepped out through the rear door into the cool of the night, and walked away from the tinny sound of the juke-box.

Why shouldn't he learn to play chess? What made it so bloody funny? Stepney said millions of people played chess in

Russia. Like a national sport. What was so sodding clever about kicking a leather ball around a park? Or killing yourself in some poxy office behind a pub taking rat poison?

He strolled through the estate past the graffiti-stained walls and the lounging groups of black teenagers, and on towards the station and the row of shops beyond the rail bridge.

Only at night did the town seem the same as ever, the old terraces and the narrow streets. As long as you didn't look up at the tower blocks, or read the newspaper reports about muggings and violence.

'Good evening, Bimbo,' said Mr Singh.

'How ya doin'?'

'I am very well. But my shop window was smashed last night. May I walk with you? This estate makes me nervous and I am visiting a friend.'

'Sure.'

'I think the neighbourhood is deteriorating. So much violence and hatred,' said Mr Singh.

'Aint it the truth,' said Bimbo.

'What is the matter with you, Bimbo?' asked Stepney, his Bishop sweeping down to remove the white Queen. 'Why you don't relax?'

Bimbo glanced up from the ornate board into the old man's face.

'Dunno, Step. Funny sorta day.'

'You must relax, in order to play. Let the body tension ease so that the brain can work.'

'Yeah? But what's the good of it? Chess, I mean.'

Stepney eased his slight frame from the high-backed chair and moved to the small workshop. He plugged in the kettle and lifted two mugs from a pine shelf. He was over seventy, bald and sparrow-boned with rounded shoulders.

'The good, Bimbo? Chess is life. Conflict. The overcoming of

8

one's opponent by stealth and cunning and force. It teaches you to think. You want tea?'

'Life don't work to rules. You make your own, or the other bloke does. And in chess everyone starts out equal. Life don't work like that neither.'

'This is so. And yet each man lives to a set of his own rules, and that makes each man the victim of his own predictability. Study his rules, know his life, and use your knowledge to conquer.'

'Conquer what?'

'Your enemy. That is what we were discussing, was it not?'

'I thought we was talking about chess.'

Stepney chuckled and added warm water to the old silver tea pot, swishing it around the base. 'Your generation is soft, Bimbo. Everyone seeks to hide from life. It is always the other man's fault, or the fault of society. You have forgotten that man is an animal. To survive and prosper he must be strong. He must conquer his enemies.'

'That can't be right. Like … say … unemployment. That's got nothin' to do with conquering people.'

'It has everything to do with it. Milk or lemon in your tea?'

'Milk, ta.'

Stepney handed him a mug and lowered himself into his seat. 'If there is one job and ten applicants who is chosen? The best one. *Verstehen*? He has to conquer the other nine. Down it always comes to strength, either of the mind or the body.'

'Maybe we should be partners,' said Bimbo. 'You got the brains, and I once turned a Volkswagen over for a bet.'

'If I needed a partner', said the old man, 'it would be you.'

'I was only joking.'

'I was not. You would like another game?'

'We aint finished this one yet.'

'It is mate in three. But you are getting better.'

'It just takes me longer to lose.'

Stepney chuckled and shook his head. 'You British won the war this way. By taking a long time to lose, you won.'

'Don't start on history. I was never no good at it.'

Bimbo sat back and stared at the small room, with its cluttered shelves and bric-a-brac, musical mugs, telescopes in brass, and tiny porcelain figures, depicting Chinese or Japanese warriors. By the far wall, beside a narrow window, was a bookcase, filled with tomes on antiques or chess.

'You ever bin married, Step?'

'Once.'

'What happened?'

'Death is what happened,' said Stepney, bleakly.

'Long time ago, was it?'

'It was yesterday, Bimbo. Just yesterday.'

'I'm not with ya. I saw you yesterday.'

'It does not matter. Why have you not married?'

'Never really thought about it.'

'You should. You would make a good husband. You care. And children like you. It is a good combination. Find a wife.'

'Yeah. I could advertise in the post office window. Wanted: Wife for seventeen-stone leg breaker. Likes children.'

'You do not like your job? Find another.'

'Yeah? Airline pilot? I fancy that.'

'Why are you so down today? It is not like you to be so negative.'

Bimbo sipped his tea and walked to the window, looking out over the rail tracks. 'Saw somebody today. Sherry Parker. Used to know her at school. She's starting to look old and worn out. But she used to have bright eyes and was always laughing. Lovely kids she's got – and a scumbag of an 'usband what walked out on her. I seen her lots of times. But today? I dunno. Maybe it was me swan. She's buildin' a nest again. And I broke a bloke's arm ... Anyway, it's all going round in me head.'

The old man nodded and quietly reset the chess pieces. Rain

began to lash at the window and Bimbo felt a draught of cold air against his chest. 'You oughta get that seen to,' he said. 'Or plug it wiv paper.'

'It is not a problem.'

'You could catch a chill or somethin'.'

'Come. Sit down and finish your tea.'

Bimbo returned to the table and idly moved the King's pawn forward two squares. Stepney introduced the Queen's knight into play.

It was after midnight before Bimbo called a halt and left the old man's flat, and he walked slowly through the rain across the common and on towards the estate. A white police car pulled up alongside him. He stopped and crouched as the window slid down.

'Where you left the body this time, Bimbo?' The voice was deep, and almost amiable. Bimbo leaned down and glanced in at the policeman. Sergeant Don Dodds was past fifty with a round florid face and knowing eyes. Bimbo liked him, though he didn't know why. Maybe it was just that Dodds was an old fashioned copper.

'I bin with a friend, Mr Dodds. No violence.'

'Won't be long before I put you away again, son.'

'That's life innit, Mr Dodds?'

The car drew away and Bimbo crossed the road on to the estate. He was half-way home when a thickset black man wearing a shiny black leather coat stepped into his path.

'Got a cigarette, man?'

Bimbo chuckled. 'You must be new 'ere, dick-brain. And if your mate behind me takes one more step I'll break 'im in half. Now bugger off!'

'No need for unpleasantness, man.'

'Damn right,' said Bimbo, moving on, his hands thrust into his track suit pockets.

He arrived at his home just as the sky was clearing. He

moved quietly along the communal hallway and opened his front door. The flat was cold and he lit the gas fire. Stripping the track suit top he towelled himself down, then plugged in the kettle and returned to the fire. A subdued tapping at his door made him smile.

'I heard you come in,' said Esther.

Bimbo stepped aside and she slipped past him into the flat, moving straight to the fire and sitting crosslegged on the floor. She was twenty-two, ebony dark and wand slim. Her hair was short and tightly curled and she was wearing a white towelling robe with a Japanese letter embroidered at the breast.

'You wanna coffee?'

'Is it all right?'

'Sure. Why shouldn't it be?'

'It's late. You don't mind?'

'If I minded I wouldn't ask.' He vanished into the kitchen and returned with two mugs of black coffee.

'There's a storm coming. I can feel it. And I hate thunder,' she said.

'Would you like to stay?'

'How come you never knock on my door, Bimbo?'

'Dunno. I should really.'

'I wish you would. Just once. I'd feel less like a whore.'

'You aint a whore! Don't ever say that! You're a friend. There's a bleedin' great difference.'

'Honest?'

'Cross me heart and hope to die in a cellar full a rats.'

'You look tired.'

'Nah. Strong as an ox. Now do you wanna stay?'

'Yes,' she said, grinning.

'Come on then. You can keep me warm.' He turned off the fire and led her into the bedroom. She switched on the bedside lamp and dropped her robe. The bed was unmade and she lay back, tugging the covers over herself. Bimbo stepped out of his jeans and boxer shorts, hurling both in the direction of an overflowing basket. He slid in beside her.

'These sheets are cold,' he said. Her warm body snuggled alongside him. For a little while he lay still, enjoying the closeness. Then she kissed him.

When he awoke she was gone, but the musky, pleasant smell of her remained. He wanted to go to her room and tap at the door. But he did not. Instead he fried four eggs and six rashers of bacon, ate them, washed the pan and dish, made some tea, bathed, and dressed in a faded blue track suit and worn down Adidas trainers. He flipped open the curtains. The sun was high and it was close to noon. For a quarter of an hour he went through the familiar stretching routine: first the hamstrings and lower back, then the quads.

Out on the street he began to run the circuit. Out past the tower blocks to New Street, left at the baker's, across the common, back along the lane, down the High Street, left into the estate, and then a figure eight past the station and over the bridge and back along the canal path.

Six miles exactly. Back home he took the weights from the rear cupboard and worked out for an hour, finishing with a hundred sit-ups.

He bathed once more then searched the flat in vain for a clean shirt. Finding nothing he pulled on a woollen jumper then checked his basket for a pair of shorts that might stretch to one more day. It was empty. Esther must have taken it before he awoke. He grinned and stepped into his jeans. They were still damp from last night's rain.

At the back of the High Street he entered the Roadster Cafe and sat nursing a mug of tea. Mac entered some twenty minutes later, pulling up the chair opposite.

'Saw you running again this morning. Not bad for a man your size.'

'Gotta keep in trim, Mac. You oughta try it.'

'Yeah,' said the fat man, sceptically. 'My heart'd love that. Anyway, down to business. There's a geezer owns a restaurant in Westbrook Street. Cypriot. Mr Reardon aint too happy with him. Normal business, Bimbo. Book a table, complain about the food and give someone a spanking. Upset the customers. All right?'

'No, it aint all right. I'm a collector. Turning over cafes aint my game.'

'Mr Reardon asked for you. There's fifty notes in it.'

'Nah. What else you got?'

'You aint getting the point, son. That's the job. Mr Reardon wants you to do it. Or should I go back and tell him you said no?'

Bimbo looked away, his face reddening. 'I'll do it. But why me? What happened to Nelson?'

'He's a known face. Anyway, what's it to you? You soft on Cypriots?'

'No. It's just ... it don't matter.'

'I'm beginning to worry about you, son. Now wear a suit tonight. It's a posh place. Know what I mean?'

Bimbo stared at the heavy, square face in the mirror, and the thick bull neck below it. Glancing up he looked into his own blue eyes. The awkward, clumsy boy from the Home was still there, deep down. He was older, sure. But he was there. Prison hadn't changed him. Even sharing a cell with Adrian and Stan hadn't affected the boy from the Home. Still a loner.

He smeared shaving cream on the broad chin and slowly shaved with a safety razor.

'It don't improve you much, son,' he told the reflected man. 'You was just born ugly.'

From a cardboard-thin wardrobe he took a white polo-necked sweater and an old Harris Tweed jacket he had bought six years ago. He had no trousers, and once more pulled on his jeans. They didn't look too bad, he thought, the sweater and the jacket giving him the impression of neatness.

His hair was close cropped and unruly. He ran a comb through it twice, but it swiftly settled back into place.

He sat on the bed, toying with the comb, uncomfortably aware that the time was creeping on.

'Complain about the food and give someone a spankin'.'

It didn't sit right. Bimbo rarely got angry, but he could feel the swelling of the ugly emotion now. His needs were few, but he still had them. Pay for the flat, buy his food. And where was he going to get it if he didn't work for Reardon, or someone like him? Dole? Not bloody likely.

He'd had enough of charity down the Home. He'd worked on the lorries for a while after leaving school. Two pounds a day as a casual. But all the drivers had their fiddles, and they'd chipped the big youngster in, giving him an extra tenner a week. Then the police raided and Bimbo was among those charged with theft. Suspended sentence that time. Three of the drivers got six months each. Then, short of cash, he joined Nobby Fletcher in knocking over a supermarket manager on his way to the bank with the day's takings. He'd made £425 – and nine months in the Scrubs. No regrets. Nobody forced him to do it. But after he got out nobody wanted him working for them. Except Mr Reardon.

A smartly dressed waiter led Bimbo to a table near the window and lit a thin red candle.

'Aperitif, sir?'

'Just some water.'

'Perrier, sir?'

'Whatever.' He tugged at the polo neck to allow some air to his throat. Around him some dozen or so diners were enjoying their meals, and a tall blonde woman was sitting at the curved bar, sharing a joke with two men. She glanced in Bimbo's direction, saw his eyes on her and smiled nervously. He nodded and turned away. He was out of place here, and the situation was moving inexorably out of control. The waiter returned with his drink. The water was fizzy, but quite pleasant.

'Are you ready to order, sir?'

'Nah. Not yet.'

'Bimbo?' said Esther. 'Is that you?'

His head jerked up. She was standing in the doorway in her nursing uniform, her navy blue coat draped over her shoulders, her white dress held at her slim waist by a wide black belt. Bimbo stood.

'Yeah. Er ... join me?'

Esther hesitated. 'You ... waiting for someone?' she asked. 'I mean, you don't often dress up.'

Bimbo grinned. 'Yeah, clean jeans. And no I aint waiting for no one.'

'That's a double negative,' she said, removing her coat and handing it to the waiter, who asked her if she desired a drink. She ordered dry white wine and he walked away. Bimbo moved round the table and helped Esther to a seat.

'I saw you through the window,' she said. 'Are you sure you're not meeting someone? It's okay. I mean we're not an item or anything. I won't get jealous.'

'No,' he told her. 'In fact I'm sorta relieved you're 'ere. Now we can just have a nice meal. You hungry?'

'It's a bit expensive, isn't it?' she whispered, leaning across the table. Bimbo summoned the waiter and ordered a fillet steak, rare. Esther chose veal with ham.

'You been here before?'

'No,' said Bimbo. 'It was recommended. Had a good day?'

'Not bad. All bedpans and bedmaking. You?'

'I had a run. Yeah, it was a good day. Thanks for doin' me washin'.'

'It was no trouble. Thanks for last night.'

He smiled, and started to relax. 'You look really great in that uniform.'

'It's the black skin, Bimbo. Goes well with blue and white.'

'You oughta bin a model.'

The steak was good, but the portions were not large enough to suit Bimbo. Esther couldn't finish her veal. Bimbo swapped the plates and ate it with gusto.

'You eat like a sparrow,' he said. 'I dunno how you manage.'

At around 11 p.m. three youths entered the restaurant, one of them sporting a Union Jack T-shirt. Esther stiffened, but Bimbo reached across the table and took her hand. The trio sat down at a nearby table. The waiter approached them.

'l am sorry, gentlemen, you cannot be served here without wearing jackets.'

'Says who?' snarled a burly, blond youngster.

'It is the rule. I do not make the rule,' answered the waiter, warily.

'We can't get a meal then?' said the youth in the Union Jack T-shirt.

'I am sorry.'

'Even though I'm wearing the flag of me country?'

'No sir.'

'But you serve niggers?'

'I think you had better leave, gentlemen,' said the waiter, steeling himself for the inevitable violence. The three stood, one of them kicking back at his chair and sending it flying into the doorway. Bimbo saw that Esther was sitting very still, her eyes staring at the table. He looked back at the trio, feeling suddenly sorry for the waiter.

'Hey you,' he said to the leader. 'Your mum know you're out this late, sonny?'

The three started forward. Bimbo stood and moved towards them.

At his advance the leader fell back, suddenly aware of the

power in the huge man. He backed into one of his comrades and the trio headed for the door, stepping over the upturned chair. In the street a semblance of courage returned to the youths. 'Fuck you, nigger lover!' one of them shouted. Then they ran. Bimbo scooped up the fallen chair and returned it to the table.

The waiter was sweating as he grinned at Bimbo. 'Thank you, sir. I hope it did not spoil your evening?'

'Don't worry about it, son. You got balls to stand up to 'em like that.'

'We have been waiting for trouble. My uncle says it is inevitable.'

'Life's like that,' said Bimbo, returning to Esther. She was still stiff and her eyes were frightened. 'Don't let them worry you,' he said, taking her hand.

'It's not nice to be hated.'

'I don't hate you, Esther. And I'll bet your patients don't neither.'

The waiter returned with two brandies. 'On the house, sir,' he said.

'See what I mean? Nobody here hates you.'

A movement outside the window gave Bimbo a fraction of a second's warning. He up-ended the table just as the first brick smashed the plate glass window. Pulling Esther from her chair he shielded her with his body. A brick struck his shoulder and bounced away. The sudden noise was followed by the sound of running feet. Bimbo stood and surveyed the damage. Esther rose alongside him.

'Take me home,' she said, sadly.

A police car pulled up alongside the restaurant. Two officers entered the building and questioned the waiter. The chef and a female cook were now standing at the back. The waiter spoke to the policeman and gestured to Bimbo. The officers walked over.

'Can you describe the men, sir?'

'I never saw who threw the bricks.'

'That's a shame, sir.'

Another police car drew up. Sgt Dodds walked wearily into the building. He spoke to the waiter then approached Bimbo. 'So,' he said, 'into the restaurant wrecking business now, are we?'

'I was just having a meal. It's nothin' to do with me.'

'Don't give me that shit, Bimbo. Mr Niazzi has been having trouble with your boss. Now you're here and the place is a wreck. You want to tell me it's coincidence?'

Bimbo's anger faded. 'I don't know who done this. They come in and insulted Esther. I never done nothin'. I never even gave 'em a spankin'. What else you want me to say?'

'Nothing at all. Just get out of my sight.'

The waiter, who had been listening to the exchange, pushed his way forward. 'So you work for Reardon eh, you bastard! Well, you tell him he don't get a penny. And don't you ever come here no more.'

'You want me to pay the bill?' said Bimbo, softly.

'Thirty-two pounds – and four hundred for the window.'

'Does that include the tip, you dago son of a bitch?'

'I want him out of here,' shouted the waiter.

Bimbo peeled six £5 notes from his roll and dropped them to the floor, adding two £1 coins. 'Come on, Esther. I'll walk you home.'

Esther waited until Bimbo reached the door, then she turned to Sgt Dodds. 'He didn't have anything to do with it. We were just having a meal.'

Dodds removed his hat and rubbed his hand across his heavy face. He was fifty-three years old and a career copper. And he was a good judge of character. He took the girl by the arm and led her to the bar.

'Nurse, I think you're a nice girl, but you're keeping bad

company. If Bimbo didn't have anything to do with tonight's fracas it doesn't mean a thing. This is his career. He breaks things. Mostly people.'

'You are wrong. He saved my life.'

'Don't get carried away by a few bricks, miss.'

'Not tonight. Two years ago. Now if you'll excuse me. I have a friend waiting.'

Bimbo sat at the Roadster cafe, staring at the £50 note on the Formica-topped table. 'Well pick it up, son,' said Mac.

'I never done it, Mac.'

'Don't be so modest. You gave them kids some verbal and they done it for you. Take the cash. Or are you that bloody rich you can afford to look a gift horse in the mouth?'

'I aint that rich,' said Bimbo, scooping the money and pushing it into the back pocket of his jeans. 'Funny though, eh, them skinheads turning up like that?'

'Dunno what you mean, son,' said MacLeeland, pulling a cigarette from his pack and lighting it.

'You aint lookin' at me, Mac.'

'Oh, for Christ's sake, Bimbo! Okay, so I sent 'em along. I knew you were wrong for the job, and I didn't want to see you get into trouble. All right?'

'No it aint *all right*. I had Esther with me. One a them bricks could have smashed her face. And I don't like being accused of somethin' I never done.'

'Doddsy give you a hard time, did he?'

'Nah, not really. He's all right.'

'What's that mean? *All right*? He's a bastard. A right pig.'

'He aint bent though, is he?'

'Course 'e's not bent. Doddsy? That'll be the day. That's the trouble with the force now. You can buy 'em for a tenner, and they'll come in a coach. No, Doddsy's old fashioned. But he's still a right pig!'

20

Bimbo grinned. 'I don't understand you, Mac. Do you like him or hate him?'

'Both. What you got planned today?'

'Gonna see an old mate.'

'Okay. Be here about three on Wednesday. I'll have somethin' for you.'

'No more restaurants, Mac. I aint in that game.'

Mac shook his head and sighed. 'What game do you think you're in, son? It's the same one we're all in. You work for a boss, and he tells you when to shit and how to wipe your arse. Don't be difficult.'

'I think I might go labourin' again,' said Bimbo. 'It's gotta be better than this.'

'I'll see what I can do about the restaurants and such,' said Mac. 'I'll see you Wednesday.'

Bimbo threaded his way through the High Street crowds and stopped at the Singhs' general store. The daughter, Shamshad, was serving at the checkout. She was around eighteen, a shapely girl wearing tight jeans and a pink sweatshirt with the words *Raw Evil* embroidered across the chest. Bimbo paid for his apple and wondered what her mother thought of the fashion. It would never beat a sari for style, he decided.

He queued for twenty minutes for a number 11 bus and climbed to the top deck. Ever since childhood Bimbo had loved sitting on the upper deck, especially at the front. In those days the windows had rolled right down and a child could push his upper body out, stretch his arms and pretend to be Superman whizzing through the air, high above the worries of the world.

There was no seat at the front and Bimbo found himself a place left of centre. A hand tapped him on the shoulder. He turned.

'How's it goin', pal?' asked Willy Norris.

'Not bad.' Norris was a thirty-three year old lorry driver with his own artic. He lived in Ramsay Road with his wife and two daughters. Bimbo had known him for around seven years, from his first stretch in the Scrubs.

'I'm goin' down again, Bim.'

'What they got you on?'

'Receivin'. Sixty fruit machines. Lovely bits of kit.'

'How long you got out?'

'Remanded fourteen days. That bastard Lynch is charging five hundred for the remand. It's a piggin' liberty. Used to be two hundred.'

'He'll get rumbled one of these days.'

'Yeah? Who's gonna rumble a copper? Anyway I need the remand on bail to set Nancy up. Gotta sell the business. You don't know no one what wants a trucking set up?'

'Sorry, mate.'

'Don't matter. I'll sort it out.'

'How long do you think you'll get?'

Norris shrugged. 'Two. Maybe three. You still got that flat by the estate?'

'Yeah.'

'How'd you get on with all them niggers?'

'Fares please,' said a large, black conductor.

'They don't bovver me,' said Bimbo, handing the man two fifty-pence pieces.

'Bloody bovver me,' said Norris. 'You can't move without fallin' over one. And they're all on bloody social security.'

The conductor moved on. 'And they're all so bloody surly. Did you see his face? If looks could kill, eh? It's envy, see. You wanna stop for a pint?'

'No. Gotta see someone.'

'Been naughty has he?' Bimbo bit back his anger and turned to face the front. A slim young woman in black leather trousers squeezed into the seat beside him.

'Tasty!' said Norris.

22

The woman turned, and raised the second finger of her right hand in an upward stabbing motion. 'Up yours, arsehole!'

'I think I'm in love, Bim,' he said, happily.

Bimbo swung his head to look out of the grime smeared window. Two miles along and the High Street had been replaced by a dismal lookalike, the same drab shops, the same idle strollers, or groups standing in doorways. Norris leaned forward and whispered something in the woman's ear. She reddened and looked around, but there were no other seats. Bimbo turned.

'You're beginning to annoy me, Willy. Shut it!'

'Sorry, Bim. Honest to God.'

Bimbo looked at the woman. 'Don't take no notice, sweetheart. Enjoy the ride.'

'Up yours as well,' she told him.

Bimbo stepped from the bus in the centre of Shepherd's Bush, moved swiftly through the crowds and on to the back roads to a secondary shopping area boasting a launderette, a newsagent, and a massage parlour-cum-health centre. The Body Spa had a pine frontage and a beautifully ornate door with a dozen leaded-glass circular windows. Bimbo pushed open the door and wiped his feet. The short hall was plushly carpeted and he padded silently to the reception area where a gorgeous brunette in a low cut dress was reading a paperback novel. She looked up as he entered.

'Hello, Bim. Adrian's out back.'

'Busy?'

'Not so's you'd notice. Sheila got busted last week.'

'What for?'

'She offered the VIP Special to a detective constable.'

'Unlucky.'

'Yeah. The pig's been here about a dozen times. How long does it take to suss out?'

'You keepin' well?' he asked, to switch the subject.

'Yes. And Mandy's doing well at school. Best reader in her class. She's going to be bright that one.'

'She's a nice kid. Is it all right to go through?'

'You know you don't have to ask.'

The rear office was clad in pine and furnished with a white desk, and black Chesterfield, with three matching armchairs set around a glass-topped coffee table. On the wall was a giant Aubrey Beardsley poster of two women arm in arm. Adrian was sitting on the sofa examining a set of computer print-outs. He smiled at Bimbo, stood and stretched.

'I dunno how you get away with that gear,' said Bimbo, taking in the blue and white silk shirt, the grey leather trousers and the shimmering shoes.

'Style, my dear Bimbo. One needs grace and flair to carry it off. Do you like the shoes? Pure snakeskin.'

'Nice.'

'*Nice*?' mimicked Adrian. 'They were six hundred pounds. I bought them in Milan.'

'I expect they'll keep the rain off.'

'You don't change, do you, dear?' replied Adrian, grinning. 'Coffee?' Adrian was twenty-four years old, and already rich by Bimbo's standards. For a year they had shared a cell and Bimbo found him to be a witty companion. And he had a marvellous talent for always finding the bright side of any problem. Some months ago a group of thugs had given him a severe beating. From his hospital bed he told Bimbo it was a heaven-sent opportunity of – at last – having his teeth capped.

'So how is life treating you?' asked Adrian, handing him a small cup in an oval saucer. The coffee was rich and unusually strong.

'Not bad.'

'Still feeding that swan?'

'Yeah. She's buildin' a nest again. Sad, really.'

'Have you had a word with the council?'

'What for?'

'To find her a mate, for heaven's sake.'

'You can't just go out and get a male black swan … can you?'

'Why not? Just about everything else in this world is for sale.'

'I never really thought about it.' He handed back the empty cup.

'My God, Bimbo, I think your hands are getting bigger. It's like watching snakes writhing around a bird's egg.'

'You oughta get some mugs. I feel like an idiot sitting here with a bleedin' thimble.'

'I don't know, you look kind of sweet. Endearing, in a murderous sort of way. You got work tonight?'

'What's on?'

'Only a stag show, but there's a live act after.'

'You know I don't like that sorta thing.'

'You don't have to watch it. You'll be on the door. It's worse for me. I'm inside.'

'Where is it?'

'You won't believe it. St Mary's church hall.'

'You're kiddin'?'

'Straight up. Hired it for the Royal Order of Antlered Stags reunion. Good eh? Thirty five notes and seats one hundred.'

'What if the vicar turns up?'

'You stop him at the door.'

'Bloody hell, Ade!'

'We're not breaking the rules. All they said was no alcohol. We've laid on some food, but they won't be eating much.'

'Not that film about pigs again?'

'Nothing like watching a man screw a sow to put you off your bacon sarnies.'

'That's vile, Ade.'

'The whole thing is vile, Bimbo,' said Adrian, suddenly serious. 'But a man has to make a living. I've got big expenses. Rich tastes.'

'Is Sally doing the live act?'

'No, she married an accountant. I've got this black chick. She's new to the game, but she's learning fast. She's agreed to take someone from the audience after. So it's a good raffle as well.'

'What am I supposed to be looking for?'

'It's all ticket, Bim. Numbered tickets. No gatecrashers. No late arrivals. No Filth. Anyone not kosher does not get in.'

'What time?'

'Eight-thirty. You know St Mary's?'

'Yeah. Alvin doin' the camera stuff?'

'No. We had a tiff. He walked out.'

'Sorry. Wasn't he the one that waited for you while you was in nick?'

'Yes. He'll be back. It was just a stupid tiff. It wasn't important. We were supposed to be going to Cyprus next week. I've hired a boat there. Now this ... But he'll be back. Four years we've been together.'

'Yeah. I'd better be going.'

'Another coffee?'

'No, ta.'

'I don't suppose you'd fancy Cyprus, Bim? No funny business. Just a holiday.'

'I never bin abroad, Ade. Don't fancy it. Anyway you're right. He'll come back.'

2

Bimbo pounded his way along the canal path, seeking to exorcise his frustration. He could feel the tightness in his calves as lactic acid began to settle, signalling that he was heading into oxygen debt, where even his huge lungs could no longer supply enough air to maintain his speed. Running magazines were his only reading now. He knew about oxygen debt, and carbo-loading, pulse rates and recovery times.

His own pulse was a steady fifty beats a minute at rest, and 150 at the end of a long run. It took about eleven minutes to return to normal, which wasn't too bad.

The tightness began to wear off and his breathing eased. He was in automatic now, moving at a steady nine-minute-mile pace, and his mind cleared.

No matter what, he'd never get involved in another restaurant caper, or indeed anything else that smacked of ... smacked of what? Was it any worse to break some poor bugger's arm because Reardon said so? And what of the pubs and clubs who paid protection? What if they decided to defy Reardon? Wouldn't Bimbo be sent in, along with Nelson, or Roache or Taggart? He thought of the Cypriot waiter. He seemed like a decent bloke, and he'd been willing to stand up against those skinheads. Sadness settled on Bimbo. There was no getting away from it, when the man had turned on him he had been right! Shouldn't have called him a dago, thought Bimbo.

He gritted his teeth and ran on. Sweat drenched his face, rolling in rivulets down his neck and back. One of these days he was going to run the London Marathon. That'd be good, he decided. That'd be worth something. The day was bright and clear, the evening fresh. Back at the flat he showered and donned his old track suit top with the tear at the shoulder. Draping his black donkey jacket over his arm, he left for the long walk to St Mary's hall.

Eighty-seven people had so far packed into the tiny hall. Bimbo shut the door and slipped the lock into place. There had been no trouble, and no late arrivals, and the films had already started. The windows were sealed with black plastic, and no prying eyes would see the Swedish extravaganzas beaming from Adrian's projector. Bimbo pulled up a chair in the hallway and sat down, resting his head against the brickwork. Another easy thirty pounds. With thirteen spare seats inside he could have watched the show, but what was the point? They never aroused him. They just made him uneasy. He didn't know why. Maybe it was that old Sunday school teacher – what was his name? Wills? Wilson? Something like that? All that stuff about sins of the flesh, and wanking making you go blind. Bimbo chuckled, as he remembered the old man, and his white, waxed moustache. 'Sex is an instrument of the Devil, yes the Devil! From sex comes wickedness and greed, covetousness and all things vile.'

Bimbo closed his eyes and thought about Sherry Parker. She'd won a sprint race once. He remembered her bursting through the tape, her face radiant with triumph, her nipples erect under the thin cotton top. He squirmed in his chair. That bastard Wilks! What right had he to marry her and then ruin her life? No, not just hers – the kids' too.

At a quarter to ten there was a tap at the door. Bimbo opened it. A young black woman stepped in out of the rain, followed by two youngsters, both white and in their late teens.

'Where can I get changed?' she asked. Bimbo pointed to the kitchen.

'How many in tonight?'

'About ninety,' he told her.

'Can we get a drink?'

'No. It's a church hall.'

'Is that supposed to make sense?'

'I guess not. Done much of this?'

'Enough. What's the crowd like?'

'About normal.'

'I don't think normal comes into it, does it?' Producing a weary smile the girl waited for his reaction. Bimbo shrugged.

'Dunno, I only watch the door.'

'I don't want no funny business tonight,' she said. 'I said I'd take one. No gang bangs.'

'Adrian's all right,' he assured her. 'It'll be okay.'

'Gay though, isn't he? Hardly the tough type. Can he keep them in order? I was nearly put in hospital by a crowd in Brixton.'

'This aint Brixton. And if you get worried just yell. I'll be in like a shot. All right?'

'I'd be happier if you were in there.'

'Aint my scene, sweetheart. But I'll be here.'

'I could do with a drink,' she said. 'Is there a pub close?'

'Across the road.'

'Tony, love, nip out and get a bottle of whisky – Bell's if they've got it.'

The tallest youth grinned sheepishly and moved to the door. Bimbo unlocked it and let him out.

'He's a bit nervous,' said the girl. 'He's not done this before. I'm Miranda.'

'Bimbo,' he said, offering her his hand. She giggled.

'That's not a name, it's a description. Nobody's called Bimbo.'

'I am. Real name's John. John J. Jardine. Call me Bim, if you like.'

'This is Daniel, Bim. He's my boyfriend.' Bimbo nodded and ignored the outstretched hand.

'What time we on?' asked Miranda.

'Adrian'll be out in a minute. They're about to serve food.' At that moment a great groan went up from the audience.

'What's happening?' asked Daniel.

'You don't want to know, son. You wanna get changed?'

'Might as well,' said Miranda. 'Is there a mattress in there?'

'Yeah.'

'Thank heaven for small mercies,' she said, picking up her bag and heading for the kitchen. Tony returned with the bottle. It was already open. He took another long swig.

'How many people did you say?'

'About ninety.'

He took another swallow, and followed Daniel and Miranda. Adrian stepped into the hallway.

'They here, Bim?'

'Yeah. Gettin' changed.'

'Good, the natives are restless. Raffle went well, but there's several blokes want to have a go at her if she's tasty.'

'One is all,' said Bimbo. 'Make that clear.'

'I have. You stay on hand though.'

'Don't worry about that. You watch that tall geezer with the gold neck chain. Don't like the look of him.'

'Good spot, Bim. He's the one asking for seconds.'

Miranda appeared, dressed in white panties and bra with pale stockings and a red suspender belt. Behind her came the two boys, in capes and leather G-strings. Adrian led them into the hall, and a chorus of wolf whistles greeted them.

The show lasted another hour. Bimbo waited on edge, but there was no trouble and Miranda reappeared. She dressed swiftly and, followed by the two youths, left without saying goodbye.

With the last of the punters gone Adrian and Bimbo cleared

away the chairs, folded the mattress and carried it to Adrian's saloon. They carefully laid the equipment on the mattress in the wide boot, covering it all with a blanket. Bimbo climbed into the passenger seat and stretched his legs. Adrian switched on the engine and pulled out on to the main road.

'Fancy a drink, Bim?'

'No. How did it go?'

'Not bad. The skinny kid couldn't get a hard on. Felt sorry for him. But she put on a great show. I'll use her again.'

'What did she earn?'

'A hundred.'

'Not bad for an hour, I guess.' Bimbo sniffed and looked out of the window, watching the deserted streets. It had begun to rain, streaking the window, making the roadside buildings and houses seem surreal, like smeared paintings.

'Nobody forced her, Bim. It's her career.'

'What? Oh yeah. You see their arms?'

'No.'

'Well streaked. I suppose shagging in front of a hundred people gets some money for dope, eh?'

'It's her life,' said Adrian. 'You studying for the priesthood now?'

'I'm sick of it, Ade. The collectin', the stag shows ... all of it. I aint even sleepin' good now.'

'You need a drink.'

'Nah. Just drop me off at the common. I got a chess game planned.'

'I didn't know you played chess. We could have played in the nick.'

'I'm just learning.'

The car was a beauty and Bimbo settled back into the wide seat and stretched out his legs. Even the rainsodden London streets looked pleasant from the luxury of the Renault. 'Watch this,' said Adrian, as the car picked up speed. He opened the driver's door and a metallic voice echoed eerily from the loud-speaker.

Front-door-not-shut.

'Bloody hell,' said Bimbo. 'I dunno if I like that. Bit creepy innit?'

'It tells you if you need petrol, or if your brakes are down, or if your lights aren't working. Magic. Pure magic! Just under nineteen grand.'

'Classy motor,' agreed Bimbo.

'Alvin said it was an old lady's car. He wanted a Jag. I told him if he liked Jags so much maybe he ought to buy one himself. He got really upset. That was the tiff. But l didn't mean it to sound like it did. It's just that I always had to work to bring in the money. Alvin concentrated on his art. His paintings are nice, don't get me wrong, but even I know they're not great.'

'Pull over, Ade.'

'Why? Not boring you, am I?'

'Just pull over and reverse up to them shops. I think I saw something.'

As the car came to a stop Bimbo climbed out and walked back to a shop doorway, where, in the shadows, it seemed that someone had dumped a bundle of old clothes. Bimbo knelt.

'What is it?' called Adrian from the car. Bimbo waved him over. An elderly black woman lay against the shop door. There was blood on the right side of her face. Adrian felt for her pulse.

'She's alive,' he said. 'Get her to the car.'

Bimbo straightened the woman's legs. Her tights were torn, her knees badly grazed. She was big, maybe thirteen stone. Bimbo eased his left hand under the woman's back, ready to lift her, then removed it. It was covered in blood.

'I think she's bin stabbed,' he said.

'Then move her quickly,' snapped Adrian.

Bimbo pushed his arms under her shoulders and knees, took a deep breath and hauled the dead weight against his chest.

Straightening his knees he staggered upright. At the car Adrian had spread a blanket across the back seat. Bimbo laid the woman gently on it.

The car roared away, the tyres shrieking against the sudden acceleration.

'Charing Cross is nearest,' said Bimbo, swinging to look at the passenger. Her face seemed grey, her mouth slack. Her false teeth had slipped and were half out of her mouth. Gently Bimbo removed them, wrapped them in a handkerchief and pocketed them.

Through three red lights the car thundered around Hammersmith Broadway and into the Fulham Palace Road. The huge hospital towered above them like a fortress. Adrian parked the car in front of the treble doors, and helped Bimbo pull the unconscious woman from the car. With a grunt Bimbo lifted her. Inside the huge reception area there was no one in sight. Blood was soaking Bimbo's jeans.

At the far end was a line of lifts. Adrian ran forward and pressed the call button, and both men watched as the light above the doors slowly approached G. The lift door whispered open.

'Which floor?' asked Bimbo.

'Stuffed if I know,' admitted Adrian, pressing One.

The two men emerged to a seating area before a corridor. A student nurse walked out, and stopped in shock. 'What's happened?'

'A mugging,' said Adrian. 'Get a doctor.' He glanced down at the blood soaking Bimbo's jeans. 'And you'd better make it bloody fast, dear.'

'Bring her through here,' said the nurse.

Bimbo followed the girl into a square room filled with flowers, surrounding an empty bed. The wall was plastered with get well cards. He laid the woman down.

Within minutes a young Indian doctor entered the room,

followed by two porters pushing a stretcher on wheels. Seconds later the woman was being rapidly carried towards the lifts. The nurse remained.

'Where they goin'?' asked Bimbo.

'To the theatre.'

'Will she be all right?'

'I don't know,' said the nurse. 'Is she a friend?'

'No, we just found her.'

'I think she might die,' admitted the girl.

Adrian lit a cigarette, and leaned back. He rubbed his eyes. 'I'm knackered, Bim.'

'Them things'll kill ya.'

'You never get out of this life alive, dear.'

'Can't argue with that.'

'While I remember, here's your cash.' Adrian handed him thirty pounds.

The nurse brought them two cups of tea and a saucer for Adrian to use as an ashtray. 'The doctor would like you to wait for a while,' she said. 'If it's not too much trouble.'

'We was gonna wait anyway,' said Bimbo.

'We were?' said Adrian. 'Why?'

'It wouldn't be right not to.'

'What does that mean? She doesn't know us.'

'There oughta be somebody who cares, you know? It aint right to be alone.'

'She isn't alone, Bim. There's all these doctors and nurses. They bloody care.'

'Nah. They see it all the time. Life and death don't mean nuthin'. You don't have to stay. I can get back on me own.'

'If you think it's important, of course I'll stay. Do you want to pray or something?'

'Wouldn't do no harm, I suppose. What you supposed to say?'

'I've no idea. Bit like a mental get well card isn't it?'

'I don't know her name,' said Bimbo. Adrian laughed.

'Well, if there is a God, mate, I think he'll probably know it.'

'Her name's Echo,' said the nurse. 'Echo Jerome. It was sewn in her coat. There's a chapel if you want to say a few prayers.'

'No, we'll wait here, sweetheart,' said Bimbo. 'Thanks for the tea.'

'It's a pleasure,' she said, smiling. 'When you want another, just come through.' Adrian stretched himself out on the long sofa and closed his eyes. Bimbo sat quietly, staring at the blood congealing on his jeans.

Police constable Ian Fletcher had been on duty since 10 p.m., and he'd been partnered with Chris Field, which was a guarantee to put him in a bad mood. Field had two topics of conversation, sex and piles, and on particularly bad nights they merged into one topic. Fletcher stepped out of the lift at Charing Cross, Field behind him. There were two men in the waiting area, a queer with blond-streaked hair and a giant in a donkey jacket. Of course you couldn't call them queers any more. Oh no! Now they were gays. It's all bullshit, thought Fletcher. The queer was asleep. The giant nudged him. He awoke, saw the officers and whispered something that rhymed with luck. The giant stood, his hands thrust deep into his pockets. His jeans were soaked with dried blood.

'Good evening, sir,' said Fletcher, adopting the deep, even tones rehearsed by police officers weaned on *Dixon of Dock Green*. 'I understand you found the lady.'

'Yeah,' said the giant. He had a broad, flat face and deep set eyes that set Fletcher to thinking of darkened alleyways and pickaxe handles.

'Whereabouts was this, sir?'

The giant turned to the queer, who gave a full description of the area and the condition in which they found the woman.

'Did you notice the knife wound?'

'We noticed the blood,' said the giant. 'Guessed it was a knife.'

'Were there any personal belongings? Bag or purse?'

'No.'

'Is that your Renault out front, sir?'

'It's mine,' said the queer.

'Better move it, sir. It's in the ambulance bay.'

The queer moved off, which suited Fletcher. He turned back to the giant.

'And why were you driving along the Broadway, sir?'

'Is the old lady gonna make it?'

'Too early to say. And you didn't answer my question.'

'No, I didn't. It's none of your fuckin' business, son.' Fletcher's eyebrows rose, and he pulled his notebook clear of his breast pocket.

'Name?'

'John J. Jardine.'

'Address, Mr Jardine?'

'Flat four, 16a Maple Road.'

Field moved forward. 'You didn't see who did it?'

'No.'

'Go and call it in, Chris,' said Fletcher, removing his peaked cap and sitting down. 'Any chance of a tea, love?' he called out to the nurse. She nodded. Turning back to the giant he decided to be conciliatory. 'The questions are only routine, Mr Jardine.'

'Yeah.' The eyes remained cold.

'You don't like the police?'

'I got nothin' against 'em, son.'

'Can I have your friend's name?'

'Ask him when he gets back.'

'I'm asking you.'

The giant sat down, leaned back and closed his eyes. Fletcher blinked and reddened. 'Perhaps you'd sooner answer questions down at the station?'

The giant sat up and slowly turned to the officer. 'You just keep pushin', son,' he said. Fletcher was about to speak when the lift doors opened and the Indian doctor stepped into sight. He looked tired.

'She is out of surgery,' he told the giant. 'I think she has a fighting chance. The knife blade wedged in the fatty tissue, and the head wound is not serious. But she lost a lot of blood.'

'Thanks, doc. What do I owe ya?'

'Owe me?' asked the doctor, removing his glasses. 'This is the National Health Service. You owe me nothing.'

'Sure. Well ... good work. I'll see ya.'

'Just a minute!' called Fletcher as the giant moved into the lift.

'You've got me name, son. Quit while you're ahead.' The doors slid shut.

'An odd man,' said the doctor. 'Not someone to argue with.'

Fletcher grinned, sheepishly. 'Not unless you were sitting in a tank.'

Sue Cater waited until morning conference was over, and the reporters had filed out. Then she approached Bateman.

'Why shouldn't I interview this Jardine?' she asked.

Bateman smiled, which made him look considerably younger than his forty-two years. Then he swept his hand through his thinning brown hair. Sue Cater was a good reporter, and very observant, and she knew the news editor's mannerisms well. When he smoothed his hair he was nervous. Her hopes lifted.

'I've already told you twice,' he said. 'You want it in French?'

'Because he's a leg breaker and a nasty,' mimicked Sue. 'Is that *Herald* policy these days? We only touch nice stories.'

'I didn't say we wouldn't interview him. What I said was you won't do it.'

'That's sexism, Don.'

'Oh,' said Bateman, leaning back and grinning. 'And when

you flash your eyes, and flutter the lashes to get a story, that's not using sex appeal? Which, I might add, in your case, is a considerable weapon.'

'How come it never works on you?'

'It does. I just hide it well.'

'Don't change the subject, Bateman! It's my story. I should cover it.'

'Sit down a minute,' said Bateman, seriously. Sue sat, and leaned forward, placing her elbows on his desk.

'The invasion of territorial space doesn't bother me,' said Bateman, amiably. 'Anyway, it was me who loaned you the book on body language.'

Sue chuckled. 'Come on then, give me the lecture. "You're only nineteen, Sue, and you don't appreciate the dangers involved in stories like these." Am I close?'

'Close enough. But there's more. Firstly he won't speak to you. Secondly, if you're pushy – which you are – he might lose his temper. The story isn't worth that to me. You interview Mrs Jerome. Andrew can see Jardine.'

'It doesn't matter if Andrew gets whacked in the mouth, I suppose?'

'You're right, it's sexism.'

'Let me ask you this: Is he more likely to hit Andrew or me?' This time Bateman smoothed his hair with both hands, and Sue knew she had won.

'I give in. Take Dick with you, in case he agrees to a picture – which I doubt.' She grinned and rose to leave. 'I expect you think I'm an old mother hen.'

'I think you're a lovely mother hen.'

'You may learn something today, young lady,' he told her.

Sleeting rain hosed the windows and Bimbo dismissed the idea of a morning run. Instead he pushed himself through a punishing series of press-ups, squats, sit-ups and weight work for over an hour. Boredom stopped him long before fatigue could set in.

He replaced the weights in the rear cupboard and sat by the window, looking out over the estate. Nothing moved in the rain. Bimbo transferred his gaze to the square living room and its bare walls. He ought to have put up pictures. Nice pictures. Happy. Like them Walt Disney posters with Thumper and Bambi. And that other one with Julie Andrews floating down from the sky holding an umbrella. Look good, they would. Brighten the place up a bit.

He switched on the kettle and dropped a teabag in a mug. A knock at the door made him curse. He knew. Esther was at work. Draping a towel round his neck he walked to the door and opened it.

In the hallway stood a young woman of around twenty. Her hair was light, streaked with blonde, and her face was pretty. She had a beauty spot on her right cheek, something like that Marilyn Monroe poster in Woolworths. She was wearing a raincoat that was drenched at the shoulders.

'Mr Jardine?'

'Yeah?'

'My name is Susan Cater. I'm from the *Herald*. Could I have a few words with you?'

'What about?'

'The lady you rescued last night.' She pulled a notebook from her pocket and opened it. 'Mrs Jerome.'

'Come in,' he said, stepping aside.

'I'm all right here,' she said, and, for the first time, Bimbo noticed the edge of fear in her eyes. It irritated him, but he had long grown used to such reactions.

'I aint in a mood to eat anybody today, and I got the kettle on for a cuppa.' Leaving her, he wandered to the kitchen. 'Put the fire on if you're cold,' he called. 'You want tea?'

'Thank you. White with two,' came the voice from the

living room. He brought her a mug and sat opposite her at the chipped table.

'How is Mrs Jerome?' he asked.

'On the mend. Her son has come down from Doncaster. It seems she was in that doorway for around an hour. You saved her life.'

'I'm glad.'

'She'd like to meet you.'

'Why?'

'To thank you.'

'I don't need no thanks.'

'We're doing a story and I'd like some details about you, if that's all right.'

'What sort of details?'

'Background colour, really. Who is John Jardine? What sort of man is he? You know. I mean, you look like a weightlifter. Sort of. Weightlifter rescues pensioner, that kind of thing.'

'You short of news this week?'

'It's a nice story.'

'Well, I aint a weightlifter.'

'No? What do you do?'

'This and that. Sort of odd jobs really.'

'You're unemployed?'

'Self employed. Pay me own stamp. I don't believe in that social security. Makes ya lazy.'

'You do some work for Mr Frank Reardon, I believe.'

Bimbo felt his irritation rise, and knew that it showed. The colour left the girl's face. 'Do you now?'

'According to our files.'

'Then you don't really need to talk to me, do you?'

She put her notebook down and smiled. 'This isn't a hatchet job, Mr Jardine. Honestly. It's just a nice story. Hard man rescues old lady.'

'Go away and write it then,' he said, standing.

'I'd like to get it right.'

'I thought you had me on file?'

'Not at all. All we've got is some old court reports and sentences, and some background notes saying you're a collector for Reardon. That doesn't spell out a man who rescues old ladies.'

'Goodbye,' said Bimbo.

'I'm sorry, I haven't put this at all well.'

'You put it well enough. Now leave.'

Reluctantly she stood. 'Can I leave you my card?'

'Sure.'

After she had gone he threw the card into a plastic wastepaper bin and returned to his chair by the window. He saw her climb into a car on the passenger side and watched the Escort pull away into the rain.

Hard man rescues old lady!

Bollocks!

Sergeant Don Dodds straightened his peaked cap as Constable Reynolds pulled the car into the kerb.

'You'd better wait here, son,' he said. 'They'll have the wheels off if it's left unattended.'

'There's nobody out in this weather, Sarge.'

'There will be if there's a profit in it.'

He opened the door and heaved his large body up and out into the storm. His hernia still troubled him – despite the operation – and he didn't run to the doorway. Fifty-four next birthday and almost thirty years of police work, and here he was facing retirement and nothing had changed for the better. The villains still owned the streets, and their reputations were sometimes better than his own officers'. Sometimes he wondered if it was all worth it.

Is the world a better place, he wondered? Is it hell! It all went wrong back in the sixties when policemen stopped chasing

41

villains and started rescuing bloody cats from bloody trees. That and a legal system that instructed judges and magistrates to restrict custodial sentences because nobody wanted to build more prisons. Cutbacks, political double talk, and an emasculated force. Be glad to get out of it, he lied to himself. He'd watched an old *Sweeney* episode last week where a villain confessed because he knew he'd get ten years for the robbery if he didn't. Nowadays it would be three. Or maybe two – if he'd killed somebody. Like that kid last month. Stabbed a boy to death, and got two years' youth custody. Twenty-four stinking months. Then he'd be out and some other poor mother's son would die.

Sure as eggs weren't pigging snowballs.

Dodds moved into the hallway and removed his cap. He was bald now, despite the strands of hair that swept from ear to ear, barely covering the cranium. He rapped at the door of flat four. It swung open almost immediately. Dodds replaced his cap and looked up. At six-foot-one he wasn't used to feeling like a dwarf, but Bimbo had that effect on people.

'It's like Piccadilly Circus 'ere today,' said Bimbo. 'You'll want tea, I suppose?'

Dodds walked in and stared round the room. 'You ought to get some pictures in here, Bimbo. It's like a cell.'

'Yeah. *Texas Chainsaw Massacre* posters.'

'You mentioned tea. White, no sugar.'

'I hear you bin ill,' said Bimbo from the kitchen.

'Gall bladder op, that's all. Stones. Sodding painful.'

Bimbo returned with a mug of tea. 'You get that hernia done?'

'Yes. Good as new.' Dodds smiled. The last time they had arrested Bimbo he had laid out four officers and Dodds had stopped the violence by walking forward and saying, 'Leave it out, son, I've got a bloody hernia and I'm not going to make it worse by wrestling with you. Get in the car and behave your-self.' Amazingly the big man had obeyed instantly.

'So whaddya want?' asked Bimbo.

'Just a chat. I been doing some research on you.'

'Yeah?'

'You know what an enigma is?'

'Some kind of West Indian?'

Dodds chuckled, then shook his head. 'It's a mystery, Bimbo. You are a mystery. Father unknown. Mother committed suicide in 1960. Barnado boy. In care at fourteen. Borstal at sixteen. First spell in the Scrubs at eighteen. Eight counts of GBH.'

'Michael Aspel gonna come in, is he? Bimbo Jardine, This Is Your Life.'

'Which brings us to Esther Jones. Registered drug addict at the age of seventeen. Attempted suicide two years ago. Slashed her wrists in the hallway. You got her to hospital. You visited her for a month. She lived with you for three months. Now she's clean and a nurse.'

'So?'

'And Mrs Jerome. Nice work. But why the verbal to the officer?'

'So that's what this is about?'

'Partly. Tell me something, why didn't you lay into me when we took you in?'

'You said you had a hernia.'

'That's what I mean by a mystery, son. Why the hell should that have mattered?'

'I dunno. Where's all this leadin'?'

'Buggered if I know,' admitted Dodds. 'Except that I retire this year, and I don't want to put you away again.'

Bimbo didn't know what to say. He finished his tea and took the mug to the kitchen, swilling it out under the tap. Dodds joined him, leaving his mug on the draining board. Bimbo washed it.

'Why don't you ditch that scumbag Reardon?'

Bimbo shrugged. 'He's bin all right to me.'

'He aint worth a light, son. He's a toe-rag.'

'You want another tea?'

'No thanks. Stay out of trouble, son.'

'I'll do me best.'

Dodds turned to leave, then swung back. 'I take it Adrian Owen was the man with you at the hospital?'

'Yeah.'

'See? That wasn't so hard, was it?'

Jeremiah Andrews was eleven years old, and he didn't lack pluck. But when five older white boys set after him, good sense dictated that he race home to the sanctuary of the estate, cutting through alleyways and across playgrounds, desperate to make the safety of Ironside Towers, where no white thug would dare to go. Jem was a fast runner, but, in his panic, he had not thought through his route.

His enemies had. Two of them had sprinted across the waste ground and over the wall. Jem ran straight into them. He sent the first boy flying with a right to the chin, but the second youth hammered a fist into Jem's stomach, doubling him over. Then the other three arrived and Jem found himself at the centre of a whirling torrent of fists and feet. He went down, but gamely grabbed someone's leg and hauled himself up, only to be smashed from his feet by a blow to the chest.

A voice bellowed and the whites scattered. Jem tried to rise, but fell forward on his face. Strangely the concrete seemed soft as a pillow. A hand touched his back. He tried to roll, and the hand helped him. His vision swam, then cleared enough to see a huge white man in a faded blue track suit kneeling over him.

'Just lie there, son. Get your breath.' The largest hand Jem had ever seen descended to his face, gently probing the bruises. 'Take a deep, slow breath.' Jem did so. 'Any pain at all?'

'No.'

'I don't think you've broken no bones. You wanna sit up?'

'l feel a bit dizzy,' said Jem, struggling to sit.

'That's only natural. You bin knocked about a bit, aintcha? You got a good right hand son. Like an 'ammer. Terrific shot that first one. He went down like he was poleaxed.'

Jem was feeling better, and the pain seemed to fade. 'Caught him good, huh?'

'A regular Ali. He'd a liked to have seen that one. You do any boxing?'

'Nah. No clubs round here.'

'There's one the other side of the green. You oughta try it.'

'You a fighter?'

'Nah. But I done a bit of ringwork years ago.'

'I know you,' said Jem. 'You're the runner, aintcha?'

'I like to stay fit.'

'Whass gowan on 'ere?'

Jem looked up to see Silver and four of his henchmen. The boy stood.

'I was in a fight. He helped me, man.'

'We doan need no help. You get on home, boy.' Jem moved back, but stayed within earshot. Silver was a tall man, wide shouldered and darkly handsome. He moved alongside the giant. But before Silver could speak Jem saw one of the other men, a newcomer called Ronald, step in.

'We doan like you runnin' across our turf. Find somewheres else,' Ronald told the white man.

The giant laughed, the sound full of contempt. His eyes raked the group. All were big men, their faces hard and cold.

'Your turf, you piggin' jungle bunny? Your turf's in piggin' Jamaica. Now get outta my face!' The men moved forward but Silver waved them back. The big man hawked and spat then continued his run across the estate.

'Why you let him get away with that, Silver?' asked Ronald.

'I didn't wanna see you get hurt, man. Anyways I kinda like him.'

'He's a bastard racist. An' he work for that Reardon,' said another man.

'Doan let yourself get taken in by all that media crap, Thomas. We're all bastard racists. You understand that? But that there Bimbo, he doan give a shit what colour you are. You step in his way and he'll stomp you like a bug.'

'You let him call me a jungle bunny,' said Ronald.

'It's just a coupla words, man. That was just his way a sayin' he doan give a good god damn.'

'You gonna let him get away with it?'

Silver laughed. 'He done got away with it already. That's why he's off enjoying hisself and we're standin' around jawin'. You gotta understand somethin', Ronald. Some men you can stop with a word. Some with a fist in the face. But him ... you'd have to kill Bimbo, and killin' aint my line. Keep away from him, he's trouble. Big T. Trouble.'

'He work for Reardon,' said Thomas. 'What happens when Reardon says to him to come after you?'

Silver's face lost its smile. 'Then I kill him, man. But not before.'

'I coulda taken him. No sweat,' said Ronald.

'Sure thing, man,' said Silver, who glanced at Jem and winked.

Stepney flipped the sign to 'Closed' and switched off the light. It had been a busy day and he'd taken over eight hundred pounds. An American woman had bought a Regency carriage clock, and a Dutchman had taken the Colt cap-and-ball pistol. Stepney slowly climbed the stairs to his flat and locked the money in the old iron safe hidden below the sink unit.

Outside he could hear the happy sound of children playing near the rail tracks, high pitched giggling and enthusiastic squealing. Their laughter, normally so uplifting, struck him like a blow, reversing the alchemist's dream, gold becoming lead.

46

His shoulders sagged. Moving to the antique bureau he poured himself a stiff drink, single malt Irish whiskey, the best in the world, from the Bushmill's distillery.

'You are a long way from home, Heinrich,' he told himself, remembering the days of his youth. Bavaria. Where the children would greet their elders with, 'Gruss Gott, mein herr!' God's greetings. Where the winter on the mountains brought a smile to the face of God.

And where the marchers in black had assembled in their scores of thousands to greet the new Messiah, who promised them glory and an unending Reich that would rule the world.

That day would long live in the memory of Heinrich Stolz, the man now known as Stepney. He and Anna had walked upon the mountainside, hand in hand beneath an untroubled sky. Her beauty had surpassed the magic of the mountains, for her loveliness was fragile and transient, like a flower, doomed to shine then fail. And he had loved her.

And he had failed her in the most terrible way.

'You should have had the courage to die,' he told himself, draining the tumbler, and refilling it.

Looking up he saw his reflection in the antique oval mirror. There was no sign of Heinrich Stolz in the time ravaged features that stared back at him; the wispy white hair, and the wrinkled, sallow skin mocked his memories. 'You have lived too long,' he told the man in the mirror.

Sipping his malt, Stepney returned to his chair and sat staring at the chessboard. Bimbo would never learn the game, for there was no subtlety in the man. How did the Americans say it? What you see is what you get. Yet still he enjoyed Bimbo's company. Such an innocent! Stepney sighed. 'The world needs more innocent men,' he whispered. His thoughts drifted back to Bavaria, to the snow and the pines, and a magical Christmas in 1938. He and Anna had ski'd on Christmas day, and then made love in a cabin, with a bright fire burning.

'Will you still love me when I am old and wrinkled?' she had asked him.

'As much as ever,' he had promised her. He drank another malt, then leaned back in his chair.

Such painful memories – only matched by the agony of the cancer that was killing him.

3

Adrian was close to tears. His hand hurt and itched beneath the plaster-soaked bandages. Everything seemed to be going so wrong. He had genuinely loved Alvin. It didn't matter that the boy was lazy, and filled with the crazy belief that his art was touched by genius. For the first time Adrian had found someone with whom he wished to share his life.

But, as usual, the fickle Fates had lifted him, only to dash him down again.

Like the day his mother had died. No one had told the thirteen-year-old boy how ill she was. He carried her food tray up to her, and watched her grow thinner and thinner. Until one day his father had stopped him outside the door.

'She's gone, son.'

'Gone? She can't walk.' And then his father had cried. Two months later his father too had *gone*. Hanging from a rope on the banister rail.

Somehow Adrian knew it was all his fault. He was to blame for his mother being sick. She had always had to shout at him, and he had never been 'a good boy' who'd done as he was told. And what a disappointment to his father he'd been. He hated football. Wouldn't box. Was useless at cricket. Then one day he was discovered behind the hut with Tony Bradshaw. That was the final straw for Dad. His son was a 'bleedin' fairy'.

Within months both his parents were dead.

Adrian had gone off the rails then. In care, and then caught as a runaway living with a man he had met at Leicester Square underground. At eighteen he and a boyfriend were found guilty of stealing a cheque and trying to cash it. Six months in the Scrubs. He would have gone mad there had it not been for Stan Jarvis and Bimbo.

Now he had money, possessions, and a future seemingly untroubled by material wants.

And without Alvin it didn't mean a damn.

Worst of all, he had found out at the club that Alvin was now living with a hairdresser in Acton, and that the affair had been going on for months. He was desolated. And that had made him stupid.

Ever since the Body Spa had opened Adrian had been waiting for the local protection gang to make an appearance. He knew how the world operated and had already put aside an amount to pay. But the day the men called had been the day he heard about Alvin. There had been two men, both large and exceedingly butch. They had explained about their security operation and how it protected small businesses from vandals and undesirables. Eighty pounds a week. It was less than Adrian had put aside.

'I don't need any protection,' he had told them.

'You'd be surprised how much protection you need, squire. Bad customers beating up the girls, petrol bombs through the window. It's not a nice area. Then there's yourself. A faggot. Lots of people don't like faggots. Harry here, for example. You don't like faggots, do you Harry?'

'Hate 'em,' said Harry.

'I think you had better leave,' said Adrian.

'Well, no hard feelings, Mr Owen,' said the man, offering his hand. Adrian accepted the handshake. The man grabbed his fingers and pulled him across the desk. Then Harry rammed a brass paperweight down on the back of his hand, and Adrian heard the bones break.

'Think it over, Mr Owen. We'll be back tomorrow.'

Melanie had come in as soon as they had gone. She closed the shop and took him to hospital. Then she rang the Stag and left a message for Bimbo. He had arrived early the following morning and was waiting outside the Body Spa when she stepped out of the taxi.

The front reception area was cold and Melanie switched on the central heating. 'You want a coffee, Bim?'

'Ta.'

'The girls won't be in till around eleven-thirty. Not much of a morning trade.'

'What 'appened, Mel?'

'Adrian'll tell you. I expect he's out back already.'

'I'm askin' you, darlin',' he said, softly.

'Let's wait for the coffee to heat up,' she answered, and they sat in silence, waiting for the red light to blink on the mahogany-fronted machine. Some three minutes later the three-pint jug slowly began to fill. Melanie busied herself opening the post and stacking the letters into separate piles – bills, accounts, settlements and personal. Finally Bimbo cleared his throat. She looked up. 'Sorry, Bim. I'll get the coffee.'

She handed him a mug and pulled up a chair beside him.

'Two men come in to see Ade yesterday. You could see they were trouble. Hard bastards. I left the intercom on and I heard them ask for £80 a week. I know Ade had £100 a week set aside. Anyway he told them he wouldn't pay and they broke his hand. He's not himself, Bim. Alvin aint coming back. He's living with some hairdresser. It's tearing Ade apart. He says he still won't pay. I mean that's not sensible, is it? Everybody pays. I think he wants them to hurt him. And they will. Really bad.'

'I don't get it,' said Bimbo.

'I can't explain it no better, Bim. It's like he's got nothing left, you know? Last night he went for a drink at the Barley. I got a call at ten from a mate. She told me he was trying to pick up a biker, for God's sake!'

'He was lucky they didn't kill him.'

'That's what I mean! He wants to get turned over. Maybe he thinks Alvin'll come back if he gets hurt. I don't know. I tell you what, though, he's better off without that spongeing little queen. I didn't like him at all. But Ade is a nice bloke. And God knows there aint many of them about.'

'I'll talk to him.'

'Get him to pay. He won't even notice eighty quid.'

'Yeah. You know who they are?'

'No. There's a big one. Harry. Near as big as you. It was him broke the hand. Then there's another one. Got a beard and a gold ear-ring.'

'When they coming back?'

'Today sometime.'

'Don't worry about it. I'll talk him into payin'.'

The intercom buzzed. 'Any coffee out there, Mel?' came Adrian's voice.

'I'll bring it in with the post.'

'Don't worry. I'll come out.' The office door opened and Adrian stepped into view. He was looking tired but was still immaculately dressed in a slate grey blazer and black trousers. He smiled.

'My, my,' he said, 'look what the dog dragged in. Bimbo, my dear, you must get yourself a new track suit.'

'Whassa matter with this one?'

'A present from an Ethiopian relative was it?'

'Quality gear this. Kosher. I paid £2 extra to have the Adidas logo put on.' Bimbo pointed to his chest. 'Just there. You can't see it now, but it was there once.'

'You'll give the business a bad name,' said Adrian, grinning. 'Now what can I do for you? It's a busy busy day.'

'Just wanted a chat.'

'Can it wait? Weekend, say?'

'No, son, it can't wait. Back office. Now!'

Adrian poured himself a cup of coffee and led the way. Bimbo pushed shut the door. 'What 'appened to your 'and?'

'Caught it in a car door.'

Bimbo sat down. 'Why are you givin' me all this bollocks? We're s'posed to be mates.'

Adrian shook his head. 'The lovely Mel been filling you in, has she?'

'She's worried about ya. And I aint surprised.'

'The world's full of worries, Bimbo. But it's nothing I can't handle.'

'You're gonna pay then?'

'Sure.'

'Don't lie to me, Ade.'

'What's it to you?' he snapped. 'What do you care? That's all I need, a piggin' butch bouncer, giving me advice. Get lost, Bimbo. Leave me alone.'

'You got it, son.' Bimbo rose and left the room.

Melanie walked into the office. 'You really are a prick, Adrian.'

'You don't like it, find another job.'

He looked away from her accusing gaze and returned to his accounts. For an hour he checked and counter-checked the figures. Profits were up on the last quarter, and tangential business – shows, imported magazines and videos – were doing better than expected. All in all the business should show a six figure profit in the next two years. He leaned back. He'd sold the Renault and bought a royal blue Jag. He'd driven it to Acton, but Alvin and his new lover had gone away for a few days in Tenerife.

He pressed the intercom switch and asked for more coffee. The door opened. He looked up.

'You bin thinking over our proposition, Mr Owen?'

Adrian smiled and relaxed. 'I've been waiting for you closet queens to come back,' he said, rising.

'I think he means no, Harry.'

'Did he call me a queen?' said Harry.

'I think that's what he meant.'

'I don't like that. That's not nice.'

'Oh dear,' said Adrian. Have I upset you? Would you like to kiss and make up?'

'You piggin' fairy!' hissed Harry, stepping forward, fist raised.

'He is, but I aint,' said Bimbo, from the doorway. The bearded man swung and threw a right cross. Bimbo blocked it, grabbed the man's jacket and hammered his forehead into the man's face. Blood exploded from his smashed nose and he sagged in Bimbo's grip. Releasing the body to slump to the floor, Bimbo saw Harry hurl himself at him. Bimbo leaned back and lashed out with his foot, kicking him in the kneecap just as the man's weight came down on his right leg. The knee shattered. Harry screamed and fell, struggling to rise, but Bimbo's fist cannoned into his jaw. The silence in the room was chilling. Adrian sank back into his seat, his face grey. Bimbo moved to the bearded man, hauling him to his feet. Blood was seeping from both nostrils and his eyes were glazed. Bimbo casually struck him across the face with his open palm, whiplashing the man's head back.

'Who sent ya?'

'Get stuffed!' whispered the man.

Bimbo's left hand held the man up by his lapels; his right dropped, his fingers gripping the man's testicles like steel pins. The victim's eyes opened wide in terror.

'I'm gonna ask once more, dick-brain, then I'm gonna rip your balls off. Who sent ya?'

'Reilly. Down the snooker 'all. Honest to God!' Bimbo hurled the man into a seat.

'Sit there and behave yourself. Melanie!'

'Yes, Bimbo,' she called from the hallway, reluctant to come in.

54

'Bring a box of Kleenex in 'ere. We've got a nosebleed. Then ring for an ambulance and say someone's collapsed on the pavement outside. Got it?'

'Yes, Bimbo.'

'Then order a cab for me.'

'Where's the cab going?'

'Reilly's snooker hall.'

'Wait a minute, Bimbo ...' began Adrian.

'Shut it!' snarled the big man.

Melanie returned with a box of tissues which she handed to Bimbo. He threw them to the lap of the bearded man. 'The ambulance is on its way. He's not dead is he?' said Melanie, staring down at the unconscious Harry.

'Nah. Sleepin' like a baby.' Grabbing Harry's belt he hoisted him and half carried, half dragged him into the outer reception area.

'Check the street,' he told Melanie. She glanced out over the top of the pine frontage.

'Just an old lady walking her dog.'

'Is she looking this way?'

'No.'

Bimbo opened the door, hauled Harry outside and sat him against the wall. Stepping back inside he locked the door. 'Pull down the shutters. No business today.'

'The girls'll be in soon.'

'Tell 'em it's a day off on full pay.' Returning to the office he sat beside the bloodied collector.

'You must be new at this game, son,' he said, patting the man on the shoulder. 'Whass yer name?'

'John.'

'My name's John too. Aint that a coincidence? You should find somethin' new. This is a specialist job. Not everybody can handle it.' Bimbo patted him again. 'It's no good pinchin' the nose. You gotta lean your head back.'

'Cab's here, Bimbo,' said Melanie.

'On yer feet, son. We're goin' home.'

They stepped over the still unconscious Harry and headed for the old yellow Cavalier parked outside. The driver cursed as he saw the blood-drenched tissue held to John's nose. 'Don't you get blood on my upholstery,' he warned.

Bimbo settled John in the back seat then slid in alongside the driver. 'Come on, son, we aint got all day.'

'What about him?' said the cabbie, pointing at Harry.

'I don't see nobody.'

'Right,' agreed the cabbie, slipping the car into gear.

'Nice motor,' said Bimbo. 'Smooth.'

'Good cars, Cavaliers. This has gone round the clock and it's still sweet as a nut, and tighter than a duck's arse.'

The car pulled up before a yellow-painted window board proclaiming 'Seagull Snooker'. Bimbo gave the cabbie a £10 note. 'Wait for me, son. And keep the motor runnin'.'

'Aint gonna be no bovver is there?'

'Not for you – as long as you're 'ere when I come out!'

Bimbo led the injured man inside. There were a dozen tables, with three in use, and several men were lounging by the bar. Bimbo ignored them and propelled John towards the rear of the hall to a small office. A thickset Irishman was speaking into a telephone as they entered. Bimbo shut the door.

'I'll call you back,' said the man, replacing the receiver. He stood. His hair was close cropped, his nose broken and pushed flat against his face.

'Well?' he said, moving round the desk. Bimbo pushed John into a seat.

'You Reilly?'

'What's it to you?' Bimbo's fist slammed into the broken nose, catapulting the man against the far wall. Bimbo followed him and delivered a second blow to the bulging stomach.

Reilly doubled over. Bimbo grabbed his shirt and hauled him upright.

'I've got something for you to think about, you cow-son,' said Bimbo. Reaching down with his right hand he took hold of Reilly's index finger. His hand snapped back. The finger broke. Reilly screamed.

'Number one! Adrian Owen is to be left alone. He took another finger in his grip. Reilly screamed once more as the crack echoed in the room. 'Number two. If he so much as catches a piggin' cold, I'll be back.' Bimbo released the man, who slumped to the floor.

'Time for a walk, son,' Bimbo told the horrified John. 'On yer feet.'

'Where we goin'?'

'Open the door.' John did so. Outside were four men, armed with snooker cues. John was about to speak when Bimbo's hands thrust at his back. He flew from the doorway straight into the group, scattering them. Bimbo walked out, picked up a fallen cue and stared at the men. No one would meet his gaze.

'What a bunch of pansies,' he said, tossing the cue aside and marching past them. He didn't look back.

The cabbie was reading a popular tabloid as Bimbo climbed in. 'Thanks for waitin'.'

'Back to the Body Spa?'

'Yeah.'

As they drew up the cabbie pointed to the doorway. Harry was still there, and still unconscious. 'Is he drunk or summink?' asked the cabbie.

'Probably,' replied Bimbo. 'How much I owe ya?'

'The tenner covered it, mate.'

'Well there's another five. I like Cavaliers.'

He left the cab, stepped over Harry, and tapped on the door. Melanie let him in.

'I was worried about you, Bimbo. How did it go?'

'No trouble, Mel. Can you call the ambulance again?'

'I did that. They say it's on its way. Shall we bring him in again?'

'Nah. Adrian out back?'

'Yeah. He's pretty angry.'

'So am I, darlin'.' Bimbo filled two mugs with coffee then carried them through to the office.

'Well, if it isn't Mr Macho.'

'Cool off, son. You can always 'ave yourself done over some other time.'

'Oh, into psychology are we?'

'Whassa matter with you, Ade? It aint enough you got money? So what if the tosser left you? He was a piggin' parasite anyway. You gone soft in the head. I don't get it.'

'What the fuck do you know about it?' screamed Adrian.

'Not much,' said Bimbo. 'But I like ya, Ade. You're a gutsy bugger.'

Adrian blinked, and sat down on the edge of the table. 'Oh shit, Bim. I think I'm cracking up.'

'You aint the type, son. Why don't you go down the club, have a drink, meet some mates, and get yourself laid?'

'That's not the answer to everything you know.'

'It's a start though, innit?'

Adrian grinned. 'Maybe. What happened with Reilly?'

'We had a chat and shook hands.'

'Is it all right then? I don't mind paying.'

'Too late for that, Ade.'

'Will they be back?'

'I aint sure. Probably not. Watch yourself, though.'

'I always do. Thanks, Bim. You're a mate.'

Bimbo nodded and headed for the door.

'Can I ask you a question?' said Adrian, suddenly.

'Sure.'

'That man – the one you took away with you …'

'What about him?'

'Would you really have ripped his balls off?'

'He thought I would. Thass all that counts.'

'I know that. But ... would you?'

'Does it matter?'

'I guess not,' said Adrian, realising in that moment that he didn't really want to hear the answer.

Bimbo was uncomfortable. Sitting on the sofa in Esther's tiny, delicately furnished flat, he nursed a glass of dry white wine and tried to concentrate on what Dr Simeon Abazul was saying.

It wasn't easy. The man's English was beautifully modulated, but many of the words he used skipped past Bimbo's ears. Esther was sitting on the goathide rug at Simeon's feet, staring up at him. Bimbo had not wanted to come, but Esther begged him.

'You're the nearest thing to family I got,' she had said that morning.

'If you like him that's good enough.'

'I want to know what you think.'

'He's a doctor, right? Can't be bad, can he? I mean, he's not the sort what goes around chalking up the nurses, is he?'

'No!'

'Well then.'

'Oh please come, Bimbo.'

'I'll be there,' he agreed.

And he was, though he would sooner be having boils lanced, he realised after only a few minutes. Dr Abazul was a tall, handsome Nigerian, educated at Eton and Oxford and, according to Esther, a fine all-round sportsman. He played football, rugby and cricket and was no mean squash player. He seemed perfectly relaxed in a sky blue, lightweight woollen suit and a dark blue open-neck shirt.

'And what do you do, Mr Jardine?'

'Call me Bimbo.'

'An odd name for an Englishman.'

'It's a nickname.'

'And how did you acquire such a nickname?'

Bimbo shrugged and grinned sheepishly. 'When I was a kid there was this film doin' the rounds. *Dumbo*. About an elephant with big ears who could fly. I used to dodge off school all the time and watch it. So I got the nickname, Bimbo. Actually it was Dumbo at first, but I cracked a few heads. Then it was Bimbo and I sorta liked it.'

'I see.' But Bimbo knew he didn't see at all and his embarrassment grew. 'Have you known Esther long?' asked the doctor.

'Coupla years.'

'She is very fond of you,' he said, leaning forward and draping his arm round Esther's shoulders. His dark eyes held a glint of challenge.

'What about you?' asked Bimbo. 'What sorta doctoring do you do?'

'Much of my work is research, Mr Jardine. Sub-fertility in men and women. You know, couples who cannot have children.'

'Really,' said Bimbo, hoping he would not be crude in front of Esther.

'The human body is a fascinating organism. In general terms a man needs to create twenty million sperm per cubic centimetre to have a realistic chance of becoming a father. Less than that and he is considered sub-fertile. With women the problems can be different, blocked fallopian tubes, irregular ovulation, poor womb placement. The list is endless.'

'Yeah, right.' Bimbo tugged at the collar of his shirt.

'Am I embarrassing you, Bimbo?'

'No,' lied Bimbo. 'Not at all. So you put 'em right, yeah?'

'Would that it were that easy. With some men we use drugs or chemicals to boost testosterone levels. That helps in some cases. At other times we might recommend donor insemination for the wife. It is a complex business.'

'Must be, yeah.'

'Would you like some more wine?' asked Simeon.

'No, ta. I don't drink much.'

'Esther tells me you are an athlete.'

'I like to keep fit.'

'No smoking, little alcohol and regular running … you should live for ever.'

'Yeah, that'd be nice.'

After the meal Esther slipped out to the off licence for another bottle of wine, leaving the two men together. Bimbo's discomfort had not faded.

'An odd evening,' said Simeon.

'Yeah.'

'Are you lovers?'

'We're friends. And you shouldn't ask questions like that.'

Simeon smiled, unruffled by the rebuke. 'Do not misunderstand me, Bimbo. I like Esther. I rather think she feels the same. But I am a jealous man. I do not share what I value.'

'Well,' said Bimbo, beginning to relax, 'I think I know what you mean. But she aint like a car, or a nice suit. You don't own people like Esther. I aint a pushy man, doc. I'm happy if she's happy. She likes ya. I think that's great. You treat her right, and that'll be fine. But if you've got any ideas of notchin' her up and throwin' her away, forget it. She's bin through too much, and bin right messed about. I won't let that happen again.'

'You mean the addiction?'

'She told ya?' said Bimbo, surprised.

'Yes. She still has the scars … inside and out.'

'Yeah, well …'

'Allay your fears. At the moment Esther and I are friends. I cannot say to you that my intentions are honourable. It may be that when we get to know one another better we will decide not to continue the relationship. It may also be that one or other of us gets hurt. That is a fact of life. You cannot cocoon your friends from life's realities.'

'That's true,' said Bimbo, meeting Simeon's dark eyes, 'but you can make sure the scumbags stay well clear.'

'I appreciate the direct manner of your speech. So let me be equally clear. I also despise the men who seek to make public conquests. Invariably they dislike women, and see them as objects for their own gratification. I would like a wife, Mr Jardine. One whom I felt would walk alongside me, not two steps behind. A partner for life.'

'You don't have to explain it to me,' said Bimbo, his awkwardness returning.

'Of course I do. Esther adores you. You are everything to her: big brother, father … friend. She talks about you constantly.'

'Yeah, well women can get on yer nerves when they go on.'

'On the contrary. We live in a sick, materialistic society, and it is extremely pleasant to find there are still men like you.'

'Look, doc, all this is makin' me uncomfortable. I've sat here like a gooseberry half the night, so I'll just leave you and Esther to have a nice time. Nice meetin' ya.' He stood and thrust out his hand. Simeon took it and responded with a firm handshake.

'I am sorry if I embarrassed you, Bimbo. I hope we meet again.'

Bimbo left the flat and found Esther sitting quietly on the stairs, a bottle of wine beside her. Bimbo squeezed alongside her.

'Go back in, sweetheart.'

'Do you like him, Bimbo?'

'He's ace.'

'Really?'

'Yeah. Hook 'im and land 'im.'

She giggled and kissed his cheek. 'And, princess …'

'Yes, Bimbo?'

62

'Stop tellin' him about me, and start talkin' about 'im. All right?'

Stepney gazed at the chessboard and shook his head. 'Not a wise move, Bimbo. You have just eaten the Poison Pawn. Now your Queen is doomed, for I can pursue her with Knight and Bishop and she will fall.'

'Poison Pawn. I don't understand.'

'It is like a sacrifice. The little pawn stands alone, unprotected, begging the Queen to eat her. When the Queen does so she has signed her own death warrant.'

'You do put a lotta colour in the game, Step.'

'It is a great game, but it is a game of death. Checkmate is a bastardisation of the Persian Shah Mat – the king is dead. Let us stop for a while. My brain is tired.'

'Balls! You're just feelin' sorry for me.'

'That too. Some tea?'

'Why not?' Bimbo glanced at the clock on the mantelshelf. It was almost midnight. 'Don' half make time fly, playin' chess.'

'Yes,' agreed Stepney, returning with a teapot and two mugs on a silver tray.

'Where'd you learn to play?'

'In Russia. It is the spiritual home of the game these days.'

'I didn't know you'd bin to Russia.'

'There is much you do not know, my friend. I was taught by a cossack. Fine man, great horseman. The game helped overcome my fears.'

'Fears of what?'

'Of being killed, or captured, or maimed.'

'You talkin' about the war?'

'Of course. Why else would a civilised man want to cross Russia?'

'Was you with the Russian army?'

Stepney chuckled, and poured the tea. 'I was with the

63

Totenkopf Regiment – Deathshead. We were an SS Panzer group.'

'Germans? I thought you was a Jew,' said Bimbo, surprised.

'One of life's ironies, my friend. God's little joke. I am a German, from a good Aryan family. But I was telling you of the war. We were the pride of the German army. Unbeatable. We crushed all resistance and swept across the Soviet army like elephants across a field of ants. Great tank, the Tiger. On firm, flat ground there was no machine on earth to match it. But – with the diesel fuel frozen solid it was just another metal monster, immobile and useless.'

'I seen a film once about the war. Winter done ya,' said Bimbo.

'That and a costly mistake. We misread the people. When we invaded we were met by cheering crowds. They hated Stalin. They looked on us as deliverers. We could have had an enormous army of cossacks riding with us. But our leaders believed in the principles of rule by terror. Jews were rounded up and slaughtered. Russian peasants were herded into slave labour camps. We proved worse than the Bolsheviks and the people turned against us. Stalingrad was a nightmare beyond description. But some of us broke out and limped home. Home? Ruins and ashes.' The old man fell silent.

'Long time ago, Step.'

'I give you some advice, Bimbo. You take it.'

'Sure.'

'Never do anything your heart is against. *Verstehen*?'

Bimbo gazed at the old man, saw the intensity in his eyes and then nodded. 'Sure,' he said.

Stepney shook his head. 'No! This is not some idle theory, and I do not wish you to patronise me. What I am telling you is about life. It is so easy to compromise, to tell yourself it does not matter. Or someone else will do it if you don't. It always matters. The world can crush us and kill us, but the most terrifying injuries are always from within. Our own deeds. They can torment us with whips of fire. Once I did a terrible thing ...'

The old man fell silent, then licked his thin lips.

'You don't have to tell me. I don't need to know,' said Bimbo, swiftly.

'Confession is good for the soul, nicht war?' But Stepney said nothing more, and sat silently, staring down at the chessboard.

'It's gettin' late, Step,' said Bimbo, rising. 'I'll see you Monday.'

'You are a good boy, Bimbo. Follow the heart, eh?'

'Yeah. Look after yourself.'

The Reverend Richard Kilbey opened the vestry door about three inches and peeped out at the congregation. Almost a hundred people had gathered for Morning Communion and he allowed himself a fleeting moment of pride. When he had first come to this West London parish three years ago the first congregation had numbered twelve. A towering figure at the back caught his eye. The vicar shut the door and smiled.

'Good congregation today,' he told Evans, his sidesman and leading baritone.

The organ sounded and Richard stepped back to allow the choir to precede him as they filed into the old church, and along both sides of the aisle to the choir stalls. Richard knelt before the podium and tried to pray. But Bimbo's face intruded on his communion with the Creator.

'Forgive me, Lord,' he whispered, 'but I cannot concentrate.' Every Sunday for a year Bimbo Jardine had stood at the back, singing with gusto in a voice that sounded like a runaway concrete mixer. Some of the regulars had, at first, visited Richard at the Vicarage, to complain about this man of violence in their midst. But Bimbo was never less than pleasant and always commented on the service when Richard shook hands with his parishioners at the door.

'It isn't right he should be allowed in,' said Mrs Collis, one day.

'The church is for sinners,' he had told her. She had not returned.

The service opened with *Jerusalem*, a particular favourite of Richard's – and of Bimbo's, judging by the power with which he launched into it. The choir rose valiantly to the task of drowning him out.

The sermon was shorter than usual, but Richard was satisfied with it. There were few coughs and the congregation seemed attentive.

After the service Richard shook hands in the vaulted, gothic doorway. Bimbo was one of the last to leave.

'Nice to see you, Bimbo. Are you well?'

'Mustn't grumble, Rev. Good service. Nice 'ymns.'

As the last of the congregation bid farewell to the vicar his sidesman, Joseph Evans, approached him.

'Do you really think we should extend a welcome to him, Richard? Mrs Collis has now convinced at least seven regulars to join her at the Baptist Hall.'

'Let me be absolutely frank, Joseph. I am not in the numbers game. And although I am sorry that Mrs Collis felt the need to take her presence to another church I cannot say it troubles me greatly. I always found her to be a mean-spirited woman.'

Joseph's eyes showed his surprise. 'That's the first time in three years I've heard you criticise a parishioner.'

'Perhaps it is time I began. Last week I told the congregation about the problems faced by the Refuge for Battered Wives. I put a tin at the back of the church. By Sunday evening it contained seven pounds seventeen pence. I estimate almost three hundred people attended our services that day. And I personally saw Bimbo put in five pounds.'

'This is not a rich area, Richard.'

'I know that well, but how many of our flock are without a

colour television? Or a video machine? Or go without foreign holidays? Last month you and Marjorie asked for help decorating a pensioner's home. How many came forward from Men's Fellowship? Two, wasn't it? You and me.'

'You sound bitter. It's not like you.'

'Not bitter, Joseph, sad. I am reminded of the rather lovely story of the woman who died. She had attended church every day of her life, but had never done a single kind deed for anyone. Still she went to Heaven. When she arrived an angel led her down a street of mansions, further down a street of fine houses, on to a series of terraced dwellings and finally to a shanty shack at the edge of an old wasteground. "Here is your home," he said. "But this is terrible," she told him. "I know," he replied, "but it was all we could build with the material you sent up."'

'You should use that in your sermon, Richard.'

'Perhaps I will.'

Outside, Bimbo surveyed the clear blue sky. All in all it wasn't a bad day, he decided. Mrs Echo Jerome was out of danger and making a good recovery, Adrian seemed to be coming out of his near suicidal depression, and the sun was shining fit to burst. He made his way to the Indian deli, bought a loaf of granary bread, and wandered to the park to feed his swan. He'd enjoyed the service, and he liked the man he still considered 'the new vicar'. Short sermons, but always punchy, coming at you like a series of left jabs, followed by the knockout right cross. Good timin', thought Bimbo. And a good choice of hymns, by God! That *Jerusalem* now, lovely words, full of colour and glory. Spears of burnished gold. You could almost see 'em shining. And chariots of fire. Made a great film title out of that one. Something about runners in long shorts beatin' the arse off the Yanks, which was no bad thing.

What was the other line in the film? Oh yeah, some geezer

who wouldn't run on a Sunday. Decent sort, especially for a Scotsman. Bimbo had watched it on a rainy Saturday night, just after he'd busted that Italian git's collar bone. Funny bloke. He'd gone straight to the Old Bill, and earned Bimbo another three months inside. No accounting for people.

The park was crowded and the swan had taken sanctuary on her island. Bits of bread still floated on the water, ignored even by the usually voracious ducks. Bimbo put his loaf away and left the park, heading down the long lane to the Stag.

It was all tower blocks now, but when Bimbo was a boy there had been rows of terraced homes, and alleyways, where cowboys and Indians had roamed at will. It all seemed colder now, and the kids hung around in groups, staring with predatory eyes at passers by.

He arrived at the pub just after 2 p.m. and was greeted with a wary smile by Jack Shell, the publican. Mac had spoken of Shell. The man didn't like the idea of paying protection and had talked of forming the other publicans into a resistance unit. They hadn't been interested.

Mac said Reardon had toyed with the idea of 'giving Shell a spanking', but had been talked out of it. Bimbo liked the bluff publican. He ordered a half-pint of pure orange juice and sat by the window watching a darts match. A black labrador nuzzled at his hand and he scratched at its ears.

'Too bleedin' friendly that dog,' said Bernie Eaves, sitting down beside Bimbo and looking with regret at the empty pint glass he carried.

'Light and bitter, Bernie?' offered Bimbo.

'That's decent of you, son.'

Eaves was well known as a sponger, but he was a pleasant old man and had once been a fairground fighter of some distinction. Bimbo brought him his drink and returned to watching the darts.

'No point havin' friendly dogs in this area,' said Eaves. 'You want something that'll take their bloody throats out.'

'Wot you talkin' about?'

'The young bastards movin' in now,' said Eaves. 'Cut your heart out for a fiver, most of 'em.'

'You aint bin mugged again?'

'Nah. They did little Ernie last week. You know Ernie? The one with the limp. Snatched his wallet and whacked him round the head.'

'How's the wife?' asked Bimbo, switching the subject.

'Fit as a bleedin' fiddle. Still giving me stick over a bird I was seen with in 1951. Never forget, women. I only gave her a bleedin' light.'

'Dunno why she stuck with you, Bernie. She must have bin a right looker when she was young.'

'She's still a looker, son. You just have to be older to appreciate it. You still with Reardon?'

'Yeah.'

'Well keep out of his way today. He's right pissed off.'

'Why?'

'Well, accordin' to Ronnie – and don't you go repeatin' it – somebody's muscled in on Reardon's patch.'

'No? No one'd be that stupid.'

'Straight up, Bim. Reardon set up this business with an Irish geezer called Reilly. Anyway, a rival firm busted up Reilly's snooker hall and broke his bloody fingers. What do you think about that? There were about a dozen of 'em by all accounts. Hard as nails. Ex commandos, they say. From the East End.' Bimbo's mouth felt dry and a strange queasiness hit his stomach.

'But that's down the Bush. That aint Reardon's patch.'

'You aint listenin', son. Reardon is backing this bloke Reilly. Expandin' the empire, aint he?'

'I don't believe it,' said Bimbo. But he did.

'You better believe this then. Reardon's only drafted in Jackie

Green. So somebody's gonna get his head cracked. You know Jackie?'

'Boxer wasn't he?'

'Bleedin' good un, an' all. Greedy bugger. Got hooked in on a Securicor caper and went down. Lost his licence.'

'Well, they don't fight Marquis a Queensbury rules round here, Bernie,' said Bimbo.

'You don't know Jackie, son. He's a piggin' killer. Near as big as you, he could beat a man to death without no pickaxe handle.'

'Nice. So what's the word now?'

'They're gonna move in on this other firm and turn it over. Expect you'll be in on that.'

'I doubt it. There aint no other firm.'

'What you talkin' about?'

'I busted the geezer's fingers. He was havin' a go at a mate of mine. There aint no dozen hard men. It was just me.'

'Fuckin' hell, son,' said Bernie, dropping his voice. 'What you gonna do?'

'I'll go explain it to Mr Reardon.'

'I shouldn't, son. He won't like it.'

'But I didn't know, did I? He'll understand.'

Bernie leaned in close. 'I may be old, Bimbo, but I aint as green as I'm cabbage lookin'. I know what Reardon's like. I've seen men like him all me life. He won't believe ya, and if he does he'll still have ya seen to. To stop people laughin' at him. I should wander off somewhere. Move over the East End or summink. You aint got no roots.'

Bimbo drained the last of his orange juice. 'I like it here, Bernie. This is me home, innit? I'll straighten it out.'

'Good luck, son.'

4

Frank Reardon was a dapper man and a keep fit enthusiast. Just under six feet tall he weighed 160 pounds, and at the age of 42 still had the same waist measurement he had had as Regimental middleweight champion. He stepped from the squash court beneath his Richmond home and congratulated his young partner on a close-fought match. That the man had allowed him to win he had no doubt, but then that was the reward of power. It was immaterial to Reardon that the younger man was more skilful. The only fact that mattered was his subservience. Reardon showered and dressed in a white silk shirt, grey slacks and a designer jacket of grey silk, and joined his guests by the pool.

Most of them were boring: local councillors anxious to taste the high life and, so, eager for his bribes, two solicitors, and several chamber of commerce social climbers But the rest were diamonds. Two came from television, four from the theatre – one of whom was strongly tipped for a knighthood in the New Year Honours list. The thought of entertaining a genuine knight at the Citadel gave Reardon a deep, inner glow.

His wife, Jean, was doing her usual splendid job entertaining the guests, moving about the poolside with unhurried style and almost regal poise. But then that's why he had married her. It certainly wasn't for the sex, which was a bloody shame. She was quite the most beautiful woman he had ever seen in the flesh, but boneless in bed. Like making love to a filleted cod. But he'd found the answer, by God. And now she knew who was the boss at the Citadel. He looked at her, his eyes raking the lines of the long dress, and pictured the bruises on that pale posterior. He turned away as arousal flickered.

'Frank, my dear, you look disgustingly fit.'

Reardon bared his capped teeth in a wide smile. 'Peter, so glad you could come. I saw the first night. Marvellous.'

'Not a bad piece, is it? There's some talk of a movie version.'

For a few minutes Reardon chatted with the actor, then moved around the guests, shaking hands, smiling, his pleasure real, his mood almost serene. For years he had wanted to cultivate people like this, and had sought to disguise his business life. And then one day he had realised that 'society folk' loved mixing with dangerous men. Subtly he allowed a few rumours to circulate. Now he was hip-deep in socialites.

One woman had even begged him to make love to her in a back room of a casino, and was hugely disappointed to find he was not wearing a shoulder holster, equipped with a Magnum.

On the far side of the pool Jackie Green caught his eye. Reardon moved through his guests and took Green by the arm, leading him through the long, architect designed conservatory and out to the marble fountain.

'Mac's called in. Bimbo is on his way over.'

Reardon swore. 'Did he give a reason?'

'No.'

'If that bastard turns up here in that track suit I'll set the bloody dogs on him.'

'l hear he's quite handy,' said Green. Reardon grinned as he recognised the light of challenge in the huge boxer's eyes.

'Not in your class, Jackie. He's a streetfighter. And a good one. Knuckle and skull. But up against a boxer ... no chance.'

'Loyal, is he?'

'Loyal, Jackie? Who the hell is loyal? He does what he's told, and he knows the rules. He's been down twice and never grassed.'

'No danger then?'

'You'd like him to be, wouldn't you? It's like watching a bull on heat. Have you always had this urge to destroy things?'

Green grinned. 'Just people, Mr Reardon. Certain people.'

'Well Bimbo's no danger. How old are you, Jackie?'

'Thirty-one.'

'You should have been British champion. Ever thought of fighting again?'

'Course I have. But I can't get me licence back, and if I did, no manager would have the guts to take me on.'

'It's not guts, Jackie. Don't feed yourself bullshit. They wouldn't take you on because you're trouble. Birds, booze, gambling. No discipline. But you stick by me, son, and you might just get your chance. You still training?'

'Five miles a day and two hours in the gym.'

'Keep it up. You do well by me and in three months we'll stage a comeback. Maybe even a stab at Frank Bruno.'

'Whatever you want you get,' whispered Green. 'I'd bleedin' kill for a chance to get back in the ring. And I could handle Bruno. No sweat.'

Reardon smiled and moved back to his guests.

The party broke up at around 8 p.m. and Reardon saw the last of his guests to the wrought iron gates, waving as the red Ferrari containing Peter and his boyfriend roared off towards Chelsea. The electronically operated gates were swinging shut when a lumbering figure in an old track suit appeared from the shadows.

'Mr Reardon. It's me. Bimbo.'

'Mac said you were on your way hours ago.'

'I saw you 'ad guests. So I waited. Sorry to bovver you at 'ome.'

'Open the gates, Jackie! Come in Bimbo. What's on your mind?'

'Well, there's bin a bit of a cock up over this Shepherd's

Bush business. I don't know how to explain it really …' Bimbo stumbled to a halt as Jackie Green appeared from the gate tower. The man was powerfully built, weighing in at around seventeen stone. His head was close cropped and his chin, powerful and square, masked the sensitive nerve ends under the jaw. Almost impossible to knock out. He was wearing a white tuxedo which showed off his massive frame to great advantage.

'Go on, Bimbo. I haven't got all night. You can talk in front of him.'

'Well, there was this geezer wot threatened a friend of mine. And some heavies done him over. So …'

'Get to the point.'

'I'm doin' me best. Like I said this friend got turned over. So I sorted the other bastards out.'

'How does this affect me?'

'It was Reilly, weren't it?'

'Reilly?'

'Yeah. I broke his fingers.'

'Who did you have with you?'

'Wiv me? Nobody. They was a gutless bunch. I just turned over his two collectors and went down the club and sorted him.'

'Reilly says there were five men.'

'He's bullshittin'. It was only me. You can check with the cabbie. He took me there with this other geezer. He 'ad a nose-bleed.'

'The cabbie had a nosebleed?'

'No, the other geezer. He was one of Reilly's collectors. I broke his nose. John, I think 'is name was.'

'You expect me to believe this crap?' But he did believe it. There was no cunning in Bimbo Jardine, no *side.* If he said he went alone, then that's just what happened.

'It's straight up, Mr Reardon. No 'arm done, though, eh?'

74

Anger flared in Reardon then. 'No harm done? You think the word won't get out? Reardon turns over his own pigging operation? Left hand doesn't know what the right's doing? I could be a laughing stock, Bimbo. You think I should just let you get away with that?'

'I never knew you was behind Reilly.'

'Get out, Bimbo. You don't work for me any more. You don't work for anyone any more.'

'Hold on, Mr Reardon ...'

'You hard of hearing, pig-brain?' said Jackie Green, moving forward. Their eyes met and Reardon saw the malice lurking in Green's gaze.

'I hear all right,' said Bimbo, backing away. The malice was replaced by triumph as Bimbo ambled away into the night.

'You want me to turn him over, Mr Reardon?'

'No. That would be like sending the SAS out to punish a schoolboy. Roache and Taggart can do it. If he takes his punishment well I'll let him back in a month or two. Good bruisers are hard to come by. And Bimbo's the best.'

'You sound like you like him.'

'Everybody likes him. But that's not the point, Jackie. You ever study Machiavelli?'

'Never heard of him.'

'He once asked Cesare Borgia, Is it better to rule by love or fear? Borgia said both were good, but love is bestowed on a ruler at the whim of the people, and can therefore be lost, whereas fear is bestowed on the people by the ruler. You understand?'

'Sure,' said Green, but Reardon knew the man was humouring him.

'What it comes down to, Jackie, is that people will need to see Bimbo pay. Then everything will get back to normal.'

'I'd really like to do it, Mr Reardon.'

'Save your energy for Mr Bruno. Now let's have a drink.'

*

Bimbo walked out of the cinema with the film only half finished. He'd seen enough. Bodies everywhere and enough blood to sink a bleedin' tanker. What was the point of it? And who the bloody hell was the hero? Jackie Green's face came unbidden to his mind. Now he would enjoy that movie. The look in the boxer's eyes that day had remained with Bimbo long after he walked home from Richmond. It was like looking into the eyes of a man-killing animal. It was now a week since Bimbo had tried to apologise – and there was no sign of work. Even Mac wouldn't see him.

Bimbo stopped in the foyer and bought a carton of orange juice. It was dripping with sugar and he left it on the counter.

'Not enjoying the movie?' asked the blonde receptionist behind the confectionery counter.

'Nab. It's all violence and killin'.'

'That's what people want.'

'You ever see *Shane*?'

'Western wasn't it? With Alan Ladd?'

'Yeah. Now that was a film. A proper film.'

She grinned. 'Where the hero always had the white hat.'

'Yeah. At least you could tell who the flamin' hero was.'

'Wasn't like real life though,' she said.

'And that is?'

She shrugged. 'It's pulling in the crowds, which makes my job safer. It's done great business. And they're making a follow-up. You going to finish that drink?'

'Nah. Nice talkin' to ya.'

He wandered out into the night and turned up the collar of his donkey jacket. The wind was cold and autumn was fast encroaching on the last days of summer. So many people in there, watching that filth. He tried to remember where he'd seen the actor before. But the memory slid around and he was unable to get a hook into it. He shivered and began to jog along the High

Street. A clap of thunder heralded a sudden downpour and he ducked into a hamburger bar fronting the arcade.

The place was empty and Bimbo sat by the window watching the rippling rain melting the illuminated Barclay's sign across the street. The film kept coming back at him. How could they sit there and enjoy that crap? Did they really think life was like that? All that hatred and death? And the actor ... Bronson! That was it! He was in that western with Yul Brynner about gunfighters what went to Mexico to save a village. He ought to be ashamed of himself, thought Bimbo. Mind you, he probably had about ten ex-wives and needed the money. And he was gettin' on a bit.

'What can I get you?' asked a sallow-faced young man in a stained apron.

'Cuppa tea.'

'After 10 p.m. you have to spend £1.50.'

'Just a cuppa tea, son, seein' as how you're so busy.'

The man thought about it for a moment then shrugged. 'Comin' up,' he said.

A cold draught touched Bimbo's back. He turned to see a young girl stepping in out of the rain, her imitation leather coat drenched, her bleached-blonde hair plastered to her face. She sat two tables from Bimbo. The manager approached her.

'What can I get you?'

'Coffee, please.'

'Just coffee?'

'Yes.'

'My night for getting rich,' he said, as he walked back past Bimbo. The girl opened a narrow black handbag and produced a purse. Bimbo watched as she tipped the contents into her hand.

'Can you make that a tea?' she called.

'I've already poured it out.'

'I haven't got enough for a coffee.'

'The evening gets better and better,' said the manager.

'I'll have the coffee,' said Bimbo. 'She can have my tea.'

'Sorry to cause you trouble,' the girl told the manager. He ignored her. Bimbo transferred his gaze to the street. The rain shone like oil on the brickwork of the buildings opposite. He heard the rustle of the girl's coat and looked up as she slid in opposite him. She was tall and slim with large blue eyes and a staggeringly pale complexion.

She forced a smile. 'Can you lend me a few quid?'

'You want somethin' to eat?'

She nodded. 'I'll pay you back.'

'It aint necessary. Order what you fancy.'

'Can I have a double cheeseburger. No onions,' she called.

'Oh happy days,' said the manager, bringing their drinks to the table.

'Bin out in the rain long?' asked Bimbo.

'About two hours.'

Bimbo drained his coffee. It was stewed and bitter.

'Do you live around here?' asked the girl.

'Yeah. Just off the estate.'

'You couldn't put me up for the night, could ya?' The manager placed the cheeseburger in front of her, but her eyes remained fixed on Bimbo

'You aint very bright, kid, are yer? Didn't your dad warn you about strange men?'

'Me dad *was* a strange man,' she said, picking up the cheeseburger and biting into it. Bimbo sat quietly, watching her eat. She was young, not yet twenty, maybe not even eighteen. Yet her eyes were world weary. She finished the burger and leaned back.

'All right?' he asked.

'Vile. But it filled a hole. Thanks. Can I spend the night? I don't mind if we ... you know ... make out.'

'Make out? I don't make out. I wouldn't even know how.'

78

'Gay, are ya? I don't mind.'

'I aint gay,' he said, without rancour. 'It don't matter. Sure you can stay. How come you got nowhere else?'

'I had a row with me boyfriend.'

'He's probably regrettin' it now. You want me to walk you back?'

She grinned. 'You're a weird one, aint ya? He aint forgotten. If he sees me again he'll punch my teeth out. He wanted me to sleep with a mate of his. A right toe-rag called Bobby. Never bleedin' washes. I said I wouldn't. He said Bobby had already paid. Then he hit me. So I walked out.'

'Sounds like you're better off out of it.'

'Yeah. Aint that the truth.'

'How old are ya?'

'Old enough to tell the time. Me name's Sharon. You?'

'Bimbo.'

'Bimbo Jardine?'

'Yeah. Do I know ya?'

'You broke my boyfriend's arm. Tony. Remember?'

'It was an accident.'

'I don't give a toss. If you hadn't done that I'd never have been able to get away. He'd a bleedin' tied me to the bed. He's done that before.'

'How come you took it?'

'Dunno. Thought he loved me. Stupid innit? Love. No such bleedin' thing. All a man wants is somewhere warm to put his willie.' Bimbo chuckled.

'You think that's funny?' she snapped. 'It aint so bleedin' funny when you have to live with it.'

'Yeah,' said Bimbo, 'I guess it aint. But the world aint full of scumbags like Tony. It just seems like it sometimes.'

'You got a girlfriend?'

'No. Not really.'

'What does "not really" mean?'

'She's goin' out with someone else. But we're still friends.'

'How come you didn't see him off, this other geezer?'

'Why should I?'

'You are weird. Can we go? This place aint too friendly.'

'Sure.' Bimbo rose and walked to the till.

'Two pounds nine pence,' said the manager. 'My cup runneth over.'

Outside the rain had eased to a fine drizzle and they wandered west.

'Is it far to your place?'

'Nah. Fifteen minutes.'

'Couldn't we get a cab then? My feet are killing me.'

'Walkin's good for you.'

'Well, at least a drink then.'

Bimbo chuckled and took her arm, steering her towards the Railway Tavern. The pub was old fashioned, which meant it had only one fruit machine and no juke-box and was packed with regulars. Bimbo eased his way to the bar.

'What do ya drink?'

'Brandy,' she told him. The barman approached, licking his lips.

'Evening, Andy,' said Bimbo. 'Brandy for the lady and a pineapple juice for me.'

Andy leaned across the bar. 'I'm sorry, Bim, but we can't serve you.'

'I 'ope this is a joke,' said Bimbo. The man's face reddened.

'It aint me, mate. The boss told me.'

'Well get 'im over 'ere.'

'It won't do no good, Bim. It's come from Reardon, innit? Sorry.' Andy moved away to take another order. Bimbo turned from the bar, looking around the packed lounge. There were several people he knew, but none of them were looking his way. He waited, but their eyes remained fixed.

'Sorry, sweetheart,' he told Sharon.

'What you done then?'

'Aint got a clue. We'll go down the Barley. It's only about a hundred yards.'

The Barley was a bikers' pub, which meant it was either full or empty. No half-way measures. Tonight it was near empty. Bimbo saw the look on the middle-aged barmaid's face as he entered, and guessed the response.

'Sorry, Bim, love. But you're barred. It's nothing to do with me.'

'Thass all right, Doreen. Aint your fault.'

'Look, my brother runs a pub in Chelsea. He's always looking for help. Why don't you go over there for a while? Nice area. And it aint Reardon's patch – not yet anyway.'

'I like it here.'

'I don't think you are going to like it here, Bim. Derek told us tonight there isn't a pub that'll serve you. And Taggart and Roache have been asking after you. There's going to be trouble.'

'Nah. It'll blow over. I aint done nothin'.'

'Taggart and Roache, Bim. Don't forget them. They aint nice people.'

'I know.'

Bimbo stood for a moment, uncertain. Sharon touched his arm.

'Can you lend me ten quid?'

'Sure. Why?'

'I got a friend in Fulham. She can put me up for the night. I'll get a cab over.'

'You're welcome to stay at my place.'

'Thanks anyway … but I think you're trouble. I don't need any more trouble.'

'Yeah.' Bimbo peeled two £5 notes from his shrinking roll. 'Good luck, anyway.'

'I don't think it's me that needs the luck.'

Bimbo shrugged and moved to the door. Sharon ordered a

brandy and sat quietly at the bar. Doreen wiped the bar top clear of beer rings.

'Known him long?' asked the barmaid.

'Just met him tonight.'

'Nice bloke, Bimbo.'

'What's he done?'

Doreen shrugged. 'It don't matter what he's done. It's enough that Taggart and Roache are looking for him. Evil pair. I watched them grow up. From tiny tots who liked pulling wings off butterflies, know what I mean?'

'Yeah. But he's no different, is he? He's a collector. He broke my boyfriend's arm.'

'Oh he's different, love. Otherwise why give you ten quid?'

'It's a loan.'

'Yeah? You don't even know where he lives, do you? How you going to pay him back? But he knew that. And don't care. Soft touch is Bimbo. Everybody knows that.'

Bimbo crossed the road and moved on to the estate. It was dark here, several of the street lights having been shot out with air rifles. The rain had stopped and thoughts of Taggart and Roache flickered in his mind. He had known both men for some years, and liked neither of them. Taggart was a huge man of Irish descent, with a mop of dark, curly hair and a handsome face. He was known to carry a ten-inch piece of lead pipe which he used with lightning speed, rendering any opponent unconscious. Roache was smaller and slimmer, six feet tall and weighing around fourteen stone. His preferred weapon was a brass knuckleduster that fitted neatly over the fingers of his right hand, adding weight and bone-crunching power to his blows.

Why were they looking for him? He knew the answer. Reardon had decided to punish him for something he had done in all innocence. He had helped a friend. And for that he must pay.

It wasn't right.

His instincts warned him to leave the area for a while, but something deeper inside snarled at such an action. He turned up his collar against the biting wind and moved on. Nothing stirred on the estate, and Bimbo's eyes took in all the shadows, wary of any sign of movement.

Once inside the downstairs hallway he relaxed and mounted the stairs. A strange, antiseptic smell greeted him as he arrived at his flat on the first floor. Esther's door opened.

'Bimbo?'

''Allo princess, how ya doin'?'

'I'm okay. I cleaned your door.'

'I didn't know it needed cleaning.'

'Someone smeared dog's mess over it.'

'Nice. Sorry about that.'

'It wasn't any trouble. Why would anyone want to do that?'

'Dunno. It's bin that sorta day. Wanna coffee?'

'Sure.'

Inside the flat he switched on the wall-mounted gas fire. Esther padded in barefoot and sat on the rug in front of the heat. She was wearing her white towelling dressing gown, and her hair shone from a recent shower.

'How's the doc?' called Bimbo from the kitchen.

'He's fine. We went to a restaurant called Valentinos. It was lovely. We're going away next weekend to a flat he owns in Sussex. I've never been to Sussex. It's supposed to be beautiful.'

'Yeah,' he said, entering with two mugs of steaming coffee. 'I had a little job there one summer. Place called Hastings. I done the deckchairs on the beach, you know, wandering around and taking the cash if people wanted to avoid sitting on the tar. Nice little number. Friendly people down there.'

'We're going to Rye.'

'That's nice an' all. Cobbled streets. Real class. You'll love it.'

'You're soaked,' she said. 'Get out of those wet clothes, you'll catch pneumonia.'

'Nah. The fire'll dry 'em.'

'Where you been tonight?'

'Went to the pictures. Bleedin' terrible film. Some bloke mowing down bikers with a machine gun. Packed out the place was. Terrible. Gave me a right headache.'

'It's what people want, Bimbo. Plenty of action.'

'You like them films?'

'No. But then I see violence all the time at the hospital. I thought you didn't like going to the pictures.'

'Nothin' else to do. I used to love the films when I was a kid. They had a telly at the Home. Old black and white thing, with doors on the front. That's where l first seen *Shane*, and *The Cisco Kid*, and *Cheyenne*. You remember *Cheyenne*?'

'No. I remember *Shane*. There was a lovely little boy in it.'

'That's right. A proper film, proper hero. Never lost his rag, never screwed nobody, and only killed the villains when there was no other way. It all seemed so right then.'

'The world changed, Bimbo.'

'Yeah,' he said, sadly. 'Guess so.'

'Maybe there never was a Shane kind of world. Maybe it's just pictures.'

'Nah. Can't believe that. There wouldn't be no point to nothin', would there?'

'I don't know what you mean.'

'No. Neither do I, really. Don't mind me, sweetheart. I'm glad you and the doc are hittin' it off.'

'He's a lovely man, Bimbo. Kind, strong. Bit like you really.'

'Yeah. I can see the resemblance.'

She laughed. 'You know what I mean. Simeon cares.' She looked up at him and he could see the concern in her eyes. 'You know what you ought to get? A video. Then you could watch all those old films you like. Might cheer you up.'

'I aint even got a TV.'

'Well they're not impossible to buy, you know. You just walk into a shop. Are you all right?'

'Sure. Fit as a fiddle.'

'That's not what I mean. You seem ... a bit down.'

'Nah. It's only the film.'

'Would you like me to stay?'

'Now what would your doctor friend think about that? No. You get on back home. Get a good night's kip.'

She kissed him on the cheek and left.

'*Maybe there never was a Shane kind of world. Maybe it's just pictures.*' The words echoed round in his mind, and he felt the cold touch of panic.

5

Bimbo woke at seven, pulled on his track suit and trainers and set off across the estate. The sun was shining and a light breeze fanned his face as he ran. Today felt like a good day. He did his normal six-mile figure eight and returned to the flat. Waiting outside was one of the young men he had seen with the black sex-show girl.

'You looking for me, son?'

'Yes. I'm Daniel, remember? The church hall?'

'I remember. How are ya?'

'Okay. Your friend Adrian gave me your address. Hope you don't mind.'

'Depends on why,' said Bimbo, wiping his sleeve across his sweat streaked face.

'Miranda's got a gig tonight. Private house in Ealing. Big place. She wants you to be there.'

'What for?'

'You know, look after her.'

'I dunno, son. It aint my game. I only done it for Ade cos he's a mate.'

'There's fifty pounds in it, Mr Bimbo. It's just that Miranda is worried. She accepted the job just after we did the church hall gig. There was this man, big chap, rings on every finger. He made the offer.'

'Yeah. I remember him. He's trouble, son.'

'That's what I think. Will you come?'

'Why don't she just send the money back and call it off?'

Daniel shrugged. 'I guess she's got principles.' Bimbo laughed aloud.

'Okay, son, you said that with a straight face. What's the score tonight?'

'She's going to do a straight strip-tease for a small party, about twenty, and then one of them gets to ... you know.'

'Yeah, I know. And she's worried about a gang bang. What's the fee?'

'Two hundred and fifty. She's already had a hundred.'

'What's the address?'

'Don't worry about that, Miranda and I will pick you up around seven. Is that all right?'

'Sure. But you tell her this is a one-off. I don't like sex shows.'

'How come you're agreeing then?' asked Daniel.

'I'm broke,' admitted Bimbo. Leaving the youngster standing, Bimbo walked into the hall and up to his flat. He showered and dressed in a white sweatshirt and jeans and walked back to the High Street where he waited for a bus to take him to the town hall. It was one of those newfangled one-deck buses where the driver took the fare. Bimbo didn't like them at all and sat at the back, his good mood evaporating.

The town hall was big and ugly, built during the middle Victorian era, and now stained by a century of filthy air and generations of loose bowelled pigeons. He mounted the stone steps and followed the sign to Reception. A middle-aged man was sitting behind the mahogany topped counter. He was extraordinarily thin with bright blue button eyes and a trimmed moustache. He looked at Bimbo and sighed.

'Do you have an appointment with someone, sir?' The voice was world weary, and his tone suggested that it would be a minor miracle if Bimbo actually had an appointment.

'No. I wanna see somebody about a swan.'

'Your swan, sir?'

'Do I look like I keep swans?' Bimbo took a deep breath, struggling to contain his irritation.

'Then whose swan is it?'

'It's one of yours. Down the park.'

'Being a nuisance, is it?'

'How can a swan be a bleedin' nuisance?'

The man sighed. 'What is it about the swan that brings you here?'

Bimbo cleared his throat, his face reddening. 'Well … it's lonely, innit? Its mate got shot a coupla years ago. It's on its own.'

'Lonely swan, right. Don't think we've got a department for that, sir.'

Bimbo leaned forward and fixed the man with a cold stare. 'I tend to be an easygoing bloke, mate. Even when I meet arse-holes like you. Now I'm goin' to ask you a question, and then I'm gonna do one of two things. I'm either gonna walk away, or I'm gonna ram your fucking face on that counter. Understand?' The man swallowed hard, then nodded. 'Good. Who do I see about swans?'

'Go down the hall, turn right, and go up the stairs. Second door on the left. Miss Owlett. Parks Department.'

'Ta. You bin a big help.'

He followed the directions and tapped at the door. There was no answer. Turning the knob, he pushed open the door and stepped inside. A young woman was sitting at a leather topped desk, writing with a smart black Parker fountain pen. Her long brunette hair was drawn back into a severe pony tail and she wore no make-up. She glanced up.

'Can I help you?' she asked, her voice crisp, the words spoken at speed. Her pen remained poised over the writing pad. Bimbo sat down. As he did so she slowly screwed the cap on the pen and laid it on the desk beside the pad.

'It's about the black swan in the park.'

'Which park?'

'Your park. Up the road by the bus depot.'

'We have five parks,' she informed him, 'but yes, I know which one you mean. Is the swan causing a nuisance?'

'I just had this with the bloke downstairs. You get a lot of people complaining about swans do ya?'

'No, actually. That's one thing people rarely complain about.'

'I'm glad to 'ear it. Well I aint complainin' either, love.'

'I am not your love,' she snapped. 'Or your darling, or your sweetheart. Now get to the point, I'm rather busy.'

Bimbo leaned back and took a deep breath. 'The swan needs a mate. She's buildin' a nest, and that aint natural. She's lonely, see. Vandals shot the male bird a coupla years ago, and all her cygnets.'

'The bird is lonely? Are you some sort of expert on swan psychology?'

'No, I'm not. But I'm pretty good at people. Good enough to know when I'm wasting me bleedin' time.' He stood and left the room, closing the door quietly.

Inside Liz Owlett picked up her pen and returned to her notes, and the costings at the Refuge Centre. Forty women were living there at present, without a council grant. But then who cared about battered wives? Or mistreated children? Liz was tired. She capped her pen and pushed her back into the deep leather chair. She could have got the cash for the centre, but then the press started bleating about money for lesbians, and the loony left. The grant was a dead duck then. Sure Pam Edgerley was gay. So were half the committee. But that didn't negate the need for the refuge. Pam would be in soon, and Liz had no good news for her. She swore. Moving to the desk by the window she plugged in the kettle. All over the area women were being maltreated by vicious, sexist bastards like ... like the brute who'd just been in.

God, the way he had called her love.

Calm down, Owlett, she told herself. You're being ridiculous.

The door opened and Pam Edgerley walked in. She was a shade under six feet tall, with short dark hair, highlighted by natural grey. She was wearing tight-fitting jeans and a chunky rust-coloured sweater.

'The news is all bad,' said Liz, swiftly. 'You want some tea?'

'Cheer up, Liz. We didn't expect to win. We had a donation of £250 this morning.'

'Who from?'

'Richard Kilbey. He invited me to talk at Meeting Point – it's the church women's group. They had a fund raising jumble sale for us. Nice man, Richard.'

Liz grinned. 'He probably gets his wife to dress up as a schoolgirl and beats her with a cane.'

'Probably,' said Pam, smiling. 'Why so down?'

'The grant mostly. But I've just had a man in here gave me a wonderful counterpoint. I'm working my guts out to raise funds for a vital project and he wanted me to waste my time on a swan. I mean a swan, for God's sake!'

'What's the matter with it?'

'Oh you'll love this. It's lonely, he says. Needs a mate.'

Pam sat down and sipped her tea. 'Why does he think it's lonely?'

'He says it's building a nest and pining for its dead mate.'

'How sad.'

'Sad? Pam, be serious.'

'I am being serious. Beautiful things, swans. You know they mate for life? My father told me of a swan whose mate died. It refused to eat and starved itself to death. What will you do?'

'I think the world's gone mad,' said Liz.

'It will,' said Pam, 'if ever we stop caring about lonely swans.'

*

Bimbo left the town hall and caught a bus back to the estate, arriving at Maple Road just as Sgt Don Dodds pulled up in the yellow and white Escort. Bimbo sat back on the low wall outside the building and waited as Dodds walked over. The sergeant's uniform was neatly pressed, with not a mark of dust or dandruff, and his buttons shone like polished silver. Immaculate. Bimbo was always impressed by Sgt Dodds.

'I want to talk to you, Bimbo, so invite me in for a cup of tea. You'll get yourself a bad name talking to coppers in the street.'

Bimbo nodded and led the way inside and up the stairs. A large cod lay on the mat outside his door, a skewer through its eyes.

'Like fish, do you?' asked Dodds.

'Somebody's been playing silly buggers,' said Bimbo, picking up the fish. As he lifted it the slit belly flopped open and a dead rat slid to the floor.

'Nice,' said Dodds. 'Check the rat. It could be like one of them Russian dolls, you know, getting smaller and smaller.'

'Very funny,' said Bimbo, picking up the remains and carrying them to the rubbish chute. The smell of the fish hung in the air and Bimbo opened the door of his flat and walked to the kitchen. He scrubbed his hands and plugged in the kettle.

Dodds carefully removed his cap and laid it on the table. 'Life's taking a nasty turn, son.'

'I aint complainin'.'

'Fallen out with Reardon, though, eh?'

Bimbo stepped into the living room with two mugs of tea. Dodds accepted one of them, blowing at the surface before sipping it. 'You didn't answer me, Bimbo.'

'Nothin' to say, Mr Dodds.'

'Nice cuppa, son. Teach you that at the Home did they?'

'Nah. Borstal. They was strong on tea in Borstal. Whaddya want?' he asked, suspiciously. Dodds shook his head.

'I'm not here to get you to grass – not that I wouldn't, but I know you're not the type.'

'Then why are you here?'

'Because I hear things, son, and I don't like what I'm hearing. You've got on the wrong side of Reardon. Now Roache and Taggart are talking about the wonderful rearrangements they're going to make to your face. Get the picture?'

'And you're worried about me, I suppose? Well you aint my fucking mother. You're the fucking Filth!' snapped Bimbo.

Dodds' eyes narrowed and he pushed himself to his feet. 'Don't you get cocky with me, son! If I wasn't worried I wouldn't be here.' Bimbo nodded. He liked the sergeant and felt ashamed of himself. It was always the same, when angry. Like with the Cypriot waiter, calling him a dago, or with the black bloke on the estate, using the term 'jungle bunny'. No way was Dodds 'the Filth'. No way. Bimbo sighed then looked into Dodds' angry eyes.

'I'm sorry, Mr Dodds. It's bin a bad day.'

'It'll get worse,' said Dodds, barely mollified. 'I've been a copper since you were soiling nappies. I've seen all the scumbags – generations of scumbags. They're all the same, Bimbo. They all think they're Jack the Lad, and they're all the bloody same. After a while you know just what they're going to do. Take Reardon. First he makes you high profile. He bars you from the pubs. That makes you interesting. Everybody looks and says, "I wonder what'll happen to Bimbo now?" Then he starts messing around in your life. Like the fish and the rat. Then maybe it's your mates. And finally, when just about every bastard in the manor knows he's after you, he'll have you turned over. Badly. And I mean badly.'

'He's got no reason.'

'Bollocks – if you'll pardon the French. I didn't come down with the last shower of rhubarb, son. You turned over Reilly. Broke his fingers. Don't insult my intelligence by denying it.

Anyway I'm not here to book you. But Reilly's got no credibility now and Reardon's Shepherd's Bush operation is down the toilet. He's got to turn you over. Can't you see it?'

'We'll just have to wait and see,' said Bimbo.

'Wait and … ? Give me one good reason why you can't leave the manor.'

'This is where I live. Aint nobody runnin' me out.'

'Not even Jackie Green?'

Bimbo looked away. 'Why mention him?'

'Did you back down for him? Out at Reardon's?'

'What if I did?'

'I'm not blaming you, son. So would I – even without the hernia. But you've got a reputation as a hard man. Now a lot of little toe-rags might start thinking they can cut you down a peg or two.'

Bimbo's smile was genuine. 'They're always welcome to try, Mr Dodds.'

'There's an old saying, Bimbo, "Never a horse that couldn't be rode, never a man who couldn't be throwed." Bear it in mind, son. You're not Superman. And you're not made of steel. You still dating that black nurse?'

'What's it to you?'

'Nothing, son, except you'd better watch out for her. She'll be on the list. And that gay filth peddler. And probably the old Jew by the station. Trust me, Bimbo. And warn them.'

'It'll blow over, Mr Dodds. You see if it don't. I made a mistake. I said I was sorry. If Roache and Taggart are lookin' for me they're probably doin' it off their own bat. No one's gonna get silly over a misunderstandin' .'

'Pity you can't get that brain of yours to do a few press-ups,' said Dodds, wearily, putting on his hat and making for the door. 'When you go out, watch yourself. Don't relax. Don't trust anybody. Especially invites to out-of-the-way places. Even from old mates. You understand me?'

'Sure.'

'And keep away from Jackie Green.'

'I don't need no advice on that score.'

Sherry Parker sat on the worn vinyl-covered sofa staring at the faded carpet. The kids were upstairs, shrieking their lungs out, giggling and jumping from bed to bed. But the sound floated by Sherry. Her head ached, and her eyes were dry and sore. She stubbed out her cigarette in an over-full ash tray, her eyes flickering to the clock on the mantelshelf.

The social security money had run out, the rent was four months behind, and tonight's supper for the kids would be cornflakes – if there was any milk left. Sherry ran her hand through her greasy hair and gazed down at her body. Once she'd been a sprinter, but now, she thought, her legs looked like upturned milk bottles. She lit another cigarette. Four left. Who cares?

'Mummy, can we have some lemonade?' asked Sarah from the doorway.

'There isn't any.'

'I could go to the shop.'

'Go away! Leave me alone!' screamed Sherry. The little girl backed away, confused and afraid, then ran upstairs. 'I'm sorry,' whispered Sherry.

She had always tried to be a good mother, a good wife. At least she thought she had. But Alan was always complaining. She was frigid, he said. Lousy in bed. How were you supposed to react to five minutes of frenzied humping? But she'd tried to change. She'd bought sexy magazines and read them, attempting to titillate him with her new found knowledge. He said she was acting like a whore. Eight years they'd been together, while he whinged and whined and came home reeking of the perfume from the women he casually screwed. Then one day he had moved out, and, on that same day, she realised just how miserable the last eight years had been. Like a prison sentence. Like a loss of life. When Alan Wilks walked out he took a part of Sherry Parker with him – eight years of her youth, and all of her smiles. He had buried the sprinter under the weight of his criticism, cut her with the knife edge of his tongue, and stolen her confidence, sucking it from her into the vacuum of his contempt.

Now he sent no money for the children, and Sherry was about to lose her home, and possibly her kids, to the care of the council.

'Oh God!' she said, dropping her face to her hands.

'When we having tea mum?' said Simon. Sherry heaved herself from the sofa and wandered into the tiny kitchen. Plates and dishes were piled high on the draining board and the rubbish bin was filled to overflowing. She opened the cupboard and stood staring at the shelves. There was a tin of tomatoes, a half-empty packet of sage stuffing, three slices of bread and some cornflakes.

'God in Heaven,' she said.

'Don't cry, mummy,' said Sarah, tears on her face.

'There's nothing to sell,' said Sherry, staring down at her hands. Her wedding ring was long gone, and she'd even sold the television – and that was rented.

'Let's go for a walk,' she said.

'I'm hungry, mummy.'

'Later. Get your coats on.'

Bimbo was feeding his swan when the children spotted him. He was wearing his old jeans and a torn blue track suit top. Sarah raced towards him. He hoisted her high and she shrieked with delight. Young Simon was further back, but he yelled, 'Me too, Bimbo! Me too!' Bimbo obliged, then transferred his gaze to Sherry, who was still some distance away. Her shoulders were bowed, her hair unkempt.

'Mummy's bin cryin',' said Sarah. 'And there's no tea.'

''Allo, Sher.'

'Bimbo.'

'You aint lookin' too good.'

'Nice of you to say so,' she snapped.

'Aint what I meant,' he said, softly.

'Yeah? What did you mean?'

'I meant you're lookin' ill, like flu or summink,' he said, carefully. 'Sit down for a minute.'

'I can't stop. I got too much to do.' But she hovered.

'Go and play on the swings, kids, I want to talk to yer mum.' They galloped off, shrieking, in a race to the slide, which Sarah, being the oldest, was bound to win. But Simon battled gamely to catch her. 'Nice kids,' he said, taking her arm. 'Sit down. Just for a minute.' Sherry allowed herself to be led to the park bench and she sagged to the seat, staring at the swan gliding through the water.

'What's gettin' you down?'

'It's none of your business. And I don't want you givin' no more money to Sarah. We aint a bloody charity case.'

'You angry with me, Sher?'

'Don't call me Sher. I hate it. No, I aint lookin' too good. But I did once, didn't I? Which is more than can be said for you. At least I had my day. You used to fancy me rotten, didn't you? I used to watch you standing in the playground. Never had the nerve to ask me out – not that I'd have gone with you. I used to wonder what you were scared of.'

'You was always too good for me,' he said. 'I thought you'd do better for yourself.'

'And didn't I just? Prince bastard Charming I got.'

'Is there anything I can do?'

'Bit bloody late, isn't it? The playground's a long way from here. Or do you just want to get into me knickers? Yeah? I'd even screw you for a tenner for some food. That what you want?

96

A quick bang for a tenner? No. Wouldn't be worth it, would it? I expect he's told everyone what a lousy lay I was. Expect I'm the talk of the town.'

She began to cry. Bimbo had no words to ease her pain, but his huge arm circled her, pulling her gently into him. Her head came down on his shoulder and he patted her back. The swan waddled up on to her island and the lonely nest, settling down almost hidden from view.

After a little while Sherry pulled away from him and dried her eyes. 'I'm sorry,' she said. 'I didn't mean what I said. I wasn't angry with you.'

'I know. How come you don't do Wilks for maintenance?'

She smiled. 'Unemployed isn't he? Everyone knows he makes a good living fencin' for that ponce in Bollo Lane.'

'What about social security?'

'I aint a good manager, Bim.'

'Rent?'

'I last paid it when Noah was buildin' the ark.'

'Tell you what,' said Bimbo. 'We'll talk about it down the McDonald's. We'll all have some burgers and chips or sum-mink. The kids'll like that. And you used to like them chocolate milkshakes, didn't ya? We'll have one of them.' She grinned, and just for a second he caught a glimpse of the girl she had been. They rounded up the children and left the park. At the roadside Sarah grabbed Bimbo's hand, while Sherry caught hold of Simon. As they crossed the road Sherry felt Bimbo's free hand at the small of her back, steering her. In that moment she caught a glimpse of herself in a shop window, the greasy hair, the short dumpy figure. But instead of resignation a tiny spark of anger flared.

As the children finished their burgers and milkshakes Sherry reached across the table and took hold of Bimbo's hand. 'I'm sorry for what I said, Bim. About you never lookin' good. Looks aint everythin'.'

'Don't worry about it. I never was a picture. But a blind man'd be glad to see me, eh?'

'I'm glad to see you.'

'Yeah … well. That's good. We better be goin'. We'll have a quick walk through Tesco's and pick up a few bits.' Sherry didn't complain and Bimbo filled a shopping trolley with food and carried the two bulging bags back to her flat.

'Would you like a coffee?' she asked, as he dropped the bags in the doorway.

'Another time. Thanks, anyway. Look after yourself, Sher.'

He ambled away, hands thrust into his pockets, heading for the High Street and home. A car pulled up alongside him, and a woman's voice called him. He turned. Inside the red Volvo estate he recognised Caroline Shell, wife of the publican who ran the Stag.

'Can I have a word with you?' she asked. She was a thin, blonde woman, with a hard face and a harder nature.

'If you're gonna tell me I'm barred don't bovver. I'd already worked it out.'

'Jack told them he wouldn't bar you.'

Bimbo was surprised, and touched. 'Well, that's nice.'

'Nice? It was bloody stupid. They said if they heard you'd been served there they'd be back to see him. So stay away. My Jack's got plenty of bottle, but not much brain. And I won't see his head kicked in over a thug like you. Do we understand one another?'

'Yeah. Thank him for me.'

'Don't be stupid. I won't even tell him I've seen you. He'd spit blood. Just stay away.' She slipped the car into gear and sped away.

He took a bus to the estate and made his way through Ironside Towers. Silver was sitting on a wall, talking to three black youths. One of them shouted something but Bimbo ignored it and strolled on. Once home he bathed and changed into a light blue roll-neck sweater and a clean pair of jeans. Delving into his wardrobe he pulled clear the old tweed sports jacket and donned it.

Just before seven a car drew up in the road outside and a horn sounded.

Miranda was sitting in the back seat. Daniel was driving. As Bimbo came down the steps she opened the rear door and he slid in beside her, his long legs cramped in the narrow space. Her perfume was overpowering.

'Make sure it's okay for me,' she said.

'I aint the Seventh Cavalry. How many gonna be there?'

'About thirty, I think. Some sort of private party.'

The house was in Perivale, a nice area Bimbo had rarely visited. All the houses were double fronted and reminded him of the old films, the black and white Edgar Wallace jobs. There were four cars in the drive at the building as Daniel drew up, two Porsches, a Jag and a Lotus. Daniel parked the battered Hillman beneath an overhanging willow and the three of them made their way to the front door. Daniel tugged on the bell pull. The door was opened by the tall man Bimbo remembered from the church hall. He had rings on every finger and his hands were wide and thick, the knuckles flat.

'The lovely Miranda,' said Ringo, his voice beautifully modulated and very public school. Bimbo was jolted by the contrast. He had expected West London cockney. The man's eyes switched to the towering figure of Bimbo. 'King Kong, I presume?'

'He's a friend,' said Miranda.

'A minder? How quaint. Fighter, are you?'

'Gonna invite us in, are ya?' responded Bimbo.

'But of course. Follow me.' He led them through to a circular library. You may change in here, my dear. We'll call you through in about ten minutes. All right?'

'How many here?' she asked.

'Just a small party.'

He left and Bimbo settled down in a wide leather chair and opened his jacket. There was a brass newspaper holder to his left and he idly riffled through the papers. *The Times*, *The Sunday Times*, *The Daily Telegraph*, and several copies of *Country Life*. He pulled clear a colour supplement and began to leaf through the pages, stopping at an article about a film star called Jack Nicholson. He was being paid ten million dollars for a film role. Bimbo wondered how much that was in real money.

''Ere, you seen this?' said Bimbo, looking up. Miranda had stripped to red panties and bra and was rolling a white stocking up her leg to fasten it to the white suspender belt. 'Oh. Sorry,' he said, looking away.

'I'm not shy,' she said. 'Have you got the cream, Daniel?'

'They might want a double ride,' he said, opening the nozzle. Bimbo stood and wandered from the library to the hall. This was the last time, he told himself. This isn't your game. Not even close.

Ringo reappeared, sliding open the doors to an inner room. Bimbo wandered back into the library in time to see the doors slide shut and hear the ripple of applause from beyond. He was about to settle down with his magazine when Ringo came back in, this time from the hallway.

'A word to the wise,' he said, offering Bimbo a thin roll of £5 notes. 'Take a walk.'

'I've already been paid.'

'Listen, old lad, we've had a dreadful time deciding which two get to split the beaver, so we've decided we'll all have a ride. You understand? Now we'll bonus the lady. And you. So let's not make this difficult.'

'How'd you mean, difficult?' asked Bimbo. The man grinned.

'I should tell you I'm a former para, and I've been trained in martial arts. I could break you in half in two seconds flat. So take the money, because I don't want to hurt you.'

'Bimbo!' screamed Miranda. Just as the scream sounded Bimbo caught a flash of movement. Ringo's fist swept up. Bimbo patted it away, grabbed the man's jacket and jerked him forward into the 'Liverpool kiss'. Their heads smashed together with a sickening crack. Ringo, his nose crushed, slid to the floor. Bimbo put his foot to the door, exploding it inwards. There were four men inside. Miranda was being held down on a white rug by two of them while the other two were partly undressed. Daniel was sitting on a nearby sofa nursing a cut lip.

Bimbo walked forward, grabbed the first man by his hair and lifted him to his feet.

'Go and sit down,' he said. The man obeyed. The others joined him. 'Miranda, get dressed. We're leaving.' She scrambled to her feet and gathered her panties from the floor.

'Look, this is a misunderstanding,' said one of the group, a middle-aged man with a pot belly. Ringo told us this was a group thing. He charged us all. He hit the boy.'

'I don't give a toss,' Bimbo told him.

'Look, we'll throw in another two hundred,' said the man.

'Not interested,' said Bimbo.

'Hey, wait a minute, man, this is business,' said Miranda.

'You aint serious?' But he could see that she was. Bimbo swallowed hard. He felt sick suddenly, and backed away towards the door. He heard Miranda speaking to the pot bellied man, but it was as if the voice was coming from a great distance.

'Give the money to Daniel – and the rest of what's owed me,' she said. The man walked to an antique dresser and opened a drawer. From it he took a bundle of notes, which he counted out to Daniel.

'Okay,' said Daniel. 'It's all here.'

'Give Bimbo an extra twenty and drop him home. I'll get a cab later,' said Miranda.

Bimbo looked at the men in the room, the elegant furnishings, the expensive fitments. 'Fuck this,' he said. Then he walked out, stepping over the body of Ringo, and striding out to the drive. Daniel joined him.

'You were terrific,' said the boy.

'Shut it, son. And give me my money.'

'Are you upset?

Bimbo ignored him and walked to the car. The drive home was made in uncomfortable silence. In Maple Road Bimbo climbed out and turned.

'I don't want to see you again, son. Or the slag. I don't wanna hear from you. Or about ya. You understand? Now get lost.'

MacLeeland was sweating as he sat in the long private lounge behind the Royal Swan. He didn't like Wednesdays much these days. Lately Reardon had taken to finding fault with every aspect of his methods.

'I see there's nothing from Williams,' said Frank Reardon, scanning the books. Jackie Green loomed behind him, saying nothing, his cold blue eyes fixed on Mac's red and blotchy face.

'Williams is dead, Mr Reardon. Car accident,' said Mac.

'You seen the wife?'

'Not worth it, Mr Reardon. She's got nothin'. Council house and no savings.'

'And you okayed the bloody loan?' Reardon shook his head. 'I really don't know, Mac. Going soft, are you?'

'Williams was a good man, always paid on the button, dead on time.'

'Well he's dead on time now,' said Jackie Green. Reardon laughed, but the humour faded from his expression as he returned to the books.

'There's three others here – all behind,' said Reardon.

'I sent Roache after one of them. He's put the bloke in hospital. Damn near critical. No chance of cash now. We need good collectors, Mr Reardon – men like Bimbo.' Mac's heart was hammering now, and he struggled to look calm.

'Speaking of which, I see he's still walking around. I told you to get him seen to. Not trying to cross me, Mac, are you?'

'Course not. It's just …'

Reardon's hand came up, and Mac stopped speaking immediately. 'I don't want to hear any more of that shit about how popular he is. Why is he still standing?'

'Roache and Taggart are on it, but I had to pull Roache for the collection. They'll see to it – if they can.'

'What does that mean? If they can.'

'You know what it means, Mr Reardon,' said Mac, mopping his face with a damp handkerchief. 'Bimbo's special. He's bloody 'andy and I'm not convinced Roache and Taggart are up to it. And anyway, what's the bloody point? Christ, the man made a mistake. We all make mistakes.'

Reardon leaned back in the chair and laced his fingers behind his neck. 'Remember at school, Mac, how if you did something wrong you got punished? And the army? Remember Germany, Mac, when they caught me stealing from the NAAFI? Fifty-six days in the glasshouse? That's what we're talking about, Mac. Crime and punishment.'

'At least you did nick the stuff,' said Mac, wearily. 'Bimbo just helped out a mate. But that's beside the point, really. I just wonder whether it's going to be worth the hassle.'

'What hassle?' asked Green. 'He's a brainless bouncer. Who's gonna fucking care?'

Mac looked up. 'I know the man, Jackie. You don't. Roache and Taggart are just thugs, and I don't think they've got the bottle to take him. What happens when they fuck up? What happens when the next pair of bouncers fuck up? How are you going to look then, Mr Reardon?'

'He might be right,' said Jackie Green. 'Let me handle it. You think I can handle it, Mac?'

MacLeeland was squirming now, and the pain in his chest was sickening.

'Forget it, Jackie,' snapped Reardon. Turning to Mac he said: 'Tell Roache I want it done before Saturday. Nothing too nasty. Maybe break his arm and mess his face a little. You understand me, Mac?'

'Sure.'

'Are you all right?'

'Yeah. Wonderful.'

'When did you have your last check up?' asked Reardon, leaning forward and scanning Mac's face.

'Last week. I'm okay, Mr Reardon.'

'I'm worried about you, Mac. Maybe this is all getting too much for you.'

'No! I'm fine. As God's my witness.'

Reardon stood and walked from the room. Jackie Green hovered. He leaned across the desk. 'You like him, don't you, this Bimbo?'

'He's all right.'

'How special is he?'

'He's not a boxer, Mr Green. He's just ... you know ... tough and willing. He's a nice lad.'

Green smiled. 'It'll come to him and me, you know. I get a feelin' for these things.'

'I 'ope you're wrong.' Mac swallowed hard and pulled a bottle of pills from his pocket. His hands were shaking as he removed the cap, placing one of the pills under his tongue.

Alan Wilks had enjoyed himself. He'd won the snooker match with the last pot of the night, a long black that he'd cut into the top pocket. It was a stroke of extreme delicacy and precision that would not have disgraced Steve Davis. He'd pocketed forty quid as a result of that shot. And he'd got rid of those Seiko watches. All in all the sort of night that couldn't fail to bring a smile to a man's face. Nine hundred quid he'd taken in three days, of which twenty per cent was his own. One hundred and eighty pounds, plus the forty from snooker, sat snugly in the inside pocket of his leather bomber jacket.

He was whistling as he strolled towards the iron bridge. That barmaid from the Clifton wasn't at all bad. Bit broad across the beam, but a lovely pair of fun bags, he thought. And she was on for it. Wilks always knew when they were on for it. Something about the eyes. He'd always been the envy of his mates for the amount of gash he could pull. People said there wasn't a bird anywhere he couldn't lay. But they was wrong. Not that he'd ever admit it. No, the real skill was spotting the birds who couldn't wait to be shafted. The ones who wanted a bit of rough handling. Wilks always enjoyed that, the spanking and the humiliation they asked for, forcing them to do exactly what they wanted to do anyway. He'd only made two mistakes. The first was with that snooty clerk from the Box Company. She'd squealed like mad and it was only at the end that he realised she wasn't play-acting. And he'd raped her. He'd lived in fear for months that she'd go to the law. But she didn't. After that he'd gone back a couple of times to give her another go. Somehow it was better than the ones who wanted it. But she'd moved away and left no forwarding address. The second mistake was the worst though – marrying Sherry and letting her have the brats. Kids! What a waste of space. I want, I want, I want! And they ruined Sherry. Right laugh she used to be until they came along. You're well out of it, son. Somebody told him that Bimbo Jardine was sniffing around her now. He'd get a shock. Like screwing a corpse.

Slowly he climbed the old bridge steps, listening to the sound of his footsteps echoing in the dark. He'd always liked the old bridge. A long time ago it had doubled as a cavalry fort for the youngsters, and then as a space station. He had a lot of good memories of the bridge. He'd got his first gash here with that Pamela bird. Ugly little cow, but a great arse.

He descended the steps and emerged by a cracked street

lamp, stopping to light a cigarette. Suddenly a weight descended on his neck and his face, rammed into the steel tube of the street light. Twice more he felt his head cannon into the metal, then all thoughts fled.

He awoke an hour later. Rain had drenched him. He struggled to rise, fell, then pushed himself to his knees. One eye refused to open and he could not breathe through his nose. His hand sped to his jacket pocket. Gone! Two hundred and twenty quid. All gone.

'Oh Jesus,' he whimpered. 'Oh Jesus! Why me?'

Bimbo stood in the queue at the building society, waiting for the red arrow to light. An elderly woman in front kept glancing back nervously and clutching her handbag. Bimbo smiled at her. She looked away. He transferred his gaze to the wall, and a huge picture of the High Street taken in 1911. It showed a tram and several horse-drawn wagons. In the foreground was a little boy in a flat cap. Bimbo liked the picture. It always made him feel good.

'You're on, son,' said a man behind him. The elderly woman had moved forward and another red arrow beckoned Bimbo. He ambled to the counter. Beyond the double screen sat a young girl, pretty, but disfigured by acne. Bimbo dropped the blue book into the tray. 'I wanna draw some cash,' he said. 'About three hundred.'

'Can you fill out this form, sir?'

'I aint got me glasses. Can you do it?' He watched the girl's pen speed across the form, then it was returned for his signature.

'How would you like it, sir?'

'Tens'll do. How much I still got?' She turned and tapped at the computer keys beside her.

'Three hundred and seventy-seven pounds 22p.'

'Not enough for a Ferrari then?'

'You could buy a Ferrari tyre,' she said, grinning. 'Build it piece by piece.'

He took his money and added it to Wilks' two hundred and twenty. Outside, the winds of autumn had scattered the rain clouds and brought a chill to the air. Bimbo took a bus to the town hall and found the rent office. A young man with tired eyes made the check he requested.

'Mrs Wilks owes two hundred and forty-six pounds 75 pence,' he said.

Bimbo laboriously counted out £250. 'Do you have her rent book?'

'Nah.'

'Can you get her to bring it in?'

'Can't the rent collector do it?'

'We don't have rent collectors any more. Too dangerous out on the streets. Most people pay by direct debit.'

'Too dangerous? There's always bin rent collectors. Even when times was really rough.'

'Not any more. That's a jungle out there now,' said the man.

'Get off! Jungle? Thass West London. It aint changed.'

'Have you seen the figures on muggings and burglaries and assaults?'

'Well … it may have changed a bit.'

The man grinned. 'If she doesn't feel like bringing the rent book in she can always post it.'

'Ta.'

In the corridor outside he saw Richard Kilbey. At first he did not recognise the vicar, for he was wearing a handsome Harris Tweed jacket, and a cravat was tucked into his cream shirt, instead of the usual white dog collar.

''Allo Rev, what you up to?' Kilbey smiled and shook hands warmly.

'I'm meeting two ladies for lunch.'

'Well, you'll impress 'em in that gear.'

'I think not. And you? What are you doing here?'

'A mate asked me to drop in and settle a bill. Are you allowed to take them collars off then?'

'Yes. Once in a while. Special dispensation.'

'Well, nice to see ya. By the way, how did things work out with that charity you was pushin'?'

'The Refuge for Battered Wives? We're still fund raising. That's what today's lunch is about.'

'It's run by dykes aint it?'

'I have no idea. Would it matter?'

'Guess not, Rev. See you Sunday.' As he was about to leave Pam Edgerley and Liz Owlett approached. Kilbey smiled broadly and shook hands. Bimbo nodded to Liz.

'You given any thought to me swan?'

'I am looking into it, Mr ... Mr?'

'Jardine.' Pam Edgerley held out her hand. Bimbo took it, gently.

'Nice to see someone cares about something,' she said. Bimbo nodded and wandered away. 'God, he's big!' said Pam. 'One of your flock, Richard?'

'Loosely speaking. I rather like him. He's blunt and honest – after his own fashion. And that makes him disconcerting at times. What was that about a swan?'

'It was nothing,' said Liz, sharply. 'Shall we find somewhere to eat? I'm starving.'

Beyond the front doors Bimbo steered his way through the lunchtime crowds. The first Christmas cards were already on display as he eased himself into Debenham's. Bloody hell, he thought. It's only September. Moving along the stalls he stared longingly at the chocolate bars he had lusted after as a schoolboy. Somewhere along the line he had lost his taste for them. Yeah, that was it! The Scrubs! Chocolate never tasted the same behind a locked door. Like eating in a toilet. At the rear of the store he saw bank after bank of televisions, most of them showing racing. But, at the end, in beautifully sharp black and white, Bimbo caught a glimpse of Gary Cooper, walking down a dusty street. There was no sound but you could see the tension in Cooper's face. Bimbo moved closer.

'Greatest western ever made,' said a young man in a Hepworth's jacket and baggy trousers.

'Nah. *Shane* was the best.'

'Didn't win Oscars though … did it?'

'Buggered if I know. What's this one then?'

'*High Noon,*' said the man, in a tone that signified, even to Bimbo, that the question should never have been asked. 'Do you have a video?'

'Nah. Aint got a telly. Never fancied one.' The man's expression moved instantly from helpful indifference to total concentration. Sincerity oozed from every pore. Bimbo grinned as the man spoke. 'Let me show you some of our bargain buys. Here we have a Hitachi colour set, eight channel, remote control, superb …'

'I'm unemployed – and broke,' said Bimbo.

Instantly alone, Bimbo wandered the store, stopping at the toy section where he studied the Transformers. He'd a loved them as a lad. Toys what changed from lorries into robots. Ace.

As the afternoon wore on Bimbo tired of window shopping. He caught a bus to the station and wandered towards Stepney's Antiques. Four doors short of the old man's business he stopped and stared into the window of Cottage Video, where a superb poster of Winnie the Pooh had pride of place beside a large portrait of Clint Eastwood. Bimbo pushed open the door and stepped inside.

The walls were covered in shelves and lined with video jackets boasting every kind of film from war to comedy, porno to Pinocchio.

'Well, Jesus Christ, if it aint the prodigal,' said a voice. Bimbo spun. A powerfully built fair-haired man walked from behind the counter, thrusting his hand at Bimbo.

'Stan? Bleedin' hell, I never knew you was in this business. I thought you left the area.'

'No way, son. Not with the money there is in this,' said Stan Jarvis, with a crooked grin. 'I started out with a suitcase and a few pornos and pirates, but that's a mug's game. I built a roll and took a chance. Talk about payin' off in spades. I got three shops now – worth near a quarter of a mill, what with stock and that. You wanna cuppa?'

'Nah, ta. I'm meetin' somebody. It's good to see ya, though.'

'And you, son. See much of Ade?'

'Now and again. He's set up a massage parlour.'

'Birds or blokes?'

Bimbo grinned. 'Women. Nice bunch, too. You wanna pop down there.'

'I would, but there's enough free round here. Too bleedin' much, as a matter of fact. I'm gettin' worn out. Tell you what, before you go, I'll give you a free membership. Then you can take films whenever you like.'

'No point, Stan, I aint got a telly, let alone a video.'

'I could help you out there. A ton the pair. I'll even set them up for you.'

'Is it straight?'

'Come off a straight lorry, son.'

'I dunno, Stan. I only like the old movies.'

'I got 'em. John Wayne, Fred Astaire, Bob Hope. Not much call for 'em now, but I got 'em. You name it, I'll drop it round.'

'You got *Shane*?'

'No, that I haven't got. But I can get it. You still at the same place?'

'Yeah.'

110

'I'll drop the gear round tonight – about ten.'

'You couldn't let me have a coupla posters for the wall, could ya?'

'Sure. Whaddya fancy? Eastwood, Stallone …?'

'That Winnie the Pooh looks good. Anything, really, cartoons mainly.'

'I didn't know you had kids.'

'I aint.'

'No, course you aint. Very colourful, them cartoons. See you around ten.'

Bimbo left the shop and found himself facing Roache and Taggart, with a third man waiting just beyond them. The three men were tense, their eyes gleaming. Taggart stepped forward.

'We got a message from Reardon,' he said. Bimbo hit him in the mouth. Taggart flew backwards into the gutter, his head ramming into the wheel of a parked car, dislodging the hub cap, which rolled into the road. Taggart feebly tried to rise, but sagged back, the lead pipe rolling from his fingers.

'Anyone else got a message?' asked Bimbo. The third man backed away, but Roache leapt forward, sunlight gleaming from the brass knuckleduster on his right hand. Bimbo blocked the right cross with his left arm and hammered a punch to Roache's solar plexus. The man folded, his head snapping down straight into Bimbo's knee which thundered into Roache's face. He was unconscious before his body slumped to the pavement.

The third man spread his hands. 'I'm out of it,' he said. Stan Jarvis came out of the shop carrying a wheel spanner.

'You all right, Bim?'

'Yeah, no sweat. Pair a pansies. See ya later.'

Bimbo walked slowly to the antiques shop, stepping into the cool, musty interior. Stepney was standing in the doorway. He shut the door, flipping the sign to 'Closed'.

'So, my friend,' said the old man. 'It has begun.'

6

'Don't you start!' said Bimbo. The old man shook his head and led him through to the back of the shop, where a chessboard was set up on a wide oak table. The board was huge, the set fashioned to represent Napoleon against Wellington. The pawns were hussars, the knights lancers, the Bishops cannons, the Rooks fortresses. Stepney's King was Napoleon.

'That's a bit tasty,' said Bimbo.

'I bought it today. I am glad you like it.' Stepney moved a hussar pawn forward. 'You know those men?'

'Yeah. Two of 'em anyway.'

'And now it is over, you think?'

'Come on Step, play the bloody game,' said Bimbo, bringing out a Knight to challenge the pawn. A second hussar was moved to defend the first.

'I am talking about a game – just like chess. Now I ask again, do you think it is over?'

'How the hell should I know?' said Bimbo. 'I'm just one of these bleedin' pawns.' He stood and moved around, idly staring at the antiques casually laid on the many shelves and tables.

'That is what you are not any longer,' Stepney told him. 'They have barred you from the places you like to go. They have sent thugs to thrash you. Now what will they do?'

'How come you're such an expert?' snapped Bimbo, returning to the table. Stepney unbuttoned his waistcoat and leaned back, hooking his thumbs in his braces, his button blue eyes fixed on Bimbo.

'At last a sensible question. My dear Bimbo, I do not like to boast, but in this matter I am indeed an expert. In my youth, when I first joined the Party, Germany could have gone two ways: Bolshevism or National Socialism. It was decided to bait the Bolsheviks, and I helped organise spontaneous riots, the hunting down of their senior men. If they could not be discredited with scandal or rumour of scandal they were killed. You understand? Later, when we won, and the war began to turn against us, I was moved from the Eastern Front to join a Gestapo intelligence unit in Belgium. Believe me, Bimbo, there is nothing your friend Reardon can teach me. I know what he is doing, and why he is doing it.'

'Not a nice bunch … the Gestapo,' said Bimbo.

'Will you listen? You think I am talking just to amuse myself? There are men still alive who would give thousands to know where I am, so that they could avenge themselves on me. You think I tell you this lightly? I tell you because I care about what happens to you.'

'Sorry Step.'

'You have begun a war, that will not end until you are defeated. Publicly. Conspicuously. In his wisdom, this Reardon has chosen you to illustrate his power. You have now thrashed his men and humiliated him once more. You should have let them beat you. It was the only sensible course. Now you must go away. Find employment in another area.'

'I aint runnin'.'

'Ach, Bimbo, I love you like a son, but your brains are not your best feature. It is not enough to have strength and courage. And what will be achieved by your staying behind to suffer, perhaps, maiming or even death?'

'I never done nothin' wrong. I just helped out a mate.'

'What has this to do with anything? You committed no crime. So what? What crime did the Poles commit, or the Czechs, or the Austrians? Yet still our armies marched into their countries and stole their freedom. Your crime is the same as theirs, you are weak. Against an army even a strong man like you is no more than a sacrificial lamb. Who will care if the lamb bleats "I am not running"?'

'And I aint no lamb.'

Stepney ignored him. 'Reardon is convinced you made him look foolish. So he decides to punish you, and puts you from his mind. A few blows, a little lost pride, and Bimbo Jardine would once more have been safe. But no! Bimbo Jardine will stand tall. He will not run. So, next time there will be four men, or five, or ten. And where does this get Bimbo Jardine?'

'I dunno, Step. I can't even tell you why I'm stayin'. I don't know meself. Maybe I should go back and talk to Mr Reardon again.'

'To what purpose? Did you not apologise? What else can you say?'

'But it's all so stupid.'

'Of course it is stupid. And Reardon is now in danger of making himself look truly ridiculous. I have a little place in Norfolk, a small cottage I go to sometimes. You are welcome to stay there for a few weeks, until this blows over.'

'You think it will blow over in a few weeks?'

Stepney sighed and shook his head. 'Let us continue our game.'

Stepney introduced a Knight into play and the match commenced. Bimbo played better than he had before, but lost easily.

'You are getting better,' said Stepney, reaching over and patting Bimbo's shoulder. 'You made me think once or twice. But still you react. Your play is passive. Still, we have a little time to work on it.'

Bimbo grinned. 'I enjoyed the game. Helps take your mind off things. Still, I could murder a cuppa tea.'

'We will go upstairs,' said the old man. Bimbo stood and

began to walk towards the shop door. 'No, not that way. Follow me.' He led Bimbo to a narrow door at the rear of the shop, which opened to a stone-wall-enclosed yard and a rickety fire escape. The two men climbed in the darkness until Stepney reached a window which was locked. The old man took a penknife from his pocket and slid the blade under the latch. The window had not been opened in years and was stiff. Bimbo forced it and they climbed inside.

'Forgotten your key, Step?'

'Come here, Bimbo,' said Stepney, moving through the darkness of his rooms and stopping at a window overlooking Station Road and the front of the shop. In the shadows opposite stood three men. Two more were lounging by a telephone kiosk.

'There will be others,' said Stepney. 'At least three, perhaps four, in the alley behind the shop. They are waiting for you.'

'How'd you know they were there?' asked Bimbo. 'I never 'eard nothin'.'

Stepney pulled down the blind and switched on a table lamp.

'Do you ever listen to me?' he asked. 'I know the way Reardon's mind works. He is a jungle animal, and, as such, entirely predictable. The present gang will wait most of the evening. Then they will go for fresh instructions. Reardon will be furious. Next, he will have men near your home. Maybe even in your home. But,' he shrugged, 'that is a problem for another day. Put on the kettle.' Removing his waistcoat, Stepney donned an old fisherman's sweater.

'You losin' weight, Step?' called Bimbo from the kitchen area.

'A little.'

'You aint got much to start with. You eatin' all right?'

'As a horse. Do not fuss. You can sleep on the Chesterfield. I will fetch you some blankets.'

'Don't worry about that. I'll get off home.'

'You are intending to fight that gang?'

'Nah. I'll nip over the station wall and cut along the tracks. It'll be all right.'

'Think for a moment. As long as you are here they must stand out in the cold, becoming uncertain, and even ... God willing ... a little afraid. Let them suffer. And keep an old man company for a while. This has not been a good day for me.'

'Business bad?' asked Bimbo, bringing a cup of tea to the old man.

'No. But I made a trip today, and I have heard better news. I went to the hospital in Fulham Palace Road. They tell me the cancer in my lungs will kill me soon.'

'I dunno what to say, Step. Honest I don't.'

Stepney smiled and put aside his tea. 'We will have some Armagnac, my friend. In fine balloon glasses. I shall bore you with the story of my life.' He moved to an ancient dresser and poured the spirit into two glasses, passing one to Bimbo. Then he switched on an old gas fire and settled back into his armchair.

'You aint never borin', mate. Never. But tell me what the 'ospital is planning?'

'I am too old for the harsher treatments, they tell me. And anyway the cancer is well advanced. But I am seventy-seven. I have had a good run, as they say.'

'Can't they cut it out?'

'No. It is at the centre, and spreading into both lungs.' Suddenly he grinned and raised his glass. 'Good health!'

'Yeah.' Bimbo sipped the fiery liquid, not enjoying the taste.

'Do not look so sad. I am not going to die tomorrow – at least I hope not.'

'But you don't even smoke or nothin'. It aint right.'

'There you go again! Right! What is right? Life is a lottery. Only the strong, or the lucky, continue to smile. Outside Stalingrad I was trapped in a burning Panzer. No way out. My comrades dead. I was ready to join them. But the Russians fired again, blowing the turret clean away. I scrambled clear. Two hundred thousand men disappeared in that battle. But not Heinrich Stolz. I was very tough. And I was lucky. I shall not complain to the Almighty merely because my time has run out.'

'I'm sorry. I'm bleedin' sorry. How long?'

'I will be lucky to see Christmas. About eight weeks.'

'You got any family?'

Stepney pushed himself from the chair and opened a small cabinet. From it he took a silver framed oval picture. He handed it to Bimbo, who saw a young woman with long dark hair and a radiant smile.

'Your daughter?'

'My wife.'

'She was very pretty.'

'She was beautiful. She was also a Jewess. She died in Ravensbruck.'

'Must have hit you pretty hard.'

'You do not understand. Ravensbruck was a death camp for Jews. I sent her there. I informed the Gestapo.'

'Jesus, Step! Why?'

'For nearly half a century I have asked myself the same question. I have no convincing answer. I was a fervent believer in a god among men; a giant sent to liberate my people. I did not know she was of Jewish stock when we married. And when she told me I felt betrayed. Sullied. I was young, and proud, and very stupid. In those days we were told the camps were work places. "Work for Freedom" was emblazoned on the gates. Only later did I *really* know. But I guessed.'

'You didn't mean to kill her then?'

'God, no. But my intentions count for nothing. As the Bible says, "By their works shall ye judge them." One day, in a village four days into Soviet territory, I was ordered to assemble a firing squad. I did so. The entire village was surrounded and all the men, women and children herded into the central square ...'

'I don't want to hear all this,' said Bimbo, but the old man was staring ahead, his eyes distant, his mind locked in the past.

'We mowed them down with machine guns, and had to walk among the bodies finishing off the wounded. And I did it. Coolly, dispassionately. Mostly the survivors were women and children. I shot them all. All.'

'I think you ought to talk about something else.'

'Tonight there is nothing else. *Verstehen*? Tonight the ghosts walk. They know I am close. They wait for me. When the allies overran Germany I escaped to Switzerland with false papers. I lived there for five years. Every day I watched for the hunters. But they never came. Eichmann they hunted down. Mengele they searched for. But Stolz was only a little murderer. His souls were measured in hundreds.'

'You aint a bad man, Step. I know you.'

'You know nothing. You are a trusting soul, Bimbo, and I bless the day you came into that cafe and watched me play chess. But you do not know me. Not at all. God has given me nearly fifty years to atone for my crimes, and in all that time I have done nothing for anyone. A wasted life. And when I die there will be no one at the funeral. An empty church and a priest who will bury me under a name that is not my own.'

'I'll be there, Step.'

'This I know. I do not deserve you, Bimbo.'

'You want another game of chess?'

'No. I think I will sleep now.'

Bimbo waited until the old man was snoring softly, then he covered him with a blanket and turned off the fire. Silently Bimbo climbed out of the window and down the fire escape, scaling the station wall and walking unseen through the rail yard.

Beyond the gates was an alley, with two broken street lamps. Bimbo stepped into the darkness and stopped, listening. For some seconds he heard nothing. Then a match flared some twenty feet away and a cigarette tip glowed fiercely.

Bimbo crept forward. Two men were sitting on a low wall. He retraced his steps, moving back into the rail yard. Vaulting a low fence he scrambled down to the rail line and began to walk along beside the tracks.

A half-hour later he was walking warily through the court-yards of Ironside Towers. A few youngsters were still hanging around in the shadows, or sitting on the stairs, and he could hear the faint sounds of pop music drifting from a distant party. He stopped and scanned the road outside his flat. From here he would have to walk out on open ground, cross the road and mount the steps. Now would be the time, should any of Reardon's men be on hand. He waited for several minutes, leaning against a wall, but there was no sign of movement in the street opposite.

'Well come on, son, you can't wait here all night,' he told himself. Swiftly he walked out into the open, crossing the road. His heart was hammering as he mounted the steps. A figure moved out of the shadows. Bimbo spun, grabbed the man by his jacket and slammed him into the wall.

'It's me, Bim!' screamed Stan Jarvis. Bimbo's huge fist froze.

'Sorry, Stan, but it's bin one of them days.'

'Yeah, I know. After you turned over them scumbags I did some checking around. You got on the wrong side of Reardon. But why don't we talk inside? I got your gear. Come on, give us a hand.'

Bimbo carried the television upstairs while Stan brought the video recorder. Once inside the flat Stan moved around, searching the walls of the living room. 'Where's your aerial point?'

'I aint got no aerial.'

'What's the point of buying a piggin' TV without an aerial?'

'Never thought about it. Anyway, I only want to watch the video.'

While Stan set up the machinery, Bimbo made some coffee.

'Come here!' called Stan. 'I got a surprise for you! Bimbo wandered out and sat down before the television. Suddenly a movie started. It was *High Noon* with Gary Cooper.

'I wanted *Shane*,' said Bimbo.

'That's what makes it a surprise,' said Stan, grinning. He froze the picture and switched off the recorder. 'I'll get the other one at the weekend. Seriously though, Bim, you need a hand with this Reardon?'

'Nab. I don't wanna see no bricks through your windows. But thanks anyway, mate, you're the first to offer.'

'Us cellmates oughta stick together.'

'I'll give you a shout if it gets too rough. But I reckon it might blow over. You know, just like with Pearson in the nick. And he was a bleedin' killer. Remember?'

'I remember,' said Stan. Pearson was the tobacco baron, and his word was law inside. Even outside. Men who had upset him would, even on release, find their lives full of constant fear. Once a young Italian had been found hanged in his cell after publicly refusing Pearson's advances, and ridiculing him. 'Pearson tried it on with Adrian, and you stood up for him. Saw the bastards off.'

'And nothin' happened did it?' said Bimbo. 'Pearson never had me topped or nothin', did he? And he was worse than Reardon.' Stan drew in a deep breath, and let it out slowly.

'He would have, Bim. But Ade went in and gave him what he wanted.' Bimbo sagged back in his chair, and rubbed at his tired eyes. Everything was so wrong, so crooked and vile.

'I never knew that. Why didn't he tell me?'

'Because he didn't wanna see you dead. But it don't matter. What I'm sayin' is Reardon's the same as Pearson. It's shit or bust, Bim. You've got three choices. Leave, and don't come back. Sit tight until they take you apart. Or hammer the son-of-a-bitch!'

''Ammer him? You been watchin' too many of your movies. He's got about thirty men on his payroll And on top of that there's ...'

'Jackie Green,' said Stan. The name hung in the growing silence.

'Yeah. Him,' said Bimbo. 'I can't, Stan. I aint no army. I wouldn't know what to do. I don't even want to know, neither. I just wanna be left alone.'

'Good luck,' said Stan, rising. 'I gotta go. I'm meeting Rose down the Barley. But, if you need me, just give a shout. By the way there's some posters for you in the video box.'

'Thanks, Stan.'

'Don't thank me, just pay me,' said Stan, grinning. Bimbo handed over the £100 and watched from the window as Stan drove away in his red VW Golf. The man was a diamond, but Bimbo didn't want him involved in this business. He settled down with a cheese sandwich and watched the first half of *High Noon*, but then he remembered that Gary Cooper had also died of cancer and his thoughts drifted. He switched off the machine and sat quietly, thinking of Stepney. He liked the old man, and he didn't much care about his past. But – Jesus! – to have your own wife topped. And to kill women. It didn't seem possible that the gentle old chess player could ever have done anything like that. Bimbo pushed the ugliness from his mind and pulled the rolled-up posters from the video box. There were three in the roll. The first was *Winnie the Pooh*. He stuck it over the fireplace using an old roll of Sellotape. The second was from *Casablanca*, picturing Bogart and Bergman. This he put in the alcove by the far window. But the last was *Shane*. Bimbo spread it lovingly across the carpet. Alan Ladd stared back at him, while Jean Arthur stood arm in arm with Van Heflin. Beyond them were snow-capped mountains and endless prairies.

He carried the poster to his bedroom and carefully positioned it on the wall, where he could see it as soon as he woke.

Back in the living room he restarted *High Noon* and watched the marshall do his duty. The man in Debenhams was right. It was a great film.

Later, as he lay on his bed staring at the moonlit *Shane* poster, he found sleep impossible. It disturbed him, for sleeping had never been a problem. Even after his first arrest he had gone to bed in the locked cell and slept like a baby. He'd just put his head down, and dropped off the world. But not tonight. Events flowed through his mind. Adrian giving in to Pearson, Miranda taking the money, Sherry, desperate and broke, Wilks unconscious in the rain, Stepney, alone and dying ...

And Jackie Green. Above them all, like a spectre, there was Jackie Green.

It took a long time for Bimbo to realise why he could not sleep. He was experiencing an emotion he had never known before.

Fear.

The next two days passed without incident, but on the Saturday afternoon, as Stepney was closing his shop, two men entered. The old man judged them in a glance and slowly made his way to the rear of the shop. He sat behind his oak desk and waited. One of them flipped the sign to 'Closed' and locked the door, then they walked towards him. Both were tall and well built, though one was running to fat. Their faces were flat, their expressions cold.

The fat one sat down on the edge of the desk staring with naked contempt at the elderly dealer.

'You're friendly with Jardine, aintcha?' he said.

'Yes,' admitted Stepney.

The second man sat back in a Regency chair, a faint smile contrasting with the malice in his eyes.

'Well, that's gonna cost ya,' he said. 'Still, all you Jews are loaded. So I guess you won't mind.'

'How much?' asked the old man.

'I like a man what gets straight to the point. Didn't I say that, Gary?' he asked the fat one, who nodded. Turning to Stepney he smiled. 'See he don't understand you Yids. I told him. You always know where your bread's buttered. Now, this is the score: We bin told to turn your place over. And we've got to do it. After that you pay one hundred notes a week. If business is bad we'll send a man in to go over the books. We aint gonna break you. You can help yourself by moving some stuff for us. That'll earn you a few bob. Understand?'

'Of course. You will have some stolen items that I can move through my contacts.'

'Exactly. But – since you helped out Jardine – you gotta be punished. What we'll do is this: You tell us the sort of stuff you wouldn't mind gettin' broke, and we'll break it. Then we can go back and say we done it right, and you won't be too put out. Couldn't be fairer could we?'

'It is very reasonable,' said Stepney. 'You are a man of intelligence. But what of my friend Bimbo?'

'What about him?'

'Are you not here to request that I invite him to my shop at a time convenient to you?'

'You see, Gary, what did I say? That's why they all get rich.' He swung back to Stepney. 'I'm beginnin' to like you, old man. I could almost forget you're a Yid. Yeah, you're right. If you do that for us, we won't even smash the shop, and the first week's money gets waived.'

'He's takin' all this a bit calm, aint he, George?' said the fat one.

'Now you mention it, he is.'

'I shall be honest with you, gentlemen. I am sure you will appreciate candour. I have been told that I have only a few months to live. I have cancer in my lungs. Therefore I have little to lose. You can destroy my shop, or break my bones. But you cannot hurt me. Would you like some tea?' The two men exchanged glances.

'You missed something out,' said George. 'We might not be able to hurt you, old man, but if we turn you over it will get right up Bimbo's nose. Cos he'll know it was his fault. So I don't really give two tosses for your cancer. You can die when you like for all I piggin' care. But you don't want Bimbo hurt, do ya?'

'You are very intuitive, young man … George. And quite correct. You will go far in your chosen profession. Once upon a time I could have used a man like you. In fact I did.'

'Yeah, well thanks for the compliment, but I don't think we're gettin' anywhere. Gary, start breaking up the place.'

'That would not be wise,' said Stepney, lifting the pistol from its hiding place beneath the desk, the black eye of the barrel staring at George. 'This is a Walther P38. It is in good working order. Now you are an intelligent boy. I think you will understand what I am going to say to you. Since I am dying I have nothing to lose. On the other hand, you are young with everything to lose. Am I going too fast for your fat friend? No. Good. Should you, or any of your comrades, visit me again, I shall kill them. *Verstehen*? You will go back to Reardon and you will give him this message. You will tell him that he is no more to me than a maggot, and, in my time I have forced better men than him to my boots.'

'You think I'm gonna say that to Reardon? You must be out of your mind.'

'Not at all. But you will repeat it to your friends. Or Gary will. The result is the same. People will know I have contempt for your boss.'

'It probably aint loaded,' said Gary, half rising.

'You are probably right,' said Heinrich Stolz, with a death's head grin.

'It's loaded!' snapped George. 'Sit down and stay cool.'

124

'As I said, you are an intelligent boy. You just missed your era.'

'Well, what a surprise,' said George, rising slowly and backing towards the door.

'We ... Yids ... are a surprising people,' said Stepney.

Sue Cater closed her notebook. The police incident book showed three burglaries, a bag snatch and a car fire for Friday, which would make only a few paragraphs for the News Briefs column. But with two page leads needed the news editor, Bateman, was not going to be too impressed. She thanked the station officer and re-checked her notebook. Maybe one of the burglaries would yield a good human interest story – widow's life savings stolen. But she doubted it. All the burglaries had taken place in the rich quarter, the plush east end of the borough.

Anyway, what are you sweating for, Cater? she asked herself. There were stories, if only the paper would have the balls to follow them up. Protection rackets, bent coppers, evil landlords. But Bateman kept pointing out that with the staff now mainly made up of junior reporters it would be dangerous to attempt any exposés.

She saw Don Dodds walking towards his car and ran down to intercept him. He turned at the sound of running footsteps and smiled as he recognised the youngster.

'What's the rush? No Great Train Robberies today, are there?'

'I thought you might buy me a coffee.'

'I'm not sure Edna would appreciate my being seen with a gorgeous young reporter. Come to think of it, neither would the Super.'

'But you're retiring at Christmas, more's the pity. Go out with a fling.'

He grinned once more and climbed into the white Escort. 'I'll see you at Mia's. But only twenty minutes, mind. And no talking shop. Still want to come?'

She nodded and ran for her car, a dark blue Escort. She beat the sergeant to the coffee shop by three minutes and was already sitting at a corner table with two cups of black coffee before her when he arrived. He removed his hat and sat opposite her.

'One of these days, young lady, you are going to be stopped for speeding. And booked.' But he knew it was unlikely. Sue Cater was pretty and blonde, with large, innocent eyes. Few men would be able to pluck up the courage to write the ticket.

'I want to pick your brains, Don.'

'I said no talking shop.'

'Not current cases. Just general info about the area. And it's off the record. No notebook. No quotes. Scout's honour.'

'There was a time, young lady, when that meant something. Reporters had a certain code. I don't believe it works any more. Too many lies and half-truths get in the papers.'

'Not from me.'

'I accept that. It's why I'm here. So ask – but I might not answer.'

'John Jardine.'

'Bimbo? What about him?'

'Is it true he's going to end up in hospital?'

'Who told you this?'

'It's all over town. In the bars, anyway. Is it true?'

'What's your interest?' he asked, sipping his coffee.

'He rescued an old lady. And I saw Liz Owlett the other day – you know, the council officer trying to help the refuge – and she said he's trying to fix up a mate for the black swan in the park.'

'So?'

'Well, he seems like a nice man.'

Dodds smiled. 'It's a relative term. You're a big girl, Miss Cater, and you know there are two worlds out there. There's the nine-to-five clerk who gets on the bus, goes to work, comes home, reads the paper, watches TV and goes to bed. The following day he starts all over again. He's your average punter. He thinks we live in a civilised world with laws to protect him and his wife and children. Then there's the real world. And Bimbo lives there.'

'But the punter is right,' said Sue. 'There are laws to protect him?'

'Not really. The law is there to punish. That means anyone is free to attack this clerk and his family. Nothing is going to stop it happening. But we try to make sure the villains are put away. The theory is that prison sentences deter other offenders. But we lost the way. Prison is not much of a deterrent. A man can admit thirty burglaries and get six months inside. Thirty burglaries can affect the lives of maybe a hundred people. And the fear never goes away. Do you know I went on a course once where a psychiatrist told me more women have breakdowns over burglaries than over rapes? Did you know that? It seems that the violation is greater when it's the home that is invaded.'

'And Bimbo's world?' she nudged.

'Survival of the fittest. Law of the jungle.'

'Run by men like Frank Reardon.'

'No names, young Sue. This is background, remember. Bimbo's world is dog eat dog. It's about muscle and fear. And he's lived in that world all his life.'

'As a leg breaker.'

'As a collector,' corrected Dodds. 'But, yes, he's cracked a few skulls. I don't want to defend Bimbo. I've put him away twice. But he's not a villain. Most people who know him like him. He helps out. Like that woman he took to hospital. And another girl he helped wean off drugs. It's a funny old world. If I was in trouble I'd want my bank manager standing by me – even though he is a pompous little sod, if you'll pardon my French. But if I was in a tight spot, with people out to break my bones, I'd want Bimbo close by. I can't really put it too much clearer.'

'You like him, don't you?'

'Well, I wasn't trying to hide it. Yes, I like him. Old fashioned, is Bimbo. Mrs Thatcher would like him. He's full of Victorian values.'

'One leg breaker recognising another,' said Sue, grinning. 'Anyway, how did Bimbo get in this mess?'

'He helped a friend.'

'I don't understand.'

'I didn't suppose that you would.'

'The word is they are going to cripple him.'

He nodded, and finished his coffee. Sue shook her head. 'But if the police know this, why don't they stop it?'

'Stop what? When I interview Bimbo in hospital he'll say he fell down the stairs. Even if his back's broken and he'll never walk again. You understand that? That's the law in his jungle.'

'But if he's no threat to them, why cripple him?'

Dodds replaced the empty cup and called for a refill, which was supplied by a portly, middle-aged Italian woman. When she had gone he leaned forward.

'It's about credibility. Bimbo's boss makes his money from other people's fear. People pay him so that they don't end up in hospital. He thinks Bimbo made him look a fool. Now he knows people are watching to see what happens to Bimbo. If he's seen to get away with it those people will – maybe – cease to fear the boss.'

'So what will happen?' she asked.

Dodds shrugged. 'If Bimbo has an ounce of sense he'll take a beating and get on with his life.'

'And has he? An ounce of sense?'

'Good question.'

'So answer it.'

'He'll force them to cripple him. He'll suffer.'

'Why? Where's the point?'

128

'Ah well, that's something your generation wouldn't understand, young Sue.'

'Try me.'

He shook his head. 'It's not worth it. Believe me.'

'How can you be sure?'

'Because you asked the question. If you were capable of understanding the reason, you wouldn't have needed to ask. And your twenty minutes are up.'

'Oh come on, Don,' she said, as he picked up his hat and stood, 'you can't leave it like that.'

'Why don't you ask him?' he said. 'Thanks for the coffee.'

She paid the bill and returned to the office, wrote up her News Briefs and completed a short feature on hang gliding. After checking the desk diary for any late entries she left the building and drove to Maple Road. For some time she sat in the car, too nervous to enter the building. She'd certainly made a bad impression the last time, and reddened as she remembered her maladroit handling of the big man. Would he give her a second chance? She checked her face in the rear view mirror. Her looks gave her confidence and she locked the car and entered the building.

She climbed the stairs, wary of the bulging, threadbare carpet, and turned into the corridor. She stopped in her tracks. A dead cat was nailed to Bimbo's door, blood leaking from its open mouth. She turned and fled, cannoning into Bimbo on the stairs.

'Steady on,' he said, catching her by the arms. She looked up and the warmth disappeared from his eyes.

'Oh it's you.'

'Someone's left ... left ... a cat. A dead cat. Nailed to ... your door.'

Bimbo released her and walked slowly to his flat.

She waited on the stairs until she heard the flap of the rubbish chute slam down. Taking a deep breath, she returned to his door. Blood still stained the old rush mat. She tapped on the door.

'Come in,' he said, from the kitchen. 'Kettle's on.'

The first thing she noticed was the *Winnie the Pooh* poster. She sat before the gas fire staring at the cartoon. 'There you go,' he said, handing her a mug of tea. He switched on the fire and pulled up a chair. He was dressed in a faded blue track suit, torn at the shoulder, and he smelt of sweat, not stale and acrid, but fresh and primal. She felt inhibited by the smell, and strangely disconcerted.

'I'm sorry about the cat,' he said. 'Not nice for a woman to see.'

'Not nice for *anyone* to see. Why was it done?'

'Dunno,' he said, avoiding her eyes. 'Prank, I s'pose.'

'Has there been much of this recently?'

'Drink your tea, love. It'll make you feel better.'

'It's a nice poster. I used to love Winnie the Pooh.'

'Yeah.' He seemed ill at ease, and she didn't need great intuition to sense his distrust of her. The tea was hot and too sweet. Sue had given up sugar two years before and now felt as if she was holding a can of heated syrup. Standing, she moved through to the kitchen and tipped the tea down the sink. There was enough water in the kettle for a fresh cup, and she spotted a small jar of coffee on a crowded shelf. The movement through Bimbo's flat made her feel more confident. It was all in Don's book about body language and human behavioural patterns. Take control!

Returning to the fire she sat once more, this time facing Bimbo. 'Look, I'm sorry about last time. Can't we start over?'

'We aint got nothin' to start.' His response was not overtly hostile, and her mind worked furiously at the problem. What was it everyone said about Bimbo? Soft touch for someone in trouble?

'I need your help.'

'Yeah? Want me to kill somebody, or maybe eat a few babies?' As he spoke he smiled, but there was more sorrow than anger in his eyes. Sue changed tack again.

'I'm sorry,' she said. 'What do you want me to say? I didn't know you. What else did I have to go on, except a few old court cases and a reputation?'

'You said you wanted 'elp. What kind of 'elp?' asked Bimbo, his eyes still wary.

'I've got an exam coming up, it's called the Proficiency Certificate. I've got to do a project for it. It's like a degree journalists have to do before they become seniors – you know, fully-fledged reporters. At the moment I'm a junior. Anyway, I'm doing this project on crime, and I wanted some advice. I spoke to Don Dodds and he suggested talking to you.'

'I aint no criminal.'

'No, that's not what I meant,' she said swiftly, feeling her way into the interview, watching his every reaction. 'Don talks about there being two worlds, the cosy nine to five, and the real world. He says you live in that real world. I just want some advice. I won't quote you. No names. It's a general piece. Not even about this area.'

'What do you want to hear?' asked Bimbo. 'I'm just an odd job man. I don't know nothin' about gangsters.'

'I'm not talking about the Mafia. Just local crime. Protection rackets, extortion, prostitution. Look ... I'll ask you some ques-tions, and any you don't know – or don't want to talk about – you ignore. How's that? It would really help me. If I fail this exam I'll be fired,' she lied.

'You can ask,' he said.

Be careful now, Sue ...

'Okay, let's take protection rackets – generally. Do you see them as evil?'

'I aint sure what you mean.'

'By protection rackets?'

'Course not. Evil.'

'You don't know what evil means?' she asked.

'Course I do. I aint much of a talker, Miss … Cater innit? … But, like you can get some right evil bastards involved in anything, can't ya? Banking, politics. Like that Hitler bloke. And there's some right nasty types in the Old Bill.'

'So you don't see the rackets themselves as evil … immoral?'

'They probably are,' he admitted. 'But it's the way the world works. Aint nothin' gonna change that.'

'It's not the way my world works.'

'Course it is. How much you earn?'

'Just over £9,000 a year.'

'Take it all home, do ya?'

'No, there's tax and stoppages.'

'Thass what I'm saying. The Government says, "Give us thirty per cent of what you earn or we'll bang you up." You aint got no choice. Like old Al Capone. They couldn't get him for running his rackets so they banged him up for not payin' for theirs. Income tax invasion or summink. Nice touch eh?'

Sue stifled a smile. 'But that money goes towards hospitals and schools and roads and pensions,' she said.

'Yeah, I know. And bombs and planes, and payoffs and freebies. What I'm sayin' is nobody gets a choice. You pay 'cos you have to. Because they're bigger than you, and stronger. It's the same around here. Same anywhere.'

'But does that make protection rackets morally justified?'

'I don't know. I don't think about it much. In fact, I don't think about it at all. It just is, innit?'

'Okay,' she said, sensing him pulling away. 'How does one go about setting up a protection racket, and why don't the police close it down? Isn't that what they're there for?'

'What do you wanna know first?'

'Sorry. Setting it up.'

'Piece a cake. Pubs, clubs, restaurants all need a quiet life. Nobody's gonna take his wife to a place where there's trouble, right? So you cause a bit of trouble. Fight or summink.' He stood and walked to the kitchen, returning with a fresh mug of tea.

'So why doesn't the proprietor go to the police?'

'I aint tellin' this right. Look, that's not the way it works. See, the first thing that happens is someone approaches the publican, and points out that it's a rough area. He tells the publican he's operating a security business that watches out for trouble and nips it in the bud. Nothing illegal about that. Let's say the publican tells him to naff off. The guy just goes. No trouble. No threats. The following night two men in the pub have a row and a fight breaks out. Smashed chairs, broken bottles, bit a blood on the carpet. Following day the original geezer is back. "Dear, dear," he says. "Hear you 'ad a bit of trouble." The publican wises up, and pays. He can always put it down to breakages. They've all got their own fiddles. And no one could ever prove the fight weren't ... weren't ...'

'Spontaneous?' she offered.

'Yeah.'

'But surely the police know how this works?'

'Course they do.'

'Then they should be able to stop it.'

'Well there's the second problem, innit. The publican – poor bugger – has got to work out if the local bobbies are bent. I mean, if he complains and the copper is on the payroll, then word will get back that he's about to grass 'em up. He could be badly hurt for that. And, at best, his business will get wrecked. Fights every night. All the customers goin' elsewhere for a quiet life. He'd be out of business in a month.'

'And there are bent policemen around here?'

'We was talkin' general, wasn't we?' he said, sharply.

'Sorry. Reporter's habit. Suppose someone refused to pay, no matter what? And he didn't go broke.'

'Don't happen much.'

'But if it did?' she persisted.

'He'd get a spankin', I suppose. Broken arm or somethin'.'

'How do you justify that?'

'I don't even try. It's his own fault. He coulda paid.'

'Suppose it's got nothing to do with money?'

'I don't get ya.'

'Suppose the boss just didn't like someone.'

'He'd get a spankin'. That's what power is, innit? Where's all this going?'

'I'm still wondering about the morality of it all. Could a man fight back?'

'He could get his own group together. It's happened before. He could knock out the other firm.'

'But if a man was on his own? Could he fight back? Is there a way?'

'No. You ever tried standing in front of a moving truck? Aint no point. It'll roll over ya. Some things you can't fight back against. You just take your knocks and put it down to experience.'

'Then why are you?' she asked, hoping her timing was right.

'I thought that's what this was about,' he said. 'Time to go.'

'No,' she said. 'Not this time. I wasn't lying to you, Bimbo. I am working on a project. And I'm not looking for a story. I just wanted some answers. I spoke to Don Dodds. He's worried about you. I don't know why, but so am I. Do you have any food in the house?'

It was a delicate moment and she kept her face calm, her eyes fixed on his. She watched his sudden anger fade and he grinned.

'I got some eggs and cheese. And some bread, but it's a coupla days old.'

'You like omelettes?'

'Sure. You mind if I take a bath first? I bin runnin'.'

134

'Not at all.' He stood and left her, crossing the room to the bathroom opposite. She wandered towards the kitchen. The bedroom door was open and she saw that the bed was unmade. Above it, on the wall, was a western poster showing Alan Ladd and Jean Arthur. The kitchen was tiny, the cupboards almost inaccessible. Designed by a man, no doubt! She found the eggs and cracked four into a plastic jug. Then she recalled the size of her host and added three more. The cheese grater was at the back of a drawer and showed faint traces of mildew. She scrubbed it clean and idly wondered whether the detergent would prove a greater health hazard than the mould. With all the ingredients prepared she moved silently back into the living room and listened. She could hear Bimbo splashing in the bath and took the opportunity to enter his bedroom. It was small and cosy and, more importantly, the sheets were clean.

She was in the kitchen when Bimbo emerged from the bathroom. She had made up her mind that if he came out dressed only in a towel she would leave. She'd known enough tacky men in her life. If not ... well, she'd play it by ear. Bimbo was fully dressed in a dark blue sleeveless top and clean jeans. And his close cropped, curly hair was still damp. He wasn't handsome by any stretch of the imagination, she thought, but there was something about him; a quietness within the strength, a softness in the eyes that couldn't be weakness. It was odd really. Huge men were almost always repellent. All that deep, manly-chest bullshit. But Bimbo was not repellent. Not by a long shot. But then he didn't look like Sylvester Stallone, or any of those looks-obsessed types. His body was not clean lined, merely colossal.

She carried in the omelette on two plates and sat beside Bimbo on the floor before the fire, her knee only a couple of inches from his own. During the meal she allowed her leg to droop so that they touched. He did not recoil, or move, or indicate in any way that he had noticed the contact.

'Tell me about the swan,' she said, as he put his plate aside.

'How'd you know about the princess?'

'Liz Owlett told me. I was interviewing her about the refuge.'

'Short of cash, aint they?'

'Yes. The council aren't interested in battered wives.'

'A lot of it goes on.'

'Isn't it the same as your protection racket theory? The husband is stronger and so he can do what he likes?'

'I guess so. Aint right though. If I caught a man doin' it I'd break his bleedin' fingers.'

'Why?'

'What sorta question is that?'

'Where's the difference between the battered wife and the publican?'

'He's a man. A man is supposed to look after himself.'

'Aren't there women publicans?'

'Probably. Look, I aint no Einstein, right? I don't know all the ins and outs. And I aint got all the answers. All right?'

'Tell me about the swan. The Princess?' He relaxed instantly.

'That's what I call her. I feed her most weekdays. You know, granary bread. Good stuff, that. Get it down the Indian deli. Anyway, her mate got killed a coupla years back. She's lonely. Builds a nest every year. Lays eggs what can't hatch.'

'But swans mate for life. Even if they found a black she might not take to him.'

'Be nice for her to have a choice though, eh?'

'You're a romantic, Bimbo,' she said, leaning forward and letting her hand fall to his thigh. He smiled and covered her hand with his.

'Yeah,' he agreed, 'but it don't make me an easy lay, if you know what I mean?'

Sue was stunned, and felt herself reddening. 'I don't think I do.'

136

'I never go to bed on a first date. Not even for an omelette.'

'You think I'm trying to seduce you?' she said, forcing a smile.

'Susan innit? Listen Susan, no one ever said I was over-bright, but I aint stupid neither. You're a lovely girl, no question, but I aint much for screwin'. I need to like somebody. Know 'em. Be close to 'em. I probably didn't put that right, and I 'ope you aint offended or nothin'.'

She leaned back and moved her knee. 'I'm not offended, though I don't know why. I don't normally come on that strong. In fact I rarely have to come on at all. You don't think you're being a little old fashioned?'

'That's the way I am. You want a coffee before you go? I noticed you didn't like me tea.'

'How are you going to get to know me if you throw me out?'

'I aint throwin' you out. Do you wanna coffee?'

'Black and strong, please.'

As he walked away she remembered Don Dodds' remark about Bimbo. *Something your Yuppie generation wouldn't understand, young Sue.* And here she was sitting below a Winnie the Pooh poster, making up to an old fashioned leg breaker, and being turned down. She felt like the female equivalent of a medallion man at a disco. She giggled suddenly, just as Bimbo returned with two cups of coffee.

'You sound 'appy.'

'I am. Nothing wrong with that, is there?'

'No. Where you from?' he asked, sitting beside her.

She told him about her family in Leeds. Her father was an accountant. Her mother had died nine years ago when Sue was eleven. She had two brothers, one of whom was blind. He was trying to become a writer of fantasy stories. She was one week from her twentieth birthday. She liked reading, writing, horse riding and archaeology. She had no boyfriends currently, having just split from Robin, a solicitor. She was left wing, but not loony, against wars, and pro-abortion.

And she talked for two hours.

She was running out of things to say when Bimbo took her hand and kissed the palm.

'You wanna go 'ome?'

'No.'

'I don't want you to either.'

'What made you change your mind?'

'I never changed me mind. I just decided I liked ya.'

'Why?'

'You make a nice omelette. Will that do?'

'For now,' she said.

Sue Cater lay awake for a long time after Bimbo fell asleep. She snuggled into his warm body and watched the moon shining beyond the gap in the curtains. That she had enjoyed the hour of lovemaking was beyond question, but the reasons for that were many and varied, spiralling inside her mind like windswept snowflakes. She half wished she were home with her typewriter, so that all these snowflakes could be captured. Outside, the wind howled against the windows, rattling them in their frames. Somehow the sound was deeply comforting.

The sex had been fine, the lovemaking wonderful. Why was it that so many men failed to understand the difference? And how did this man come to know the truth? What was there in his past that had led him to the knowledge all women carried?

She compared him to Robin – ex-lover, ex-friend. Bimbo certainly couldn't match Robin's technique, or the variety of his skills with hand and tongue. But Bimbo's strength was just that, she realised. His lack of technique. All he had done was hold her, before and after, drawn her to him and loved her simply, becoming part of her in a very real, almost Biblical sense. Biblical? What are you thinking of, Cater?

'God! I wish I had my typewriter!'

She slid from the covers and donned Bimbo's old dressing

gown. Slipping from the room she quietly shut the door and switched on the gas fire, settling down with her thoughts. Rummaging in her bag she found her pack of Bensons and her lighter. The smoke felt good in her lungs. Here, away from Bimbo, there was more perspective. Could she ever love a man like him? Now there was a thought! And it saddened her. Bimbo was a man who would adore children, and home, and little wife. He'd pop out Sundays for his pint before the roast dinner, and grow old and contented without ever noticing the passing of life.

She shivered. Better to stick with the Robins of this world, the laughing, mocking, subtle, carefree Robins, whose cunning quips and rapier wit allowed no morbidity. The ash on her cigarette toppled to the rug. Guiltily she rubbed it into the pile and wandered to the kitchen, dousing the stub under the tap and throwing the remains into a bin.

Returning to the warmth of the bed, she turned her back on Bimbo and stared at the moonlit poster on the wall, trying to remember if she'd seen the film. Wasn't it the one about an evil rancher trying to terrorise farmers? And didn't Alan Ladd fall in love with Jean Arthur? She couldn't recall much about it, except a scene where Alan Ladd and Van Heflin struggled to remove a huge tree root from the ground before the cabin.

Idly she recalled her previous lovers, counting them. Fifteen, beginning with the disco man when she was just fourteen years old. He had seduced her in the back of an old Ford Transit, on a rug that smelt of jasmine. God, that had been good! Her thoughts flicked back to Bimbo. He hadn't even asked her the normal, boring question. How was it for you? Most men seemed to need their prowess re-affirmed. Or the other old perennial: Did you come? The truly fragile partner would also seek comparisons between his performance and previous lovers'. But not Bimbo.

And Sue found herself regretting that the questions were not asked.

Silly cow, she told herself.

Bimbo groaned and rolled over, facing her now and breathing deeply. Sue could smell his breath. It was sweet. Lifting her arm she gently stroked the flesh of his flank. His breathing became more shallow and his eyes opened. In the moonlight she saw him smile. 'Can't sleep, eh?'

'No.' His left arm circled her shoulder, drawing her in, then his hand moved down her body over the outside of her thigh. She tilted her hips, and the hand slid obediently down between her legs.

The strength and suddenness of the orgasm took her by surprise, and even before the last quivering bursts of pleasure had subsided he reared above her. Her legs felt stretched as she tried to circle his hips, and then he was inside her, moving, moving. Sue found herself floating in a sea of warmth and pleasure, and in one strange and special moment she experienced, for the first time, a feeling of total oneness with a lover. His strength was hers, his body was hers, his life was hers. Christ! she thought. I hope I can write this! And in that moment feeling fled, and she was Sue Cater, the reporter, once more.

7

Bimbo awoke at six. Raising himself on one elbow he looked down on the sleeping girl. Her left arm was outside the covers and he gently stroked the cold skin. He lifted the blankets over her and rose. It was bitingly cold in the room and he padded to the window, staring down over the rain-polished street. The sky was still dark. Closing the bedroom door softly he switched on the fire in the living room. His body felt loose and relaxed as he pulled on his track suit and trainers. Leaving the front door on its latch he set out on his route, past the tower blocks to New Street, left at the baker's, across the Common, back along the lane, down the High Street, left into the estate and then a figure eight to the right, past the station and over the bridge. It was a good run and, for the first time in days, his mind was empty of fears.

Back in the flat he took the weights from the rear cupboard and worked out for forty-five minutes, finishing with a hundred sit-ups. He bathed and dressed in jeans and a grey sweatshirt, dropping his track suit in a holdall by the door, ready for the launderette. Then he made two mugs of tea, and carried them into the bedroom.

Susan was awake.

'You sleep all right?' he asked.

'Like a log. I had a lovely dream, but I can't remember it.'

'Water should be hot again in about twenty minutes. Once you've had a bath you'd better go.'

'Used, abused, and thrown aside,' she said, grinning.

'It aint that.' Bimbo was genuinely aggrieved.

'I know, you're just frightened the neighbours will see me and give you a bad reputation?'

'Nah! Well, it's just … things aint bin goin' too well lately, what with dead cats and that.'

'You're talking about Reardon?' His expression changed, his eyes growing cold and distant. 'Don't misunderstand me, Bimbo. I'm not talking about a story. But it's all over the pubs that you're in deep trouble.'

'Yeah?'

'Yeah,' she said, mocking his accent. He grinned.

'It'll blow over.'

'That's not what you said last night.'

'I didn't talk about it last night.'

'No? Wasn't it you who was talking about people who get a spankin', whether they deserve it or not? Wasn't it you who said that's what power is? Ordering someone to beat up someone else?'

'Maybe. But I never done nothin' wrong.'

'It doesn't matter, does it?' she said. 'Right and wrong? What the fuck does Reardon care about right and wrong?'

'You didn't oughta swear. Don't sound right.'

'I'm not getting through to you, am I? You said there was no sense fighting back. You said that, didn't you? Or is there one rule for the rest of the world and another for Bimbo Jardine?'

'I said you take the knocks and get on with it. I aint lookin' for no trouble. I never asked for it. I just wanna get on with me life. I don't need no aggravation. Not from Reardon. Not from Dodds. And not from you.' He stood, his face red and angry.

But Sue was also losing hold of her temper. 'Dodds said if you had any sense you'd take the knocks. But you're not going to are you? You're going to make them kill you.'

'It aint none of your business!'

'You're not bloody Shane!' she shouted. 'And this isn't some stupid western.'

'What do you know about it? What do you know about anythin'? Your dad's an accountant. You went to a private school and lived in a posh area. Had a gardener, didn't ya? Well, I never 'ad none a that. I never 'ad nothin'. Probably never will have. All I got is in here,' he said, thumping his chest with his fist. 'Aint no bastard ever taking that away. A western? I know *Shane*'s a film, darlin'. But somebody wrote it, didn't they? And whoever he was, he knew. He bloody knew!'

'What did he know?' asked Sue. 'Answer that!'

'He knew broken bones wasn't so special. Somebody gives that to ya. But they'll mend. But when they make you eat shit, they're taking somethin' away. And you don't never get it back.'

'Jesus Christ!' she screamed, kicking the blankets from the bed and standing to face him. 'Not the old "A man's gotta do" crap?'

'Yeah. But I don't s'pose reporters have a lot to do with that, do they? I mean, there's not a lotta time, is there? What with yer face stuck in somebody's dustbin looking for juicy bits a rubbish. Buncha bleedin' vultures, the lot of ya. I don't know why you come here. But you know where the bloody door is. Use it!'

Without another word Bimbo left the room and Sue Cater heard the front door close. She sank to the bed, all anger flowing from her.

'Congratulations, Cater, you handled that ever so well.'

She wandered to the bathroom and filled the tub. Lying back in the hot water she began to relax.

'Just what did you expect of him, you dimwit?' she asked herself. 'He's a leg breaker, for God's sake. Violence is his trade. Stupid, stupid woman. Just because of one night's gentle lovemaking, did you see him as some sort of poet?

'*All I got is in here!*'

And that was the key to everything. Heart. In the Attic Greek sense. Soul. His lovemaking had been slow and gentle, full of soft touches and warmth, a seemingly inexhaustible well of giving. How could she have been so naive as to try to ram home her middle-class reasoning? She felt like a missionary trying to explain to a tribal chieftain why he suddenly needed trousers and a Bible. Climbing from the bath she dried herself and dressed. She stopped in the bedroom on the way out and stared at the rumpled linen.

'Good luck, Shane!' she whispered.

And left.

Liz Owlett carried two cups of lemon tea into the bedroom, laying them on the pine dresser before moving to sit on the bed. Pam Edgerley was asleep and Liz hesitated before waking her, staring at the angular face. It was a beautiful face, thought Liz, the face of a fighter, strong and yet caring, the strength coming from a combination of self mockery and an ability to understand the funny side of life's tragedies. Leaning forward, she kissed Pam's cheek.

As always, Pam awoke with a smile. She rubbed at her eyes, yawned and stretched. 'You spoil me,' she said, reaching for the tea.

'You're worth spoiling. What do you want to do today?'

'Nothing. And everything. Let's just wander.'

'You don't fancy window shopping in Ealing?'

'God, no!' said Pam. 'Let's go to the park and feed the ducks.'

'It's raining,' said Liz.

'All the better. We'll be on our own.'

'You have the weirdest idea of a good time. I think I'd sooner stay in bed.'

Pam chuckled and sat up. 'Not the greatest testimony to my lovemaking. Given a choice between being drenched and

144

making love to Pam Edgerley, Ms Owlett chose the latter ...
eventually.'

'Okay, you talked me into it – we'll feed the ducks.'

The clouds were breaking up and the rain had eased to a fine
drizzle when the two women entered the park at the western
end, past the boating pond and the white war memorial. Pam
was wearing a bright red anorak with the hood up, while Liz
was dressed in a leather coat and jeans. They walked arm in
arm for a while, until Pam leaned over and kissed the younger
woman on the cheek. Liz blushed and pulled away.

'Still yearning for the closet?' asked Pam, masking the hurt.

'I'm sorry.'

'It doesn't matter. It's a big step. But it's not irrevocable. Mr
Right need never know – if you find him.'

'It's not that,' Liz told her, forcing herself to link arms.

'Then what?'

'It's my mother. She's so old fashioned. You know, "Where
are my grandchildren?" sort of thing. I really want to tell her
about us ...'

'Don't!' said Pam. 'Not ever!'

'But why? I'm not ashamed of what I am.'

'It has nothing to do with shame. It has everything to do with
strength. Sometimes you have to be strong enough to be weak.
When I first realised that I was gay I had this urge to confess
it to the world. If possible I would have stood on the stage at
the Royal Albert Hall and shouted it out. But it's not worth it. I
know what I am. I am proud of what I am. And what I do. Pam
Edgerley has finally become a person I like. But I should never
have rammed it down my parents' throats. You understand?
We can accept what we are. Sometimes they can't. So leave
them with their fantasies.'

'And live a lie?' asked Liz.

'What sort of crap is that? Live a lie. You don't walk to work
in the morning and say, "Hi, I was a bit down last night, so I

played with myself. It was lovely." Privacy has nothing to do with lying. And what if it did? How many times have you told a lie to avoid hurting someone's feelings? "What do you think of my new coat?" "It's very unusual." When what you might say is, "It makes you look three times fatter than you are."'

'It's not the same thing.'

'It's exactly the same thing,' said Pam.

'Oh no!' whispered Liz, stopping in her tracks.

'What is it?'

Liz pointed to the bench by the duck pond. Bimbo Jardine was sitting there, hurling lumps of bread to the water where a black swan was feeding.

'Do you want to go back?' asked Pam. Liz nodded, but at that moment Bimbo turned. He waved. The black swan glided back to her island and Bimbo stood. The two women approached.

'Mornin',' said Bimbo. 'Come to 'ave a look at the princess, did ya?'

'Yes,' said Pam, swiftly. 'Nice to see you again, Mr Jardine. Are you well?'

'Yeah. You?'

There was something uneasy about the big man, a tension in his face. Pam looked into his eyes, read the hurt.

'She's very lovely,' said Pam, pointing to the swan. 'I've been reading up on them. They have quite a few black swans at Leeds Castle in Kent. Might be worth approaching them for a mate.'

'Guess so,' said Bimbo.

'Have you been coming here long?'

'Coupla years. I never got to know her really until she was shot. Poxy vandals done it. Dunno why. She's lucky to be alive. I keep waitin' for the bastards to come back and finish her, you know?'

'I do know. People can be very cruel.'

'Yeah. Course you'd know that, wouldn't you? The refuge and all.'

146

'Yes. Would you like a coffee?'

'Sure,' said Bimbo. Pam felt Liz tense at her side, but ignored it, and the three strolled up the short hill to the snack bar. There were no other customers and a Calor gas fire was unlit. Bimbo carried three plastic cups of coffee to a window table. Liz was shivering. Bimbo swung in his chair.

'Oi, pal!' he called to the bearded man behind the counter. 'Put the fire on.'

'We don't light it until eleven,' replied the man.

'Excuse me,' Bimbo told the women. He stood and ambled to the counter. Pam watched the scene from the corner of her eye. The man listened as Bimbo spoke to him, then opened the counter flap and wheeled the fire to their table. Once it was lit he retired to his counter without a word.

'God, that's better,' said Liz.

'You must be a diplomat, Mr Jardine,' said Pam. 'How did you convince him about the fire?'

Bimbo smiled and shrugged. 'Just told him you were cold, like. You work for the council?'

'No. I'm unemployed.'

'I thought you ran the refuge.'

'I do, but it's a voluntary scheme. We don't get any grants. We rely on donations. Also I earn a little from freelance writing.'

'How many women you got there?'

'At the moment ... seventeen. It's far too many, but they've nowhere else to go. There are also twenty children.'

'That's a lotta sad people, innit?'

'It is the tip of the iceberg, Mr Jardine.'

'Call me Bimbo. So, what do you do for 'em?'

'We counsel them. But there's not much we can do – except be there. Give them a haven for a while.'

'But they gotta go home eventually though, eh?'

'Sadly yes. Are you married ... Bimbo?'

'Nah. Maybe one day. Who knows? You?'

'l was once. Divorced.'

'Knocked you around, did he?'

'No. He was charming. But I married young and it was a mistake. We all make mistakes. I'm a lot happier now. More fulfilled.'

'Yeah. Are you one of them lesbians?' he asked.

'Good Heavens, you are direct.'

'No offence meant. It just slipped out,' said Bimbo, reddening

'None taken, Bimbo. Are you gay?'

'Nah. Got a mate who is, though, and he don't seem too happy with it. Just busted up with his boyfriend. Funny business really. He's got this massage parlour, see, beautiful girls. And he's bent. Odd innit?'

'How did you get to be friends?'

'We was in the Scrubs together … you know, prison? … I was doin' two years, and he was in for a few months on some cheque fraud or somethin'. We was cell-mates.'

'How did you feel about sharing a cell with a gay?'

'How do you mean?'

'Did you feel threatened?'

'Nah. He's only a little bloke. And he aint violent.'

'So it didn't bother you?'

'Why should it?'

'Suppose he'd made a pass at you?'

'He did, as a matter of fact. I just told him to leave it out.'

'But you remained friends?'

'Sure,' said Bimbo. 'Is she your girlfriend?' he asked, nodding to Liz, who was now staring out of the window.

'You are an unusual man, Bimbo. What do you do for a living?'

'Not much at the minute. You know, between jobs. Not got a trade. Not much good with me 'ands.'

'How do you get by?'

148

'Odd jobs. Collectin'. Mindin'. Casual labour sometimes.'

Pam finished her coffee and smiled. 'It was nice talking to you, Bimbo, but we have to go. Good luck with the swan.'

Liz stood and moved away without a farewell. Pam caught up with her outside. The sky had cleared to a glorious blue.

'What's the matter with you?' asked Pam. 'How could you be so rude?'

Liz swung on her. 'Rude? Jesus Christ! How could you ask him for a coffee? It was so humiliating. Now he thinks I'm your girlfriend.'

'I thought you were,' said Pam, softly.

'That's not the point.'

'Then what is? Before we met him you were talking about living a lie. Now you're angry because someone knows the truth. Make your mind up, Liz.'

'I just don't like sitting around with the likes of him.'

'The likes … ? I think you have the wrong idea about him. He's not wife-beater material. Not by a long way.'

'Oh yes?' snapped Liz. 'I was talking to Sue Cater a few days ago. She told me all about Bimbo Jardine. Collecting? Indeed he does. Protection rackets, leg breaking. He's a thug, Pam! He works for Frank Reardon.'

'Small world,' said Pam. 'We had Reardon's wife in last week. And I still think you're wrong about Bimbo. You take the car. l want to be on my own for a while.'

'I didn't mean to upset you,' said Liz swiftly, her eyes wide.

'You didn't,' Pam assured her. 'I'll see you later.'

Liz looked around then tentatively kissed Pam's cheek. The older woman watched as Liz walked from the park.

'Will you ever learn?' whispered Pam, when Liz was out of earshot.

Stepney sat in the narrow office watching Dr Matthew Adams reading his notes. Adams' bald head was gleaming with sweat and his glasses had slipped to the tip of his nose. It seemed odd to Stepney that he should be sitting here so calmly while a man he hardly knew was reading about his death. Adams looked up and fixed his gaze on a point somewhere to Stepney's right.

'We are not achieving the result we hoped for,' said Adams, his speech clipped and formal to the point of coldness.

'Speak plainly, doctor, and look at me when you speak.'

Adams jerked and gave a nervous smile. 'I am sorry, Mr Stepney. These conversations are never easy. I pray they never will be.' His watery eyes met the old man's gaze, then swung away. 'The radiation, as you know, did not shrink the tumour in your lungs, and we now have a cerebral metastis to deal with at the base of the brain.'

'And what is that?' asked Stepney.

'It is a secondary tumour. It explains the numbness in the fingers of your right hand. I think it is time you agreed to come into hospital.'

'For what purpose?'

'I think you understand the purpose very well, sir. The paralysis will continue, and also cause disfunction in your thinking. Have you noticed any difficulty remembering words?'

'A little,' admitted the old man.

'Anything else?'

'Memory lapses. Some chess moves I cannot recall. And yesterday ...' Stepney's voice faded to silence.

'What happened yesterday?'

'I forgot how to move the knight. And you say this will get worse?'

'I am afraid so, Mr Stepney. As the growth continues to expand these disfunctions will become more severe. For your own sake you should come in today.'

'Stolz.'

'I beg your pardon?'

'Stolz. My name. Henry Stepney is a ... business name. My

real name is Stolz. Heinrich Stolz. It is important to me that you use my name.'

'Of course, Mr … Stolz? Can you come in today?'

'No. I shall go home. I shall die there. It is what I want. I wish to see the things I love around me. You understand this?'

'Yes,' said the doctor, sadly. 'Your family. Are you Jewish, Mr Stolz?'

'No. Why do you ask?'

'You have a number tattooed on your right armpit. I thought perhaps you were a survivor of the camps.'

'No, I am not a Jew. My tattoo is from my regiment.'

'I see.'

'Be assured that you do not, Herr Doktor. Good day to you.'

Adrian left the massage parlour a little after 9 p.m. and entered the multi-storey car park some ten minutes later. His Jag was on level four and he took the steps at a run. Life was beginning to look up. On Thursday he had met a young man at the club and they had struck an instant rapport. Tonight, he had arranged to meet him at a small pub in Shaftesbury Avenue. The car park was deserted as Adrian pushed open the swing doors on level four. His footsteps echoed in the concrete chamber. A man moved from the shadows. Then another.

Adrian turned and sprinted for the doorway. Two more men came into sight. He swerved and ran down the incline towards level three, his pursuers close behind. A large man in a donkey jacket stepped into his path. He was carrying what looked like a pickaxe handle. Adrian leapt feet first, hammering the man from his feet. Hitting the ground hard, Adrian rolled and sprang upright, continuing his flight. He had always been swift and he thanked God that he'd stayed fit. He didn't recognise any of the men, and had no idea why they should be chasing him. But their reasons were immaterial. Their intent was obvious.

A car screeched into his path, headlights blazing. He tried

to stop, but he was running downhill. At the last second he leapt high on to the bonnet, crashing into the windscreen. The car doors opened and he felt himself dragged clear. A fist cannoned into his face, his head thundering against the car's wing. The other men arrived.

And the nightmare began.

It was Melanie who brought the news to Bimbo early on Monday morning. They shared a cab to the hospital, where neither of them were allowed in to see the patient. Melanie found out that Adrian was on the critical list and unconscious. A policeman was sitting by his bed. He came out when a ward sister told him there were visitors.

Police Constable Ian Fletcher sighed as he recognised the giant. Ever since the night he and Field had interviewed the two men who had brought in the mugged woman he had wondered about John Jardine, and entertained the fond hope he would be arrested in the manor and brought to the cells resisting. Now the queer was in a coma and the concern on the giant's face made Fletcher's animosity vanish.

'How bad is he?' asked Bimbo.

'Very bad. Fractured skull, both legs and arms busted. Broken ribs and a collapsed lung.'

'He'll make it though, won't he?' asked Melanie.

'I have no idea, madam. I hope he does.'

'Is he awake?' asked Bimbo.

'No. He's groaned a couple of times. Look, I've got to get back in there. It's not worth you waiting around. Believe me.'

'I'll wait anyway,' said Melanie. 'Is it all right to sit in with you?'

'Are you family, miss?'

'I'm his fiancée.'

Fletcher read the lie but ignored it. 'All right. But not you, Mr Jardine. Sorry.'

'Any idea who done it?'

'Not yet, sir. There was a note pinned to his chest. Excuse me, miss,' he said, pulling Bimbo out of Melanie's earshot. 'When I say pinned to his chest, that's exactly what I mean. They used a staple gun. It didn't make a lot of sense, but I have a feeling you might just understand it. It said "Does this look like a cold?"' Bimbo stiffened. 'I thought so,' said Fletcher. 'Would you mind explaining it?'

'Sorry, pal. That's not the way it's done.'

'Do I take it we're going to find a lot more people busted up?'

'I hope not,' said Bimbo. 'But you can never tell, can ya?'

'Are you still at the same address, sir?'

'Yeah. Why?'

'We may need to talk again.'

Bimbo nodded and made for the stairs. Once out of sight he stopped and rammed his fist into a wall. He could still see Reilly in that dingy office behind the snooker hall, still hear his own threat ringing in the air.

'If he so much as catches a piggin' cold I'll be back.'

Well they'd called his bluff. In spades!

For three days Reilly had extra men laid on at the Seagull, and he had taken to carrying a snub-nosed Colt Python in a hip holster under his jacket. Reilly had grown up in a tough area of Liverpool and was no stranger to violence. In his youth he had been as hard as any man, and had fought and suffered, won and lost, and taken his knocks. But now he was forty-seven years old, with a wife and four children. He was softer now, more aware of his mortality. A heart attack in '82 and ulcer operation in '84 brought that home to him. When Jackie Green had relayed Reardon's instructions about hitting the queer he had looked for every reason to refuse. Green allowed him none; he'd even insisted on using two of his own men to back up Reilly's team. Roache and Taggart. They had damn near killed the queer and Reilly had dragged Taggart away at the last, sickened beyond fear.

'You're a maniac!' Reilly had screamed. Taggart had turned on him, his eyes glittering, the blood-drenched lead pipe raised! Two of Reilly's men had stepped between them.

'You've got to restore credibility,' Green had said. Credibility? What they'd done was insane.

The door opened and a towering figure moved into the office. Reilly scrabbled under his coat, his hand hooking round the target grips of the pistol and swinging it clear. Jackie Green gave a mocking grin.

'My, my, we are jittery.' The ex-boxer sat down and poured himself a generous measure of Scotch. 'Looks like you're doing good business tonight. Must be a dozen tables in use out there.'

'Friday's a good night,' said Reilly, pushing the gun back into its holster.

'That should get the job done,' said Green. 'If you get a chance to use it.'

'You sent two piggin' maniacs!' said Reilly. 'You've no idea what they bloody did.' He poured himself a Scotch and drained it.

'They did what they were told – what they're good at.'

'A broken arm and a few bruises would have been just as good,' said Reilly, filling his tumbler. 'There was no need to damn near kill the poor bugger.'

'You want to tell that to Reardon?'

'I'm telling it to you. About the same thing these days, isn't it?'

'Don't get flash with me, Reilly,' said Green, softly. 'It don't pay. You're frightened of Bimbo. Well, believe me, I'm ten times worse.'

Reilly nodded. 'I don't doubt that for a second. I've seen men like you before. They never last. The police'll stand back for a few rackets. But they won't take the likes of you. Fucking mad dogs filling the streets with blood.' Green rose from his chair, his face white. The snub-nosed Python flashed up, the black eye of the barrel pointing at his forehead. 'If I had to do it again, Jackie, I wouldn't tie in with Reardon. I thought he was a businessman. But he wants to be a gangster. Now get out of my office.'

'You aint got the nerve to pull that trigger,' said Green, locking his gaze to the older man's. Reilly smiled, and, just for a moment, the old Liverpudlian street fighter rose from memory.

'No? Then it's lucky for me you haven't got the balls to try me. Piss off, Jackie.'

He eased back the hammer. Green said nothing, but he turned and left the room, pulling the door closed behind him. Reilly sank to his chair. It was all getting out of hand. A cold shiver passed through him, like someone walking over his grave. Events had moved out of control now, like a runaway train heading downhill. Nothing was going to stop it.

And someone was going to die.

Bimbo sat in his flat staring at the fire, unsure of what to do. Adrian was hanging on to life by a thread. The only thing the doctors were sure of was that, if he did survive, his hearing would be impaired in his right ear, and one of his kidneys was damaged. Bimbo was lost. He couldn't march around the manor with a machine gun. He wasn't Charles Bronson. And if he thrashed Reilly what would it achieve? Who would be next? Stepney? Esther? Sherry? Maybe it was time to leave, to find a job in some other city. A tap at the door disturbed him. He thought it might be Esther, then remembered she was in Sussex with her doctor boyfriend.

'Who is it?' he called.

'It's me. Stan.'

Bimbo opened the door. Stan Jarvis stepped inside. Bimbo closed the door behind him and put on the kettle. Jarvis joined him in the small kitchen.

'Sorry, mate. What can I say?'

Bimbo shrugged. 'I reckon he'll pull through. Tough little bastard.'

'Everybody's talking about it. They're all wonderin' what you're gonna do.'

'What can I do, Stan? Ade started it all by refusing to pay. I got involved and I made things worse. I can't make 'em no better. I aint no one-man – bleedin' – army.'

'You don't have to be. There's two of us.' It was said simply and Bimbo looked into the man's square face and nodded.

'I know you mean that, and it's good to know. But there aint no point, Stan. Stay out of it.'

'You aint gonna let 'em get away with it, are ya?'

Bimbo didn't reply. He made the tea, handed Stan a mug, then walked past him and back to his chair by the fire. Stan joined him.

'I know you aint scared, Bim, so what is it?'

'I can't stop it. They got me beat. I aint a killer, Stan. I'll crack a few skulls if necessary, but that aint it anymore, is it? I'm on me own. No offence, Stan. I know you'll stand with me, but there aint no point to it. We aint a gang. We aint the Krays. We got the muscle, but we aint got the evil, know what I mean?'

'No, mate, I don't. All I know is a friend of mine's had the shit kicked out of him. You don't do nothin', then I will.'

'What you gonna do, Stan?' asked Bimbo, softly. 'You bin watchin' too many videos. You wanna take on Reilly? Or Reardon? They'll be waitin'. Knives, pickaxe handles, maybe a shooter or two. You wanna take on Jackie Green? He don't even need no weapons. Go 'ome, Stan.'

'Stuff it!' said Stan. 'Don't lie down and die, son. You're worth more than all the rest of 'em put together. And anyway, you said it yourself, you can't stop it. You bought the ticket. Now see the ride out.'

'Don't get me wrong, Stan. I aint runnin'.'

'Didn't think you would. Now hear me out. Reardon's movin' off the manor. Chiswick, Hammersmith, the Bush, Ealin'. They say he's even moving in on Southall. And he's bought a club up west. Big Time Frankie!'

'So? The rich get richer. What does it prove?'

'I said hear me out. I'm in business now. I know the way these things work. He's borrowin' money to finance his operations. Now's the time to hit him.'

'With what?'

'Trust me, Bim. Each to his trade.'

'Your trade's videos.'

'No, that's just what they call a vocation. My first trade: arson.'

Bimbo closed his eyes. 'That's what got you put away in the first place.'

'Only cos some bastard squealed. Now, I done some checking. Reilly is under-insured. Place is a fire trap. Fire brigade went in and gave him two months to bring the place up to scratch. He won't get a piggin' penny if it comes down.'

'You can't torch the Seagull. There's flats above it.'

'Empty. Waitin' for renovation. I told you, I done some checking.'

'It aint worth the risk.'

'He's just had sixty grand's worth of new tables and electronic gear. Paid cash up front. Know where he got the money? Borrowed it from Reardon. Now that should hurt.'

'But the insurance?' said Bimbo.

'You don't understand the insurance business, son. Legalised theft. If the building is unsafe they'll void the policy. They'll find any way they can not to pay up. They'll claim contributory negligence.'

'And you're sure no one's going to get hurt?'

'Absolutely.'

'I don't know, Stan. You can't be sure about a thing like that.

Some dosser asleep round the back. Squatters in the flats.'

'No one will get hurt.'

'What about the fire brigade? Some fireman going in?'

'Trust me.'

Bimbo thought about it, and pictured Adrian in the hospital bed. 'Where will it end, Stan?' The video club owner spread his hands.

'It's like buying a ticket on a runaway train. You never know.'

'Okay. Let's do it.'

'Jeez, I'm glad you said that. That's a weight off my mind.'

'Why?'

'I torched the place before comin' 'ere. It was goin' a treat when I left. Fancy a beer?'

Stepney rubbed at the numbed fingers of his right hand and carried on reading. The young reporter had been very kind allowing him access to the files for his book on royal visits to the town. She had brought him a cup of tea and shown him the filing cabinet marked L-R. He had thanked her and removed the 'ROYAL' file, settling down at the small iron desk in the filing room.

'If you want anything just shout,' said the girl.

'I will. Thank you so much.'

When she had gone he returned to the cabinet and tugged open the drawer, pulling out the file marked 'REARDON, FRANK'. It was mostly full of old cuttings, but someone had added a foolscap page of notes, giving basic details like date of birth, army record, and business interests.

Stepney carefully copied the dates of interest into a small, leather bound notebook. The times may have changed, but the methods never vary, he thought, with a wry smile. Mussolini had known how to deal with enemies. Goebbels had learned from him, and refined his methods. Now, half a century later, Frank Reardon was to learn a terrible lesson.

'But only if you live long enough, Heinrich,' he told himself. It was difficult making the notes. His fingers felt swollen and numb, the writing was spidery. But he persevered. At 3.40 p.m. he returned both files to their place and left the office. It was cold outside, frost in the air. He thought of the geraniums in his window box. Time to take them in.

What for? He would never see them bloom again. Still, someone might.

He hailed a taxi and arrived home at 4.20 p.m. He was tired and weak, his strength fading. He wanted to sleep, to rest. But there was no time. Life was now measured in days. In his flat he fed a sheet of paper into an old typewriter. Just like the old days. A sense of deep pleasure swept through him as he thought of Frank Reardon's face. Stepney worked for an hour, revising, polishing. The secret was not to go over the top. No adjectives. Simple statements always seem more real, and therefore retain the illusion of truth.

It was something the Party understood from the very earliest days. You didn't need a gun to destroy an enemy. What was it the Führer had said? Faced with a choice between the truth and the big lie, people will always believe the big lie. With men like Reardon it was easy to find the weak spot. Everything they had was built on their strength and their ruthlessness. There was a certain glamour, Stepney knew, that attached itself to gangsters. So then, destroy the glamour, and create … what? Contempt, disgust, and outrage.

Oh yes, Frank Reardon, you have some surprises in store.

The big lie is going to bring you down.

At last satisfied, he folded the three sheets and lifted the telephone receiver. Beside the phone, on a large note pad, he had written the number he had found in Yellow Pages. He dialled it slowly.

'Hedges,' came the disembodied voice.

'Mr Hedges of Oriol Printing?'

'Yes, who is this?'

'My name is Stepney. Be so kind as to call upon me at six-thirty this evening. My address is ... do you have a pen?'

'I'm a very busy man, Mr Stepney.'

'Too busy to earn a swift, tax free thousand pounds?'

'How swift?'

'That will depend on you. But there is a second thousand to be earned almost as swiftly.'

'Give me the address.'

Hedges arrived five minutes early. Stepney watched him from the upstairs window, smiling as he saw the man step from a five year old Ford Capri. The old man walked to the top of the stairs and called down.

'Come in, Mr Hedges, the door is open. Shut it behind you, if you please.' Stepney waited as the man climbed the stairs. Hedges was a man in his mid-fifties. His face was red and blotchy, his eyes sunken and dark-ringed. He looked a man with troubles. Stepney hoped they were financial. 'Follow me, please.' He led the printer into the back room and sat down, beckoning him to a straight-backed chair.

'Mind if I smoke?' asked Hedges, pulling a pack of cigars from his pocket.

'Yes I do. You may smoke in five minutes when you are away from here.'

'Okay, down to business then: you mentioned two thousand pounds.'

'First tell me of your printing set up.'

'I can do anything you want. Posters, leaflets, small magazines, cards. You name it.'

'I want a single page leaflet set in 12pt. Times Roman.'

'I see you know your type. How many words?'

'Four hundred and fifty.'

'How many leaflets?'

160

'The first run will be one thousand. The second the same, but different text. The third need only be five hundred.'

'Sounds simple enough. What else?'

'That is it.'

Hedges leaned back, his face taking on a sad expression. 'That's not cost effective for me.'

'Do not insult my intelligence, Mr Hedges. It will take you one hour to set the type, another two perhaps to run off the thousand. You could handle all three in a night, for which you would quote me perhaps three hundred pounds. But we will not quibble. You will receive five hundred pounds for the first printing. Two hundred and fifty more for each of the others. And there is a bonus, as I said, of another thousand.'

'There is?' said Hedges. 'Why?'

'Read this,' said Stepney, passing the sheet to the printer. Hedges fished in his pocket for his glasses and settled back to read.

'Jesus, Joseph and Mary!' he whispered. 'I can't print this.'

'You can,' said Stepney firmly. 'You will deliver these to me tomorrow morning at nine. No later. Here are the other two pages.'

'I don't even want to read them,' said Hedges, rising.

'That's where the bonus comes in,' said Stepney. 'Call it danger money.'

'Do you know what could happen to me if word got out that I printed these? Stuff me gently! I'd be wearing me nuts as a necklace. Get somebody else.'

'Firstly, there will be no way to trace the leaflets to you, because there will be no way to trace them to me. Secondly, you will set the type yourself when everyone else has gone home. You will work alone. No one need know you had a hand in the production.'

'You don't think Reardon is going to check all the printers? I'm not risking my balls for a piddling two thousand.'

'How much then are your balls worth?'

Hedges sat down, and Stepney held back the smile of triumph. 'What you want these for?'

'To be read, Mr Hedges.'

'I take it it's all true. I suppose it must be.'

'I suppose it must. How much?'

'Give me a minute.' Hedges pulled a cigar clear and tore off the cellophane wrapping. Stepney did not stop him. Hedges lit the cigar with a Zippo lighter and drew deeply on the smoke. 'Five thousand,' he said at last, but his eyes betrayed him.

'Two thousand five hundred,' said Stepney.

'It's not enough.'

'I think so. For a little danger? It is enough.'

'How can I be sure he won't find out?'

'Nothing is certain in this life, Mr Hedges. That is why the rewards are greater than normal. But if it will make you feel happier let me tell you that I am negotiating for a third party, who does not know where the printing is being done. He has been commissioned by a fourth party. You understand? By the time the leaflets arrive at their destination you will be twice removed from the scene. Also, there are five printers in the immediate area, and another fourteen in outlying areas. You are from the far end of Chelsea. They will not come to you first. They may not come to you at all. There are over fifty small print shops in this part of London.'

'Three thousand. That's my lowest.'

'I am sure you have bills to pay. And I wonder, in these days of recession, when next you will have the opportunity of earning this amount for one night's work?'

'I must be mad,' said Hedges. 'What are you offering up front?'

'Ten per cent. Two hundred and fifty pounds. The rest on delivery.'

'And no one will ever know?'

162

'No one but you and I.'

'Are the other two sheets as bad as this one?'

'Yes.'

'Jesus! Reardon will go apeshit.'

'One lives in hope, Mr Hedges.'

'I'd better get going if I'm to be working all night.'

'You better had.'

8

Stan Jarvis unlocked the shop door, turned on the light, switched off the alarm and prepared the start-of-day discs in his computer. Every customer, every film, every transaction was fed into the new Amstrad 8512, and Stan knew, almost to the penny, how much he'd made in the last year. He was on the verge of becoming rich – at least by his standards. He'd opened a second shop in Fulham, which was doing nicely, and had taken lease on a third in Ealing. The Porsche was getting closer all the time.

'Not bad, Stanley,' he told himself. Especially for the boy who went through school labelled 'stunningly stupid' by his headmaster, and was the butt of many jokes by his contemporaries. Three weeks before his school ordeal ended, a young, gifted teacher had finally diagnosed the reason for Stan's torment. He was dyslexic, unable to memorise letters, or recreate written words from sounds.

Stan had left school twenty-five years ago at fifteen and journeyed out into the wild East End with no qualifications and no future. He had taken several casual jobs, working on the lorries, or building sites, but money was tight and his £2-a-day was no great help to his widowed mother. Then he had met up with some schoolfriends who had other ideas about wealth, and Stan found himself heading for degree honours in burglary. He was careful, swift and cunning. And he was never caught. Then, twelve years ago, he had discovered his real talent. A timber merchant facing financial ruin needed a fire to cover his stupidity. Stan supplied it, and from the heat earned a cool £1000. It was a straight paraffin and rags blaze, but it was a beginning. Before the end of four years Stan Jarvis was the best professional 'torch' in London. Electronic igniters, failsafe cut outs, and clean alibis left Stan owning a nice house in Perivale, a solid bank account and guaranteed foreign holidays in places like Miami and Barbados. It also brought him a wife, Cora, and a Dobermann called Prince.

Prince was a strange dog, incapable of being trained, lacking all loyalty, and a permanent cause of devastation in house and garden. But that still put the dog ten points ahead of Cora. She had been – probably still was – the best screw in London. And she'd certainly screwed Stan. She and her latest lover now had the house, the bank account and the foreign holidays. She had also 'grassed' on her husband and earned Stan Jarvis five years at one of Her Majesty's less salubrious hotels.

It was while at Wormwood Scrubs prison that he had met Bimbo Jardine and Adrian Owen. Stan liked them both – but especially Bimbo. The man had not an ounce of malice in his colossal frame.

There were few absolutes in Stan's life. He wasn't patriotic, his morals would have disgusted a sewer rat, and anyone who lent him money had to have less brain cells than an amoeba. But when it came to 'mates in trouble', Stan moved into a class of his own.

He knew what Bimbo Jardine was facing. It could be summed up in one word.

Pain.

And there was no way he'd allow Bimbo to suffer alone. Trouble was, he knew, that Bimbo would never believe just how far the likes of Reardon and Green would go. Stan, on the other hand, was under no illusions.

And when Jackie Green walked into the shop at 11.15 that morning Stan was well prepared. The boxer was wearing a white Lacoste sweatshirt and beautifully cut grey trousers. Stan grinned at him, his expression open, honest and welcoming, giving no hint of the tension he felt. Any mistakes in the next few minutes would see blood spilled on the shop's new carpet. ''Ello Jackie, how ya doin'?'

'Not bad, Stan. Yourself?'

'Can't complain. You got yourself a video?'

'Yeah.'

'Couldn't have come to a better place. We've got all the latest. And for you there's a free membership.'

'That's nice,' said Green, moving to the door, dropping the latch, and switching the sign to 'Closed', 'but I wanted a chat.'

'What about?'

'About a fire.' Green's pale eyes fixed on Stan's face.

'Sorry, mate, I quit that game. No point now. I'm doin' pretty nicely. But I can put you in touch with a couple of old mates. Good geezers. They won't blag.'

Green sat down on the stool beyond the counter and leaned in. 'I don't want a fire done. I'm talkin' about last night.' Stan's heart began to beat faster, but he was also a fine poker player.

'You lost me, Jackie.'

'The snooker hall?'

'Fred's place? I drove past that this mornin'.'

'Not Freddie,' said Green, his eyes losing their malice. 'Reilly's. The Seagull in the Bush.'

'Ah, insurance job was it?' said Stan, knowingly.

'What's that mean?'

'Reilly. Short of money is he?'

'Not as far as I know. You think he done his own place?'

'Dunno,' said Stan. 'Thass the normal way, innit?'

'Talk me through it,' said Green. 'The "normal way".'

Stan rose and walked back to the electric kettle, checking it for water, then switching it on. 'Okay. Talkin' general, right? A guy owns a snooker hall and it aint doin' too well. He orders a

166

load of new equipment: tables, carpets, decorations, panellin',
anything that costs a few bob. Then, late one night, he ships a
load of it out, brings in the old rubbish what he's kept in store.
Then the place is torched. If he's sensible he'll have taken out a
bloody great insurance policy about a month before.'

'Bit obvious, innit? Big insurance policy? Wouldn't they
smell a rat?' said Green.

'Maybe,' agreed Stan, 'but it would also be strange if he
didn't – having put in a load of new equipment. Wouldn't you
increase your insurance?'

'How do you know he put in a load of new equipment?' said
Green.

'Who? I thought we was talkin' general.'

'Forget it. Go on.'

'Well, that's about it. Insurance people send an assessor
down, and as long as the torch has done his job well they
should pay up.'

'What do you mean, done his job well?'

'Made it look like an electrical fault. Set the blaze to a socket,
like a plugged in TV. Accidental.'

Green nodded. 'So you reckon they'll pay up?'

'They don't like payin' up. They'll look for some loophole,
but then if the job's been done right they should have no
option ... unless ...'

'What?'

'Unless they can claim negligence on the part of the manage-
ment. You know, lighted cigarette left burning on top of a glass
of paraffin, or a building that's already been labelled a fire
hazard by the Fire Brigade. That sorta thing.'

'That's all very well,' said Green, 'if Reilly torched his own
club. But what about enemies?'

Stan shrugged.

'Easy to find out,' he said.

'Yeah?'

'Sure. Look at all the facts. I don't know nothin' about the way the Seagull operates, but, if it was a rundown hole and then it was torched I'd say the bloke … Reilly? … was turned over. But – and this is the big but – had he bought any new stock? Had he increased his insurance? Is he lookin' to retire in Barbados? Cos if any of that is true then you can count out enemies. I mean people who don't like you don't go round doin' you favours, do they? You want tea or coffee?'

'Nothin'. But you go ahead.'

Stan made a mug of strong tea and returned to the counter. He could see that Green was undecided, but he wasn't out of the woods yet.

'You seen Bimbo lately?' asked the ex-boxer.

'Yeah. Saw him Saturday. He bought a video recorder. I dropped it round. Why?'

'He had a grudge against Reilly.'

'He never mentioned it to me. But anyway, he aint a torch. It would never occur to him. And if it did he wouldn't do it himself – he'd come to me.'

'Exactly the thought that crossed my mind, you and him bein' cellmates and all.'

'Oh, I see,' said Stan, keeping his reaction muted, but allowing an edge of anger to show. 'That's it, is it? Nice. What you gonna do then Jackie? Break me 'ands? Smash me shop?'

'I don't think you did it, Stan,' said Green. 'You're not stupid. But I thought it was worth a trip out here. And it was. You've given me a lot of food for thought. You still mates with Bimbo?'

'I won't lie to you, course I am. We spent a coupla years in the same cell. But he fights his own battles, and I aint walkin' on the other side of the street to avoid him just cos he's got on the wrong side of his boss. It'll blow over.'

'Don't bank on it. You stick by your friends, then?'

'When I can – and when I don't have to suffer any pain.'

'Adrian Owen was a friend of yours.'

'ls, Jackie. He aint dead yet.'

Green nodded. 'It was Reilly that turned him over. Him and Roache and Taggart, and a few others.'

'Yeah? Takes a lotta men to turn over one queen, don't it?'

'You knew then?'

'No, but I'm beginnin' to see how it all hangs together. And if you're tellin' me this so I can report it to Bimbo, forget it. I don't want to see the lad gettin' himself into more trouble.'

'You think he'd go after Reilly?'

'Probably. I don't see where all this aggro is gettin' anyone.'

Green shrugged. 'Some people like aggro, Stan. What about the old Jew next door?'

'Stuff me, Jackie, what is this? Twenty questions?'

'Don't make me angry,' said Green. Stan drew in a slow breath.

'He's just that, an old Jew. Where does he fit in?'

'He's another friend of Bimbo's. And he pulled a shooter on two of Reardon's lads.'

'Jesus, Jackie. There's a man on the critical list, a place has been burnt down, and now there's a shooter? Leave me out of it.'

'You are out of it, Stan. For now. I should stay that way. I should cross the road to avoid Bimbo Jardine. Cos if I hear you've even waved at him, I'm gonna be back. And then we won't talk. I'll just bust your bones and nail your bollocks to the wall.' Reaching down, Green lifted Stan's tea and slowly poured it on to the computer keyboard. The screen shorted out and the programme disappeared. 'Have a nice day, Stan.'

Sherry Parker was frightened, with the fear born of weakened nerves and destroyed confidence. The house was clean, though it had taken four solid hours of effort to bring it to its best. The wallpaper needed changing, and the paintwork was flaking, but everywhere else was bright. Even the kids had helped.

Sarah had tidied her room and Simon had bundled all his toy soldiers in a cardboard box, tied it with string, and forced it under his bunk bed.

Sherry herself had stuck rigidly to a diet, and had lost three pounds in the last four days. Not much – but enough to allow her to squeeze into her favourite blue dress. Her friend Joan had cut her hair, and even added gentle blonde highlights. The mirror in the lounge confirmed that she looked better than she had in years. But the fear remained.

Wilks had taunted her with words of acid; had blamed her for his infidelities. She was 'clumsy in bed'. She had 'no understanding of a man's needs', 'no imagination'. She was 'the worst lay I've ever had'.

Now, with the meal over, the children asleep, and the coffee half finished, her nerves were at breaking point. Seemingly oblivious to her mental anguish Bimbo sat staring at the coal fire. He was dressed in light blue jeans and a new white rollneck sweater. He seemed totally at ease, sprawled in front of the fire.

'I love this,' he said, suddenly. 'We had a real fire at the Home. They used to give us our milk at night sitting in front of it. And there was this woman – not the matron, a sorta helper – she used to tell us stories. It was great. Yeah,' he said, his voice fading, 'good days them. All went bloody wrong somewhere.'

'You wanna talk about it?' asked Sherry.

'Not much to say, love. There's a friend of mine on the critical list, and another one dyin' a cancer. I can't do nothin' for neither of 'em.'

'You done a lot for me,' she said. 'Don't that count for somethin'?'

He smiled, but his eyes still had a faraway look. 'Yeah. It counts. But it weren't nothin', Sher. It was only money.'

'No it wasn't. It was carin'. You don't know how good it is to have somebody care whether you live or die.' She stood and

170

began to gather the dishes from the table. Bimbo rose to help.

'You just sit there,' she said. 'I'll do it.'

'Nah. I'll wash, you wipe. Then you won't have to worry about it in the mornin'. I always 'ate that. Gettin' up to a chock-a-block sink and all that cold grease.'

In the kitchen Sherry's nerves returned. Bimbo scrubbed at the plates and pans and whistled the theme from *High Noon*, his enormous frame making the tiny kitchen seem even more like an over-extended cupboard.

'Lovely meal, Sher. The kids were great, weren't they?'

'On their best behaviour for uncle Bimbo. They like you, Bim. You're very good with 'em.'

With the last of the dishes cleared away Sherry led Bimbo back to the lounge and poured him a glass of Sainsbury's cheapest brandy. Bimbo took a sip and put it aside. 'Don't be on edge,' he told her, as he resumed his seat in front of the fire. 'I aint gonna rape you, or nothin'. So relax for a minute, eh?'

'I didn't know it was that obvious.' She sat beside him and drained her glass. He stretched out his hand and she took it.

'It's nice 'avin' friends. So you just sit there, enjoy the fire, and we'll have a chat, then I'll be on me way. All right?'

'It's a long time since I've had a man round for a meal. You don't know what it's like. Wonderin' if the chicken is cooked through, or the puddin's a disaster, or the house is a mess.'

'And the sex bit,' he said.

'Yeah, specially that,' she agreed.

'It used to bovver me when I was younger. It don't anymore,' he said. 'It aint that important. It's nice, don't get me wrong; but it aint the be-all-and-end-all.'

'It is to some people,' she told him, refilling her glass. 'Wilks used to go on and on about it. Always braggin' about who he was pullin' and how good they were in bed.'

'He's a scumbag. He always was.'

'You aint drinkin' your brandy. Don't you like it?'

'Not much of a drinker.' Lifting the iron tongs he added two more lumps of coal to the fire.

'I don't know why I'm talking to you like this. It probably aint right,' she said. 'I think I'm getting drunk. Why'd you pay me rent?'

'That's what friends are for. Anyway, I come into a bit of money I weren't expectin'. Don't worry about it.'

'One of these days I'll pay you back. Honest!'

'It aint important. You lost weight, aintcha? Looks good.'

'It's not enough. I need another half a stone. Maybe then I'll try sprintin' again.'

Bimbo chuckled. 'I remember that race you won. You beat Maggie Ames – and she was County. You was so 'appy. I thought you was gonna do a lap of honour.'

'It was the only time I did beat her. Everythin' was right, like I didn't weigh nothin' and I was floatin'. That was the only time. I was me and I won and everythin' was right. Nothin's bin right since.' She drained her glass and stared into the fire. Bimbo reached out and switched on the table lamp. Then he rose and flicked off the main light. The room was more cosy now, flickering red in the light of the fire. Sherry tensed, but Bimbo just sat as he had before.

'I aint very good in bed,' she whispered, the words hanging in the air.

'Me neither. We probably don't get enough practice.'

She giggled and poured another brandy. 'You got a girlfriend, Bim?'

'Nah. Aint much of a ladies' man. Bit of a loner really. There was this girl I used to like. But I never said nothin'. I just used to watch her. She won a race once.'

'You shoulda said. Maybe that's what she was waitin' for.'

He moved to sit alongside her and lifted her chin. The kiss tasted of brandy. She lay back on the rug and he stretched out beside her, kissing her cheek and her brow. His hand rested on her hip, without moving, and she could feel the warmth from his touch. A large lump of coal split and fell apart, yellow flames licking at the chimney. Sherry's arms circled his neck, pulling him down. For a long while they lay there in the firelight, his hand stroking her back and her hip. She sat up and unfastened the blue dress, lifting it over her head, then stood and moved to the sofa.

'Give me a hand,' she said. Together they opened it out into a large double bed. Turning to him Sherry tugged at his sweater, pushing it up his chest. He chuckled and pulled it off. Leaning down he swept his arms around her, lifting her from her feet. Laying her on the bed, he unfastened his jeans and stepped from them. She removed her bra and panties. Lying down beside her, he drew her to him.

They made love for more than an hour, sometimes slowly and gently, stopping often to kiss and touch, sometimes with fierceness and driving passion. Then they lay, arm in arm, in comfortable silence as the fire slowly died.

'Are you happy?' she asked him.

'Yeah. You?'

'I think you could say that.' She rolled on top of him, her arms resting on his chest. 'You lied to me. You said you were no good in bed.'

'So did you,' he said, pulling her into an embrace. She struggled free and straddled him. He smiled and slid his hands down her waist, pulling her into position.

'Again?' she asked, as she felt the movement beneath her.

'Seems like a good idea.'

Later, as Sherry slept, he lay awake feeling content. Ever since his teenage days he had wanted to make love to Sherry Parker; from the moment he saw her joy at winning that race. That she had faked the first climax bothered him not at all. It had allowed her to relax, and maybe the second one was real. The clock on the wall showed 1 a.m. Bimbo eased himself from the bed and dressed. It wouldn't do for the kids to come down and see uncle Bimbo in bed with mummy. Gently he roused her from sleep and kissed her goodbye.

'You will come again?'

'Try to keep me away.'

She smiled sleepily. 'Can I get you a coffee?'

'No. Go back to sleep.'

After he had gone Sherry got up and stirred the fire to life, adding more coal. The evening had been too pleasant to allow it merely to fade away in dreams. She wanted to burn the enjoyment into her memory so that at any time in the future she could relive every moment.

The phone rang. She glanced at the clock. It was 1.20 in the morning.

'Hello?'

The voice was low, the words vicious and terrifying. She listened in frozen terror until the line went dead.

'Oh my God!' she whispered.

Bimbo jogged home from Sherry's, enjoying the inner warmth of a dream satisfied. No, not satisfied, he realised, but begun. Thoughts of Reardon and Jackie Green were far away as he pounded into Ironside Towers, across the dark courtyard, towards the beckoning street lights outside his home.

A match flared.

Bimbo swivelled, fists raised and ready. Silver moved away from the young woman he was with and walked towards him. In the moonlight the tall, slender black man looked almost feral, his movements smooth, his eyes gleaming.

'Cold night,' said Silver.

'Yeah,' agreed Bimbo, embarrassed by his show of fear.

'Three men hangin' about your door. I think they busted your place, man.'

'Recognise 'em?'

'All you ghosts look alike to me.'

'Thanks for the tip.'

'It didn't cost nothin'.'

'No. You're keepin' the lady waitin'.'

Silver grinned. 'The bitch don't mind. I hear you're in deep shit, man. I hear Reardon is out for your ass.'

'What's it to you?'

'Nothing to me, man, ceptin' it bring trouble to my turf. I don't want no ghost gangs bringing down the Filth, you dig? What you do anyway? You steal from him, man?'

'I never stole nothin'. I never done nothin'. And I don't need to explain it to you, do I?'

'Damn shame you aint black,' said Silver. 'I could use you. But,' he shrugged, 'that's the breaks. You moving out?'

'No.'

'You a fool, man,' said Silver, wandering away to the girl.

'Yeah,' Bimbo told the night.

He moved out onto the street and swiftly crossed the road, alert for any movement. There was none. The main front door was still open and he entered, dropping the latch. He stood for several minutes, eyes closed, listening for any sounds. There were none. He moved up the stairs, keeping to the wall, avoiding any loose boards that might betray his arrival. On the landing he waited once more, finally pressing the two-minute light. The landing was empty, and there were no bloody messages outside his flat.

He turned the key in his front door, hurling it open and stepping back into the landing. The door crashed into the wall beyond. Silence. Reaching round the doorway he flipped on the light and entered.

Nothing. The flat was empty, and just as he'd left it. He shut the door and searched every room. A £10 note he'd left on the table was still there. He sat by the window until the hammering in his chest eased.

He awoke at seven, ran six miles, and worked out until 9 a.m. Then he bathed, dressed and took a bus to Charing Cross Hospital. A different policeman was seated by the bed. Bimbo opened the door and stepped in.

The constable looked up and waved him away. Bimbo ignored him and pulled up a chair. Adrian's face looked more human now, the swelling subsiding, but both eyes were blackened. His arms were both encased in plaster and his legs were in traction. A tube was pinned to his right arm, and another had been inserted into his nose.

''Ang in there, son,' said Bimbo. The constable touched his shoulder. Bimbo looked up.

'I'm sorry, mate, but you can't stay here.'

''Ow is he?'

'The next few days are crucial. That's what they say. He's bleeding internally and too weak to be operated on. You're Jardine, yeah?'

'Thass right.'

'Sgt Dodds said you might be round. Now come on, move yourself. You're not going to do any good sitting there. He can't hear you.'

'I come in every morning. Just for a coupla minutes.'

'Okay. I'll leave a message with the next man. He'll let you in. But only for a couple of minutes. Right?'

'Yeah. Ta.'

Bimbo left and walked back to Shepherd's Bush, stopping to view the Seagull Snooker Club. It was completely gutted and timbers had been erected at the side, preparatory to demolition.

Stan certainly knew his trade.

Bimbo took a bus back to town and stopped off at the deli for a loaf of granary bread. As he stepped back outside a white Jaguar screeched to a halt in the kerb and two officers leapt out. 'John Jardine?' asked the first.

'Yeah?'

'Get in the car,' he said, taking hold of Bimbo's arm. Bimbo shrugged him away. The officer lunged at him, and, without thinking, Bimbo grabbed his jacket and spun him to the pavement. The second constable dragged his truncheon clear.

'You better put that away, son, or I'll make you eat it!' Bimbo warned him. The man swallowed hard and advanced. A second car pulled up.

'Bimbo!' roared Don Dodds. 'Stop soddin' about and get in the car!'

The big man walked to Dodds' vehicle.

'What the bleedin' 'ell's 'appenin'?'

'Get in, son, we'll talk at the station.' Bimbo slid into the back seat.

'Wait a minute,' he said, as the car moved away. 'What about me bread? I dropped it.'

Dodds said nothing and the car picked up speed. It was a short ride to the new building, and a longer walk to the interview room on the lower levels. Don Dodds remained with him while the custody officer advised him of his rights and his pockets were emptied. Then he was left sitting at a metal topped desk, a young uniformed constable standing by the door. After about fifteen minutes two CID officers entered. One was young, about twenty-one, with sandy hair and a face that seemed never to have come in contact with a razor. The other was Eric Lynch, a 48-year-old Geordie, well known in the manor. Bimbo didn't like him.

'Where were you last night?' asked Lynch, sitting opposite Bimbo and lighting a small cigar.

'None a your business.'

'That's how we're going to play it, is it?'

'Looks that way. And there's no point lookin' for back 'anders. I don't pay pricks like you. And I don't need no four-hundred-quid remand neither.' Lynch reddened. Then he smiled.

'Remand, Bimbo? You couldn't get bail on this if you was Prince Charles. Now tell me about last night.'

'I got nothin' to say.'

'The custody officer told you why you're here. It's murder, son. The man you beat up last night .... Reilly. You caved his skull in. Not very wise. Understandable, though. After all he did have your queer mate turned over. You queer, Bimbo?

'No.'

'Just didn't know your own strength, eh? That gonna be the defence?'

'There aint no defence. I never touched him.'

Lynch turned to the younger man. 'What you are witnessing here, Ian, is the ultimate triumph of brawn over brain.' He swung back to Bimbo. 'Watch my lips, dick-head. You – killed – Reilly – last – night. Now, before you deny it again, I'm going to run through some facts. At eleven-fifteen last night Mr Reilly was walking home to his house in Hammersmith. His wife, who was waiting for him, heard a noise and looked out of her window. She saw a man – she described him as being a bloody giant. Ring a bell, does it? – who was wearing a light-coloured track suit top. He was beating up her husband. She screamed and the man ran away. She remembers the track suit top being torn at the shoulder. Do you have a track suit top torn at the shoulder?'

'Yeah. It's back at me flat.'

'No, son. It's here. All your clothes are here. And I suppose you are going to be amazed to hear that your track suit top is all covered in blood.'

Bimbo said nothing.

'Oh go on, son,' said Lynch. 'Detective Constable Sunley is new to CID, and he's never heard anyone say, "this is a stitch-up, guv."'

'I wanna see Sgt Dodds.'

'That's a new one. Think he can get you off, do you? Well,

what do you know? Old Dodds. Old white-as-bloody-snow Dodds. I suppose you want a confidential chat?'

'Well, I couldn't have one with you, could I? Your nose is so far up Reardon's arse when he coughs you sneeze.'

'Under normal conditions, Bimbo, I'd make you eat those words. But there's no need is there? What do you reckon? Ten years. At least with your record. Maybe life.'

'I'd like to see Mr Dodds. And that's the last word you'll hear from me, you scumbag.'

'You're not using the brains God gave you, Bimbo,' said Lynch. 'Reilly had your mate put on the critical list. You went to sort him out. In the fight that followed he died. If you admit it you could get off with manslaughter. Maybe only do two, three years. The judge would take it kindly that you admitted the offence.'

Bimbo stared into Lynch's eyes.

'Look,' said the younger man. 'What the inspector says makes a lot of sense. You've been identified on the scene, the blood is on your clothes, and you have the motive.'

Bimbo looked into the younger man's face. 'Okay, son. I was with a lady named Sherry Wilks last night. I went round for dinner and stayed till after midnight.' He gave the address.

Both men left the room, returning twenty minutes later. Lynch was wearing the kind of smile that could curdle milk.

'Have you had time to work out a different alibi, Bimbo?' he said.

'What you talkin' about?'

'Mrs Wilks says she hasn't seen you in days.'

For the rest of the day Bimbo refused to speak, maintaining a sullen silence and staring at the far wall. He was finally taken to a cell, where he sat on the narrow bed, his face impassive, his feelings masked.

Why would Sherry do that to him? Was it all a set up? Was

that why she had invited him round, so that he could be put away for a crime he didn't commit? He'd taken many knocks in his life, but this hurt worse than any. Betrayal. All he had done was try to help her, and she had repaid him with a savagery he could not comprehend.

He was still sitting in the same position when the cell door opened at midnight.

'I hear on the grapevine you want to talk to me,' said Don Dodds, stepping inside with two mugs of tea.

'It don't matter now,' said Bimbo.

'Of course it matters. I know you didn't mean to kill him.'

'I didn't do it, Mr Dodds. If I had done it, I'd admit it.'

Dodds removed his cap and sat beside the big man. 'Drink your tea.'

'You know about Sherry?'

'I heard.'

'Why would she do that? Why would she say I wasn't there?'

'Did you see anyone else last night?'

'No. Yeah. I seen that spade, Silver, when I come home. About one o'clock. He said he saw someone in my flat.'

'What about the track suit top?'

'I left it in a holdall by the front door. I was gonna take it to the launderette. I just never got round to it. I never done it, Mr Dodds. But I'm goin' down for it. Two pound to a bent penny Reilly's wife fingers me.'

'Show me your hands,' said Dodds.

'Why?'

'Don't keep asking questions, son. It's nearly midnight and I'm on again at eight-fifteen.' Bimbo put down the tea and lifted his hands, palms upwards.

Dodds turned them over, examining the knuckles. They were flat and hard. 'All right, Bimbo. You just sit tight. Say nothing. I'll see what I can do.'

'Too late for that, Mr Dodds.'

'You know what the Yanks say, son, it's not over till the fat lady sings. I'll see you tomorrow.' Dodds stood and tapped at the door. 'Get some sleep,' he said.

Outside the cell, Dodds waited as the officer locked the door, then walked with him back to the desk.

'Thanks, Wilf.'

'Don't worry about it. What's your interest?'

'I don't think he did it.'

'Evidence is a bit overwhelming, isn't it?'

'Only on the surface. Bimbo's no actor. And he wouldn't be able to get away with lying to me.'

'Come on, Don. We've got his track suit top and a witness who said she saw a giant. We know he's had trouble with Reilly – and threatened him.'

'Anyone who hits a man so hard he smashes his skull in ought to have bruised hands. Bimbo doesn't. Added to that, where are the jeans he was supposed to have been wearing? Why no blood? Why only on the track suit top?'

'Maybe he threw the jeans away.'

'What, and kept a torn track suit top? What for, nostalgia?'

'It's a bit thin, Don.'

'Then there's the woman. Why give such a bum alibi?'

'Panic?'

'No. Something smells here. Who tipped us off?'

'No idea. Lynch took the call. That's all I know.'

'That says a lot,' muttered Dodds.

He left the station and glanced at his watch. It was almost ten-to-one and the night was chill to the point of frost. He climbed into his car and drove to Ironside Towers. Interviewing Silver was a problem. The man was a known villain and would give no information to the police.

The lift was out of order and Dodds slowly tramped up to the fourth floor, stopping outside the green-painted door with the brass numbers showing 114c. He pressed his finger to the bell and left it there. After about a minute a light came on in the hall beyond and the door was wrenched open by a tall negro wearing a white dressing gown. The anger faded from his eyes as he saw the dark uniform. 'Good morning, Mr Silver. Hope I didn't wake you.'

'What the fuck you wan'?' asked Silver, in an angry whisper, stepping from the hall on to the landing. 'My kids is asleep.'

'There was a raid on a pharmaceutical firm last night in Fulham. One of the witnesses said she saw a tall negro with a white leather jacket and tassles. A jacket just like yours, Mr Silver. So my Super suggested I ask you along to the station to answer a few questions. Get dressed please.'

'I was here all evenin'.'

'It's not the evening, Mr Silver. It was about this time of the morning.' Dodds consulted his notebook. 'About 1.11 a.m. to be precise.'

Silver pulled the door to and stepped away from the house. 'This is a crock of shit, sergeant. I was nowheres near Fulham.'

'I'm sure you can produce witnesses, sir. Now come along, get dressed.'

Silver's voice dropped to a hoarse whisper. 'Jesus, man, I was with a woman. My wife she's crazy. She'd cut my balls with a razor.'

'Dear, dear, wouldn't that be a shame? Still, better than going inside, eh? There's no one else to give you an alibi?'

'Nobody who would. Hey! Wait a minute! I seen Bimbo – you know, the big guy from over the way. I seen him about that time.'

'Bimbo Jardine?'

'That's him! Yeah. We spoke down in the courtyard.'

'What about, sir?'

'Who gives a shit? We spoke. You ask him.'

'He's another villain, sir. He might just back you up – and

be lying. Tell you what, you tell me what he was wearing when you spoke.'

'White sweater, jeans. He don't seem to feel the goddamn cold.'

'And what did you talk about?'

'I told him some men were hanging round his flat. He's in trouble, you know?'

'So you were just doing a good deed for a white neighbour?'

'Yeah. You wanna arrest me for that?'

'Not at all, Mr Silver. You get back to bed, sir. You'll catch your death in this weather.'

'That's it?'

'That's it, sir,' agreed Dodds. 'We'll see if Mr Jardine backs up your story. Goodnight, sir.' Dodds left the stunned Silver and walked back to his car. So far, so good, he thought, but it proved little. Bimbo could well have come home from killing Reilly and changed his clothes. At least that would be the prosecution argument.

He drove home for five hours' sleep and at 7.45 a.m. was outside Sherry Wilks' front door. There was no bell and he rapped sharply with his knuckles. The door was opened by a young girl of around eight or nine. Dodds removed his cap and crouched down.

'Good morning, miss,' he said. 'Is your mummy home?'

'She's in bed.'

'Well, you go and tell her a nice policeman is here to have a few words with her.'

The girl ran off, leaving the door open. Dodds stepped inside and made his way to the living room. Two minutes later Sherry entered. She was wearing a towelling robe, and her face was flushed and angry.

'How dare you just walk in here,' she stormed. 'Have you got a warrant?'

Dodds stood. 'Put the kettle on, madam, and let's not have a scene. I'm a very busy man and lying to the police is a serious business – even for a young mother.'

For a moment Sherry stood her ground. Then she backed away to the kitchen. Dodds followed.

'Two sugars, madam, and keep it weak. I've always had a fondness for weak tea.'

'You said I lied.'

'Now my wife makes tea so strong you could melt the spoon. Thirty-three years we've been married. You'd have thought she would have learned by now.'

'I didn't lie. Honest to God.'

Dodds said nothing. Sherry poured the tea into a white mug and Dodds sipped it appreciatively.

'Shall we go back into the lounge?' he said. Once there he sat down and stretched his legs. 'I did a little checking on you yesterday, madam. Sad case, isn't it? You married that sleaze Wilks. He left you destitute. You got behind with your rent, and then met a nice man. That must have lifted you, eh? A good, soft article like Bimbo. Suddenly all your problems disappear. Rent paid, food in the house. Amazing what some men will do for a poxy little gold digger. For a slag! And make no mistake, that's what, you are – a slag! I've seen your sort for twenty years. And you still make me sick. Nice cup of tea, though.'

'You've no right to talk to me like that. You don't know me,' said Sherry. 'You've no right.'

'Oh, right doesn't enter into it, madam. We're talking facts. Night before last you entertained a man here.'

'It wasn't Bimbo.'

'No? It was a man in white sweater and jeans. So your neighbour tells me. Built like a brick outhouse. Huge.'

'My friend is big. But it wasn't Bimbo.'

'Now isn't that strange? Here was I thinking Bimbo Jardine was a friend of yours, and now you tell me there are two giants in your life. Got a thing about big men have you?'

'Get out! Get out of my house!'

Dodds didn't move. Sipping his tea he looked around the room. 'I retire soon, madam, and perhaps you can do me a favour. Perhaps you can tell me what makes people like you. Was it being married to Wilks? Or was it that sleaze-bags tend to attract each other? And one other thing. How is it that your little girl can't tell your boyfriends apart? She told me, when she answered the door, that it was Bimbo who was here.'

Sherry's face lost its colour and she sagged back into the armchair, her hand over her mouth.

'Cat got your tongue, madam? Well … you know what they say, "Out of the mouths of babes and sucklings". Looks like you'll have to give the money back, won't you? And then, just for dessert I'm going to book you for obstructing the police in the pursuit of a murder inquiry. I don't doubt you'll get off with probation, but your picture will look nice in the local paper, and your neighbours will be able to point at you and say, "That's the slag who tried to put Bimbo away."'

Sherry's eyes filled with tears that ran down her cheeks.

'I shouldn't bother with the tears,' said Dodds. 'They don't work on me. I've seen it a thousand times. Now, what time did Bimbo arrive, and what time did he leave?'

'It isn't like you said,' sobbed Sherry. 'Not anything like it.'

'Just answer the question, madam.'

'You don't know what it's like. They threatened my kids. There wasn't any money. They said they'd hurt my kids.'

'Who said?'

'I don't know. Just after he left there was a phone call. And this awful voice said they knew he'd been here, and if l told anybody, they'd get my kids.'

Dodds sat and finished his tea. The tears seemed genuine, but then most women could turn on the taps, he knew.

'So it was Bimbo,' he said. She nodded. 'And what time did he leave?'

'Just before one.'

'Thank you, madam. I'll be going then.' He rose.

'What about my kids?' She shouted, rising from the chair to grab his jacket. 'What happens now?'

'I'll see someone is sent round. Now calm yourself down. Nothing is going to happen to the youngsters. l promise you that. It was an empty threat. But we'll look after them. Now calm down.'

'I didn't want to let him down – especially after all he's done for us. I'm not a slag. I'm not. I'm not!' He led her to the chair and settled her into it. The little girl came in, her eyes blazing.

'You made my mummy cry. You're not a nice policeman.'

'You make her a nice cup of tea, and she'll feel better,' said Dodds. 'Go on now. You know how to make a cup of tea, don't you?'

'Go on, Sarah,' said Sherry. 'Do what the policeman says.'

Dodds passed Sherry a clean white handkerchief. 'I am sorry, Mrs Wilks. But I needed to know. Right now Bimbo is sitting in a cell looking forward to a murder trial and maybe fifteen years. You understand?'

'I understand. But he won't will he? I let him down. After all he'd done. And I do like him a lot. I thought … you know, maybe we'd get together. Maybe even get married.'

'Don't worry about Bimbo. As far as he's concerned I came here this morning and you told me everything. Now I'm going to call and get a couple of officers round. Okay?'

'I'm not a slag. I'm not!'

'Thank you for your help, Mrs Wilks.'

Chief Inspector Frank Beard was forty-seven years old, and not only skilled in the arts of police work, but also a fine reader of men. Before his oak-topped desk sat two men he could read very well. One was an old fashioned copper, who, despite his cynicism, had never lost his understanding of duty, nor his compassion. The other was a first rate case solver and bent as a three quid note. Frank Beard would have loved to be able to prove a case against the Geordie, to kick him from the force, to see him serve a stretch. But Lynch had been surreptitiously investigated on four occasions, and always came up whiter than snow. He was sharp, and he was crafty.

'Outline it for me,' said Beard. Lynch flicked open his notebook.

'Reilly was killed late the night before last. His wife described the assailant. I received a phone call early yesterday morning saying that one John J. Jardine had threatened Reilly several weeks ago and broken two of his fingers in a fight. It seems that Reilly was running a small-time protection racket, and had put the squeeze on a gay friend of Jardine's. I was told that Jardine had killed Reilly. We obtained a warrant and searched Jardine's flat. We found his track suit top, covered in blood. The lab says the blood is Reilly's. We picked up Jardine in the High Street, where he assaulted P.C. Daines. We've questioned him and he obviously denies the killing, but he gave us an alibi which has subsequently been shot down.'

'No it hasn't,' said Dodds. Beard leaned back. Lynch swung on the sergeant.

'What do you mean it hasn't? My D.C. rang the woman. She denied he was there.'

'I went to see her. She'd been threatened. She's now willing to swear he was there – from seven until one.'

'So that's why Jardine wanted to see you alone. To set up an alibi.'

Dodds ignored him and turned to the Chief Inspector. 'She was terrified, sir. She had a phone call after Bimbo left saying that if she told anyone he was there her kids would be hurt.'

'Bullshit!' said Lynch.

'I also saw the man Silver – you know, the pimp on Ironside Estate – he saw Bimbo at around 1 a.m., coming home. He was wearing a white sweater and jeans. He also said he saw some men hanging around Bimbo's flat.'

'New career in CID is it, Dodds?' asked Lynch.

'I'd be no good at it, Lynch. I've been saving for two years for a new greenhouse.'

'You bastard! What's that supposed to mean?'

'Enough!' roared Frank Beard. 'Now, Don, what makes you sure the woman isn't lying?'

'I had to trick it out of her, sir. She denied he was there, but I told her that her daughter had told me different. I also said her neighbours had identified Bimbo as leaving the house at 1 a.m. And I know terror when I see it.' Lynch made to speak but Beard waved him to silence.

'Then what is going on – in your estimation?'

'It's hard to say, sir. As far as I can piece together Frank Reardon is … was … behind Reilly's operation. When Bimbo moved against Reilly and broke his fingers, Reardon took that as insubordination and decided to have Bimbo punished. Reilly then organised a vicious assault on Bimbo's friend, Adrian Owen. A short time later Reilly's snooker hall was burnt down. Insurance company refused to pay up. Place was a fire trap. Now Reilly is dead.'

'Which all points to Jardine,' said Lynch.

'I accept that,' said Dodds, 'but there are pieces missing.'

'Like what?' asked Frank Beard.

'I'm satisfied Bimbo didn't kill Reilly. But someone did. And someone torched his place. I reckon Frank Reardon lost a lot of money when the snooker hall went up. My bet is he had Reilly topped.'

'And your view?' Beard asked Lynch.

'It's a damn sight less complicated than this fairy story. We've a man on the manor who served time for arson. His name's Stan Jarvis. He was good at it too. He now runs a video shop.

But, more importantly, guess who he spent two years sharing a cell with?'

'I'm not into guessing games, Inspector.'

'Bimbo Jardine,' said Lynch, triumphantly.

'So you're still asking for Jardine to be kept in custody?'

'Yes, sir.'

'But you, Don, think he's been set up?'

'I'm convinced of it, sir. I think we should let him out. He's not the type to "flee the country". And I believe this can of worms will explode if Bimbo is on the street. Reardon still hasn't managed to punish him. His credibility is slipping, and we could find ourselves putting him away.'

'I'm not interested in any more murders,' said Beard. 'One is quite enough to be going on with. But I wouldn't mind seeing Reardon's arse in a sling. What's this about Jackie Green?'

'Reardon brought him in – a sort of partner,' said Lynch. 'There's some talk of Reardon financing him so he can get back into the ring.'

'I saw him fight McNab,' said Beard. 'Good puncher. Didn't he get pulled in over a Securicor job?'

'Yes, sir. He did three years.'

'Where is he now?'

'I understand he's flown to Tenerife for a short holiday,' said Lynch.

'Convenient,' said Dodds.

'What does that mean, Don?' asked Beard.

'Well, sir, he's another giant, isn't he? I wouldn't have minded examining his hands for bruises this morning.'

'I'm ordering Jardine released, pending further inquiries,' said Beard. 'And I want a close eye kept on the situation. Any developments, come to me instantly.'

'I think it's a mistake, sir,' said Lynch, reddening.

'We all make mistakes,' said Beard, softly. 'I can live with it.'

9

Hedges carried the boxes up to Stepney's front door and rang the bell. For some minutes he waited, then rang again. The old man opened the door and Hedges swallowed hard. The flesh had vanished from Stepney's face, his skin stretched tight over skeletal features. His eyes were bright, his clothes dishevelled, and his right arm was tucked inside a broad belt he had buckled about his waist.

'*Wer bist du?*' asked the old man.

'I've got your stuff.'

'*Was? Ich versehe sie nicht.*'

'Don't fuck me about. I've been up all night. Now let me in.'

The old man swayed in the doorway. 'Here, are you all right?' said Hedges.

'*Sprechen sie Deutsch!*' ordered Stepney.

'I don't speak German. It is German, isn't it?'

Stepney rubbed his hand across his eyes. 'German? Yes. German. I am sorry, Mr ... Mr ...?'

'Hedges. I've got your leaflets.'

'Yes, of course. Bring them in.' Stepney struggled up the stairs ahead of the printer and sank into a leather armchair.

'Now where's my money?'

'First show me the merchandise.' Hedges ripped open the four boxes, producing a selection of A4 leaflets. Stepney ran his eye over them and smiled. 'You have done well.' Reaching into a drawer he produced an envelope which he passed to the man. Hedges opened it and counted the money.

'You ought to see a doctor,' he said. 'You don't look well.'

Stepney chuckled, a dry sound that brought a shiver to the printer. 'Goodbye, Mr Hedges. You may rest assured no one will ever know of your part in this.'

'I could take you to the hospital,' said the man.

Stepney reached once more into the drawer, picking up a loose bundle of notes. Slowly, with his left hand, he counted out ten £50 notes, pushing them across the table.

'What's that for?'

'That? It is for caring. Now go.'

Stan was at the station to pick up Bimbo at 8.15 a.m. He said little until Bimbo had squeezed himself into the passenger seat of the Cottage Video van. As they drove out into the High Street, Stan outlined his conversation with Jackie Green.

'Now you know me, Bim, born conman. I talked Jackie into the idea that Reilly torched his own place. But, Jesus, son, never expected Jackie to top him. This is all gettin' out of hand. You gotta do a runner. Broken bones is one thing, undertakers is another.'

'l don't get it,' said Bimbo. 'This is all so stupid. One mistake. One piddlin' mistake. And it aint as if I didn't say sorry. Now Adrian's smashed up, Reilly's dead, and you're tellin' me to run. I don't believe this.'

'Don't try to work it out, Bim. It aint your strong suit. Just trust me and vanish for a while.'

'I aint runnin'.'

Stan pulled over and parked. He turned to Bimbo. 'Listen to me. If you woke up in the night and the flat was on fire you'd leave, right? You wouldn't stay and tell the fire "I aint runnin".' This is the same thing. It's out of control. Reardon's gonna destroy ya. You understand that?'

'It aint the same.'

'You think you can stand up to Jackie Green?'

'No,' admitted Bimbo.

'Then what you gonna achieve by stayin'?'

'I dunno, Stan. But I aint leavin'. It wouldn't feel right.'

'Whass that mean? Feel right.'

'I aint much on explainin'. I can't stop the world crappin' on me. I can't do nothin' about the way I am. I can't even protect me mates. But no one aint gonna ever get the satisfaction a sayin' they run me out. No one. You understand?'

'No, son,' said Stan, sadly. 'There's a time for fightin' and a time for runnin'. But, that's it, I aint gonna try and convince ya no more. You need me, I'll be there.'

'You stay out of it. Drop me off at Stepney's will ya?'

'Sure, and that reminds me: Jackie was askin' about him.'

'They aint startin' on him now?'

'They already did, son. He saw 'em off with a pistol. Gutsy old Jew, eh?'

'He aint a Jew, but it don't matter.' Stan switched on the ignition and the van pulled away.

Stepney's shop was closed, but his front door was on the latch. Bimbo and Stan made their way upstairs. Stepney was sitting in his old armchair, staring at a chessboard. He was un- shaven and his shirt was dirty and rumpled. The chess pieces had been set in a crazy pattern diagonally across the board.

'You all right, Step?' asked Bimbo, kneeling beside the old man.

'*Ja, mein freund. Sehr gut.*'

'I'm sorry, mate, I don't speak the lingo.'

'All the pieces,' said Stepney. 'I make a new game, yes? The old game is gone for good.' He leaned forward and swept a knight diagonally across the board and Bimbo saw that his right arm was hanging limp and useless in his lap.

'Oh God!' whispered Bimbo. 'I'm gonna get you to 'ospital.'

'No!' shouted Stepney. 'I will die in my home. But you, Bimbo my son, you will do something for me, yes?'

'Sure. You name it.'

'I wish for some peppermint. You buy some now. I will speak with your friend, Stan.'

'I'll be right back,' said Bimbo. 'Look after him, Stan.' As the big man ran down the stairs Stepney waved Stan close.

'Anything I can get ya?' asked Stan, nervous and uneasy.

'Nothing. But listen closely. I know you are a man of intelligence, and I also know you are aware of the trouble our large friend is in. Over there are four boxes of leaflets. One is on yellow paper, the second on pink, the third on white. Repeat it to me.' Stan did so. 'Good. They are to be distributed – and no one must know how, or by whom. You follow me?'

'No. Sorry, I don't know what you are talking about.'

'They will help destroy Reardon. They will take his mind from Bimbo. You understand? Read one. The yellow box. Take one and read it. Aloud.'

'I aint much on readin'. To be honest I aint much on readin'.'

'Then pass one to me. We must be swift. I do not want Bimbo to know of them.'

Stan passed a sheet of yellow paper to the old man, who took it in his left hand and held it before his eyes.

'There is a headline which says "The Evil Among Us". Then it reads:

"For centuries there has been no more evil a crime than that of abusing young children. Yet here, in our own area, there is a man who has been convicted of sexual crimes against young children, crimes too hideous to reproduce.

That man is FRANK REARDON, who was first convicted of abusing in 1964 and was dishonourably discharged from the army in 1971 for assaulting a boy aged three years and four months.

Reardon now poses as a businessman, and still carries on his evil and corrupt practices, procuring young children from his many contacts in the criminal underworld.

A case of the death of a child in Munich in 1970 was recorded, but the culprit never brought to justice. It was thought to be a serving soldier. Reardon was questioned, but an alibi was registered by a homosexual drug addict Reardon was liaising with, and the case was dropped through lack of evidence.

How can this man be accepted among us, with all the inherent danger to our children?

For the sake of our young we must demand the police act. And swiftly!"'

Stepney finished reading and sagged back.

'Bloody Hell,' whispered Stan. 'How did you find all that out?'

'I made it up,' said Stepney, smiling. 'It is good, *nicht wahr*?'

'It's bleedin' brilliant. But won't he scotch it at the start? I mean you can't prove none of it.'

'He will not be able to disprove it. That is the beauty of the blatant lie. Did you notice the age I gave for the child? Not three years. Not four years. But three years four months. It has the ring of truth. And that is all it needs.'

'What do the others say?'

'The second talks of his perversion in more detail with six case histories. The third deals with his liaison with the homosexual child molester Jackie Green.'

'Jesus, Joseph and Mary!'

'You can see these are distributed?'

'Where they gotta go?'

'Every public house, shop, cafe, and as many private homes as possible. But nothing to the press. They alone can declare his innocence, should they so desire.'

'All hell will break loose.'

'It is already loose.' Stepney laid his head back on the chair top. 'I think,' he said, 'you should take me to the hospital now. I cannot feel my legs.'

'I'll get you there,' said Stan, rising.

'There is a letter in the cabinet. See that Bimbo gets it.

You know, my friend, that I am very frightened. I have never died before. I wonder who will be waiting to mock me. So many.' Softly the old man began to sing. '*Oh Tannenbaum, Oh Tannenbaum, wie grun sind deine blatter, du grunst nicht nur in Sommerzeit, nein auch in Winter wenn es schneit, Oh Tannenbaum, Oh Tannenbaum, wie grun sind deine blatter.*' He looked at Stan. '*Ist gut, ja?*'

'Yeah. It's good. What's it mean?'

'It was a song we sang before the war. Would you pour me some Armagnac?'

'Sure,' said Stan. Locating the bottle, he searched for a glass. Returning to Stepney he froze. The old man's eyes were unfocused, and Stan knew instinctively he was dead. As he had seen in so many movies, he closed the dead eyes. Bimbo came pounding up the stairs.

'I got 'em, Step. I got 'em.' He stumbled to a halt.

'He's sleepin' aint he?'

'He's gone, son.'

'But I got 'em. Here, look. I got his peppermints here. Step!' Kneeling by the chair he took the old man's hand. Stan lifted the first box of leaflets and carried them down the stairs.

Bimbo stayed with the old man for a long time, holding his hand and talking to him. There were no tears, for it seemed to Bimbo that Stepney had not gone. The silence in the room was curiously reassuring, and Bimbo could not take his eyes from the old man's face. It was so still. You couldn't mistake that stillness for sleep. There was not the tiniest movement. He understood then what people meant when they talked about serenity. He didn't know if Stepney was at peace or burning in the fires of Hell. All he knew was that after today, after these few quiet moments, he would never sit with his friend again.

Stan came back after a while and Bimbo failed to hear his arrival.

'I called the ambulance, Bim.'

'Bit late for that.'

'I know, but it wouldn't do to leave him sittin' here, would it? They'll take him away and sort out the death certificate and that. You better find his keys, then we can lock up.'

After the ambulance had left Bimbo wandered into Chiswick, strolling the High Street through to Hammersmith and along the Fulham Palace Road to Charing Cross Hospital. Here now were two of the few friends he had. One was dead, the other, perhaps, dying. He made his way to Adrian's room. The policeman came out to him. He was a middle-aged copper that Bimbo hadn't seen before.

'Mr Jardine?'

'Yeah.'

'He's not doing too badly. Blood pressure is up and the doctors say the internal bleeding is slowing down.'

'Thanks, pal. Nice of you to let me know.'

'Well, you don't get many friends in life, do you?' said the policeman. Bimbo shook his head and walked away. A receptionist directed him to Dr Adams, who had been on duty when Stepney's body was brought in.

The doctor sat with Bimbo in the reception area and lit a cigarette. 'I shouldn't,' said Adams, 'especially knowing what I know, but I don't think I could get through a day without a smoke.'

'It gets some people that way,' agreed Bimbo. 'What's the score, doc? About Step, I mean.'

'Are you family?'

'Yeah. Near as. There aint nobody else.'

'You'll need a death certificate. You can collect the necessary documents from here tomorrow morning before 11.30. Then you'll have to go to Fulham Town Hall to register the death. Have you ever arranged a funeral? No? Well, you'll need copies of the death certificate. The undertaker will want one, so will

196

the banks, or building societies, or wherever he kept his money. You'll have to notify the pensions office.'

'I'll sort it out.'

'Were you close?'

Bimbo nodded and looked away.

'He was a tough old man,' said Adams. 'And he possessed enormous courage. If it's any help I don't think he regretted dying. I saw him several times before the end. He wanted to die at home, with his family. At least he did that.'

'I was out gettin' peppermints for him. I wasn't there.'

'You were there, Mr Jardine. He knew you were there. Was he insured?'

'Dunno. I don't know nothin' about his private life. Why?'

'Funerals can be expensive, you know, but you can get a grant.'

'He was my friend. I aint countin' no cost.'

'That wasn't what I meant. He was a very organised man. I would imagine he made arrangements with a solicitor. Check his papers, you'll probably find the man's name.'

'Yeah.' Bimbo felt as if he was coming apart. The muscles of his face were tight, while his stomach trembled. He breathed deeply, then turned to the doctor. 'Look, doc, no offence, but I can't talk about it now. I'll be seein' ya.'

Bimbo stood and moved away, stepping out into the cold night. The wind was picking up and, uncharacteristically, Bimbo hailed a cab to take him home.

The following morning he was back, sitting in a waiting room to collect the death certificate. He was ushered through to a small office where a middle-aged woman with greying hair sat before an untidy desk. She smiled nervously and lifted a large brown envelope.

'I'd like you to verify these personal belongings,' she said, tipping the envelope and emptying the contents on to the table top. There was a fob watch, a gold ring, and a slender golden crucifix on a narrow chain. The ring spun on the table top. Bimbo stared at it.

'I'm sorry,' said the woman. 'But we have to be careful. It's necessary that you agree all his belongings are here.' She took a pen and read out the items, ticking each one's description as it was recorded on the sheet before her.

'I never knew about the cross,' he said.

He took the death certificate to Fulham Town Hall and waited with four other people. One was an old man with sad, empty eyes. He was dressed in a suit and a wide kipper tie. Alongside him were two young women, and there was a baby in a new pram.

It didn't take a genius to work out that the old man had come to register a death and the women to register a birth. Bimbo smiled at the man who looked at him, then away without acknowledgment.

'It aint right,' Bimbo told the clerk who registered the deaths and births. 'It aint right we should all be sittin' together.'

The clerk was elderly, with wispy white hair and a long, ascetic face.

'I appreciate your point, Mr Jardine. But this is life, isn't it? We are born and we die. It's a circle. Some people find it a great comfort to sit outside and see the joy of life. Many comment on it.'

'I know,' said Bimbo. 'I just did. And it still aint right.'

The man at the undertaker's was tall, grey-haired and punctiliously polite. He took the documents and showed Bimbo a series of brochures highlighting coffins.

'Is it a burial or cremation, sir?'

'Cremation. It's what he wanted.'

'Then I should avoid the oak. It's a lovely casket, but it does not burn very well. But this one is nice. It has oak veneer and simulated brass handles. Will you be keeping the ashes?'

'What for?'

'Some people like to. However, we will have Mr Stepney's scattered in the Garden of Remembrance.'

'Yeah. That sounds nice.'

'Will you wish to view?'

'View?'

'The deceased. If you wish we can place him in an open coffin in the chapel.'

'No. No, I don't want that. And his name's not Stepney. It's Stolz. Heinrich Stolz. He wanted his real name used.'

'I am afraid we must go by the name on the death certificate.'

'I want his name on the coffin. I promised him.'

'I could put Henry Stepney, born Heinrich Stolz.'

'That'd be fine,' said Bimbo.

'When would you like the funeral?'

'Whenever's convenient.'

'Friday?'

'Fine.'

'At Mortlake then. 2 p.m.?'

'Sure. Look, who does the talkin'?'

'Talking?' said the man, bemused.

'You know, says the words over him. I want somebody good.'

'They're all quite reasonable, Mr Jardine. They do this a lot.'

'I don't want "quite reasonable",' snapped Bimbo, feeling his anger rise.

'No, no, of course not. If there is someone you'd like to suggest ...'

'I'll sort it out. Now, how much?'

The man slid an estimate across the table. 'That's kosher is it?' asked Bimbo.

'We're not overcharging you, sir. There is a cheaper coffin if you wish.' Bimbo sighed, and wondered how he could raise the money.

'You want it in advance?'

'No, sir, we'll send the bill to your home. Will there be flowers?'

'Only from me.'

'What about cars?'

'Cars?'

'To carry the mourners.'

'There aint no mourners. Only me. And I'll make me own way there.'

The Reverend Richard Kilbey had thought his library cum study quite spacious until this afternoon, when the towering figure of Bimbo Jardine seemed to cause the walls to shrink. Bimbo was clearly uncomfortable and Richard seated him in his own wide-bodied chair.

'So how can I help?' he asked.

'There's a funeral Friday. I was 'oping you'd do the words.'

'Well, Friday's my day off ...'

'It don't matter then,' said Bimbo, half rising.

'Sit down, please, and let me finish. What I was going to say was that it should be all right. Because it is my day off I have no other commitments. Look, let me get you a cup of tea, then we'll talk.' Kilbey patted Bimbo's shoulder and left the room. His wife, Sheila, was standing in the long kitchen, her slender face set in an expression of distaste.

'What is that man doing here, Richard?'

'He wants me to perform a funeral service.'

'Someone he killed, no doubt.'

'Sheila!'

'Honestly, Richard, you are so naive sometimes. He's an awful man. You should hear some of the stories. And yesterday he was being questioned by the police about that murder in Hammersmith.'

'Would you bring some tea in?'

'You really have no idea what I'm talking about, do you?'

'We'll discuss it later,' he said, returning to the study. Bimbo was standing by the bookshelves. Most of the volumes were scriptural, Barclay Essays on the Gospels, discussions on Greek syntax, historical tracts of the early church, the works of St Thomas Aquinas. But on the shelves by the window was a series of tomes on twentieth century history.

'Tea is on its way, Bimbo. Now tell me about the funeral.'

'It's at Mortlake at two. Be nice if you could do it.'

'Why me?'

'Cos I know ya, Rev. I don't know nobody else what could do it right.'

'Do it right?'

'I want somebody who cares. And you care, dontcha?'

'I hope so. Who is the deceased?'

'A friend of mine. Henry Stepney. He run the antique shop up by the station.'

'Was he Jewish?'

'No. Not by a long shot. His real name was Stolz. 'Einrich Stolz. He changed it after the war, but he told me he wanted to be buried with his real name.'

'Tell me about him'

'Is that important?'

Kilbey smiled. 'If l don't know about him, how can I speak of him, or declare him to God?'

Sheila Kilbey entered with a tray, bearing a teapot and two cups, a small jug of milk, and a bowl of sugar. She did not speak or look at Bimbo. When she had gone a red-faced Richard Kilbey poured the tea. Bimbo said nothing.

'Go on, please.'

'What, everything?'

'As much as you know.'

'Well, he was a nice old geezer. He taught me to play chess. And he was ever so sorry about bein' a Nazi, and that.' Kilbey closed his eyes and leaned back in his chair as Bimbo's story continued. At last the big man's voice faded to silence. Kilbey opened his eyes. He stood and walked to the shelf by the window, scanning the history books and finally pulling one clear. Returning to his seat, he flipped through the pages for some minutes. Then he nodded.

'Have you ever heard of Kraniskow? No, I suppose you haven't. It was quite famous in the days after the war. It was a Russian town. Every man, woman and child was butchered by the SS. The officer in command of that vicious massacre was one Heinrich Stolz.'

'Yeah, he told me about that. It played on his mind a bit.'

'A *bit*? It says here that Stolz was such a committed party member he had his own wife taken to the gas chambers when he found she had Jewish blood.'

'Yeah, I know. He was sorry about that and all.'

Kilbey put the book to one side. 'Bimbo, if this was anyone but you I would think I was the victim of some bizarre practical joke. You are asking me to intercede with God Almighty for the soul of a mass killer, a dark legend who has been hunted for fifty years?'

'He's bin good to me. It should count for somethin', shouldn't it?'

Kilbey was about to speak, but he hesitated and thought through his words. 'Don't misunderstand me, Bimbo, but for some people Christianity is like a club. They meet on Sundays and sing a few hymns and make a play at worship. But to me, and many others, God is real, and not to be mocked. Heinrich Stolz was a man of consummate evil. No minister could recommend him to God. And that, essentially, is what a funeral service is for.'

'You could say a few words though, eh?'

'But they are not just words, Bimbo. Did he ever say he repented? That he regretted his deeds? And I don't mean a bit sorry.'

'Yeah. He cried about it once. And he was a tough old bird, know what I mean? One time he told me God had given him forty years to atone for his crimes, but he'd wasted it. He'd

202

never done nothin' for no one. But he was good to me, Rev. And I never 'ad no family.'

'He mentioned God? Look, give me a day, Bimbo. I need to think about it.'

'Sure. I'll come back in the mornin'.' Bimbo paused in the doorway. 'He once said to me that you shouldn't never do nothin' if your heart aint in it. So if you can't do it, Rev, no 'ard feelins, eh?'

Kilbey sat in the study long after Bimbo had gone. Sheila joined him there. The tea was untouched.

'Are you all right, Richard?'

'In a word? No.'

'What did he want?'

'I told you, a funeral service.' He outlined Stolz's history and saw the horror reflected in her eyes.

'You can't do it,' she said.

'You're probably right.'

'There's no *probably* to it. It would be a mockery. And what if it gets out? You'll be a laughing stock – or worse.'

'That's hardly material.'

'You'll have to tell the police.'

'Why?'

'The man was a war criminal. There's probably a file on him somewhere. Actually,' she said, brightening, 'this could work out very well. There'll be masses of publicity when you turn it down.'

'There will be no publicity. I have no wish to get my name known in that way.'

'And I have no wish to spend the rest of my life in this seedy little town,' she told him. 'You could have been – should have been – a Bishop by now, like Sandy. You have all the talent. And you're very good with people.'

Kilbey took a deep breath, and swallowed his anger. 'The reason I am good with people is because I like them. And sometimes – thank the Lord –I love them. I have no wish to be a Bishop. As far as I can see, there is little evidence that God ever attends a meeting of the General Synod. Furthermore, I will not court publicity on this matter, and I forbid you to tell a living soul.' Sheila Kilbey stood and stalked from the room. Kilbey filled his ornate pipe with St Bruno and settled back to think the problem through.

'Did anyone speak for Judas?' he thought.

Pam Edgerley was caught between fury and compassion. The woman weeping before her was dressed in a blouse of fine yellow silk, a skirt of soft wool, and shoes that were hand made in Italy. Her handbag was of a leather so soft and exquisitely tooled it must have cost more than the weekly food bill at the refuge. But the side of her face was bruised, her lip was split and her eyes were bright with panic and fear.

'I don't know what to do,' she sobbed. 'I don't know any more.'

'You are not alone in this,' said Pam. 'And you do at least know you have to do something.'

'Oh God, if he finds out I've been here.'

'Let him find out. Leave. You are not short of money. Go somewhere. A hotel.'

'He'd find me. He'll kill me.'

'Listen to me. The last time we spoke you said he had begged forgiveness, and you believed him. He said nothing like this would ever happen again. Well it has. You must leave him, or you'll be right. He will kill you. Or cripple you.'

'You don't know him. You don't know what he's capable of.'

'I think I can see what he's capable of.'

'No,' said the woman, 'you don't. When he did this, he … he …'

'You don't have to talk about it.'

'I want you to understand. He called one of his men into the room. Then he ripped my clothes off and ordered the man to rape me. Then they both did it. And more.'

'God! You must go to the police.'

The woman smiled. 'You still don't understand, do you? Last week we had two senior policemen round for dinner. My husband pays them. He pays lots of people. Councillors, solicitors, policemen, thugs. My husband is an important man. Highly respected.'

'I know who your husband is, Mrs Reardon. I know what he does. But it's what he is doing to you that frightens me.'

Jean Reardon nodded. 'He wasn't always like this. He was charming, and thoughtful. He once surprised me with a second honeymoon trip to the Bahamas. It was the most beautiful time. But he's changed.'

'Changed?' said Pam. 'He has just seen you abused in the most terrible fashion. And he'll do it again. Maybe next time it will be two of his thugs, or all of them. Do you want to go through that again?'

'No,' she said, softly. 'But I haven't a lot of choice. I left him the last time and went to a friend's house near Leeds. Two men brought me home. He was fine for a while, then he turned. Things haven't been going well with him.'

'I still think we should call the police,' said Pam.

'No!' Terror shone in Jean Reardon's eyes. 'I'll deny it all.'

'Then why did you come here?'

'I just wanted to talk. You know? I just ... God, I wish I had the courage to kill him.'

'That would be one answer,' agreed Pam. 'Look, I have a friend in Somerset. She has a farm. I'm sure she would put you up while you think this through. Why not give it a try? Do you have a cheque book?'

'No,' said Jean Reardon. 'He took it away and closed my account.'

'Barclaycard?'

'American Express. Gold card,' she said.

'Okay,' said Pam. 'I want you to go and buy the most expensive piece of jewellery, and then sell it. Take the money and come back here. Then we'll get you to Somerset.'

'I don't know. I just don't.'

'Then trust me.'

The door opened and two men walked in. Pam stood. 'What the hell?'

'Come on, Mrs Reardon, we'll take you home,' said the first, a tall, broad-shouldered Irishman with dark curly hair.

'Get out,' ordered Pam, 'or I'll call the police.'

'You aint bad lookin' for a dyke,' said the man. 'You know what you need, don't ya?'

Pam's fist cracked into his face. He backhanded her into the wall.

'Stop it!' screamed Jean Reardon, standing. The man backed away from the stunned Pam. 'I'm sorry,' said Mrs Reardon. 'I shouldn't have come.'

Gathering up her bag she left the room. The Irishman grinned at Pam.

'That's not a bad punch you got there,' he said. 'I like a woman with a bit of spirit. I may see you again. Yeah. I think you'd like that.'

As the door closed behind them Pam sank into her chair.

Marie, one of her helpers, rushed in.

'I couldn't stop them, Pam. Are you all right?'

'I'm fine.'

'Should I call the police?'

'No. You'd find there were no witnesses. You know, for the first time in my life I wish I'd had a gun. I'd have blown that bastard away without a second's hesitation.'

'Just as well you didn't then,' said Marie. 'It wouldn't have solved anything.'

'True,' she said. 'But it's a nice fantasy.'

10

Frank Reardon downed his scotch and placed the lead crystal tumbler on the circular table that surrounded the centre-piece log fire. MacLeeland sat in discomfort on the Regency chair nursing a tonic water. The lounge in Reardon's home was forty feet long and furnished with impeccable taste. It didn't suit the man who owned it, Mac realised, but then Jean had chosen the furniture and the trappings.

'How could he be so bloody stupid?' raged Reardon. 'Topping him, for God's sake.'

'I don't know, Mr Reardon,' said Mac, realising it would be unwise to remind the man that he had been warned on several occasions that Green was more than a little unhinged.

Reardon picked up the single sheet of paper supplied by Detective Inspector Eric Lynch. 'He plants a bloodstained top in a bag, and he doesn't think about trousers, shoes, towels, and all the other vital ingredients. Just as well he's in piggin' Tenerife!'

'It doesn't look good, Mr Reardon.'

'Damned right about that, Mac. Jesus! Why didn't he go the whole way? He could have had a bath in Bimbo's flat. Left some blood on a towel. And then to threaten the Wilks woman. God, if she'd just admitted he was with her the whole business would have looked like a set up alibi. But no! He's got brains of shit.'

'It did look like Reilly double-crossed you.'

'Bullshit! He knew he'd get nothing if he torched the place.

We talked about it. You think he set out to bankrupt himself? No. I'll tell you why Jackie Green killed Reilly, it was because the man pulled a gun on him and called him a mad dog. Reilly rang me the same day.'

'You should get rid of him,' said Mac.

Reardon looked away, and Mac realised it was all too late.

'Now what about Bimbo?' asked Reardon. Mac sighed.

'That's not good for you either, Frank.'

Reardon grinned, and poured himself another Scotch. 'You're right, Mac. I should have listened to you. I'm not too big to admit I made a mistake. But it's gone too far. Bimbo's out there making me look a prize prick every time he walks out on the street. He's got to be seen to. And it's too late now for a broken nose and a few bruises. He's got to be in traction. Or dead.'

'Dead?' said Mac. 'What are we doing? There's one man dead already.'

'How many men will be with Taggart tonight?'

'About a dozen.'

'And they all know Bimbo,' said Reardon, 'so most of them will be carrying pickaxe handles, or hammers. You can't get away from it, Mac. There's a chance they could kill him.'

'It's got to be stopped, Frank. It's going to destroy you.'

'Too late to worry about that. I hear Jack Shell's making noises again about not paying. If that happens, how long before the other publicans and club owners start following suit? No. The cards are dealt. Now we play the hands.'

'You know what Lynch said, Frank. The Filth are just waiting for you to do something, stupid.'

'After Bimbo's sorted things will calm down. Then we'll get back to business as usual.'

'And if he dies tonight?'

'It's a hard life,' said Reardon. 'We'll send flowers.'

*

Bimbo wandered disconsolately around Stepney's flat, gazing with new eyes upon the possessions he had seen so many times before: Dresden plates, small Japanese figures in carved ivory, ornamental daggers, and a silver tankard inscribed in German. Stepney had said they were all of sentimental value. But not any more. Now they were just dead objects, like the man who had loved them.

Bimbo sat down in the chair opposite the chessboard and carefully put all the pieces into place. On the table beside the board was an envelope. Bimbo picked it up and read his own name. It was hand-written in shaky script. He opened the letter. It was typed.

My dear friend,

You read this because I am now gone to whatever purgatory the wise Lord has consigned me to. I know you will feel some sadness at my passing, and, in a way that is pleasing to me. Until I met you there was no one who would shed a tear for Heinrich Stolz. I am content that you will mourn for me, for you are a kind soul and a man of deep feeling. I used to believe, when I was young, that I was also such a man. I never was.

I think we can never be what we dream to be. We either are, or we are not. Like the holy man, who is always the last to speak of his own worth, for that is what makes him holy. So with the kind man, the caring man.

But why am I writing this to you, who will not understand? It is because I have no one else to hear my meagre philosophy, and I look upon you as my son.

And now to the other matter. You live your life like you play your chess; you react. In your present trouble this is not enough. You have two choices. You can run – or you can fight. But if you choose to fight you must understand the necessity of carrying the battle to the enemy. Go after him. Harry him. Destroy him.

You can no longer stand like the rock against the tide. It will wash over you.

And as for this Jackie Green. Do not be frightened. To be what he is means he has no soul. And a great warrior must have soul. When you come to fight him, as I fear you must, take all he can offer. Absorb it all. Every second you withstand him he will grow weaker, and he will defeat himself. Trust me on this.

I wish, my dear friend, that I had known you longer. It would be nice to think that, in some future time, we could meet again. But I doubt the wise Lord will send you to my destination.

Think of me once in a while – and do not neglect your chess.

It was signed simply, 'Stepney'. Bimbo read the letter three times before folding it and returning it to the envelope. Sitting in the old leather armchair he recalled his first meeting with Stepney two years before. It had been raining hard and Bimbo, soaked through, had stepped into the haven of a small cafe in Chiswick. There were perhaps twenty people inside and two men had been playing chess. One of the players, a young man in a bright red shirt was giving a running commentary on the game, much to the chagrin of his opponent.

'Admit it, John, you're out of your class. Mate's inevitable.'

Nursing a cup of coffee, Bimbo had sat down at a nearby table and watched the rest of the game without any real interest. The man in the red shirt grinned at him. He was obviously trying to build an audience. Finally the other man knocked over his king and passed a £5 note across the table. The winner pocketed the money and took a small notebook from his shirt pocket. 'That makes forty-nine straight wins,' he said. 'Anyone want to bring up the half ton?'

He looked at Bimbo, who shook his head. 'I don't play.'

'Greatest game on earth,' said Red Shirt. 'Skill, daring, and lateral thinking. I don't want to brag or anything, but you've got to be a bit special for this game. I learned it in Russia.

Everyone plays it there. The name's Francis, George Francis,' he said, extending his hand to Bimbo.

Bimbo decided the rain was preferable to this prick's company and was downing the last of his coffee when an elderly man moved into view, seating himself opposite Francis. He was slender, of medium height and balding. His face was sharp, his eyes small and button-bright. He was wearing an old pinstripe suit, and a gold watch chain showed on his waistcoat. 'You would perhaps accept a challenge?' he said, his voice clipped and precise, but unmistakably of East European origin.

'I only play for money, grandad. Don't want to steal your pension, do we?'

'How kind of you, but it is not necessary. It is a rainy day, and we will, perhaps, offer some amusement to these travellers. Money, you say?'

'A fiver a game, and I give odds of three to one. That's fifteen quid if you win.'

'How much are you carrying, young man?'

Francis grinned and pulled a wad of notes from his jacket. He spread the money theatrically on the table. There were fifteen £5 notes and four £10 notes.

'One hundert and fifteen,' said the old man. 'Call it one-twenty.' He opened his own wallet and counted out eight £5 notes. 'That, I believe, is approximately one third of the total and therefore the bet is accepted.'

'Do what?' said Francis. 'Hang on a minute, I said a fiver.'

'You said odds of three to one. I accept. We will play for it all, for it is only money.' He turned to Bimbo. 'Be so kind as to hold on to this small fortune.'

Bimbo grinned and swept up the stake. 'Be a pleasure.'

'Which colour do you prefer?' asked Stepney.

'White.'

'Then play. I notice that you like to chatter during the game.

Please continue it. You could perhaps outline the state of play to the audience.'

People gathered round, moving tables for a better view. Even the cafe owner left his counter. Stepney spotted him. 'Before you get comfortable, my friend, be so kind as to give everyone a drink and perhaps a sandwich. The winner will pay from his winnings.'

'Thank you, sir,' said the owner, smiling.

Bimbo concentrated on the board. He had no idea of the rules. Red Shirt's white pieces at first seemed to be sweeping forward, while black could only block, but gradually the game settled down and Bimbo's fascination began to fade. The old man sat largely unmoving, hunched over the table, his gimlet eyes fixed on the pieces. Red Shirt, after a quiet start, soon got into his stride.

'Ah yes,' he said, 'the Sicilian opening. Capablanca always used that. He was a chess star you know, years ago.'

The old man said nothing. Francis grew more at ease, his face mobile, a little smile here, a raised eyebrow there, a gentle, knowing, shake of the head.

Bimbo was growing bored, and had he not been holding the money, would have left. The challenger lost two pieces to Red Shirt's one, and Bimbo didn't think he could bear watching the braggart win again. His white pieces were all around Stepney's king now, which was sheltering behind a row of pawns and a couple of figures shaped like horses' heads.

'Now this is fascinating,' said Red Shirt. 'We are entering what is called the "endgame". All the manoeuvring for position is over. All that's left now is the kill!'

'Check,' said the old man, sweeping his Bishop up the board and taking a pawn before the enemy King.

Francis smiled. 'Do I detect a note of panic?' he said, taking the offending Bishop with the King.

'Check,' said the old man, moving a Knight into position. A

flash of irritation darkened Francis' features. He stared at the board and swore. He moved his King, and the Knight took his Queen. 'Check,' said Stepney, his eyes shining now with undisguised malice.

'Moved too fast, didn't I?' said Francis, forcing a smile. 'Now let me think.'

'Think all you like, young man, but it is mate in three,' said the old man.

'Play it out!' snapped Francis. Stepney did so. Applause burst from the spectators.

'How much for all the coffees and sandwiches?' said the victor. The cafe owner consulted his pad.

'Eighteen pounds twenty.'

'Give him twenty pounds,' Stepney ordered. Bimbo did so, then handed the man his winnings.

'Walk me to my home,' said the old man, striding away. Bimbo followed and soon found himself outside an antique shop near the station. He had often walked past it, and stopped to look at the old swords and pistols.

'My name is Stepney. Come in and have some tea.'

'You gave him a right turning over,' said Bimbo. 'Nice, that was.'

'His arrogance annoyed me. Playing for money, indeed!'

'He wasn't no good then?'

'He was not bad. But I am not bad either, and he was a fool. He should not have played a man he did not know – especially not when the stakes multiplied.' With the tea finished, Stepney offered Bimbo £10. Bimbo shook his head.

'I never earnt it.'

'Never reject a gift, when the giver is sincere. Many people find such refusals offensive,' said Stepney, returning the money to his pocket.

Bimbo had never known why the old man took to him, and he never cared much. Every now and again he would turn up at the shop, just before closing time, and enjoy a cup of tea and a chat. They would talk about sport or the weather, or Stepney, with wit and humour, would sound off about politics, morality and the stupidity of man. Now, in the cold flat, surrounded by the residue of a man's life, Bimbo wished he'd spent more time with the old man.

'Gonna miss ya, Step,' he said.

It was a little after six when he arrived at Sherry Parker's front door. He knocked and waited but at first there was no answer. He knocked again. Then he heard Sarah's voice from upstairs.

'But it's Bimbo, mum.'

Sherry opened the door, but did not step aside to allow him in, nor did she meet his eyes.

'I don't think you'd better come round any more,' she said.

Bimbo had expected an apology, or a welcome. Her question stunned him. 'Why?'

'You know why! You're trouble. They threatened my kids over you. I can't have that. I won't have that.'

'I aint blamin' ya,' said Bimbo. 'I just thought ...'

'Just go away,' she said, tears streaming. 'Just bloody go away.'

It seemed a long walk home, and Bimbo found it inconceivable that all his current problems should have emanated from the simple desire to help a friend in need. He wasn't in love with Sherry, but he knew he could have been, given a little time. Now she was lost to him. As Esther was lost to him. And Stepney.

He zipped his padded windcheater against the cold and crossed the road to the estate. The wind was picking up, but at least the rain was holding off. The estate was dark and gloomy with yet another street lamp knocked out of commission by a stone, or an airgun.

Who'd wanna live here? he asked himself.

214

A cloud moved back, like a veil lifted from the moon's face, and the drab grey buildings suddenly shone like silver, giving the estate the momentary grandeur of a ghostly castle. A sudden movement from the left caught Bimbo's eye. Instantly his fists came up – then he recognised the young black boy he had seen taking a beating. 'Late to be out, son,' said Bimbo, relieved.

'I bin practising,' said Jeremiah Andrews, holding up his cricket bat.

'Daylight's best for that,' said Bimbo, moving on. Two men stepped from the moon shadows several yards ahead. Both were carrying pickaxe handles. A whisper of movement from behind. Bimbo swivelled and ducked. A club whistled over his head. His right fist thundered into the man's belly, bringing a great whoosh of air exploding from his lungs. Bimbo left fist clubbed the back of the man's neck and his assailant's face hit the concrete. The man did not move. Reaching down, Bimbo swept up the pickaxe handle, just as the other two moved swiftly to the attack. The three-foot club flashed out, catching the first of the attackers in the ribs. He fell back. The second man aimed a slashing blow which Bimbo blocked. Releasing the club with his right hand, Bimbo lunged and grabbed the man's jacket, dragging him forward into the dreaded 'Liverpool Kiss', his forehead smashing the man's nose and half blinding him. Stepping back, Bimbo lashed the pickaxe handle into the man's temple, catapulting him from his feet.

The man with the injured ribs staggered back a few steps. Then he began to shout.

'He's here! Over here!'

The sound of running feet came from several alleyways. With no time for thought Bimbo charged into the first alley, cannoning into a group of men in the dark. His club slashed left and right. He heard a bone snap, followed by a satisfying scream. Something hit him a wicked blow in the back and he stumbled. A face loomed before him. Bimbo smashed it from sight. Blows were raining in on him now, mostly glancing from his huge shoulders, but one pickaxe handle cracked into his temple. He spun back, losing his grip on his club. In the darkness he stumbled and fell. A man tripped over him. Bimbo grabbed him, hauling him on top of his body, and the blows hammered down. Hurling the screaming man from him, Bimbo rolled, his hand touching the fallen club. Grabbing it, he lurched to his feet and ran. There was no time now for plans, or coherent thought. He was a hunted animal, and he was in pain. Outnumbered and outmanoeuvred, he could only fight until he fell.

Emerging from one alleyway he found himself in the main courtyard. He staggered to a stop in the eerie light of the single street lamp. Blood streamed from the cut to his temple, and his cheek and forehead were badly swollen. His body ached from the blows he had taken. Two men rushed at him. He swept a blow to the first man's stomach, doubling him over, but before he could finish him the second man's club cracked into his left cheek, hurling him from his feet. Another man ran in and kicked him in the stomach. As the boot swung for a second kick Bimbo grabbed his ankle and wrenched. The man flew backwards, cannoning into his comrades. Bimbo made it to his knees, but was drop-kicked from behind. He rolled to his back. A wooden club flashed for his face. Throwing up his right hand he caught the weapon. His foot lashed out and the man fell. With the club in his possession Bimbo once more made it to his feet, parrying and hitting out where he could. A sharp pain lanced his arm as a strike thundered home above his elbow. He dropped the club and charged into the midst of the mob, where their weapons were of little use. His huge fists smashed left and right, and for the first time he recognised some of his attackers. Blows hammered into him, and he screamed like a wounded animal, lunging at his tormentors. But now they had him, and they formed a circle around him. Blood dripped into Bimbo's eyes. He tried to wipe it away. Pain was swamping him.

'Finish him!' screamed Roache, rushing in, his knuckle-duster gleaming in the lamplight. With his strength fading, Bimbo grabbed the man's jacket and crashed a wicked punch to Roache's belly. A club swung for him. He twisted Roache into its path and found a short moment of satisfaction as the weapon exploded against Roache's mouth, snapping his head back, his teeth bloody and broken, his jaw smashed. Bimbo hurled the body aside and charged for Taggart.

But there was no strength left in the giant frame and he stumbled under the blows and toppled.

The world spun in blackness and pain. As he slid from consciousness Bimbo heard Taggart's shout of triumph. 'Now break the bastard!'

For several seconds no one moved. The eight men still standing were breathing heavily. Several had bleeding wounds, others were experiencing the swelling numbness of broken arms, fingers or ribs.

There had been thirteen at the start. Five were down and unconscious, with who knew what injuries. Roache lay beside Bimbo, blood streaming from his shattered mouth, his jaw hanging at a horrible angle.

'I think that's enough, aint it, Tag?' said one man. 'We don't wanna kill him.'

'Kill him? He aint even started to hurt yet,' said Taggart, moving in and launching a vicious kick into Bimbo's unprotected side. Taggart kicked him twice more, then took a knife from his pocket.

'Stuff that!' said another of the men. 'I aint stayin' for this!'

'Then fuck off back to mummy, Phelps. This bastard's had it comin'. Now we'll see what he's like without any balls!'

*

Ten year old Jeremiah Andrews sped from the shadows. He had not forgotten Bimbo helping him against the white thugs, and now he was ready to repay the debt. No one heard his silent charge, until his cricket bat thundered into Taggart's head, knocking the man from his feet. Taggart rolled and came up snarling, blocking the next blow with his forearm and punching the boy from his feet.

'You little black bastard! I'll piggin' show you!' Suddenly the courtyard was alive with men, many carrying knives.

'Jesus!' whispered Phelps. Jem scrambled to his knees, and tried to rise. Silver pulled him upright. The twenty men of Ironside Towers spread out around the whites.

Silver eased his way forward, and leaned down to pick up a fallen club. Taggart backed away and the eight men formed a rough fighting circle.

'You're on my turf,' said Silver, smiling.

'Private business,' said Taggart, pointing to Bimbo's body. 'He aint one of yours.'

'No, but he is, man,' said Silver, swinging the club back to point at Jem.

'That was a mistake. He come outta nowhere.'

'No shit?' said Silver. The pickaxe handle shot forward in a straight thrust that clove into Taggart's mouth, punching him from his feet.

'You other men better be gettin' off home,' said Silver, 'while I'm still full of Christian charity. You just leave him here,' he added, pointing to Taggart.

'What you gonna do with him?' asked Phelps.

'I'm gonna teach him a little pain,' said the black leader. 'Course you may all be close friends a his, and you may wanna stand by him. That's your choice.'

'He aint no friend of mine,' said Phelps, dropping his pick-axe handle. The others followed suit. Taggart was on his knees now, blood staining his mouth.

218

'You can't leave me 'ere!' he shouted.

No one spoke, but one by one the gang drifted away.

'Take him round the back,' ordered Silver. Three men pounced on Taggart, dragging him away into the darkness. Silver moved to where Jeremiah was sitting. 'You okay, boy?'

Jem nodded.

'How many fingers am I holding up?'

'Three.'

'That's good. Now tell me, shit-for-brains, just what you was gonna do with all them bastards?'

Jem shrugged. 'He helped me out, Silver. I owed him.'

'You don't know nothin' about how the world works, boy.'

Bimbo groaned and several men moved to help him.

'Leave him alone!' ordered Silver. The men backed away. Leaving Jem, he walked to Bimbo and squatted down beside him. Blood was pooling on the ground beside Bimbo's face. 'Can you hear me, man? This is Silver. We just saved your ass. You wanna hand to get up, big man?'

Bimbo forced his arms beneath him and pushed. He groaned and dragged his knees under him, pushing himself to his knees.

'You wanna hand?' mocked Silver.

'Get stuffed!' whispered Bimbo.

Silver grinned. 'One tough son-of-a-bitch. Better go home, tough man. You aint in no condition to tackle a sick cat.' Bimbo stood, tottered and fell to his knees. Jeremiah Andrews ran to him.

'Lean on me, man,' he said, and together the giant and the child moved slowly towards the road.

Silver strolled back to the waiting group. 'That is one great kid,' he said. 'Now let's see about our friend Taggart.'

A large black BMW pulled up as Jem and Bimbo reached the far side of the road. Jem was sweating heavily, and taking more and more of Bimbo's huge frame as Bimbo's fragile hold on consciousness began to slip. Esther leapt from the passenger side of the car and ran to Bimbo.

'Oh my God!' she shouted, as she saw his battered, bleeding face. Dr Simeon Abazul arrived just as Bimbo toppled. The doctor grabbed him, taking the weight.

'I'll be okay. Get me to me flat,' mumbled Bimbo, his voice slurred. Simeon manoeuvred him to the car while Esther opened the door. Carefully Simeon eased Bimbo to the back seat where he slumped across the leather upholstery. The doctor turned to the boy.

'With what were these injuries inflicted?'

'They looked like baseball bats,' said Jem. Simeon pulled a £5 note from his wallet and offered it to the boy.

'Up yours!' said Jem. Without a word the boy stalked off into the night.

Simeon climbed into the driver's seat and gunned the engine. Esther was sitting alongside Bimbo, his bleeding head in her lap. The BMW roared away.

Four hours later Bimbo was back in his own bed, the wounds to his head having required twenty-two stitches. Against all advice and entreaties he had refused to stay in hospital and Simeon had reluctantly brought him home.

The tall doctor quietly pulled shut the bedroom door and joined Esther by the living room fire. He took the coffee she had made and sipped it.

'At least nothing is broken,' she said.

'He has an amazing constitution, but the bruising is pro-digious, and he really should have stayed in hospital. He has suffered a serious concussion and reaction may set in. I think you should stay with him tonight. I would stay with you, but I am on call. You have my number?'

'Yes.' She took his hand. 'Thank you, Simeon.'

'Why did he refuse to have the police called? I do not under-stand.'

'It is not his way.'

'I see. The law of his particular jungle. Such a sad end to a beautiful evening. I will see you tomorrow.'

'You had better,' she warned him, forcing a smile. She stood and kissed him lightly on the cheek. Outside in the hallway he fished in his pocket and came up with a small black box. He flipped it open. Within lay a solitaire diamond ring. Closing the box he returned it to his pocket and walked down to his car.

As he opened the door a small, dark blue Ford Escort drew up. A pretty, blonde white woman stepped from it and approached him.

'Excuse me, are you the doctor?'

'Yes. What can I do for you?'

'How is he?'

'Oh, I see,' he said. 'You mean Mr Jardine?'

'Yes, I heard he was injured.'

'He is in bed resting. My fi ... girlfriend is with him. I am not his doctor. I was merely close by when he was hurt.'

'I'm sorry,' said Sue Cater. 'I saw the BMW and thought ... well, you know. Not many people around here can afford those!'

'Do not apologise, ' said Simeon. 'You took me rather by surprise. I thought perhaps you were clairvoyant. Are you a friend of Bimbo's?'

'Yes. Is he all right?'

'He was badly beaten by a gang of thugs armed with pickaxe handles. Miraculously nothing is broken. Why don't you go up? Esther would be pleased to have company I am sure.' She nodded and he walked her back to the flat, introduced her to Esther, and left.

Sue Cater followed Esther silently into the bedroom and recoiled when she saw the swollen, twisted features of the sleeping Bimbo. Outside Sue outlined to Esther the tale she had heard in a local pub.

Bimbo Jardine, so the story went, had been thrashed to

221

within an inch of his life and was now in traction and on the critical list. Three of his attackers were also in hospital, one with a smashed jaw, another with crushed ribs, and a third with a fractured skull. Two more had broken arms, and a sixth, a man named Taggart, had not been seen since the incident. Several others carried various injuries from broken noses to heavily bruised features.

'I don't know why all this is happening,' said Esther. 'He's such a nice man.'

'He annoyed his boss. It's that simple,' Sue told her. For a while the two women sat in silence. Sue took in the dark elegance of the negress, the shining skin, the huge, beautiful eyes, while Esther was impressed by the willowy grace and the poise of the blonde, white woman.

'Are you his girlfriend?' asked Esther, suddenly.

'No. I'm a reporter from the *Herald*. I've been seeing Bimbo about … the swan in the park. He's been trying to find a mate for her.'

'Yes,' said Esther, 'he cares about things.'

'I'm sure. How do you know him?'

'I'm his neighbour.'

'Oh.'

Esther smiled. 'Why lie? I was, sort of, his lover for a while. But not any more. Simeon is my boyfriend. In fact I thought he was going to propose to me tonight.'

'Would you have said yes?' asked Sue.

'Faster than a speeding bullet,' said Esther, grinning.

'What does Bimbo think of him?'

'He likes him. He told me to *'unt 'im and bag 'im,'* she said, copying Bimbo's broad cockney. Both women chuckled.

'It's not often one lover recommends another,' said Sue.

'Bimbo's a bit special. A long time ago I was on drugs. Pretty hard stuff. I tried to kill myself. Bimbo was there. He saved my life, and he took me in. He sat with me day after day, listening as I ranted. He pulled me through. Sounds easy when you say it like that, but it wasn't. I was hateful. Three times I slid back, but he was always there. I lied and I cheated. I stole his money. But he stuck by me. Big and loving. Better than a father, better than mine anyway.'

'You love him?'

'Of course I love him. Wouldn't you?'

'I don't know.'

'Maybe not,' said Esther, 'but you know more than you're saying. You've slept with him, haven't you?'

'Yes,' admitted Sue. 'But only once. But I know what you mean.'

'They don't make many men like Bimbo,' said Esther. 'He's a one-off.'

'How does Simeon feel about him?'

'He likes him. He was jealous at first, but then he got to know him. When I get married Bimbo will give me away. He'd like that.'

'I thought that was reserved for family.'

'He is family,' said Esther.

'Do you mind if I stay with you?'

'Why should I? Nice to have the company. We'll have to check him every half-hour or so. There could be a reaction to the concussion.'

'What do we do if there is?' asked Sue.

'We call Simeon. There's a phone in my flat.'

Esther rose and, followed by Sue, entered Bimbo's bedroom. His pulse was strong and he was sleeping deeply.

Outside once more Esther turned on the TV. There was no picture. She picked up a video box.

'You want to see *High Noon*?' she asked Sue.

Bimbo awoke in the middle of the night to nausea and pain. His stomach surged and he groaned, swallowing back the bile.

His head pounded and he found he could only open one eye. He tried to roll over. Agony exploded from his back and ribs, his chest and his arms. Eventually he made the full turn and lay on his stomach. His belly surged once more, and he vomited to the floor beside his bed.

Hearing his distress Esther came into the room. Sue Cater was asleep, wrapped in blankets before the fire. Esther settled the big man back on the bed and fetched a bowl of warm water and some towels, clearing the mess and scrubbing the bedroom rug with disinfectant. She left a clean bowl by the bed and checked Bimbo's pulse. It was regular at around forty-eight beats to the minute. His head felt warm to the touch.

'My poor Bimbo,' she whispered. Three times more he was violently sick, and each time Esther cleaned him and emptied his bowl. On the last occasion she noticed spots of blood among the bile. She was on the verge of ringing Simeon when Bimbo at last fell into a deep sleep.

Returning to the living room Esther watched the dawn slowly break over Ironside Towers. The beating Bimbo had taken was savage. At the hospital she had seen his injuries, huge purple and yellow weals where the clubs had struck him. His upper back and ribs were massively bruised, as were his chest and arms. His face was swollen and almost unrecognisable. The casualty doctor had been stunned to see the victim was still walking, and even more surprised when the X-rays showed the absence of broken bones.

Bimbo slept on until almost eight o'clock, by which time Sue Cater was awake, and making use of the bathroom. Esther, hearing sounds from the bedroom, moved into the doorway in time to see Bimbo struggling to rise from the bed. 'What do you think you're doing?' she asked.

''Allo, princess.'

'Get back into bed.'

'Got things to do, aint I?'

'Nothing that can't wait.'

'Get my running gear, will ya?'

'Listen to me, Bimbo, you've been hurt. You have to rest. You can't go running.'

'Just get the gear, princess. Don't give me a hard time.'

'Lie back,' she urged.

He shrugged away her hand. 'Get the gear, or I'll get it me bleedin' self.' He tried to rise, groaned, stood and stumbled to his knees. She helped him back to the bed.

'Sit still. I'll get it.' She found his running clothes and a grey sweatshirt. 'I can't find your blue top,' she said.

'It don't matter. Help me get into 'em.'

'Look, I'll make a deal with you. I'll make you a cup of tea, and we'll talk for a little while. Then I'll help you dress. Okay?' He nodded and she ran to the kitchen. The kettle took an age to boil, but she made the tea, adding extra sugar and milk to Bimbo's pint-sized mug. When she returned Bimbo was lying on his back on top of the bed. Sue Cater walked into the room. Esther tried to cover Bimbo's nakedness, but his body had trapped the blanket.

'Don't worry about it,' said Sue. 'I've seen him naked before. But never in that state. God he looks dreadful.'

'Ta,' said Bimbo. He stared at the two women from his one good eye and sipped his tea. 'I look that bad, eh?'

'Worse,' said Esther.

'I'll feel better after a run.'

'You're joking,' said Sue. 'You'd never make the stairs.'

'Don't put money on it, sweetheart.'

'But it's stupid, Bimbo,' Esther told him. 'It won't matter if you miss your programme for a day or two. Or even a week.'

'It aint that, princess.'

'Then what?'

'It's Reardon, innit? I mean, the word'll be out, won't it. Bimbo's bin done over. Well he's in for a bleedin' shock. I'll be out there like normal, which is more than you can say for some of the buggers who done for me.'

'And then what'll happen?' snapped Sue Cater, moving to sit on the bed alongside him. 'Then they'll have to come back at you again, won't they?'

'No, darlin'. Not again. Not ever again. I 'ad a mate wot played chess. He could a told ya wot this is now. This is the endgame. Cos I've taken all I'm gonna take. From now on, it's my game, my rules.' He turned to Esther. 'Come on, help me get dressed.'

'Oh, Bim …'

'You promised, princess. And I've drunk me tea.'

'You could kill yourself. You know that? One blood clot into your heart. That's all it will take.'

'And you can guarantee that won't happen while I lie in bed?'

'I guess not.'

'No. Come on then, girl. Get me shorts on. This is embarras-sin', you know.'

Esther helped him into a pair of white shorts, then slid his old track suit trousers over his legs. While she was carefully easing his arms into the sweatshirt Sue Cater pushed his trainers on and tied the laces. At last fully dressed Bimbo lay back on the bed, breathing heavily.

The two women left him and returned to the living room. They said nothing. The bed springs creaked, and Bimbo groaned as he made it to his feet. The women turned to see him looming in the doorway, one hand gripping the frame. His face was grey beneath the bruises.

'I'll be back in about an hour. Do me a favour and have an 'ot bath ready.'

'This isn't clever, Bimbo,' said Sue Cater, sternly.

'Nobody ever said I was clever, darlin'.' The front door closed behind him.

'He'll never make it to the estate,' said Esther.

'I think he will,' said Sue. 'As he said, it's important.'

'I don't understand it. Do you?'

'No. I expect Shane would.'

It was an ordeal for Bimbo's stiff limbs, but he struggled down
the stairs, holding hard to the banister rail, and paused in the
open doorway, breathing deeply and readying himself. The
pain was intense, but he forced himself to relax. A runner
needed good lungs to supply oxygen to the blood, strong legs
to carry him, and a sound heart. All three he had. Though his
ribs and chest were bruised his legs were largely untouched.
He shook his arms at his side and rolled his head, seeking to
ease the stiffness in his neck. Pain thundered and settled over
his right eye, lancing into his mind. He allowed anger to flow.
Anger against Reardon, against Taggart, against Stepney for
dying. Against himself for being weak.

Opening the door he stepped out into the grey daylight. The
first few steps were faltering and unsteady, but muscle memory
took over as he pushed himself into his stride. In his belly the
bile churned, but he fixed his good eye on the pavement before
him and counted the steps in his mind, measuring his breathing against the pace.

His calves were tight, and he realised he had not completed
his stretching routine. His head ached, and he knew within
seconds he had made an arrogant mistake. His body screamed
at him to turn back. To lie down. To give in.

NO!

Never!

Out past the tower blocks and on to New Street, which
stretched ahead like a marathon course. Some early morning
shoppers stopped to stare at the big man lumbering along his
course. Most ignored him. Another man, with a black eye and
a swollen nose, cursed and ran inside a shop, where he picked
up a phone.

Bimbo turned left at the baker's, crossed the road to the common and pounded across the grass. His calves were on fire now as oxygen debt built up. This would pass, he knew, once his body stopped fighting him and accepted the inevitable. He could hear nothing above the rushing of blood in his ears, and the hammering in his head. Sweat leaked under the plaster that covered his stitches, burning into the wound.

With only one eye Bimbo found his sense of perspective had gone, and twice he stumbled over kerbs, but he retained his balance and kept moving. He knew he was nowhere close to his nine-minute-mile pace, and roughly figured that his lack of speed would add twelve agonising minutes to the run.

Stop, and rest. Lie down! Give up!

NO!

Out through the common gates and into the lane. In the distance he could see The Stag. It seemed to get no nearer and his heart sank. Stare at the pavement, he told himself. Don't think of distance. Just one pace at a time.

Jack Shell, the publican, was chatting to a lorry driver delivering barrels of beer when he saw Bimbo. Shell, a burly, grey haired ex-docker ran towards him.

'Go on, my son!' he yelled. 'You show the bastards!' Bimbo heard the shout and gave a feeble wave. The pavement slid slowly by beneath him. Other shouts of encouragement came, but he could not tear his eyes from the pavement. It was a far more personal battle now between Bimbo's will and his beaten body.

The phone beside Phelps' bed rang. His head ached and he snatched the receiver from its rest.

'What is it?' he roared. 'What? You're joking!' Hurling the phone aside he clambered from the bed, wincing as the bruised ribs reminded him of the night before. He moved to the window and dragged back the curtains. To his right he saw the crowds gathering, and then the lumbering figure of Bimbo Jardine, jogging without a care in the world.

Phelps swore, and watched until the runner was out of sight. He picked up the phone and dialled swiftly.

Bimbo cut through the alley and on to the High Street, his vision blurring, his chest encompassed by a band of searing heat. He crossed the estate and out past the station. On the bridge, out of sight, he stumbled to a halt and fell to his knees, retching violently. His stomach heaved and he spat the last of the bile from his mouth. Hauling himself to his feet he was forced to walk for a while. Then he lurched into his stride and turned into the canal path, and round the tree-lined corner and on to the estate. Windows were open everywhere, people leaning over balconies and clapping him. He waved and ran for the sanctuary of his home. Outside, Jack Shell and about a dozen others had driven to Maple Road, and they applauded as he ran through them and up the steps. Esther and Sue Cater were in the hallway. They helped him up the stairs and into the flat. Esther undressed him, but it took both women to ease him into the bath, where he lay for almost an hour, between sleep and dreams. He managed to climb out unaided and sat on the edge of the bath, weakly towelling himself dry. The effort was too much and he went back to his bedroom and lay down. Sleep took him almost immediately. Esther covered him with fresh sheets and a blanket.

Two hours later Stan Jarvis arrived. Sue Cater had left for work, but said she would be back later, and Esther was nervous alone with the stocky video dealer. She could see from his eyes that he was a 'ladies' man' and did not like the frank appreciation that showed in his gaze.

Stan followed her into the bedroom, his eyes lingering on the rounded hips and long, sleek legs. But all amorous thoughts fled as he saw Bimbo's wounded face. 'Jesus!' whispered Stan, backing out of the room. 'He's got more guts than brains. You're the nurse, right?'

'Yes,' said Esther. 'And this nurse has to go to work. Will you stay with him?'

'Sure. What do I look for?'

'Any slurring of the speech. And check him every half-hour or so. You know how to take a pulse?'

'Yeah.'

'His pulse rate is around 48–50. Any irregularity and you call the number on that pad by the door. Ask for Dr Simeon Abazul. There's a phone in my flat and the key is by the pad.'

'Okay. He's very proud of you, you know. Talks about you a lot,' said Stan.

'Have you been friends long?'

'Yeah,' said Stan. 'We used to share a room.'

'Why did he run today?' Stan saw the concern in her eye, and shrugged.

'They wanted to 'urt him. Bad. Put him in traction. That was just his way of tellin' 'em he couldn't give a toss. Some of 'em are in hospital. Others aint lookin' too comfortable. But Bimbo? Well, he's out runnin'.'

'Then it's not over?'

Stan stared into the beautiful eyes. 'No, darlin'. They found Taggart this morning. Both arms and both legs broken, his fingers smashed. Reardon will go apeshit.'

'And Bimbo is alone.'

'He aint alone. I'm here. I aint much. But I aint no pussycat neither.'

'If he is attacked again, they will kill him.'

'There won't be no gang. Don't worry about it.'

'What then?'

He toyed with the idea of lying to her, but there was no point. 'It'll be one man. His name's Jackie Green,' he said.

*

Richard Kilbey sat in Pam Edgerley's tiny office, trying to screen out the discordant wailing of a baby in the room alongside. 'You look tired, Pam.'

'I am tired. Bloody tired. No council grants, press harassment, and now they say we have to move out because we haven't got enough fire doors, or some such rot. Why can't we get help? Every one of the women here has been savagely abused, and there's nothing they can do. Why does no one care, Richard?'

'I wish I could answer that,' said Kilbey, softly, wishing he could say something to lessen the despair in her eyes. 'How much will it cost to bring the building up to requirements?'

'The cheapest estimate is eight thousand,' said Pam. 'But it wouldn't matter if it was eight hundred. We haven't got the money. The well's dry.'

'If I had money ...' said Kilbey, then stopped. There was no point in going on.

'I know, Richard. You're a good man. But we close a fortnight on Friday.'

'I'll have another few words with the Boss,' said Kilbey, his eyes flicking upwards. 'He's been known to work a miracle or two.'

Pam smiled. 'I don't think He likes me. I'm some sort of abomination, aren't I?'

'I sometimes think He gets a little irritated by the people who claim they know His mind.'

'I don't believe in Him, Richard.'

'But He believes in you, Pamela.'

Pam stood and wandered to the window. 'You have no idea what this place means to the women here. You know, there's a young girl out there, deaf in her left ear from a beating she took. There's another one who miscarried after her husband hit her in the stomach. We had one the other day whose husband, and another man, raped her. And she's gone back home. Can you believe that? She was here, and he sent two men to bring her back.'

'You should have called the police.'

'What would they have done about Frank Reardon? He terrorises the town and they do nothing. Why should they care if he does it at home?'

'The world is an evil place,' agreed Kilbey. 'Look, I'll have another collection at the church.'

'There's no more time,' said Pam.

Kilbey felt depression hit him as he walked to his car. So many people lived in suffering, and so few were willing to help. He looked back at the old Victorian house, and the badly painted sign above the front door: 'REFUGE'.

His own wife had criticised him for getting involved with 'those lesbians', and one parishioner had written a letter of complaint to his Bishop. Kilbey started the car and drove to Maple Road.

Bimbo's door was opened by a stocky man with fair hair and a moustache.

'Yeah?'

'I'm the vicar. I'm here to see Bimbo.'

'He don't need no last rites, mate.'

'I'm sure,' said Kilbey. The man stepped aside and Kilbey entered the flat. Bimbo was in bed. He was awake and sipping a glass of milk.

''Allo, Rev. Sorry, I couldn't get round to ya.' Kilbey was stunned by the big man's appearance. His face was swollen and discoloured, and one eye was closed.

'Good Lord, Bimbo, what on earth happened to you?'

'Fell down the stairs, didn't I? It's better than it looks. Fancy a cuppa? Stan, make yourself useful.'

'No,' said Kilbey, swiftly. 'I just came to talk about the funeral.' He was about to go on to say that he could not, in all conscience, officiate, but Bimbo immediately brightened.

'You're a mate,' he said. 'I really appreciate it. Look in my coat there. He left me a letter. That'll give you some idea of what he was thinkin', you know, towards the end. He mentions God a coupla times.'

Kilbey removed the letter and read it through twice. There was warmth in the words, and compassion. Kilbey smiled.

'Who is this Jackie Green he writes of?'

'Don't worry about that, Rev. The old boy got the wrong end of the stick there.'

'I see. Do you have any money, Bimbo?'

'Some. Why? You need payin' for the service?'

'No. The funeral parlour put all that in the bill. No, I was thinking of the refuge. They're being closed down. But don't worry if you're short.'

'Nah, thass all right. Twenty be enough?'

'That would be handsome.'

'I'll give it ya Friday. Okay?'

'I'll see you there,' said Kilbey.

The vicar returned to his car. There were several black youths lounging by it. One of them walked up to him. 'We bin lookin' after it for you, man,' he said.

'That is very thoughtful of you, my boy,' said Richard. 'It is good to see people who care for one another.' He patted the youth on the shoulder and climbed into the car.

How nice, he thought, as he drove away.

At the upstairs window Stan chuckled. 'You oughtta have seen that, Bim,' he said.

'What?'

'That priest. Gang of louts by his car. You know the scene – sting him for some cash for lookin' after it.'

'What happened?'

'He just patted the leader on the shoulder and drove away.

You should see the geezer's face.' Stan laughed. 'They're all arguin' now. Dunno 'ow he got away with it.'

Stan walked back into the kitchen and emerged minutes later carrying a tray, on which sat a plate heaped with overdone eggs and underdone bacon.

'You aint no cook, Stan.'

'No, and I aint no nurse neither. Get it down ya. I gotta go to the shop. You gonna be all right?'

'Yeah. Thanks for stayin'.'

'No trouble, son.'

'And don't forget me *Shane* film.'

'I'll get it. I'll be back tonight.'

Stan did not go straight to the shop. First he called on an old flame named Elsie. She invited him in and offered him a beer.

'You do those leaflets all right?' asked Stan.

'Yeah. Me and Tracey delivered 'em around 1 a.m. Nobody saw us.'

'You're sure?'

'Absolutely. You don't think I'd want Reardon to find out, do ya? What a pig, eh? Doin' that to children. Deserves hangin'.'

'Don't he just? The second lot go out tomorrow. Okay?'

'Sure. Where's my hundred?'

'Don't you trust me, girl? After all we've been through?' he asked, putting his arms around her and pinching her ample backside.

'No, Stan, I don't. Especially after what we went through.'

He grinned and pulled a wad of cash from his jacket, peeling off ten £10 notes. 'Be careful, Elsie.'

'And you,' she replied.

Next, Stan went to his lock-up behind the shop and took an old AYA side-by-side twelve bore shotgun from the hidden rack. In his garage workshop he carefully sawed away the butt, leaving a pistol grip which he sanded smooth and taped. Locking the weapon in a vice, he took up his hacksaw and reduced the barrel lengths by eighteen inches. He filed them clean, and pressed the release lifting the weapon clear, then armed it with number six loads before snapping it shut. With a length of leather he fashioned a sling which he attached to the pistol grip, and hung it over his shoulder. It nestled against his hip. He put on his jacket and checked in a mirror to see if the gun bulged. It did, but not enough to arouse suspicion.

'You come for me, Jackie, and you'll be walking on stumps,' he said.

Mac sat staring in disbelief at the A4 sheet before him, his face white, his mind racing. Phelps said nothing.

'Where did you get this?' asked Mac, pushing it away from him across the desk, as if it carried some alien germ.

'It was pushed through me door. Everybody in the street got 'em. Bit rich, innit? I never knew none a that.'

'It's not true,' snapped Mac. 'I've known Frank Reardon for years. He came out of the army with an honourable discharge. And he served with distinction in Malaya and Germany. I was with him. He got a bloody medal, for Christ's sake.'

'Sure, Mac. I didn't mean nothin'. Course it's not true.' Mac stared stonily at the man, reading his thoughts. Phelps believed it. He believed Frank Reardon messed about with children.

'We've got to find out where this came from – before Frank sees one,' said Mac, wiping the sweat from his fat face. He lit a cigarette and looked once more at the damning words. 'And I want to know how widespread it is. I want to know exactly how far this has been distributed. Got it?'

'Sure, Mac. Evans got one in South Acton, but Ryan never. He's over east. As far as I know they done the Lane down to the park and up to the High Street.'

'I don't believe this,' said Mac, sighing. He took a deep breath. 'It's like a bloody nightmare. I'll have to scrape Frank off the ceiling when he sees it.'

'He'll be able to put it right, won't he?' said Phelps. 'I mean there's got to be official records and that.'

'That's just it,' said Mac. 'There won't be. Because it's not true. Don't you see it? Frank can talk till he's blue in the face. But you can't produce non-evidence. There never was a court case. He hasn't got a record for this.'

'What I mean', argued Phelps, 'is that he can prove that, can't he? I mean the Old Bill will have to admit he's in the clear.'

Mac nodded, but doubt remained in his eyes. 'You get off and check out where they've come from. Get back to me every hour. I'll wait for your calls.'

After Phelps had gone Mac read the offending leaflet once more. The police wouldn't deny it. At least not immediately. They'd have to check with the central computer. But not everything was stored on computer. There'd be calls to other stations, other areas, delays. And every day Reardon failed to nail the lie, more people would believe it.

God in Heaven, he thought, I almost believe it, and I know it isn't true.

11

By mid-afternoon one of the reporters at the *Herald* spotted the leaflet while having a late lunch at the Roadside Cafe. It was lying on the seat next to him. He took it back to the office and passed it to Sue Cater. She took it to Don Bateman.

His words were hardly encouraging. 'It's a lovely story, but we can't even chase it up.'

'Why? That doesn't make any sense.'

Bateman was forty-two years old, and had been a provincial journalist for twenty-five years. Many of the youngsters he had trained had gone on to Fleet Street, or good provincial papers. Sadly, many others had gone to lucrative posts in public relations.

Bateman was a good journalist, who loved local newspapers and never regretted his commitment to small weeklies. He pushed the layout sheets aside and lit a cigarette. He liked Sue Cater, both for her personality and her talent. Otherwise, with three deadlines looming, he would have sent her off with a flea in her ear.

'It makes sense. Believe me. The story is libellous. If you ask anyone about it you will be repeating the libel and Reardon will be able to sue the paper. You understand that, yeah? Now, what you can do is check whether the police have seen the leaflet, and – if so, and only if so – ask them what they are doing about it.'

'But it's news, isn't it?' she argued. 'Isn't that what we're supposed to be about?'

'It's what we used to be about. Now we're about pushing the adverts apart. That's why there are only half the reporters there used to be and twice the advertising reps. But I don't want to get on my hobby horse. I know what you think. We haven't got the balls to publish tough stories. You're probably right. But we haven't got the resources either. There's not a senior reporter on the staff. And I can't send juniors out getting involved with slime like Frank Reardon.'

'What about the Bimbo angle?' she persisted.

'What angle? Bimbo himself wouldn't admit that Reardon had him turned over. There aren't any angles. Everyone knows Reardon runs a protection racket, and no one wants to talk about it. You get a publican to come forward and name Reardon in a sworn affidavit and we'll consider it. Get two and we'll publish. You only have one problem, though.'

'What's that?'

'That sourpuss Bateman forbids you to go near the story.'

'I wish you'd stop treating me like a child. And I also wish I'd joined a *real* newspaper,' she said, turning and stalking from the room.

'It used to be a *real* newspaper,' Bateman told the empty office. He gazed down at the layout sheets and the packed advertising on his news pages. Seventy per cent of local newspapers were now in the hands of the salespeople. He wondered how many readers knew just how far the integrity of their newspapers had slumped over the past ten years.

How many thought the editor still had any control over what used to be his product?

Why do I take this bullshit? he asked himself.

He took up his *em* rule and continued to lay out the pages – weddings, council reports, court cases, news briefs – keeping the layouts tight and modular. When he'd finished he pushed the copy and photographs into a canvas bag and carried it downstairs for the courier.

238

'He's late today,' said Fiona, the part-time receptionist.

'Give me a shout when he gets here. I may be able to squeeze a few more paras in.'

Returning to his office he picked up the phone and dialled Chief Inspector Frank Beard's private line. The police chief answered immediately.

'Frank, it's me, Bateman.'

'What can I do for you, old lad?'

'Frank Reardon.'

'What about him?'

'There's a leaflet doing the rounds saying he's a child molester.'

'I've seen it,' admitted Beard. 'You printing it?'

'No.'

'Very wise. Not a man to get on the wrong side of.'

'Is it true?'

'Who knows? Personally I don't give a shit – but don't quote me. The man's a scumbag.'

'Yes,' agreed Bateman. 'But is there a chink in his armour?'

'Isn't this a bit heavy for your rag?'

'Probably. Tell me anyway.'

'You wouldn't have the nerve to print it.'

'Too true. Times have changed.'

'Then why go after it?'

'Because I'm a fucking romantic,' snapped Bateman, 'who remembers what newspapers used to be like.'

There was silence for a moment. Then: 'You're not a romantic, Bateman, you're a dinosaur, just like me. Try Jack Shell at the Stag. From what I gather he's ready to jump. He only needs a push in the right direction. But be careful, Bateman. Reardon's sliding off his trolley. Going rogue, if you know what I mean.'

'Thanks for the tip.'

'What tip? We never had this conversation.'

Bateman rang off, then pressed Sue Cater's extension number. She answered immediately.

'Have you got a night-job tonight?'

'No.'

'Now you have. Ring Jack Shell at the Stag and make an appointment for an interview. Don't tell him what it's about, but say there'll be two of us.'

'Coming along to hold my hand?'

'Let me know what time he can see us.' He cleared the line and rang home. 'Hi, kid. Sorry, but I'm going to be late. I'll tell you about it when I see you.'

It wasn't often these days that he treated Mary. But tonight was a bonus. She could have an uninterrupted evening of passion with Larry next door. He wondered if Mary knew that he knew. He wondered if she cared.

He did. But then who cared what a dinosaur felt?

Bateman grinned as he stepped from his car and saw the hand painted sign in the window of the Stag: 'BIMBO WELCOME HERE!' Sue Cater joined him on the pavement.

'I always liked this pub,' she said.

'Your Bimbo's becoming a legend.'

'Well, that's pretty typical isn't it?' Sue told him. 'After all, it's always the men of violence who capture the public's imagination.'

'So much cynicism in one so young,' he said, shaking his head.

The long saloon bar was pretty crowded. Jack Shell and two barmaids were serving customers. Shell was a burly man in his early fifties, with silver hair. The perfect publican, he could smile faster than a politician and remember the first name of any man who had bought a pint of beer in his four years at the Stag. He saw Sue and waved her to the back room and the stairs.

'Go on up,' he said. 'I'll be with you in a moment.'

The stairs led to a private bar that Shell often rented for receptions or lodge meetings. Tonight it was empty and cold. Sue drew her leather coat more tightly around her.

'It'll warm up in a minute,' said Bateman, grinning. 'You see. And I don't want you to take part. Just introduce me, sit quietly, and learn something.'

'Like what?'

'Like how it used to be, when journalists knew their jobs, and how to do them.'

'Thanks very much, O wise and all powerful one.' He chuckled and loosened his tie. Jack Shell joined them. He apologised for the cold and switched on a wall-mounted gas fire.

'Can I get you a drink?' he asked, moving behind the U-shaped bar. Don ordered a Scotch, Sue a Bacardi. Shell gave himself a slimline tonic.

'Okay,' he said, as the journalists settled down on two bar stools, 'let's make this brief. You can see I've a full house downstairs. What is it you want?'

'This is my boss, Donald Bateman,' said Sue, dutifully. Shell offered his hand. Bateman shook it.

'Okay, Mr Bateman, I take it this is your show?'

'That's right. Thanks for seeing us at such short notice. Now – since, as you say, you're a busy man – I'll come straight to the point: Frank Reardon.'

Shell grinned, lifted his tonic and added a double measure of gin. He glanced at Sue who had opened her notebook. 'You can put that away for a start. What we are going to talk about now is strictly off the record.'

Bateman masked his annoyance at Sue's maladroitness. 'Absolutely, Mr Shell. Now let me be frank. Two publicans have approached us with complaints against Reardon, and they have agreed to sign affidavits claiming Reardon is running a protection racket. Both men mentioned your name as someone who might corroborate their stories.'

'And who are these heroes?' asked Shell.

Bateman smiled. 'I think you'll understand, Mr Shell, that we cannot name names. Suppose, for example, that these men are wrong and you are not a man to be trusted.'

'You don't mince words, do you, Bateman?'

'Not often, Mr Shell,' answered the news editor, holding the man's gaze. 'But then we're not playing pat-a-cake are we? We're talking about a vicious criminal organisation.'

'I know what we're talking about,' snapped Shell. 'Ever since I came here I've been trying to get the other publicans to stand up to that bastard. Twenty years ago I'd have done it by myself. But people get older, don't they, and their bones get brittle. Still, with luck he'll get put down for child molesting, the dirty little sod.'

'Then you are not interested in corroborating the story?'

'I didn't say that. Listen, Bateman, I know about men like Reardon; I worked the docks for twenty years. What are you going to achieve with your story? What will Reardon get? A smack on the wrist from some magistrate that's in his pocket? But the publicans who speak out will get worse than that. They'll get petrol bombs through their windows.'

'Evil thrives when good men do nothing,' said Bateman. 'Reardon's organisation only works because people are too frightened to band together. But now we've got two men willing to speak out. A third would be conclusive.'

'Why not go with the two?' said Shell. 'Then we'll see. If that sticks I might just come in.'

'No. They won't go all the way without you. You're the linchpin. Without you there's no story.'

'It's Jim Wright at the Railway, isn't it?' said Shell. 'He's always talking a good fight against Reardon. I don't know about the other one. McKay?'

'As I said, no names.'

'Yeah. As you said. Why won't they go without me?'

'They say you've got bottle, Jack. Have you?'

'Have *you*, Bateman? Do journalists risk petrol bombs – against their families?'

'You come with us, and you'll find I don't walk away,' said Bateman, softly.

'I need time to think about it.'

'There's no time,' said Bateman. 'Make a choice, Jack, yes or no.'

'You're a pushy bastard.'

'I can't argue with that.'

'Okay, it's yes. But I want to meet the other two.'

'I'll arrange it,' said Bateman. 'Nice talking to you.' Bateman shook hands and led the bewildered Sue back to the car.

'What are you doing?' she asked, as he started the engine and pulled away. 'We haven't got anybody else. And Jack will pull out when he knows he's been shafted.'

He tapped his nose. 'Wait and shee shweetheart,' he told her.

'That's the worst Bogart I've ever heard.'

'I'm not surprised, it was supposed to be Clark Gable in *Teacher's Pet*.'

'Oh. Where to now, Mr Gable?'

'The Railway and Jim Wright.'

Wright was in his middle thirties, round shouldered with a heavy beer belly. He reluctantly agreed to leave the bar and took them past the kitchen to a small sitting room.

'Make this quick,' said Wright.

'I've been told you're a man with bottle,' said Bateman.

'Yeah? So?'

'So we're going to run a story nailing Frank Reardon. We've got two publicans ready to swear he runs a protection racket. We need a third.'

'This is a gag, right?'

'No gag,' said Bateman. 'Reardon's going down. Now our two men are showing a lot of courage, and one of them suggested you might have the nerve to join them.' Bateman emphasised the word one. Wright bit immediately.

'What about the other one?'

'It doesn't matter about the other one,' he said.

'Come on, you opened this can of worms. What about the other one?'

'He said you ... talked a good fight,' said Bateman, reluctantly. 'But let's not get involved in personalities. Reardon's the main thing.'

'Bleedin' Shell. I talk a good fight? What's he been doing for four years? Payin' on the dot every week. He's got a bloody nerve. It's these leaflets isn't it? Now everybody knows what a sleaze Reardon is. Now Shell wants to make himself a hero. Grand standing bastard.'

'I haven't said it's Shell. You're jumping to conclusions. That could be a mistake.'

'Not likely to be anybody else. Who is the other one?'

'No names, Mr Wright.'

'I want to know who I'm coming in with.'

'You'll know. I'll arrange a meeting. All the affidavits will be written first, then we'll get together and discuss them. Now it's imperative that you don't discuss this with anyone else – not even people you think might be the other two. You understand? The slightest leak and you know what you could be facing?'

'I know. Have you spoken to Charlie at The Anvil?'

'Not yet.'

'I think he might come in, now he knows there's three of us.'

'Okay. Could you give him a ring and say we're on our way round? But don't tell him what it's about.'

'Sure. I'm going to enjoy nailing Frank Reardon.'

'And you will, Mr Wright. Sue will come back tomorrow to arrange the affidavit.'

Once more in the car, Sue Cater leaned across and planted a kiss on Bateman's cheek.

'What's that for?'

'Didn't the girl always kiss Gable in the final reel?'

'This isn't the final reel, but you're learning, shweetheart.'

The evening's work was an unqualified success. Charlie Harris, Jim Wright and Jack Shell had all agreed to complete and sign sworn affidavits, and the story was well and truly on its way. Bateman sat in his office staring at the blue sky through the grimy window. It had been good to get back 'on the street', and his ego had been massaged by the look of admiration in Sue's eyes.

His phone rang. He answered it and listened, white faced, as the receptionist poured out a swift explanation. His door opened.

'It's all right, Debbie,' he said, replacing the receiver.

'Can I help you?' he asked, hoping his face was not betraying his panic.

'I want to see the editor,' said Frank Reardon. 'Now!'

'He's away, but I'm his deputy. What can I do for you … Mr … ?'

'Reardon. Frank Reardon. I want to know what you're going to do about these bloody leaflets. I expect you've seen them.'

'As a matter of fact I have.'

'Well this is today's,' he said, hurling a crumpled sheet of paper to the desk. Bateman smoothed it out and read the contents. There were six case histories of sex abuse cases against children.

'And it's all lies,' said Reardon. 'That and yesterday's.'

'Have you been to the police?'

Reardon pulled up a chair and sat down. 'I saw Chief Inspector Beard this morning. He said they were looking into it. But I don't believe it. What are you going to do?'

'l don't see there is much we can do.'

'I thought you were interested in printing the truth. I'm a

local businessman, and I'm being harassed and libelled. There must be a story in that.'

'Of course there is, Mr Reardon,' said Bateman, smiling. 'Hold on a moment.' He picked up his phone pressed Sue's extension. 'Miss Cater, could you come down and make a couple of cups of coffee. Do you take sugar, Mr Reardon?' Reardon nodded.

'I'll be right down,' whispered Sue.

'You see, Mr Reardon, our problem is one of resources. Ten years ago I could have put a reporter on the story and sent him to each of the towns mentioned in the leaflets to check the truth of the matter. Unfortunately, these days, I only have three staff, and two of them are juniors.'

'What sort of newspaper is this?'

'By today's standards it's pretty good. But I can't help you in the way you want. I can't print they're untrue unless I can prove they're untrue.'

'This is fucking insane! I'm an innocent man. These things have appeared out of nowhere and everyone believes them. There must be something you can do. Do you know how much I spend on advertising with your paper every year?'

'No, I don't. But I'm sure it's significant. But this is the editorial department, and as you say, we're interested more in truth than capital. Mind you, you could put up the money for a freelance reporter. If it was someone I nominated I would accept his findings.'

Sue Cater entered with three cups of coffee and sat down behind Reardon. 'This is Miss Cater, one of our journalists. Do you mind if she sits in?'

'I couldn't give a monkey's if you brought the Dagenham Girl Pipers in. What freelance could I use?'

'I'll contact him for you. It'll cost around a hundred pounds a day and expenses. And be warned Mr Reardon, it's going to take some time.'

Reardon put down his coffee. 'I really don't believe this. How can this happen? How can somebody just print a load of lies?'

'Yes, it must be dreadfully upsetting for you,' agreed Bateman.

'I got a medal in Northern Ireland. I was honourably discharged. You could check that, couldn't you?'

'Of course, but people would only say you'd fixed it, or that someone was lying to protect you.'

'So, until your man comes home with the goods I've just got to take it? Is that what you're saying?'

'I'm afraid so.'

'I'll find out who's printing these. I'll bloody find out.'

'I hope you do. While you're here, Mr Reardon, do you mind if I ask a couple of questions?'

'Not at all.'

'Do you have any enemies?'

'All businessmen have enemies. Successful businessmen anyway. You think one of them is behind the leaflets?'

'It's unlikely to be one of your friends,' observed Bateman. 'What sort of enemies are they? Business rivals?'

Reardon shrugged. 'There are a lot of people who feel hard done by. Losers most of them. That's how the world's split, isn't it? Winners and losers. The losers whine and moan, the winners just get out and do.'

'And you are a winner?'

'I got a six-hundred-and-fifty thousand pound house and a yacht moored in Malta. Do I look like a loser?'

'In fairness, no, you don't. I'll get my man to call you, Mr Reardon. Will you be at home this evening?'

'Yeah. After nine.'

'He will require ten days' fee in advance, and one hundred pounds travelling expenses. But he's good. If the stories are false he should find out in the next week or so.'

'Thanks for your time. And you'll print the story when he comes up with it?'

'I guarantee it.'

'That's good,' said Reardon. 'Look, you'll have to come out to the house one of these days. I have lots of parties. You know, show-biz folk, local celebrities. You'd enjoy yourself. Bring the young lady here.'

'That's very kind of you. I'll look forward to it.'

Reardon shook hands and left. Sue and Bateman watched from the window as he climbed into a silver Mercedes parked on double yellow lines outside the office.

'I thought I was going to die when he walked in,' said Bateman. 'I was convinced he knew about the story.'

'He will next Tuesday when we publish.'

'Oh, well, bang goes the invitation to meet the showbiz crowd.'

'We will publish won't we, Don?'

'Of course. Why shouldn't we?'

'He is a major advertiser. Eighty grand last year for his clubs and property holdings.'

'l know we're sliding, kid, but I don't think we've slid quite that far yet.'

'You say that, but Mark's feature on bad car servicing last year was dropped like a hot brick.'

'I know. That hurt. And not only because he quit over it. But this is different.'

'I hope you're right.'

'Trust me,' he said, but the seeds of doubt had been sown.

Bimbo was standing in the porch at Mortlake Crematorium when the hearse drew up. It was a large, sleek motor with glass sides, and a single wreath could be seen on the oak veneer coffin.

Four men lifted it clear and carried it into the building, their footsteps echoing in the empty hall. Richard Kilbey smiled at Bimbo and climbed to the lectern. Bimbo watched as the pall bearers walked to the back of the chapel and sat down.

Kilbey cleared his throat and began to speak, his voice soft, but resonant.

'We are gathered here to witness the passing from life to death of a friend. Not my friend – or yours,' said the vicar, gesturing towards the pall bearers, 'but a friend to Bimbo Jardine. Henry Stepney lived among us for many years. He lived peacefully, quietly, and regretfully.

'As a young man he had another name, and he lived in another country. He grew with a burning dream, and, as with so many burning desires, it led him to forsake all that civilised men hold dear. And the flames blazed brightly for a while, until, at last – as they always will – they consumed the young man. His dreams became ashes, his life grey and void of flame.

'He committed great evils, and they returned to haunt him.

'But he found a friend and, perhaps, rediscovered a little of the young man who once cared. And let us hope that a new flame caught in his long-cold soul. A true flame, not of ambition, or lust for glory, but of love. For that is the flame that enriches, and burns without burning.

'I would like to think that Heinrich Stolz has gone to meet his maker with just such a flame. I cannot say that his crimes will be washed away, but I believe he has already suffered his own personal purgatory, and the Lord is all forgiving.

'Let us pray'

Bimbo eased himself to his knees and closed his eyes. After the service he shook Kilbey's hand warmly.

'Thanks, Rev. Nice words. He'd a liked them. By the way,' he added, fishing in his pocket, 'here's the twenty notes for the refuge.'

'You're a good man, Bimbo. Try not to fall down any more stairs. How are the bruises?'

'I heal quick. Don't you worry about me.'

An elderly man in a heavy black woollen overcoat approached Bimbo at the gates.

'Mr Jardine?' he said, his voice clipped and sibilant.

'Yeah?'

He handed Bimbo a card. 'My name is Muntford. Cyril Muntford. I was Mr Stepney's solicitor.'

'You shoulda bin in the chapel.'

'He was a client, Mr Jardine, not a friend. Could you call on me on Monday at four?'

'Why?'

'For the reading of the will, Mr Jardine. Surely you know you were his sole beneficiary?'

'No. What's that mean, exactly?'

'It means that he has left you his estate. At four on Monday then?'

'Sure.'

Stan Jarvis was waiting beyond the gates, listening to a Dire Straits album on his car's cassette player. Bimbo slid in beside him.

'Good service?' asked Stan.

'Yeah. Empty though. Wish you'd come in.'

'I never knew him. And I don't like funerals. Morbid. Where do you fancy goin'?'

'Drop me back in the High Street. I wanna get some bread for me swan. Then you better get back to the shop.'

'You didn't oughta be wanderin' about on yer own, son. It aint healthy.'

'I don't need no minder. Anyway, what with these scandal sheets goin' around Reardon's got other things on his mind. They true, you reckon?'

'Dunno,' said Stan. 'Can't read, can I?'

'Any idea who's behind it?'

'No. And I don't wanna know,' said Stan. The car pulled away, and Stan turned up the volume of the stereo.

The walk to the park helped Bimbo stretch his aching muscles, and he was pleased there was no one at the pond.

The black swan saw him and glided gracefully from the island. Normally she swept back and forth, approaching hesitantly. But today she came straight to the land and waddled ponderously on to the grass. Bimbo groaned as he lowered himself to sit on the ground. He broke some bread and threw it to her, but she ignored it, and spread her wings before settling down some five feet from him. 'Just want a chat, do ya, princess?' he said, softly. Bimbo's injured eye was partly open now, but the bird's blind eye would never heal. The thought hit him, adding to the heavy sadness the service had induced in him. His throat tightened and tears welled in his eyes.

'What a bloody Jessie,' he said, but he could not stem the sobs that tore from his throat. Strangely the bird was untroubled, and she sat close, head tilted, her good eye fixed on the friendly animal before her.

Sgt Don Dodds stood unnoticed at the bench some thirty feet away, watching the two lonely creatures. He had wanted to speak to Bimbo, but now was not the time. He walked silently away, up the short hill to the car where D.C. Sunley was waiting. Retirement was only four weeks away for the veteran sergeant. It would begin with a winter cruise in the Caribbean, which Edna had been longing for. Dodds thought about the cruise, and realised, not for the first time, that he would sell his soul for another five years on the force.

Sunley started the engine. 'That was quick. How did he take it?'

'I must have missed him,' said Dodds.

'There's a call just come in, Sarge. There's a tramp who saw a man running from Reilly's place. He's at the nick now.'

'What you waiting for, son?'

The interview was going badly when the two arrived. The tramp, an ancient black man named Hezedekiah, was just emerging from a nine day drunk. He admitted he was smashed at the time he saw the man; and hadn't realised it was the day of the murder until another tramp had told him about the killing yesterday. He had been walking along by the church graveyard when a huge white man crashed into him. Hezedekiah had fallen back and hit his head on the wall. He remembered the man had blood on him, because some of that blood smeared his own coat. A good coat. Had it for years. Never got no blood on it before. No way. 'Ceptin' the nose bleed. But that was different. Yes sir. That was his own blood. That had a right to be on his coat. But not no other blood. And not, as it turned out, no dead man's blood.

D.I. Eric Lynch was deeply unimpressed. 'Would you recognise the man if you saw him again?'

'No, sir. No way. Big as a house, though. And it wouldn't do to recognise no man as big as a house.'

'But you saw that he was white?'

'I seen that, all right. Face shone in the moonlight.'

Dodds left the room for a cup of tea and returned some quarter of an hour later. The questioning was still in progress, but Hezedekiah was growing increasingly agitated.

'Don' wanna be here no more. I had my say. You dig that? These walls is shiverin'. Gonna smother me.'

'One last time, Hezedekiah,' said Lynch. 'What happened after you fell?'

'He kep' on runnin'. I done tol' you that.'

'Did he run to a car?'

'I didn't see nothin'. I was looking for my bottle. I didn't hear it break.'

'Never mind the bottle.'

'Goddamn easy for you to say. But he had no right. I never done nothin' to him.'

'Excuse me, sir,' said Dodds. 'May I ask a question?'

Lynch was annoyed, but he nodded. Dodds sat on the desk, looming over Hezedekiah. 'What did he do to you, sir?'

'He lost me my bottle.'

'How?'

'He done threw it away.'

'How?'

'When we collided I was carryin' my bottle. Still had the god-damn cork in it. You know how long it is since I had a bottle with a cork? Picked it up Kensin'ton.'

'And how did you lose it, sir?'

'It was in my hand. Then crash. I grabbed him to stop myself fallin' but he pushed me. I let go the bottle. And it was up against him, sort of. Anyways he just grabbed it and threw it over the churchyard. I never heard it break, and I went to look. I never found nothin'. Goddamn!'

'And whereabouts were you at the time?'

'I was comin' round de corner.'

'Was the man wearing gloves? Did you see that?'

'No gloves,' said Hezedekiah. 'I wanna go now.'

Ten officers were organised to search the site, and Dodds accompanied them. Lynch and Sunley got there first and the elder man seemed anxious to get started.

'Let's wait for the others, sir,' said Sunley.

'You can wait, son,' said Lynch. 'I'll have a look around.'

'I'll come with you then, sir.'

'There's no need for that, laddie. You stay by the car.'

'With respect, sir, I'll come with you. Less chance of anyone saying we planted the evidence.'

'There won't be any evidence,' snapped Lynch. 'You think that old drunk could remember what day it was? He just wanted a free meal.'

'I'll come anyway, sir,' said Sunley. Lynch reddened, but as he was about to speak the other cars drew up.

They quartered the ground and searched inch by inch through the long grass and the overgrown graves. Finally Lynch called the search to a halt. 'Even Daley Thompson couldn't have thrown it this far,' he said.

'One last time, lads,' said Dodds. 'Back to the wall.' Dodds got one of the men to give him a hand, and climbed on to the six foot wall. From here he tried to judge the possible trajectories. The killer was large and strong. He was also angry, or panicking, at the time. It wouldn't have been tossed, but hurled. There was a tree close by. Dodds stared at it. A piece of bark was dislodged about seven feet up the trunk. He clambered down from the wall and examined it. It could have been anything from squirrel tearings to a thrown stone. But it could also have been caused by a bottle striking it. He looked around. There was no sign of broken glass. On the point of giving up he spotted a broken gravestone that had snapped and fallen forward, creating an upturned V. He walked to it and knelt. There, hidden from sight and safe from harm, lay the wine bottle. Remarkably it was unbroken, and, better still, dried blood was smeared on the label.

'Over here!' called Dodds. 'And bring a bag.' Carefully he lifted the bottle clear, holding it at the cork and under the base. The white label was damp, but the blood stain showed a clear print.

'By God,' said Sunley, 'that's beautiful.' Dodds placed the bottle inside the bag, and glanced up to see Lynch hurrying over.

'You remember what I told you, son,' he whispered to Sunley.

'Don't worry about that,' said the young officer.

'You found it?' asked Lynch.

'Yes, sir,' said Sunley. 'And there's a clear print. I'll get it back for the lab.'

'Good work,' said Lynch, forcing a smile.

Knowing Bimbo would no longer be in the park, Dodds drove to Maple Road. He was about to get out of the car when he saw a movement at Bimbo's window, and recognised Sue Cater drawing the curtains.

'You really believe in doing your research, young lady,' he whispered.

Susan turned from the window.

'What ya doin'?' asked Bimbo.

'Take your shirt and trousers off and lie down by the fire.'

'I don't think I'm up to this,' said Bimbo. 'Give me another few days.'

'You're up to what I've got in mind, cowboy. Now do as you're told.'

Bimbo groaned as he pulled the T-shirt clear. The bruises were fading, but they were still unpleasant to the eye: deep purple, yellow or angry red. Sue opened a earner bag and removed a large plastic bottle of scented massage oil. Then she took off her own blouse.

'Is that necessary?' he asked.

'You complaining? I just don't want oil on my clothes.'

'I aint complainin'. Honest to God.'

She warmed the oil in her hands and smeared it across his back and shoulders in smooth, circular motions. Bimbo closed his eyes. The warmth from the fire and the massage made him drowsy. Skilfully her fingers found the knots in his muscles, easing them clear with a minimum of discomfort.

When she had finished she leaned back. He turned to his side and grinned at her.

'Maybe I don't need a few more days after all,' he said.

At that moment there was a knock at the door. Sue swore. Bimbo rose and walked to the door while Sue gathered her clothes and made her way to the bedroom.

'Who is it?'

'Sgt Dodds. Get your arse alight and open this bloody door.'

He stepped inside and removed his cap. Glancing at Bimbo's wounds, he grinned. 'I've seen horses put down with less injuries than those.'

'Look, could we make this quick? I got things to do.' Dodds' smile faded, replaced by an expression of regret. 'Put the kettle on, son. We're both going to need a cup of tea.'

Bimbo was about to speak, but Dodds raised a hand. 'Just the kettle for now, all right?'

Bimbo moved into the kitchen and washed two mugs. The kettle took an age to boil, but at last he returned with the drinks. Dodds was sitting by the fire.

'Okay, Mr Dodds,' said Bimbo, handing him a mug. 'Whass on yer mind?'

Dodds sniffed and took a deep breath. 'No easy way to say this, son. But Adrian Owen died this morning. I'm sorry.'

'Died? Whaddya mean died? He was in 'ospital, for God's sake. He was gettin' better!'

'He had a relapse, Bimbo. It was very quick. He didn't know anything about it. The officer on call got the doctor in, but there was nothing they could do.'

Bimbo turned away and wandered to the window.

'I'm sorry, son.'

'Yeah,' said Bimbo. 'Me an all. I just buried one friend this mornin'. What's happenin' with Adrian? Do you know?'

'His parents have been notified. All the arrangements are being made by them.'

'Has anyone told Melanie? The girl he worked with?'

'No, I don't think so.'

'I'll do it then.' He sat down by the window, leaning on the sill. 'He was a good lad, you know. Gutsy. Jesus, he wasn't even thirty.' Bimbo swung towards Dodds. 'I should never have done it. If I hadn't got involved he'd still be alive.'

Dodds moved into the room, acutely aware that Sue Cater was in the bedroom. He sat down beside Bimbo. 'I haven't got the answers, Bimbo. Never have had. But sometimes we do things for the best and they don't work out. When I was younger I had a trial with QPR. I was a goalkeeper. I wasn't bad. But in that trial I got beaten by five goals. Now the thing is that a goalkeeper can only cover two thirds of his goal at any time. He's just got to pick which two thirds. I did everything right and got beat five times. They never signed me.'

'Whass that got to do with Adrian?'

'The right thing doesn't always bring the right results. If I'd done the wrong thing I'd have saved those goals. Maybe. Then I'd have been a professional footballer. If you hadn't helped Adrian he would still be alive. But it would have been wrong. For you, that is. You helped a friend, Bimbo. You didn't do it for profit. You just did it. You've nothing to be ashamed of.'

'Aint like the movies, is it, Mr Dodds?'

'Nothing is, son. This is life. I heard about the run. That was good. It rubs Reardon's face in it.'

'Big deal. Wish I could go back. Change a few things.'

'We all wish that. Probably just as well we can't. You going to bear up all right?'

'Yeah. You know me, Mr Dodds, strong as an ox. I'll be okay.'

'I wish there was something I could say, son.'

'Nah,' said Bimbo. 'Don't worry about it. It was nice of ya to come. You didn't have to do that. I'm not family or nothin'.'

'Don't do anything rash either. Reilly had Adrian turned over. And now they're both dead. I don't want any other deaths. Least of all yours.'

'No. Me neither. Don't worry, Mr Dodds. I'm not the killing kind.'

'No, but the bastards you're up against are.'

Bimbo smiled. 'I aint that easy to kill neither.'

'With luck it may all be over very soon,' said Dodds. 'And you won't have to be involved in it.'

'Don't count on it,' said Bimbo.

'So what's the big deal?' shouted Jackie Green, his square face twisted in anger. 'So the bastard died. So what? Even if they find out it's me – which I doubt – it'll still be manslaughter. I'll be out in a year, eighteen months at the most. It's not like the old days, is it? I mean, killing someone's no big deal nowadays.'

Frank Reardon took a slow, deep breath, holding down his anger. MacLeeland sat quietly on the sofa watching the two men. He knew Reardon was frightened of Jackie, but Jackie needed Reardon to give him a chance at returning to big-time boxing. Still, unhinged as he undoubtedly was, even this slender chain was unlikely to leash the mad dog for long. Reardon was walking a fine line.

'You're an idiot, Jackie,' said Reardon, softly. 'The courts may not care too much about killers these days, but the police do. It's like shining a torch into the dark places. Now they're looking. And do you know who they're looking at? No? They're looking at me. All my operations are going to come under the microscope – all because you haven't the brains to wipe your arse unless someone tattoos a route map on your leg.'

Green's eyes blazed and he moved forward. Mac tensed, but Reardon stood his ground and spoke again. 'A lot of people said you were mental, Jackie. A lot advised me to get shot of you.' Green stopped, his hands trembling.

'I did it for you,' he said, at last.

'Bollocks! You did it because he insulted you. You did it because you like doing it.' Reardon swung away. 'Go downstairs, Jackie. Play a little pool. I'll see you later.'

The big man turned and meekly left the room.

Reardon sat alongside Mac and grinned. 'Thought he was going to rip my throat out, didn't you?'

Mac nodded. Reardon chuckled. 'Not while I've got what he wants. But you were right, Mac. I should never have brought him in. Getting rid of him is not going to be easy.'

'You could give him over to the law,' suggested Mac.

'And have him tell everything he knows about me?'

'You think he'd blag?'

'Course he will. There's no one in Jackie Green's life that means anything to him – except Jackie Green.' Reardon poured his fourth large Scotch of the evening and downed it in two gulps. Mac was growing increasingly nervous. Reardon was so hard to read these days, and his mood swings were sometimes terrifying. At the moment he seemed calm enough. 'So, bring me up to date. What's new on the leaflets?'

'We've been to all the little printers. They all deny it, naturally. We've also spoken to some of the workers, you know, offered big money for tip-offs. The paper is standard A4. You can get it anywhere. The printing is something called Times Roman. All printers have it. It's an old process called letter press. Hot metal. There's only seven that still use it. We're still checking them. My bet is a man called Hedges. Got a wife that likes to spend.'

'Who saw him?'

'Phelps. He says the guy was sweating.'

'Have him seen to.'

'Sure. From what Phelps said it won't take much.'

'What's happening nearer to home?' asked Reardon.

'There's rumblings from the pubs. Something's happening. Shell, Wright and Harris have all refused to pay. Still, compared to the takings from the night clubs and the interests in Southall, it's small potatoes at the moment.'

'See that Shell is turned over. The rest will fold.'

'Okay, if you think it's a good idea with all the other business going on,' said Mac, carefully.

'I do. Now tell me again about Bimbo being in traction.'

'He was beaten to a pulp. They damn near took him apart. I was told he was in hospital.' Mac shrugged. 'But everyone knows he was right turned over. He's out of it.'

'So badly turned over that he did a six mile run the following day?'

'He's not been out since, Mr Reardon. That was just bravado.'

'Have him hit again.'

'I don't think that's wise,' said Mac, pulling a handkerchief from his pocket and mopping the sweat from his face.

'Not like you to argue, Mac. Wrong time of the month, is it?'

The insult hardly registered on Mac. He'd heard so many during the past few years. But something inside him just gave way, and he looked up at Reardon. 'I've tried to be loyal, Frank. And I've done my best to give you honest advice. Bimbo was a bloody mistake. You said that yourself. Ever since we went after him we've had nothing but trouble. Now the pubs are blowing out, the Old Bill are all over the manor, and we've got a corpse to boot. It's crazy to hit him again!'

'Crazy? You calling me crazy, you fat worm?' Reardon's hand snaked out, cracking against Mac's face and knocking him sideways across the sofa. 'Don't you ever call me crazy!'

Mac pushed himself slowly to his feet. The left side of his face was red and his eye was beginning to swell. He began to gather the papers strewn on the desk, then stopped and straightened, leaving them where they were.

'We've known each other for a long time, Frank,' he said, sadly. 'I remember when you first started. You did your own collecting. You were a hard man. But you had a great sense of humour. People liked you, Frank.'

The fat man slowly made his way to the door.

'Where the hell do you think you're going?' roared Reardon.

Mac turned. 'I'm going home. I just quit.'

'Nobody quits on me!'

'You want Jackie to turn me over, or will you do it yourself? One punch should be enough, Frank. What's one more stiff, eh?'

'Fuck you,' said Frank Reardon. 'Who needs you? I've been carrying you for years. You hear me?' he yelled, as the door swung closed.

Reardon adjusted his cravat and stalked downstairs.

Jackie Green was playing pool on the full-sized table by the poolside bar.

'You hear any of that?'

'I heard the shouting,' said Green. 'Sounds like he quit. Want I should talk to him?'

'Jesus, no. He's a friend of mine. You know I saved his life two years ago. Heart attack. I gave him mouth to mouth, and I carried him to my car – an old BMW. I got him to the hospital in four minutes.'

'No gratitude some people,' said Green, lining up a shot and cracking it away into the top pocket.

'He'll come back. I'll give him a couple of days to cool down.'

Jackie moved to the bar and poured a large Scotch, which he carried to Reardon. 'You need something to relax you,' he said. 'You know what I mean?'

'What?'

'Give the bitch a goin' over. I've got a few ideas meself.'

'I can't,' said Reardon, downing the Scotch. 'I promised her. I was pissed. It shouldn't have happened.'

'Good though, weren't it?'

'Squealed, didn't she?' agreed Reardon.

'I reckon she liked it, you know. You can tell from the eyes. She's just waitin' for it again.'

'No. No, I couldn't.'

'Have another drink, Mr Reardon. We'll talk about it.'

Bimbo sat in Cyril Muntford's elegantly furnished office, before the Victorian mahogany desk, gazing down at the pale sherry in the lead crystal glass. Beside him Stan Jarvis thought he was dreaming.

'How much?' said Stan.

The elderly solicitor gave a wintry smile. 'Two hundred and sixteen thousand pounds, that is if all the equities were to be realised immediately. But there is forty thousand currently liquid – cash, if you prefer. Then of course there is the lease to the shop. Would you wish to continue it, Mr Jardine?'

'What?'

'The shop, sir. Do you wish to continue the lease?'

'I don't know nothin' about antiques.'

'We have a complete inventory of all stock and personal items. A swift evaluation is that they will bring about seventeen thousand, but collectors will no doubt bid a fortune to own the Knight's Cross won by the infamous Heinrich Stolz.'

'I'm sorry, Mr Muntford, I can't take all this in. It's a bit sudden. I can't exactly get a grip on it, if you know what I mean.'

For the first time Muntford's smile had real warmth. 'Totally understandable, Mr Jardine. On top of your very real loss your emotions must be mixed. In a nutshell, my dear sir, after death duties are paid you should realise some one hundred and ninety thousand pounds.'

'I don't understand. Where'd he get all this dough?'

'He played the market, Mr Jardine. And very successfully.'

'And it's all mine?'

'No, sir. He left forty thousand to the RNLI – the lifeboat people – and twenty thousand to Cancer Research. But, as I said, you should realise around one hundred and ninety thousand. With careful investment you could earn some seventeen thousand per annum, before tax.'

'How much is that a week?'

'Around £350, say about £210 after tax.'

'Every week?' said Bimbo.

'Yes. And that's without touching the capital.'

'Is it all right to have some now?'

'There is no caveat against the will, Mr Jardine. The money is yours from the moment I transfer the funds and close Mr Stepney's accounts.'

'I dunno what to say. Honest to God, I don't.'

'Congratulations, Mr Jardine. In relative terms you are now a moderately wealthy man.'

On the following Wednesday morning the Reverend Richard Kilbey, moving with uncustomary speed, raced up the stairs of the Refuge and burst into the committee room, where Pam was chairing a meeting.

All eyes swung to him. 'I'm sorry,' he said. 'I'm sorry. But it's very urgent. I must speak to you, Pam. Right away. Sorry, ladies.'

'Excuse me,' Pam told them. 'I'll be right back.' She led Kilbey into the small office alongside the committee room. 'What is it, Richard? I've some very depressed people in there.'

Kilbey was almost beside himself. 'It's a miracle, Pam. My first. Well … not mine, but the Lord knows what I mean.'

'He may, but I don't, and I have some women in there who think the world's about to come to an end.'

'It hasn't come to an end. It's just beginning. Look. Just look.' He reached into the inside pocket of his tweed jacket and produced a bulging brown envelope, which he dropped to the table. 'Look inside.'

Pam picked it up and flipped it open. 'Dear God,' she whispered, as she slid the fifty £20 notes on to the desk top. She counted swiftly. 'There's a thousand pounds here!'

'And that's just the deposit for the workmen. The other money for repairs is promised. Nine thousand. Or as much as we need.' Kilbey stepped forward and clumsily embraced the astonished Pam, planting a kiss on her brow. 'I'm sorry,' he said, stepping back and looking sheepish.

'I don't understand any of this,' said Pam, sitting down and staring at the money. 'Where does it come from? And don't talk about God.'

Kilbey smiled. 'What does it take to make a believer of you? I can't tell you where the money comes from. It's an anonymous gift. He came to see me late last night and just put the thousand pounds on my desk. It was sitting there, just like it is now. And he promised the rest as soon as we need it.'

'Why?' whispered Pam.

'Does it matter?'

'No, of course not. I'm just trying to think of something intelligent to say. Do I know him?'

'It's best not to go into that. I know you don't believe in God, Pam, but this is an answer to prayer. We needed it, and here it is. I actually wept last night. I tried to call you, but the lines were out.'

'We've been cut off,' said Pam. 'I don't know what to say. You're sure about the other nine thousand?'

'I'm sure. Look, don't stay in here with me. Go and tell the other girls ... sorry, co-workers. Go on!'

Pam reached out and took both his hands. 'God, Richard, I wish all men were like you. You've kept us alive!'

'Nonsense,' he said, colouring deeply. 'But I'm very happy for you.'

She left then and returned to the committee room. Within seconds there were screams of joy, reverberating around the building. Richard Kilbey sat back and glanced out of the window. The sky was clear blue. Alone now, he said a short prayer of thanksgiving. Somehow it seemed so perfect that the legacy of Heinrich Stolz should come to the aid of man's cruelty; like a cosmic balance coming into play.

He thought of Bimbo, and his generosity.

'It aint generous, Rev. It aint like it was my money. Go on, give 'em the good news. Make a change to 'ave a bundle of notes in their 'ands, eh?'

'Come with me, Bimbo. Share the joy.'

'Nah, keep me out of it. Tell 'em it's out of church funds or summink.'

'I can't do that. It would be lying.'

'Well, whatever. How much you reckon they'll need?'

264

'Anywhere from eight to ten thousand.'

'I got the money, so you come to me, yeah? We'll sort it out.'

'God bless you, Bimbo.'

'Don't start all that, Rev. Anyway I have bin pretty well blessed all me life. Good health and that. Good friends. Aint much more to life is there? Now I got another favour to ask.'

'Not another funeral, I hope?'

'No, a weddin'. Friend of mine. I'm givin' her away. Sorta like the bride's father, you know? You aint got nothin' against spades, have ya?'

'Good Lord no!'

Bimbo shrugged. 'Thass good, cos they're both spades. Esther and Simeon. He's a doctor. They aint really of this parish, but I asked 'em if they wouldn't mind gettin' 'itched in my church. They said all right, so it's up to you. I'll be bookin' a reception at the Stag.'

'I think before you book the reception you ought to let me meet the bride and groom, so that we can arrange a convenient date.'

'Yeah right. I'll sort it out. I aint ever given anyone away before. I'm a bit chuffed, you know? Nice of her to ask, though.'

'I'm sure she had good reason.' The vicar stood and took Bimbo's hand. 'Remember what I said about stairs, won't you?'

'Only one more flight to go, Rev.'

Kilbey still wasn't sure what that meant. Now Pam Edgerley walked back into the room, disturbing his thoughts.

'I take it they were pleased,' he said.

'Yes. We want to write a letter to the benefactor. Would you take it for us?'

'Of course.'

'There's no danger of him changing his mind?'

'None whatever,' he reassured her.

*

As Don Dodds entered the room Chief Inspector Frank Beard stood up and walked round the long desk to shake his hand. 'That was a nice job of work, Don. And a great result. You know it was Jackie Green?'

'I guessed it would be, sir.'

It was a little before 7 p.m. and Beard offered the burly sergeant a drink.

'No thank you, sir.'

'You mind if I do?'

'Not at all, sir.'

'Sit down, Don,' he told the officer, returning to his own seat with a measure of Scotch in an Esso tumbler. 'You have heard what they're going to call our SOCOs?'

'Scene Investigators aren't they? Is it true they're taking on civilians for the work?'

'Yes,' said Beard. 'Course they'll be trained, intensive courses and all that.'

'I think I preferred Scenes of Crimes Officers,' said Dodds. 'At least you knew they were coppers.'

'My sentiments exactly. Look, Don, I'll come straight to the point. Without your work I doubt we'd have nailed Green. We'd certainly have booked Jardine. But it's not just that. You're a bloody fine copper, and I don't want to lose you.'

'I don't want to get lost, sir. But I've no choice. I've done my thirty.'

'Then how about staying on as an SOCO – dammit, I mean a Scene Investigator?'

'Bit long in the tooth for that, sir.'

'I can pull a few strings. And I need men like you. I'll be buggered if I'm going to get left with just the Lynches of this world.'

'I'll talk to Edna, sir. She's got her heart set on the retirement cruise.'

'You can still take it. Look, I don't want an answer now, but what's your first reaction?'

'I'd love to, sir.'

'Good man! Now, what's the latest on Green?'

'He flew in just before the lab positively identified him from the print. Now he's gone to ground. He knows we're on to him. Reardon's got too many friends around here for him not to know.'

'What do you suggest?'

'I suggest keeping an eye on Bimbo. The two of them are going to meet, sure as eggs are eggs.'

'Okay. Keep me in touch.'

Bateman stood in the composing room watching the waxed bromides cut into shape and pasted to the pages. He loved this day of the week, when all the work came together and the newspaper was born. It wasn't quite so dramatic as the old days when the words were translated into hot bars of lead, zinc and antimony, and placed in steel frames. When rough pages were 'pulled' by being smeared with ink, covered with a sheet of paper and a felt blanket, then hammered. But it was still thrilling.

And today was the best day in five years. The whole of the front page was filled with a huge headline – 'TERROR BOSS' – under which was a picture of Frank Reardon. To the left of this was a reverse strip of white on black with the words, 'Herald Team Exposes Vicious Protection Racket'. The story began on page one and moved to the centre pages, where interviews and pictures of Jack Shell, Jim Wright and Charlie Harris adorned the layouts.

Don watched the pages coming together, hoping the copy would fit the space. He didn't want to cut a single word. He had estimated the story at seventy-three column centimetres. With a five per cent margin for error he could be up to four paragraphs out.

He was twelve paragraphs over.

'You don't get no better, Bateman,' said Tom, the senior charge hand, who was working on the centre. 'You want me to trim these pix to get all the copy in?'

'Thanks, Tom. I'll get it right next week.'

'Yeah. Tell that to Brian. He's working on page eleven, which is about the biggest cock up since Mons. We're having the copy reset.'

'I had other things on my mind. It's looking good, eh?'

Tom leaned back, and toyed with the idea of a putdown line. 'It's looking good, mate,' he admitted. 'Just like the old days when we printed real newspapers. A word to the wise though. That new advertising guy, Lander was down. He didn't look best pleased.'

'It's nothing to do with advertising,' snapped Bateman.

A half-hour later, as Bateman, Sue and a young reporter called Andrew Evans were reading the proofs, the phone rang and Bateman was summoned to the third floor. He said nothing to the others, but gathered the page roughs of the Reardon story and climbed the stairs.

The *Herald* had recently been taken over by a new syndicate, and Bateman instinctively knew they were cowboys with no interest in the integrity of the profession; just another lot of greasy businessmen out to milk the dying cow.

He tapped at the Marketing Director's door. 'Come in.'

He entered.

'Sit down, Bateman. You do prefer to be called Bateman, I understand?' said Ray Lander.

'That's right, Mr Lander. Is there a problem?'

Lander was short, stocky and bearded. He looked more like a bouncer than an advertising man. 'You didn't much like the take over, did you?'

'Nothing I could do about it.'

'Care to tell me why you were against it?'

'Why not? I'm a newspaperman. I love journalism. At its best it's the soul of a community, fighting the battles that keep that community just and caring. But somewhere along the way we got bogged down, Mr Lander.'

'How?' asked Lander, hooking his arms behind his head.

'Well, there used to be a horse called journalism, and somebody suggested wouldn't it be great to pin a rosette behind his ear extolling the virtues of some poxy little enterprise. Then there were two rosettes, and then a little cart. Then a bigger cart. A piled up, ten ton cart. And the horse never got fed, but the cart kept getting bigger. You catching my drift, Mr Lander?'

'You'd have to be a moron not to, Bateman. But then you're a dreamer. Newspapers aren't cheap to print any more. We have to recover the cost. We sell the *Herald* at 25p an issue. It costs us 47p an issue to produce it. Advertising pays the bills. But then you dreamers don't much care about paying the bills, do you?'

Bateman grinned and lit a cigarette. 'Nice touch, Mr Lander. But I didn't come down with the last shower of rhubarb. During the last twenty years the sales of local newspapers have slumped. That's because people are sick to death of poor products. If it costs 47p to produce, then we should be charging 50p.'

'No one would pay it,' said Lander.

'That's right, because people like you have made them crap products. But that's where we differ, you see. People would pay for a good paper. Jesus Christ, they pay nearly £2 for a jar of coffee. Anyway, nice talking to you, but I've got a paper to get out.'

'Tell me about Reardon,' said Lander.

Bateman's smile was icy. 'Ah. That's the preamble over, then?'

'That's the preamble over,' agreed Lander. 'I had a call from Reardon's solicitor. He says we're planning to publish a libel against his client and if we do he'll take us to the cleaners.'

'There's no libel. We have three affidavits from local publicans. Once we publish the others will come forward.'

'You may not be aware, Bateman, but the *Herald* is currently losing money. That's why we picked it up cheap. Now Reardon is currently negotiating advertising contracts that could be worth upwards of eighty-seven thousand a year.'

'I don't give a shit,' hissed Bateman. Lander's face reddened.

'What do we get out of printing this story?'

'We get respect, Mr Lander. We get seen as a newspaper that lives up to its name.'

'TV coverage?'

'Probably.'

'How probably?'

'The affidavits will be presented to the police as soon as we're on the presses. They'll have to arrest Reardon. BBC local will pick it up. Then there's the trial. More coverage for us.'

'Show me the proofs,' said Lander. Bateman passed them over. Swiftly Lander ran his eye over the front page. Taking a pen from his pocket he circled a word.

'What's that?' asked Bateman.

'Spelling error. There's an 'e' in Brooke Street. You should have known that.'

Finally Lander finished reading and passed the proofs back. 'Good story,' he said. 'The pictures look a little cramped, but it balances quite well.'

'The copy overran. I had to have the pictures cut down.'

'I guessed that. Okay, that's all, Bateman.'

'Then we run it?'

'You say it's all accurate. Go with it.'

'Thanks.'

'Don't thank me,' snapped Lander. 'You think you're the only bloody newspaperman in the world?'

Bateman shrugged. 'Sometimes it feels like it.'

Downstairs once more Sue Cater leapt to meet him. 'Do we run it?' she asked.

'We run it,' he said.

Stan called for Bimbo at 8 p.m. on Wednesday evening. Bimbo's face was set and tension showed in his eyes.

'You sure about this, son?' asked Stan.

'I'm sure. No choices left, Stan.'

'What sorta condition you in?'

'I bin better. But I run this morning, and it was okay. I did an hour on the weights, an' all. I'm okay.'

'Let's be at it then, before I lose me nerve.'

The two men climbed into the VW Golf and Stan headed out on to the Richmond road. Bimbo said nothing during the journey and Stan found his own throat terminally dry. 'Wanna stop for a swift half, Bim?'

'No.'

'Aint got a mint, have ya?'

'You don't have to come in, Stan. I've told ya before it aint your fight.'

'Can't a man even have a dry mouth now?' Stan's heart was beating at a terrifying rate as they drew up outside Reardon's large house. Bimbo stepped from the car. Stan followed.

'Wait here,' ordered Bimbo.

'Not piggin' likely.'

The two men walked swiftly up the gravel path, stopping before the ornate door. 'You gonna kick it in?' whispered Stan. Bimbo pressed the bell. The door was opened by Phelps. Before the man could react Bimbo reached out, grabbed him by the front of his sweater and dragged him on to the porch.

'Two quick questions, son. Is Reardon here?' Phelps nodded. 'What about Jackie Green?'

'He's in hidin'. Police want him for toppin' Reilly.' Bimbo nodded, smiled, then cracked a wicked uppercut to Phelp's chin. His head snapped back and his knees gave way. Bimbo lowered him to the ground and entered the house, Stan behind him. Reardon was sitting in the lounge. He was dressed in light beige slacks and white shirt with fawn cravat. He was watching television. He looked up, saw Bimbo, and scrambled to his feet.

Bimbo advanced into the room.

'You bastard!' screamed Reardon. He ran forward, throwing a punch. Bimbo blocked it with ease and crashed a right handed blow to Reardon's chin. Stan heard his jaw snap and winced. Reardon stumbled to his knees. Bimbo's foot lashed up, cracking into the smashed jaw. Reardon toppled back, unconscious.

'Now what, Bim?'

'I don't bleedin' know.I was 'oping Green would be here.'

Jean Reardon walked into the room – and froze. She was a tall woman, elegantly dressed. The left side of her face was horribly bruised, and her right arm was in a sling.

'Don't worry, love, we aint gonna hurt ya. We're just leaving,' said Bimbo.

'You must be Mr Jardine,' she said, coolly. 'I have heard so much about you. I don't think it would be wise to leave the job half done. Do you?'

'Looks more than half done to me.'

'But when he wakes up he will come after you.'

'I aint gonna kill him. It's not my game.'

'Who's talking of killing?' snapped Jean Reardon. 'I'm talking of finishing him. Get his clothes off.'

'Why?' asked Bimbo.

'Because we're all going out,' said Jean, moving to the far wall and opening a drawer beneath an oval mirror. She pulled a length of leather and a large steel-studded collar clear and walked back to the body, dropping the dog leash on it.

'I think she's a nutter, Bim,' said Stan.

'Trust me, Mr Jardine. Please. I know what I'm doing. And I can lead you to Jackie Green.'

'Where?'

'First do as I say. Strip him.'

'Why the hell not?' said Bimbo, kneeling down by the unconscious gang boss.

It was 9.45 p.m. when the call came to Dodds as he was sitting at home watching re-runs of *Hill Street Blues*.

'Jackie Green is at the Royal Swan, Mr Dodds. He's on the top floor. And he's got a shooter. He took it from Reilly. It's a magnum.'

'Thanks, Georgy. I owe you.'

'You look after yourself, Mr Dodds. Wouldn't do to get shot so close to retirement, would it?'

Dodds replaced the receiver and looked at Edna. 'Have to go out, love. I'll give you a call later.'

'I'll be glad when you're away from all this,' she said.

'Me too.'

He was at the station by 10.03 p.m.

It was 10.29 p.m. when Jean Reardon guided her husband's grey Mercedes into the car park of the Royal Swan. She pulled on the handbrake and waited until Stan's VW pulled alongside.

Jean swung in the seat to look into the rear of the car, where Bimbo sat with the naked Reardon. She smiled at her husband, enjoying the fear in his eyes.

'Time to go, Frank,' she said.

Bimbo opened the rear door. 'For God's sake,' mumbled Reardon through his swollen jaw. 'Don't do this to me!' Bimbo tugged on the leash and the dog collar cut into Reardon's neck. Feebly, the gang boss grabbed at the car seat, struggling to stay inside. Bimbo jerked the lead hard. Reardon tumbled to the cold tarmac. He came up screaming and rushed Bimbo, who thudded a blow to the man's belly. Reardon stumbled to his knees, all air gone from his lungs. He began to wheeze. Bimbo grabbed him by the arm, hauling him upright.

Bimbo pulled him to the lounge door and opened it, stepping inside. The bar was packed, and all noise ceased when the regulars saw the naked man. Reardon closed his eyes and fell to his knees. Bimbo hauled him on all fours to the centre of the room.

'Hey, Danny!' he called to the barman, his voice booming in the new silence. 'Get me a pineapple juice and bowl of water for the dog.'

No one moved. All eyes were fixed on the whimpering Reardon. In the doorway Jean Reardon began to laugh, the sound chilling and almost hysterical.

'Come on, son,' Bimbo told the barman. 'Can't you see he's thirsty?'

The barman stepped back out of sight and pressed the intercom button to the flat above. Bimbo looked around at the stunned faces. 'Not very lively in here tonight. I think we'll go down the Stag. Come on, boy!'

He tugged the leash. Reardon covered his face with his hands and refused to move. From the far corner MacLeeland moved into sight, holding a raincoat.

'You've made your point, Bimbo,' he said. 'Let it go.' He draped the coat over Reardon's shoulders.

'Let it go?' hissed Bimbo. 'Let it bleeding go? Adrian's dead, Mac! This fucking piece of shit had him beaten to death. Enough? It wouldn't be enough if I took him round every poxy pub in London.'

'You want to beat me up too, Bimbo?' asked Mac. 'Cos you'll have to. I'm not letting him be left like this.'

'Oh shit, Mac!' said Bimbo, releasing the leash and letting it fall to the floor.

'Let it go, son. This aint your style, is it?'

274

Bimbo gazed down at the broken man on the floor. 'Get him out of here, then. Go on, before I change me mind.'

Mac lifted Reardon to his feet and led him from the bar. A door at the back of the lounge opened and Jackie Green stepped into view. He moved through the silent crowd and saw Reardon being helped from the pub.

Stopping before Bimbo, he grinned. 'I was hoping you'd come,' he said. 'He should have sent me after you at the start. It would have saved all this bother.' He slowly removed his navy blue blazer and handed it to a man behind him. From the doorway Stan Jarvis saw the butt of the magnum protruding from the inside pocket. The man holding the jacket nodded to Green. The boxer was now side-on to Bimbo. With astonishing speed, he whipped a right hand blow to Bimbo's chin. Bimbo flew backwards, hit a table and rolled to the floor. Green ran for him. Bimbo came off his knees in a lunging dive – straight into Green's upraised knee. He spun to the floor. Green stepped back.

'Get up, arsehole, the pain has only just started.' Bimbo wiped the blood from his broken nose and slowly climbed to his feet. He moved forward. Green stepped in, feinted a left, then drove a right-hand blow that opened the stitches over Bimbo's left eye.

The plaster was still in place, but blood began to seep through. Still Bimbo came forward, this time walking into a combination of lefts and rights that snapped his head back. An upper cut flew towards his chin. He rolled left, the fist flashing past his face, and thundered a chopping right that exploded against Green's ear, hurling him into the bar; Green shook his head and grinned.

'Not bad, Bimbo,' he said. 'You know how to hit. That's good.'

Green advanced, ducking under a roundhouse right and hammering lefts and rights into Bimbo's wounded face. Bimbo was forced back towards the door, blows raining to his face at bewildering speed. He tried to roll with the punches, block them with his forearms, but they came too fast.

He swayed back. In his anxiety to finish the contest Green leapt forward. A piledriving left from Bimbo caught him flush on the jaw. He staggered back into the crowd. Bimbo moved into the centre of the room, still dazed.

'Don't box the bastard!' shouted Stan. 'Play your own game, son!'

Green advanced, a thin trickle of blood seeping to his chin from a split lower lip. Bimbo took a deep breath, then launched himself into a drop kick, his feet smashing into Green's face and catapulting him into the doors, which exploded outwards. Bimbo rolled to his feet and followed Green into the car park. The boxer was cut now over the right eye, and glass from the door had ripped into his back.

'I'll kill you for that!' he screamed. Bimbo raced forward into a solid wall of combination punches. Blows hammered at him. He raised his arms to block them, and Green transferred his attack to the body, doubling Bimbo over. An overhand right cracked against his ear and he fell heavily across the bonnet of a car. Green was on him instantly. Bimbo's knee lashed up into Green's groin. The boxer screamed in rage and pain. Bimbo dived forward, grabbing Green's sweater. Twice Bimbo's fore-head cannoned into the boxer's face, half blinding him. Green backed away. Bimbo followed. A straight left crashed into Bimbo's broken nose, the pain lancing into his head.

The two men circled one another slowly within the ring of spectators. Both were bleeding. Both had felt the weight of the other's blows. Green's arrogance was gone now, his mind locked in total concentration. He moved in with straight, telling jabs, hunting the opportunity of landing the killer right, the blow that would end Bimbo's resistance for good. Three times he threw it, but on each occasion Bimbo managed to roll, or block.

276

Across the road, in his white Escort, Don Dodds sat with Detective Constable Sunley. Two other cars were parked close by waiting for the signal to move in.

'Shouldn't we stop it, Sarge?'

'What did you say, son?'

'I said we should stop it. They'll kill each other.'

'Stop what? We're looking for a dangerous criminal with a gun. We can't allow ourselves to be sidetracked by a display of high spirits.'

'Oh come on, Sarge. That's Jackie Green.'

'You ever read Plutarch, Ian?'

'No. Russian is he?'

'Greek. Clever man. He pointed out that great empires are not destroyed by great events. It's always the small, seemingly insignificant things that cause worlds to crumble. You ought to read more.'

'You've lost me, Sarge.'

Dodds sighed. 'Listen, Ian, we will take in Jackie Green. Count on it. But let me ask you something. Would you sooner take him fresh, or as he's going to be, win or lose, at the end of this little encounter?'

'I think I take the point,' said Sunley.

Back in the car park the two fighters were slowing down. The crowd had ceased their shouting and the battle was being fought in a grim, bloody silence. Jean Reardon watched from the grey Mercedes, her face betraying no emotion. Stan Jarvis went to his car, gathered his gear, and put on his overcoat, before pushing through to the front, his eyes glued to the man holding Green's coat.

Green himself was growing desperate. Despite hitting Bimbo three times for every punch he himself had had to take, the other man kept coming. Green knew Bimbo had broken at least two of his ribs, and he could picture the jagged bone resting against his lungs. His left hand was lower now, protecting his injured side. All he needed was the one big right. He fought for calm – and stepped back. As expected, Bimbo pushed forward. Green's left flashed up. Bimbo's head moved. The killer right hammered down in the knockout blow, landing solidly behind Bimbo's left ear like a pole-axe. Triumph surged in Green. It was over! He stepped back, making room for Bimbo to fall.

But he didn't fall. He shook his head, staggered and came upright. Green's jaw dropped. It wasn't possible. It wasn't bloody possible!

Leaping forward, he crashed two more blows to Bimbo's face, only to feel a bone-crunching upper cut to his injured ribs. Agony lanced him. He backed away, eyes scanning the crowd. He held out his hand. The man holding his jacket tugged the magnum loose and threw it into the circle. Jackie caught it.

Bimbo wiped the blood from his face – and saw the pistol levelled at him.

At that moment Stan Jarvis stepped forward, his coat flapping, the sawn-off shotgun clearly in sight. 'Jackie! I should put it down, son – or I'll blow you in half!'

The crowd behind Green scattered. The boxer looked into the twin muzzles and pictured the red-hot buckshot ripping through his stomach. He licked his smashed lips, tasting the blood.

'Drop it!' said Stan, bringing the shotgun up and pointing it at Green's face. Green obeyed. 'Now kick it over 'ere!' Green did so.

The boxer transferred his gaze to Bimbo – and charged.

Bimbo let him come, whipping a punch to his belly. Green doubled over, his head snapping down into Bimbo's upraised knee. Green's knees buckled and he hit the concrete face down. His body jerked once. Then he was still. Bimbo staggered back into the powerful arms of Don Dodds.

'How you feeling, son?'

Policemen moved through the crowd, hauling Green from the floor. D.C. Sunley lifted the pistol from the ground by the trigger guard and transferred it to a plastic bag. Then he turned to Stan Jarvis.

'Excuse me, sir. I'm sure somebody dropped a sawnoff shotgun round here somewhere. You didn't happen to pick it up, did you?'

'Yeah,' said Stan. 'Careless, some people.' He handed the weapon over.

'Thank you, sir. Very public-spirited.'

Dodds helped Bimbo to a set of steps leading to the rear garden, and sat him down. 'I didn't think you could beat him,' said Dodds.

'I don't think I could again.'

'You won't have to. He's being booked for the murder of Reilly.' Dodds pulled a white handkerchief from his pocket. 'Wipe some of that blood off your face, and I'll take you to the hospital.'

'It's over, Mr Dodds. It is over, innit?'

'It's over, Bimbo. What you going to do now?'

'Well, I got this wedding to arrange.'

'You getting married?'

'Nah, who'd have me? No, it's Esther. The nurse you met. Wanna come to the reception?'

'Sure, son. I'd love to.' Bimbo sank back against the stone steps. Dodds patted his shoulder. 'You know, Bimbo, just sometimes ... not often, mind, it can be like the movies. All it takes is a man with heart.'

The sun was shining in a clear blue sky as Bimbo sat on the grass watching the two black swans and the six grey cygnets cruising the pond. He had been there on that day in February when the black male had been released to the water. Sue Cater had written the story, and there was a great picture in the paper of the two swans facing each other, their necks shaped like a heart. Sue had the picture blown up and framed and Bimbo had placed it beside the Winnie the Pooh poster in his flat.

And now there were cygnets, grey and fluffy like miniature storm clouds.

'You're doin' all right now, princess, eh?' said Bimbo. 'Enjoy it while you got it.' The black swan slowly turned, the cygnets furiously paddling after her. She came close to Bimbo, staring at him from her good eye. He tossed her some bread.

She scooped it up and moved away. The male swan cut across, coming between her and Bimbo. 'Don't worry about me, son,' said Bimbo. 'Her and me are just old friends.'

A child clambered over the eighteen-inch fence and crept noisily up behind Bimbo. He swung just as Simon pounced. 'Gotcha!' he said, swinging the boy to his shoulder. Simon squealed as Bimbo carried him back to the path. Sarah ran from the swings.

'Mum says we got to go, or the dinner will be ruined,' she told him.

'Guess you better had, then.'

'Does the swan understand what you say?' asked Simon.

'Course she does, son. She's magic, aint she?'

'Will she miss you when you move into your new house?'

'No. I'll still come visit. I aint movin' far. It's only Chiswick. Come on, let's get an ice cream.'

'We can't. There's mum.' Bimbo glanced up to see Sherry walking towards him, arm in arm with a tall young man.

'Time to go, kids,' she called. The young man smiled at Bimbo. 'This is George,' said Sherry.

'I 'eard you got hitched again, Sher. Hope it works for the pair of you.'

'We're doing all right so far,' said George, leaning down and kissing Sherry's cheek. 'Come on kids, I'll buy you an ice cream.'

Bimbo watched as George and Sherry led the way up the short hill, the two youngsters trailing behind.

Behind them the swans and their cygnets continued their cruising.